W9-AQQ-872

Praise for *The Greenstone Grail*

"Intriguing characters and a mythic feel make this series opener a solid addition to most fantasy collections." —*Library Journal*

"Takes some of the stock material of children's fantasy and infuses it with a sensual intensity that makes it entirely a book for adults . . . a lot more than a conventional collection of fantasy plot tokens."
—*Time Out London*

"Whether it's clumsy teenagers, ancient guardians, calculating immortals, or menacing supernatural entities, Hemingway's a dab hand at character and evokes atmosphere deftly and vividly."
—*Starburst* (UK)

"A promising start." —*Kirkus Reviews*

"[A] dreamy and elegant book . . . in the Harry Potter vein."
—SF Crowsnest

By Amanda Hemingway

THE SANGREAL TRILOGY

The Greenstone Grail
The Sword of Straw

The Greenstone Grail

Amanda Hemingway

DEL REY
BALLANTINE BOOKS
NEW YORK

The Greenstone Grail is a work of fiction. Names, characters, places, and incidents are the products of the author's imagination or are used fictitiously. Any resemblance to actual events, locales, or persons, living or dead, is entirely coincidental.

2006 Del Rey Trade Paperback Edition

Copyright © 2004 by Amanda Hemingway
Excerpt from *The Sword of Straw* by Amanda Hemingway copyright © 2006 by Amanda Hemingway

All rights reserved.

Published in the United States by Del Rey Books, an imprint of The Random House Publishing Group, a division of Random House, Inc., New York.

DEL REY is a registered trademark and the Del Rey colophon is a trademark of Random House, Inc.

Originally published in Great Britain by HarperCollins Publishers Ltd., London, in 2004. Subsequently published in hardcover in the United States by Del Rey Books, an imprint of The Random House Publishing Group, a division of Random House, Inc., in 2005.

This book contains an excerpt from the forthcoming book *The Sword of Straw* by Amanda Hemingway. This excerpt has been set for this edition only and may not reflect the final content of the forthcoming edition.

Library of Congress Cataloging-in-Publication Data
Hemingway, Amanda.
The Greenstone grail / Amanda Hemingway.
p. cm.
ISBN 0-345-46079-0
1. Albinos and albinism—Fiction. 2. Gifted children—Fiction. 3. Homeless women—Fiction. 4. Immortalism—Fiction. 5. Villages—Fiction. 6. England—Fiction. 7. Grail—Fiction. I. Title.
PR6058.E49188G74 2004
823'.914—dc22   2004049396

Printed in the United States of America

www.delreybooks.com

9 8 7 6 5 4 3 2

Text design by Niqui Carter

The Greenstone Grail

This is the cup the Devil made
to hold the lifeblood of a god,
the cup from which the phantoms sprang
that followed where his story trod.

They wrought it in the Underworld—
an older world, a younger day—
before the God of gods was born
and angels stole the cup away.

They filled it with eternal life,
undying death, unsleeping dreams.
Its draught unsealed the shadow-gate
between the World that Is, and Seems.

This is the cup to loose the soul,
the blood that sets the legends free,
and we who dare to drink must taste,
each in ourselves, eternity.

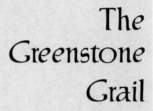

The
Greenstone
Grail

Prologue: The Chapel

There were three things moving through the wood that evening: the boy, the dog, and the sun.

The slope faced northwest, and as the cloud shadow retreated the sun's rays advanced through the trees on a collision course with the two companions, who were descending on a more or less diagonal route toward the light. The boy was dark, too dark for the Anglo-Saxon races, his skin a golden olive, his hair so black that there were glints of blue and green in it, and green and blue flecked the blackness of his eyes. His face was bony for his eleven years, a strange, solemn, mature face for someone so young. The dog was a shaggy mongrel, long-legged and wayward of tail, gamboling beside his friend with one ear pricked and the other lopped, his brown eyes very intelligent under whiskery eyebrows. He was known as Hoover from his habit of mopping up crumbs, though it was not really his name. The boy was called Nathan, and that *was* his name, at least for the moment. He had spent much of his short life exploring the woods, and around

Thornyhill he knew every tree, but here in this folded valley was the Darkwood where no paths ran, and he could never remember his way from one visit to the next. He sometimes fancied the trees shifted, rustling their roots in the leafmold, and even the streamlet that gurgled along the valley bottom would play curious tricks, switching its course from time to time as such little streams do, but without the excuse of sudden rain. It was very quiet here: few birds lived in the Darkwood. All this land had once been the property of the Thorn family (spelled Thawn in some of his uncle's ancient books), and they had built a chapel down in the valley, in the long-ago days of chivalry and legend before history tidied things up. It had been struck by lightning or otherwise destroyed after a renegade Thorn sold his soul to the Devil, or so it was rumored, but the ruin was still supposed to be there, in some secret hollow beneath the leaves, and Nathan had often looked for it with his friends, though without success. It said in one of the books that an ancient cup or chalice was kept there, some sort of holy relic, but his best friend, Hazel, said he would never find it, because it could only be found by the pure in heart. (The other boys said he couldn't have a girl for a best friend, it *wasn't done,* but Nathan didn't understand why, and did what he pleased.) He wasn't really looking for the chapel that evening, just walking with his uncle's dog, the foot companion he preferred, sniffing along the borders of some undiscovered adventure. There was a dimness among the trees, more shadow than mist, and as they went deeper into the valley the branches grew gnarly and twined together into nets, or reached out to snag fur and clothes. Nathan had to pick his way, but he rarely stumbled and never fell, and the dog, for all his casual gait, was swift and sure-pawed. Concentrating on the ground, they did not see the cloud edge passing until it slid over them, and the sun struck, slanting through the leafless boughs, filling their vision with a golden haze. For several moments Nathan strode on, half dazzled, uncertain where he was going. And then the woodland floor gave beneath him, and he was falling in a shower of earth crumbs and twig crumbs, bark scratchings and leaf crackle, falling down into the dark.

He fell perhaps ten feet, landing on more tree debris that softened the impact. He seemed to be in a hollow space, like a cave, but the quick changes from dusk to dazzle, from dazzle to semidark, proved too much for his brain and his sight took a while to adjust. He glanced upward and saw a ragged hole filled with sunlit wood, and a dog-shaped head peering down. He tried to say *I'm all right,* but the fall had winded him and his voice emerged as a croak. His arms and legs felt bruised but not broken; his jolted insides gradually settled back into place, and a brief queasiness passed. There was a scrabbling noise from above, followed by a slither as Hoover came down to join him. Nathan's eyes had adjusted by now and he could see they were in a rectangular chamber some twenty feet long, too regular in outline for a cave. Above them the ceiling consisted of a tangle of roots sustaining loose earth, but beyond he made out stubby pillars curving upward into arches, and a glimpse of man-made walls on either side, with pointed window holes choked with leaf compost and snarled tubers. Nathan reached in his pocket for the small flashlight that had been part of his Christmas stocking. The beam was weak and the gloom was not deep enough to enhance it, but it cast an oblong of vague pallor that traveled over the squat columns, the chinks of wall. The stone looked dry and crumbly, like stale bread. He stood up, rather stiffly, and followed the beam into the dimness, Hoover at his side. The soil underfoot thinned, revealing flagstones, some cracked, some thrust upward by burrowing growths. The beam picked out fragments of carved lettering on the floor and a strange little face peeping out from an architrave, its features blunted with erosion, leaving only the bulge of pitted cheeks under wicked eye slits, and the jut of broken horns. "This is it," Nathan whispered. There was no need for him to whisper, but in that place it was instinctive. "This is the lost chapel of the Thorns. That face doesn't look very Christian, does it?"

Hoover made a snuffling noise by way of agreement and thumped his tail against the boy's leg.

At the far end they found three steps up to a kind of dais—"This is where the altar was"—and above it a recess in the wall overhung with a fringe of root-filaments and silted up with earth-dust. "Perhaps that was where it stood," Nathan said. "The holy relic . . ." He felt inside, but the recess was empty. As he withdrew his hand, he heard a sound so alien he felt his skin prickle. A low, soft growling, deep in the throat. Hoover never growled. But he was staring at the recess, his lip lifted, backing away step by step. The hairs along his spine bristled visibly. "What's the matter?" Nathan demanded, but the dog did not even glance in his direction. All his attention was focused on the vacant hollow in the wall.

Nathan didn't say, "It's all right. There's nothing there." He knew that if Hoover sensed something, then there was something to sense. The dog had been his friend for as long as he could remember, and had never been seen to growl at anyone, human or animal. Canine hostilities were conducted in barks. He had always seemed to be the sort of dog who was good with small children, did not bite the postman, and would deal with a burglar by licking his face. But he understood everything people said, Nathan was sure of that, and would follow him into every adventure. And he was old. *Older than me*, the boy thought, and for the first time he wondered how old, since eleven was a fair age for a dog. He found himself backing away, too, keeping close to Hoover. Watching the recess.

Afterward he couldn't recall which came first, the light or the voices. Perhaps they weren't voices, just sounds, soft, whispery sounds, word-shaped though he couldn't make out the words, thread-like ghosts of noises long gone. Hoover ceased growling and froze;

there was froth around his mouth, and all his teeth showed. Nathan had a hand on his neck, and found he was trembling. He had switched off the flashlight and they were both staring at the light, a tiny green mote that had appeared in the back of the recess. But either the cavity was much deeper than he had thought or the light was coming from somewhere else, somewhere dark and very far away. It grew slowly, as if it were drawing nearer, emerging from an abyss of blackness, until they could see it consisted of a nimbus encircling some small object. The whispering increased, becoming a chorus of hissing murmurs. And now Nathan could make out the words, or rather a single word, repeated over and over again: he thought it was *sangré*, but the voices were so blurred he could not be certain. His heart was beating very hard, bumping against his ribs. His bruises were forgotten.

The green halo filled the hollow and spilled over. The object within it seemed to be floating, not resting, in the cavity, a cup or goblet with a short stem and a bowl as wide as it was deep. It looked as if it was made of some greenish stone, polished to a metallic luster, or even opaque glass. There were designs engraved on it that appeared significant, though what they might signify he could not guess, and here and there the gleam of furtive gemstones, but all green. He found he was drawing closer, or being drawn; his body seemed to have no will in the matter anymore. Now he could see inside the cup. He had expected it to be empty, but it was full almost to the brim. In that light the liquid looked black, but it wasn't. It was red.

Behind him, the dog gave a strangled whine of protest. He reached out, and the cup began to drift toward him, and he knew with a knowledge beyond understanding that he must drink. (*Only the pure in heart* . . .) It was full of blood, and he must drink . . . The voices sounded like a host of snakes murmuring with forked tongues. *Sangré, sangré, sangreal* . . .

With a supreme effort the dog broke free of the spell and sprang forward, seizing a mouthful of Nathan's jacket. The boy stumbled backward. The snake voices fragmented into a crackle like radio interference and were gone, vanishing on a snarl. The green light was abruptly extinguished. "Where is it?" Nathan cried, and as Hoover released him he flung himself down on hands and knees, groping on the floor for the cup. Then he stopped, and confusion slid like a cloud from his mind. He turned back to the dog, who was regarding him with vivid concern, tail motionless. "Let's get out of here."

It was easier said than done. Earthfalls and woodland detritus had built up a slope close to the hole where Nathan had tumbled through, but it was steep and sliding soil made purchase difficult. It took at least half an hour before he and Hoover managed to climb back up, enlarge the gap, and scramble into the open air. Nathan had no idea how long they had been down there, but the last of the sunset had faded and the night-filled wood lived up to its name. He switched on the flashlight but in the dark it was impossible to be sure of his route and he let the dog guide him, trusting to Hoover's instincts. Only when he had gone several yards did he realize that he had not marked the location in any way. He had found it walking blindly with the sun in his eyes and had emerged into darkness; he hadn't even registered the appearance of the trees in the vicinity. He tried to turn back but Hoover wouldn't accompany him, insisting with short, staccato barks that they should go on. *I know the direction we came,* Nathan reflected, *and there's a big hole in the ground now. I can't miss that.* "Okay," he told the dog. "We'd better go home." They went on up the slope.

At the edge of the Darkwood where the ground leveled out and the trees changed, becoming taller and friendlier, making way for paths and glades, Hoover suddenly stopped. His fur ruffled though there was no wind. Something like a shadow passed over his eyes and fled, leaving them bright and unworried. When he set off again, it was with his customary lolloping stride, without the air of prudence and purpose that he had shown since they'd left the chapel. Nathan could not know it, but the whole incident had been wiped from his mind.

The boy remembered—he remembered every detail—but when he tried to speak of it, to Hazel, or his mother, or Barty, the man he always called uncle, his tongue would not form the words, and the chapel and its contents stayed locked in his head, a guilty secret that he did not want to keep. He would dream of it sometimes, and wake to hear the snake whispers calling to him from the corners of the room for seconds after: *Sangré Sangreal* . . . Once in his dream he lifted the cup and drank, and his mouth was full of blood, and the sweat that poured off him was red, and when he opened his eyes it was a relief to find himself wet with nothing but perspiration.

He looked for the place again, though always with a friend, not saying what he was searching for, half afraid of finding it. But even the hole seemed to have gone, and the sun stayed out of his eyes, and the chapel had vanished into the secrecy of the wood.

smiled. "Perhaps you'd like to come in. It's ge[...]
making tea. If you need to feed the little one [...]

"Thank you so much!"

She stepped into the hallway, and the closing of the door [...] the dark and its phantoms. Long afterward, she knew she had tru[sted] him without thinking, on instinct. Maybe it was because he was [...] and benevolent looking, and she was desperate and alone, or becau[se] the blue twinkle of his eyes had worked a charm on her, but in the en[d] she realized it was because he had looked behind her, and seen some-thing, seen *them*. He showed her into a room with oak beams, shabby capacious chairs, firelight. A large dog was sprawled on the hearth rug, a dog with shaggy fur and waggy tail, plainly a mongrel. It got up as they came in, stretching its forelegs, rump in the air, tail waving. "Why don't you leave the child by the fire?" the man said. "Hoover will look after him. I call him Hoover for obvious reasons: he cleans up the crumbs. My name is Bartlemy Goodman."

"Annie Ward." She lifted the baby out of the sling and set him down on the hearth rug, which was as shaggy as the dog and so simi-lar they might have been related. "This is Nathan."

Baby and dog surveyed each other, wet black nose almost touch-ing small brown one. Then suddenly Nathan laughed—something as rare as his tears—and she imagined they had formed a bond that tran-scended any differences of species or speech. "I'd like to heat his milk," she said. "Would—would you mind watching him for me?"

"Hoover will take care of it. He's like Nana in *Peter Pan*. The kitchen's this way."

Looking back, doubtfully, she saw the dog gently nudging the child away from the fire with his muzzle. "He must be awfully well trained," she said.

"He's very intelligent," said her host. Afterward, she thought it wasn't really an affirmation.

The kitchen was heavily beamed and flagstoned as she might

The Fugitives

At the dark end of a winter's afternoon early in 1991 a young woman climbed down from a truck on the road through Thornyhill woods.

"Are you sure?" said the driver. "I can take you on to Eade."

"I'm sure." He had placed a hand on her knee. That was enough. She had insisted on being set down.

"It's a lonely stretch of road," he said, hefting her bags out of the cab, too slowly for her taste. She reached up, tugging her suitcase from his grasp and stumbling under the sudden weight. The baby sus-pended in a sling about her neck woke at the jolt but didn't cry, only staring about him with wide-open eyes. They were very dark, the irises so large they seemed to have almost no whites, like the eyes of some small nocturnal animal. But the truck driver wasn't watching the child. He thought the woman looked very young to be a mother, little more than a girl, her round face unmade-up and somehow vul-nerable, framed in a soft blur of hair, her coloring far paler than her baby. He wanted her to stay in his cab for all sorts of reasons, some kindly, some less so. "I thought you were going on to Crawley."

"I know where I'm going." Her determination belied her softness. She didn't know, but it didn't matter. She slammed the door, hooking the strap of her carryall over her shoulder and dragging the suitcase behind on inadequate wheels. After a few minutes, the truck drove off.

They were alone now. It was a relief the truck had gone, but one fear was swiftly replaced by others. She *had* been going to Crawley—she had a contact there, a babysitter, the friend of a friend, and the possibility of a job—but instead here she was, miles from anywhere, with little hope of another lift even if she had the courage to accept one. The baby was quiet—he cried so rarely it worried her—but she knew he would soon be hungry, and it was growing darker, and the road was lonely indeed. The suitcase trundled awkwardly at her heels, swaying from side to side, regularly banging against her leg, and the woods seemed to draw closer on either hand, squeezing the road into a narrow slot between thickets of shadow. She was a country girl with no real fear of the night, but she thought she heard a whisper of wind on the windless air, the crack of a twig somewhere nearby, strange stirrings and rustlings in the leafmold. Since the birth of her child she had been subject to nervous imaginings that she had not dared to confide in anyone, dreading to be called paranoid. There were footsteps pattering on empty streets, doors that shifted without a draft, soft murmurings just beyond the reach of hearing. And now the woods seemed to wake at her presence, so she thought the branches groped, and shreds of darkness slithered from tree to tree. *They* were there, always following, getting closer, never quite catching up . . .

When she saw the lights, she thought they, too, must be an illusion, and she was becoming genuinely unbalanced. Twin gleams of yellow, twinkling through the trees, the yellow of firelight, candle-

electric light. As she drew nearer she feared they would vanish, they grew clearer, until she could make out the source. Windows, windows in a house, and the yellow glow between half-drawn curtains. The house appeared to be set in a clearing among the trees: she could see gables pointing against the sky, and the dim suggestion of half-timbering crisscrossing the facade. It looked a friendly house, even in the dark; but she wasn't sure. "What do you think?" she whispered to the baby. "Shall we ask for help? Maybe they'll offer us tea . . ." Maybe it was a witch's cottage, made of gingerbread, and the door would be opened by a hook-nosed crone who would show them the shortest way to her oven.

Footsteps. Footsteps on the empty road. She looked around but could see nothing. Yet for a moment they were quiet and clear, softshod feet, or padded paws. And in the gloom there was a deeper dark, like a ripple running through the woods, and the sound of breathing, very close by, as if the wind itself had a throat and was panting on her neck . . . Her suitcase bounced and lurched as she tugged it up the path to the door. There was a knocker, and an old-fashioned bellpull that dangled. She tried both.

The door opened, and there was no hook-nosed crone but a large, comfortable-looking man with a looming stomach, shoulders to match, and very graceful hands. His hair was pale, his complexion a faded pink. His face wore an expression of vague benevolence, or maybe the benevolence was in the arrangement of his features, since his manner was initially hesitant, almost guarded. His eyes were periwinkle blue between fat eyelids.

"We're lost," the young woman began, uneasily, "and I wondered . . ."

He was looking beyond her, into the night, where the footsteps were, and the breathing of the wind. For a fleeting instant she imagined that he, too, heard or saw, though what he saw she didn't know; she didn't look around. Then his gaze came back to her, and he

have expected, with an old-fashioned cooking range on which something that resembled a small cauldron was simmering. A drift of steam came from under the lid, bringing with it a rich, meaty, gamy, spicy smell that made her mouth water. She had eaten nothing but a sandwich at lunchtime, and it occurred to her that she was very hungry; but the baby came first. Bartlemy provided a saucepan and she heated milk while he made tea and set out a tray with earthenware mugs, pot and jug, fruitcake. She longed to ask what was in the cauldron but was afraid of sounding too greedy, or too desperate. The room was of irregular shape and there were many small shelves on every angle of wall, bearing hand-labeled bottles and jars containing pickled fruits, chutney, strange-looking vegetables in oil. Herbs grew in pots and dried in bunches. There was a bowl of onions, white and purple, and another of apples and clementines. No dirty dishes stocked the sink, and the drain board was very clean.

Back in the living room, she gave Nathan his bottle and some bread and butter with no crusts that her host had prepared. "You're being very kind," she said. "You must think . . ."

"I think only that it's dark outside, and cold, and you seem to be in difficulty. You can tell me more when you're ready, if you wish to."

She drank the tea, bergamot-scented, probably Earl Grey, and ate a large slice of the cake. Perhaps because she was famished, it seemed to her the nicest cake she had ever tasted.

"Do you feel you can tell me now where you're going?" Bartlemy asked.

"I was heading for Crawley," she said. "There are jobs there—at least I hope so—and a friend of mine knows a good babysitter. Before, we . . . we were staying with one of my cousins, but things got awkward—I felt I was imposing—and she didn't really want the baby. So . . . I thought it was time to move on. Be independent." She didn't mention the pursuing shadows, or the whispers in the night. In this warm, safe haven they seemed almost unreal.

If it was safe. If it was a haven. She trusted him, but that very trust disturbed her, and she feared her own weakness, her cowardice—she feared to go back into the dark.

"What about your parents?"

"They're in the West Country. I don't see them much since my—my husband died."

"I'm sorry."

He asked her nothing more, nor did she volunteer any further information. They watched the child on the hearth rug, romping with the dog, pulling his floppy ears. "Do you want to continue your journey tonight?" Bartlemy said. "You can stay here if you wish: I have plenty of space. There's a bolt on the bedroom door, if that would make you feel more comfortable."

She opened her mouth to say that she couldn't, she couldn't possibly, but all that came out was: "Thank you." And: "I'm not worried." And she knew that, for a little while at least, she wasn't.

For supper he filled a mug from the cauldron—it was some kind of broth, with so many mingled flavors she couldn't identify them—and it flooded her whole body with warmth and ease. She slept side by side with her son, on a mattress that was both firm and soft, sliding the bolt because she knew it was a sensible precaution, though she didn't really feel it was necessary. And somehow they stayed the next night, and the next, and she forgot to bolt the door, and Hoover woke them in the morning, plumping his forepaws on the quilt so he could lick Nathan's face.

THE GOODMANS had lived at Thornyhill for as long as anyone could remember. In the village of Eade, about two and a half miles down the road, the most venerable residents claimed they could recall Bartlemy's grandfather, or even his great-grandfather, but people were vague as to which generation was which: they were all called

Bartlemy, or some similar name, and they all looked alike, fat and placid and kindly. None of them ever seemed to be very young, or to grow very old. It was assumed that womenfolk and childhood were details that happened somewhere else, and they gravitated to Thornyhill in middle age. They had money from some unspecified source, and they appeared to live retired, reclusive but not unfriendly, mixing little in local affairs. They were regarded as mildly and acceptably eccentric, part of the scenery, arousing no curiosity, subject to no prying questions. The dog, too, was said to be one of a succession, all mongrels, strays perhaps, rescued from dog homes. If they had been asked, the villagers might have said that one had been part retriever, another part wolfhound, a third had shown traits of Alsatian or Old English sheepdog; but no one would have been sure. Hoover had a retriever's brown soulful eyes, the long legs of a hound, a coat shagheaded, maned, tufted like anything from an Afghan to a husky. He chased cats from time to time to prove his doghood and slobbered a good deal over friend and stranger alike. It was inferred that the present generation of both dog and master had been at Thornyhill for some twenty years, doing little, staid and respectable as hobbits in a hobbit-hole, aloof from the workaday world. If twenty years was a long time for a dog to live, nobody remarked on it.

Once, Thornyhill had been the property of the Thorns, a family that was ancient rather than aristocratic, tracing their line back long before the Normans. Local historians said there had been a house on the hillside where now the Darkwood grew, a house that dated from Saxon times with a sunken chapel where Josevius Grimling Thorn, called Grimthorn, had traded with the Devil, though what he had traded, or why, remained a mystery. But the tales about him were confused and confusing, stating he had lived nearly two thousand years ago yet died around A.D. 650, and the house had been razed, and the chapel was lost, and Josevius faded into legend, and the Darkwood had grown over all. In the Tudor age later Thorns had built the surviving house, where the woodland was lighter and greener, and bluebells carpeted the ground in spring, and there were woodpeckers and warblers, and deer in the thickets, and squirrels in the treetops. The house was crisscrossed with half-timbering, showing glimpses of plaster and brickwork in between, and cloaked in creepers that turned fire red in autumn; tall chimneys jutted higgledy-piggledy from the pointed roofs. There the family had lived for centuries, keeping their secrets, until the eldest son died in the First World War, and his brother in the flu epidemic that followed, and presumably it was then the Goodmans came, though none could be found to remember clearly. There were still offshoots of the family in and around the village: the Carlows were known to be descended, on the wrong side of the blanket, from a black sheep of the Jacobean era, and the widowed Mrs. Vanstone, now in her late fifties, was invariably called Rowena Thorn in acknowledgment of her antecedents. She would visit Bartlemy from time to time and talk about the past, and she was always impressed by how much he knew, in his unassuming way, about her more distant ancestors. It occurred to her, once or twice, that his residence there seemed to be a kind of guardianship, though what he was guarding, or for whom, she could not imagine, and she put it down to imagination.

Occasionally—very occasionally—Bartlemy had visitors who were not from the village or its environs, visitors who came late at night, and stayed indoors, away from the gaze of locals, and left after one day or many in the predawn hour when no one would see them go. Sometimes an early riser or a reveler returning late from the pub at Chizzledown would catch sight of a hooded stranger striding along the road through the woods, or glimpse an unfamiliar figure on the twisty path to Bartlemy's door, but gossip took no interest, since there was neither sex nor scandal afoot, and such sightings were too rare to be thought significant. There were beginning to be Londoners in the area now, high-earning, high-spending Westend expats, generally with media connections, who bought into the country lifestyle as pictured in the glossy magazines, and installed Agas in their kitchens, and filled their fridges with Chardonnay, and invited their city friends down for summer parties in their carefully sculpted gardens. Some of them made inquiries about the Goodmans, and Thornyhill, but their questions went unanswered, and the house was not for sale. Nothing seemed to happen there for a long long time, until Annie Ward and her baby came to the door on a dark afternoon in 1991, and found sanctuary.

BARTLEMY HAD a car of sorts, a blunt-nosed Jowett Javelin from the 1950s. It was dirty and tired looking but it always managed to go, and in it he drove Annie to Crawley, and waited while she visited the babysitter and the job center, and came away disheartened. "What do you do?" he had asked her.

"I'm a computer programmer," she told him; but it appeared there were plenty of computer programmers, and she was just one in a long line.

"I'm planning to open a secondhand-book shop in the village," he said later that evening. "I want someone to manage it for me. I've got my eye on a suitable property: there's a little apartment upstairs. I'll need a manager who's good with computers to catalog stocks and keep the accounts; I'm afraid technology's a little beyond me."

What about them? she thought. They're *always out there* . . . But when she looked through the window the woods were still, and door and curtain did not stir, and no mutterings came to trouble her sleep.

"I couldn't," she said. "You've done so much already."

"Exactly. So this is something you can do for me."

She knew it wasn't true, but he seemed so matter-of-fact, his generosity unobtrusive, almost invisible, and the property materialized somehow, a tiny slot of a building between an antiques shop and a delicatessen for the Londoners, with rooms that went back and back, and odd little stairs going nowhere, and bedrooms the size of cupboards and cupboards the size of bedrooms, all in the best tradition of secondhand-book shops. She moved in, and there was no rent, and her slender salary stretched to cover everything. The villagers assumed she was a relative of Bartlemy's, a niece or distant cousin, and eventually she almost came to believe it herself, half forgetting, under the spell of his protection, that she had ever been a homeless wanderer who knocked on his door purely by chance, if chance it was. Nathan would grow up to call him uncle, and Annie walked through the woods on summer nights, and *they* were gone, vanished like an evil dream in the moment of awakening, until she barely remembered that they had ever been.

But for all her trust, it was many months before she confided fully in Bartlemy. Winter came around again, and on firelit evenings at Thornyhill she watched Nathan grow.

"Is he like his father?" Bartlemy asked once.

"No," she said. A silence fell, laden with waiting. "He's like himself. Daniel . . ."

"Your husband?"

"He wasn't my husband. We just—lived together. I took his name when he died for Nathan's sake, I suppose. I wanted my son to have something of his father to hold on to, something to remember him by. Or maybe it was because my family didn't . . . they weren't happy that Daniel and I didn't marry, and when Nathan came, they . . . didn't want him."

"Why not?" Bartlemy inquired. "He's a beautiful, intelligent child. Exceptionally so, I would say."

"Isn't he?" For a minute her face lit; then recollection clouded it over again. "The trouble was . . ." Suddenly, she looked directly at him, and there was a kind of pleading in her eyes. "Daniel was white. Nathan's far too dark—he looks half Indian or something. But I'd never had an Indian lover. There'd been no one but Daniel since we met. We were together eight years, and I was faithful to him. I wouldn't want to play around. After Daniel died, when I found I was pregnant, I was very happy. And then the baby came, and he was beautiful, so beautiful, but—since then, I never seemed to stop running. Till I came here." After a few moments, she went on: "Please believe me. I can't explain why Nathan looks the way he does. I can't explain any of it."

"How very interesting," Bartlemy said at last. "Don't fret: I know you wouldn't make it up. You're not that type at all. Anyway, why should you? There would be no real point. Can you tell me how Daniel died?"

"It was a car crash. He'd been working late—he often did—and they said, the police said, he may have fallen asleep at the wheel, but he wouldn't. I know that. They said at the inquest another vehicle hit him, a van or a truck, and must have just driven away. He only had a little Renault: he was knocked off the road into a tree . . ."

Her mind was carried back to the pale hospital room, pale as a sepulchre, and the still figure in the bed, with his battered face almost unrecognizable between the bandages, except she would have recognized him however he looked, however bruised and broken. She held his hand, tight, tight, and the tears ran down her cheeks unwiped, and she begged him to live in a running whisper that she knew or dreaded he would not hear. Looking back, she thought she had sat there forever, that a part of her was still sitting there, trapped in a moment of time, with his hand in hers, imploring him in vain: Don't go, don't give up, live. *Live.* And then he had opened his eyes.

They had given him morphine for the pain; the nurses thought he would not wake again. But somehow his body rejected the drug, and he came around, looking at her with love, so much love that she thought her heart would burst, and then the pain came, the price of that instant, that love, because he had shaken off the influence of the morphine. His face was wrung with it, scrunched up in the final agony, and she reached out with all that she had, all that she was, with mind and heart and soul, reached into his pain, into his death, and in that second she would have given life and happiness to save him, to spare him even an atom of suffering. But the pain was smoothed away, and his life with it, and when at last she drew back it was another age, another world.

"Nathan was born exactly nine months later," she told Bartlemy. "I always thought . . ."

"You thought you became pregnant in the moment of Daniel's death," he said. "I understand."

"Something happened then, something I can't remember. I don't mean there are blanks: it wasn't like that. It's as if there's a scar, a scar in time, or a fold, and inside it there's the memory, the forgotten thing. Afterward, I was *different*. I was . . . *more*. I knew I was pregnant, I knew it immediately, though I hadn't known it before. I couldn't even grieve properly. I missed Daniel—I'll always miss him—but the differentness, the moreness, filled me up."

"Life out of death," said Bartlemy. "It makes sense. Yes. There is a Gate we pass when we die"—she could hear the capital *G*—"a Gate out of this world. What lies beyond it no one knows. Religion invents, philosophers speculate, and the rest of us merely hope. If there are other universes, other states of being, then that is the only way to reach them—the only way we know of. But none may pass the Gate alive, or ever return. So they say. But even the Ultimate Laws may be broken, by the very wicked, or the very rash, or those whose love takes them beyond fear—or by the Powers themselves."

"Is this your philosophy?" she asked him. "A Gateway between worlds, and unearthly powers making laws for us to live by?"

"I'm not so original," he responded. "Others have done my thinking for me, long ago. I simply follow a well-worn path."

"I like the sound of it," she said. "People say they see a tunnel, but I prefer a gate. A gate opens both ways. Maybe I did pass through, and return . . . But then, why doesn't Nathan look like Daniel? Have you a philosophy to answer that?"

"No," he said. "Not at the moment. There could be many explanations. I will give it some thought."

THE YEARS of Nathan's childhood passed in something close to an idyll. Of course, the trouble with a happy childhood is that you are much too young to appreciate it. Nathan, with the unthinking acceptance of youth, assumed happiness was the lot of most human beings: the unhappy were few and far between, and after a period of suffering they, too, would be helped to find contentment. He had never known a father so he couldn't miss him, but his mother's talk of Daniel gave him a feeling of security, of being watched over by a friendly ghost, though strangely she had no photographs to show him. Otherwise, his Uncle Barty filled whatever space there might have been—filled and overfilled it, his solidity a protective wall, a quiet strength behind his placid manner. And Annie, trying her best always to be firm and fair, determined not to lose her temper under the stresses and irritants of parenthood, found it, much of the time, unexpectedly easy. Money was not plentiful but there was always enough, and the little feuds and fracases of village life could not disturb her comfort. Nathan went to the local school, excelled at his studies, played soccer in winter and cricket in summer. The other children admired him but were also wary of him, slightly daunted by his effortless intelligence and something about him that set him a little apart, a sort of calmness, an inner certainty. The few who became his particular friends felt themselves somehow special, singled out, though Nathan was friendly to all and never seemed to do any visible singling. His most frequent companions were George Fawn and Hazel Bagot—something that surprised his classmates, since he could have hung out with the most popular boys in the school. George was chubby and shy, regularly picked on by pupils and even some of the teachers, given to stammering when he was nervous, which was often. He was cornered in the playground one day by the school bully, Jason Wicks, when Nathan came to his defense. "Leave him alone. He's never harmed you. Why should you want to hurt him?"

There was a chorus of laughter from Jason's backing group. "'Cos he's fat, and he s-s-stammers, and his mother's a—"

"Don't talk like that," said Nathan, not angrily, but with a kind of set look on his face. "I told you, leave him alone."

"You're going to protect him, are you?" Jason bunched a big fist.

"I'll try."

The fist shot out, knocking him against the wall. George moved to help him and then shrank away, too frightened to aid his champion. When Nathan straightened up, there was blood on his lip.

"Now fuck off," Jason ordered. He had learned both his manners and his vocabulary from his seniors at home.

"No."

This time Nathan dodged the blow, grabbed the lunging arm, and drove it past him, with both his weight and Jason's behind it. Knuckles rammed into the wall—Jason screamed as flint cut his flesh to the bone. "I'm sorry," Nathan said, "but in the future, leave George alone." The backing group could have jumped him, but they didn't. Maybe they had read enough of the right books, or at any rate seen enough of the right movies, to know that this was how a hero behaved. George would have become his willing slave from that moment, if he had wanted one.

As for Hazel, she and Nathan were near neighbors, nursery playmates, squabbling companions, sharers in adventures both imaginary and real. Mrs. Bagot worked in the deli, and Hazel was frequently left at the bookshop, in theory under Annie's eye, the two children chasing each other up steps and stairways in rowdy games, or mysteriously quiet as Nathan showed her wonderful books with yellowing pages and illustrations shielded in tissue paper. Without his encouragement Hazel would have read little: she came from a household where reading was something that happened to other people, her mother preferring the television, her father the pub. She was an only child, given to strange introverted moods when she wouldn't speak for hours, or would climb a tree and refuse to come down, "watching" she would explain later when asked what she'd been doing, or "thinking." But she would always talk to Nathan. She had occasional outbursts of temper that alarmed other children, but these were rare. To look at she was a little below the average height for her age, sturdily built, with a lot of untidy brown hair that her mother was always trying to restrain in a braid or ponytail or twist, but the shorter ends invariably worked loose, and Hazel would pull them over her face to hide behind. Nathan's male classmates scorned her as a best friend because she was a girl, but it made no difference to him. Both his companions and his mother were learning that nothing anyone said or did made any difference to Nathan, once he had made up his mind.

But before George, even before Hazel, there was Woody. "Your imaginary friend," Annie called him, and Nathan accepted this, although with a note of doubt, since he thought *imaginary* meant "not real," and Woody was quite real. They would meet in the garden at Thornyhill—a garden that seemed much bigger than its actual size, with trellises overgrown with beanflowers, and herb beds, and rambling shrubs, and curious furtive statues hiding in leaves, and wild corners where wood and garden ran together and an infant Nathan found no boundaries to his playground. Annie learned not to worry about him: Hoover was always around, if he strayed too far. But even Hoover never saw Woody. Woody was very, very shy, an odd little creature with an elongated face, all nose and slanting eyes that looked sideways from his head, like the eyes of an animal. His body was thin as a twig, his skin brownish and slightly mottled, varying in tone according to his background. Hair bristled on his scalp and straggled down his back. If he wore clothes, they were so close to his skin color that Nathan never noticed. He explained that he was a woodwose, but if he had a name he couldn't remember it, so Nathan called him Woody.

"Have you lived here a long time?" the child asked him once.

"Always."

"How long is always?"

"I'm not sure. Not very long I think, but I can't remember being anywhere else."

"Do you have parents?"

"Parents . . . ?"

"A mummy and daddy. I have a mummy, but my daddy is dead. And I have Uncle Barty, and Hoover. Who do you have?"

But Woody didn't seem to have anybody.

"Then you can have me," said Nathan.

They would crawl through gaps in the undergrowth into the woods, where his imaginary friend showed him the secret worlds in the hollows of trees, and under last year's leaves, and they would watch new shoots growing, and the tiny lives of insects, and the green beginnings of things. Sometimes birds would come and perch on Woody's fingers—long, brown, knobbly fingers—or his shoulder, as if he were no more than a sapling sprouting among the roots. When Annie first heard of these explorations she was horrified. "He mustn't go wandering off on his own like this. Anything could happen to him!"

"He appears to be looked after," Bartlemy said. "You don't have to worry. No harm can come to him here."

And somehow, she believed him.

When Nathan's friendship with Hazel grew he told her about Woody, but she never met him. And gradually, as he became more preoccupied with school and other activities, he saw less and less of his strange companion, and Woody faded with early childhood, until, without really thinking about it, Nathan came to accept his mother's definition, that the woodwose had come from his imagination, and had no substance of its own.

WHEN HE was eleven Nathan won a scholarship to Ffylde Abbey, a private school run by monks about an hour's drive from Eade. Annie had dredged up the long-forgotten Catholicism of her youth to enable him to apply: it was one of the best schools in the area, patronized largely by the sons of the rich and privileged, but with high academic standards for those who wanted to attain them and superb sports facilities for everyone else. Nathan went as a weekly boarder: the distance was too great for him to come home every evening. Jason Wicks and his gang jeered at him for being a swot and a snob, but they soon grew tired of it, since Nathan appeared genuinely indifferent to their mockery and never responded to provocation. At the new school he made new friends, and inevitably saw less of some of the village children, but his closeness to Hazel and George was unaffected. They would gather on weekends in their special meeting place in the bookshop, known as the Den. There was a kind of storage space, like a very tall, thin cupboard, between two stacks of shelving, and they had discovered that if you climbed up inside with the help of a stepladder you would find yourself in a tiny loft area tucked under the slope of the roof, with a skylight through which you could scramble right outside. This was their secret headquarters where they would go to plan games and adventures, or just sit and talk out of the range of grown-up ears. They kept a cookie tin there with emergency supplies, three mugs for Coke or lemonade, and a lantern with colored glass in the sides for dark winter evenings. Nathan had even made a cardboard screen to put over the skylight at such times, so no passerby would see it illuminated. Annie sneaked up there occasionally and dusted, when she was sure they weren't around, to prevent them getting too obviously grubby. She didn't think either Hazel's or George's parents would be pleased if an afternoon in Nathan's company invariably resulted in gray clothing.

Sometimes on clear nights they would extinguish the lantern and open the skylight to look up at the stars. "I wish we had a telescope," Nathan said. "Then we could see them much bigger and closer." He'd been doing some astronomy at Ffylde. "Look, there's the Great Bear."

"It never looks like a bear to me," Hazel said. "More like a saucepan with a bent handle."

"Maybe we could see a comet," George said hopefully. "David"— his older brother—"showed me one once, through binoculars, but I couldn't really see anything. I thought it would be very bright, with a tail, like a firework, but there was just a bit of a blur."

"Where's Orion?" asked Hazel, naming the only other constellation she had heard of.

"I'll show you." Standing on a box with her, leaning against the edge of the skylight, Nathan pointed upward. "*There*. That string of stars is his belt."

"What about the rest of him?"

"I'm not sure . . ." His pointing finger wavered; in the dark they couldn't see him frown. "That's funny."

"What's funny?" said George. There wasn't room for him on the box, and he was trying to gaze up past the other two, and failing.

"There's another star, just below Orion. It wasn't there before: I'm sure it wasn't. I was up here last night."

"Show me," said Hazel. Nathan pointed again. "Perhaps you remembered wrong. Or there was some cloud or something."

"It wasn't cloudy."

"Perhaps it's a comet!" George said excitedly.

"If there was a comet it would've been on the news," Nathan said. "Besides, it looks like a star."

"It's not very twinkly," Hazel explained.

Nathan climbed down, switched on the lantern, and consulted his star map. "There's nothing here," he said. "There shouldn't be a star there at all."

"It must be a UFO," George declared. "They can look like stars. Let me see." Now that the others had come down, he scrambled onto the box. "It'll whoosh across the sky in a minute and disappear."

But it didn't.

"It could be a whole *new* star," Hazel suggested. "I've heard how they can have huge explosions out in space, and that makes new stars."

"A supernova," Nathan said knowledgeably. "If it is, it'll be on Patrick Moore."

But there was nothing about a new star on any program, and when Nathan looked the following evening it had gone. He didn't say much to the other two, but on his own he wondered and wondered, and would steal up the stepladder late at night to look, just in case. It was not until the next spring, when he had almost forgotten about it, that he saw the star again.

THAT WINTER a new couple moved down from London, causing a minor flutter of interest among less glamorous residents. They were in their thirties: he was a lecturer in history at East Sussex University and a writer of upmarket period novels, popular enough to be stocked in most bookshops instead of having to be specially ordered, and she was an actress of the intellectual type who had appeared regularly on stage and television. His name was Michael Addison, hers Rianna Sardou (Rianna reputedly shortened from Marianne), but they were assumed to be married, though she seemed to be away a great deal, on tour with a play or on location shoots for a TV drama or bit-part film role. Michael was around most of the time, however, and people pronounced him pleasant and friendly, and began to call him Mike, and he would have a pint in the pub of an evening, and chat to Lily Bagot in the deli, and to Annie. He was rather good looking, in a tousled, don't-give-a-damn sort of way, with a one-sided smile that might have been irresistible if he had been inclined so to employ it. He wore country clothes—Barbour jackets, wellies, sneakers—and glasses for reading and driving. His wife on the other hand, when actually seen, was something of a disappointment. The rumpled, unmade-up look that suited Michael so well was not what the village expected of an actress, particularly not one with a name like Rianna, and local opinion found her aloof and unapproachable. She had the appropriate cheekbones, but they displayed more angularity than beauty, and her hair, though long and dark, was usually scraped back into a tight coil, with loose ends spraying over the crown of her head. Gossip said she neglected Michael, and local attitudes became tinged with an unexpressed sympathy when he was around.

They had bought an oasthouse on the edge of the village, with two round towers under pixie-hat roofs and a long building in between, wood-paneled, antiques-furnished, expensively heated and replumbed. The River Glyde flowed past it on its meandering way through the water meadows, and their garden ran down to the bank, with mooring for a couple of boats, though they appeared to have only a dinghy, left behind by a previous owner. The house had been empty for a while before they moved in, and Nathan, George, and Hazel had once "borrowed" the dinghy, almost coming to grief in the grip of a current too strong for their oarsmanship. They had had to ram the boat into the bank in order to avoid being swept away—or sinking, since the planking proved far from watertight. Nathan, seeing Michael in the shop one day, felt obliged to mention these hazards, though he would have preferred it if his mother hadn't been within earshot. "You—took—that—boat—out—without—permission?" Annie had paled from a mixture of anger and terror.

"It wasn't stealing!" Nathan protested. "We put it back afterward—and anyway, it didn't seem to belong to anybody then."

"Boats are *dangerous*," Annie said, dismissing the issue of theft unconsidered. "You could've drowned. What were you thinking of?"

"We can all swim. We wouldn't drown, honestly."

"There are weeds under the water that can drag you down . . ."

"Never mind," Michael intervened. "Thanks for warning me, Nathan. That was very thoughtful of you. Actually, I was thinking of getting a boat of my own, just a small one, an inflatable maybe, with an outboard motor. You could come for a ride with me, if your mother doesn't object."

"Of course I don't," Annie said hastily. "It's very kind of you, but—I mean, you don't have to—"

"I'd like to," Michael assured her, turning up the twist of his smile.

"Could I bring my friends?" Nathan asked.

"Nathan—!"

"It's okay," Michael said. "Friends are fine—if the boat's big enough, and there aren't too many of them."

"Just Hazel and George. When will you get the boat?"

"Oh—in the spring, I expect. Too chilly on the river now. Don't worry, Nat: I won't forget about taking you out, I promise. I'm not a forgetting kind of person."

"I wasn't worried," Nathan said. "No one calls me Nat. It sounds a bit American."

"I won't if you dislike it."

Nathan thought about it. "I don't mind," he decided, "if it's just you. And if Mum doesn't mind?"

"It's your name," Annie smiled.

He told the others about this, in the Den the following weekend. George was both excited and rather scared at the prospect of going out in a boat again, but Hazel looked thoughtful. "What's the matter?" Nathan asked her.

"D'you think he likes your mum?" Hazel said, pulling her hair over her eyes as if to hide from his response.

"Why shouldn't he?"

"You know what I mean." She still wouldn't meet his gaze.

"He's married . . ."

"Don't be silly. Married people often like other people; they get divorced; they marry someone else." She added, rather gruffly: "I sometimes wish Mum would divorce Dad. He doesn't love her very much. Great-Grandma Effie says he's no good and never was."

There was a short silence. Mention of Effie Carlow, Hazel's great-grandmother, always commanded respect, since few people had great-grandmothers, and age had given her opinions the aura of wisdom, whether they deserved it or not. What that age was, no one was certain: her piled-up gray hair was still abundant, her walk vigorous, her face wrinkled but not withered. She had a sharp nose and a sharper tongue, and her eyes, under heavy lids, were as keen as a hawk's.

"Even so," Nathan said at last, "I don't think you should put your dad down."

"Only to you." She wouldn't have chosen to confide in George, but Nathan had made him part of their group, and she treated him a little like a favored pet. George being there counted no more than Hoover. Probably less.

"Anyway"—Nathan reverted to the original subject—"Mum wouldn't . . . she wouldn't want someone else's husband."

"My mum says Michael's very attractive," Hazel stated. "And Annie's pretty. She ought to have boyfriends."

Nathan didn't answer. This was a point that had troubled him occasionally. He had friends with single mums, both at the village school and at Ffylde—even some with single dads—and boyfriends and girlfriends were always a problem. Children had to sort them out, encourage the good ones, fend off undesirables. They tended to buy lavish Christmas presents, woo the children with hamburgers, and then shoo them from the room so they could indulge in kissing and fondling while their audience giggled outside. Some new partners brought unwanted brothers and sisters in their train. It was a hazard of modern life. Nathan knew he was lucky not to have these problems, but . . . *but* . . . "Do you want a father?" Annie asked him once.

"I *have* a father," Nathan responded. "He's dead, but he's still my father. I don't need another one. Only . . . well . . . if you have a boyfriend that's all right. As long as he's a nice person, and he loves you. Is there—is there someone?"

"When there is," Annie had said, "you'll be the first to know."

And now there was Michael Addison. Who was nice. And Lily Bagot said he was attractive. He had a wife, but she was an actress, and everyone knew actresses had affairs and got divorced a lot: it went with the territory. Still . . . maybe he loved his wife, and missed her when she was away, turning to Annie only for comfort. Nathan decided he didn't like the situation whichever way you looked at it. *If he starts to give me presents and take me for hamburgers,* he thought, then *I'll know.*

The years in Eade had turned Annie from a girl into a woman. Time had firmed her softness and tapered the planes of her face; her fluffy hair was cut short and fell over her forehead in light brown feather curls. She still wore little makeup, but the country air gave her pale skin the glow of health. Once in a while some man from the village, or one of the city expats, would be extra friendly, and she would smile politely and distance herself, in manner if not words, asserting in thought that it was for her son, knowing—in her more self-analytical moods—that Nathan was an excuse. Perhaps Daniel still had all her heart; perhaps there was something else, lost in that fold of time, that kept her alone and separate, unresponsive to all men. When Michael Addison took to dropping in, to browse among the books and chat, she liked him without reserve, confident that liking was all it would ever be. She was not cold, merely absent in some fundamental place in her spirit, like a nun who, wedded to the idea of God, seeks no mortal husband. But Annie had always been doubtful about God—the Catholic God of her childhood, demanding, faintly patronizing, immersed in ritual. She preferred Bartlemy's theory of the Ultimate Powers, maintaining some kind of equilibrium throughout all the worlds, but exacting neither blind worship nor interminable repentance. Since the moment of Daniel's death she had known with the certainty of experience that there were things out there beyond the range of ordinary human knowledge, other dimensions—universes—beings, and maybe some of them had a foothold on her memory, and a handhold on her heart.

That Christmas Michael and Rianna went to stay with friends in Gloucestershire and afterward went skiing; Hazel's father got drunk and hit Lily, causing her, for the first time, to consult a lawyer; and George was given a pair of binoculars, which were almost, though not quite, as good as a telescope. Annie and Nathan spent the day as they always did, with Bartlemy and Hoover, eating what was, had they but known it, the best Christmas dinner in the country. Bartlemy could do mysterious and wonderful things with food: children would fight to eat their greens when he had cooked them, his roast turkey was moist inside and crisp outside, oozing golden-brown juices, his potatoes crunched and melted, his plum pudding magically combined both airy lightness and dark fruitiness. Afterward, Nathan always remembered that Christmas as especially perfect. It didn't snow, in fact it rained, but they were indoors and the rain was out, and the fire filled the room with warmth and radiance, and his huge dinner disappeared into an elastic stomach and slender body, leaving no visible trace.

Bartlemy had a television, and he picked up channels no one else ever received, and they watched a fairy tale in a foreign language, about an arrogant king who was forced to wander among his people in the guise of a beggar, and learned wisdom and humility, then they played chess, and Nathan almost won, and Annie watched them affectionately and thought: *How lucky I am. How* lucky. And suddenly she was afraid, though she had never been afraid before, in case the luck would change.

And in the New Year Nathan found the sunken chapel, and saw the whispering cup, and then everything was different.

Dreams
and
Whispers

In February, Michael Addison got a new computer and asked Annie if she would come around to help him set it up. "I hear you're the resident expert," he said.

"In a place like Eade," she retorted, "that isn't saying much."

"I'll pay you . . ."

"Don't be ridiculous. I'd do it for the chance to look at your house. The whole village wants to know if it's been transformed like on one of those TV makeover shows."

"The village," he said, grinning, "is going to be very disappointed."

Annie closed the shop early—Bartlemy had always encouraged her to keep whatever business hours she liked, but since Nathan had become a weekly boarder, she had tried to stick to ten till five—walked along the High Street, and turned into the lane to Riverside House. The route ran between hedgerows that were brown and shrunken in their winter barrenness, with meadows on either side; Annie knew one was a conservation area because of the presence of a rare butterfly or orchid. The house lay beyond: she could see the pixie-hat roofs some way off. From the outside, it presented an image of rustic desirability, but when Michael admitted her, leading her through the hallway into what was clearly the main drawing room, she thought it looked curiously unlived-in, the furniture too perfectly arranged, the rugs untrodden, everything clean, immaculate, untouched. "I don't use this room much," Michael said, as though reading her mind. "My domain is in one tower, Rianna's in the other. We meet occasionally in the bedroom." Annie assumed he was joking, but she wasn't sure. She followed him down some steps and into the round chamber that was evidently his study. Units had been designed especially to fit the curve of the wall, and a wooden desk supported the latest thing in computer technology. "Here we are," said Michael. "Tea first, or work first?"

"Work," said Annie.

In the end, it took far longer than she had intended. "To me, this machine is just a glorified typewriter," Michael said, so she spent some time sorting out his files, teaching him to use search engines, surfing the Internet. When they finished it was dark, and Michael declared it was too late for tea, offering her a drink instead, and a quick tour of the house, if she wanted. "So you can tell the village grapevine about all the redecorating we haven't done." Even the master bedroom, Annie thought, looked unslept-in: Michael had a couch in the upper room of his "tower." The bathroom boasted a circular bath almost the size of a swimming pool; there were several guest bedrooms, though they never seemed to have guests; the kitchen had the latest kind of Aga, but the microwave appeared to have seen more use. Except in Michael's rooms there was luxury without personality, and a strange coldness, as if the whole house was an exhibit rather than a residence. Annie didn't get to see inside Rianna's tower: that was kept locked. "Rianna's very intense about her privacy," Michael explained. "Even I don't have a key."

"Bluebeard's Chamber," Annie said before she could stop herself.

"Stacked with the bodies of her ex-husbands?" Michael laughed. "There's only been one, he's a producer, I've met him. He's about sixty now and married to a blonde of twenty-three."

"Sorry," Annie said. "I didn't mean to be rude, or . . . or nosy."

"You weren't," said Michael. "I suppose it does sound a bit odd, to people who don't know Rianna. She's—I expect you would call her temperamental. Personal space is very important to her. We have a wonderful maid, a Yugoslav émigrée who comes over from Crowford, but Rianna won't let her in there; she prefers to do the cleaning herself. Now, what would you like to drink? There's whiskey, gin, beer . . . whiskey, more whiskey."

"I'll have a whiskey," Annie said with a smile.

They had their drinks in the sitting room above Michael's study, with the couch "for those short kips between periods of not working," a couple of worn leather armchairs, and a view over the conservation area in one direction and down to the river in the other. Since it was too dark to see very far, Michael took some pains to explain about the benefits of the view. When they dimmed the light Annie saw a shiny new moon in a sky full of crispy stars, and shadowy fields stretching away toward the village, and the twinkling of illuminated windows in the nearest houses. She turned back, and there was Michael's crooked smile, soft in the dimness, and his glasses hiding the expression in his eyes. He turned up the light, and she found herself looking at a picture of Rianna on a sideboard, a very glamorous picture, black and white, with a cloud of hair framing her artistic cheekbones, and deep-set eyes darkly made up under the flying line of her brows.

"She's very beautiful," Annie said politely.

"I know," said Michael. It might have been her fancy that he sounded almost rueful.

When their glasses were empty, he said: "I'll walk you home." And then: "Damn. It's later than I thought. I've got a call coming in, from the States."

"I'll be fine," Annie assured him.

I like him, she thought, *but I don't like the house. Apart from his bit. There's something wrong about it, something . . .*

Something to do with Rianna Sardou.

She set off down the lane, hugging her coat around her in the cold, lost in her own reflections. The awareness didn't come upon her suddenly; rather, it was a gradual feeling, a creeping change in the night, a slow prickle down her spine. There was a moment when she stopped, and glanced back, seeing nothing, and felt that the wrongness she had sensed in the house had come with her, following her, becoming a shadow at her heels, a listener on the edge of hearing. There was a horrible familiarity about it. And then a shiver seemed to run through the hedgerows, as if a darkness slipped between the leafless stems, and she caught the whisper of words that could not be discerned, a whisper quieter than quiet, so close to her ear she expected to feel the chill of its breath on her cheek.

Them.

She didn't run: there was no point. She walked very quickly, trying not to look back again, counting her paces in heartbeats. The lane dipped as it ran through the meadows and for a few minutes she could see no lights ahead, and she was alone, or not alone, and behind her she knew the shadows were playing grandmother's footsteps, and the whisper was so intimate she could imagine disembodied lips moving within an inch of her face. She fancied there was a cold touch on her nape, as if a groping hand reached out to seize her—and then she saw the lights of a house in front, and the fantasy withdrew, and she began to run as though released from a spell. Past gardens and back gates, into the village street, down the road to the bookshop. She shut and locked the door, but she knew it would be no use: no door had ever kept *them* out save that of Thornyhill. She stumbled to the phone and pressed out a number with unsteady fingers.

Ten minutes later Bartlemy was sitting in her little back room, filling much of it, a quiet, reassuring presence.

"After Nathan was born," Annie was saying, "I always thought I went a little crazy. *They* were part of the craziness—that was what I told myself. Until now. But *you* saw them, didn't you? The night we came to Thornyhill. You saw them following me."

"Oh yes," he said calmly. "I saw them."

"What are they? Who are they? Why have they come back?"

"If I knew the answers to those questions," said Bartlemy, "I would be a wiser, if not a happier man. I know only what I have observed or deduced. They seem to have no real substance, yet they exist. They are made of shadow and fear. There are always many together, a swarm rather than individuals. They are like nothing I have ever seen before, and I have seen many strange things. I was able to keep them away from Thornyhill—my influence is strong there—and I hoped they were gone for good, but clearly that isn't so. Yet why should they reappear now? Where have they been? In hibernation, maybe, until some call or need drew them forth. You were visiting Riverside House?"

"Yes. I wondered . . . if they were there waiting. There's something not quite right in that place. Not creepy, just rather peculiar. A feeling as if—something was out of kilter. I think it has to do with Michael's wife."

"Rianna Sardou . . . A theatrical name. A name for a witch. I believe she looks like one, too, at least on screen: all darkness and glamour. A storybook witch. But stories can lie."

"Do you think there's a connection between Rianna and—*them?*"

"I don't know," he admitted. "I don't know why they pursued you in the past, or why that pursuit resumed today. As I said, I don't know any of the answers, but I can think of another question."

"What's that?" Annie could think of several.

"Why don't they ever catch up?"

Annie shivered. "*Don't!* I thought—something *touched* me, back there in the lane . . ."

"Nonetheless, they didn't catch you. They followed you for months, all those years ago, and they didn't catch you. Why not? They are far swifter than humans. They hunted you with darkness and terror, but you always eluded them. Are they chasing you, or simply watching you—spying on you? Or else—"

"Can we not discuss it anymore?" Annie pleaded. "At least for now. I want to sleep tonight."

"You can stay at Thornyhill, if you wish."

"No," she said. "I'll stay here. This is my place."

In bed later, she lay awake a long time, but no movement stirred the curtain, and the night was empty and still.

NATHAN DREAMED. Not the now familiar nightmare of the cup, with the hissing snake voices and the taste of blood; this was a dreamscape he had known since early childhood, once vague and surreal, now increasingly vivid. A city. A city at the end of Time. Towers soared up a mile or more, many-faceted, topped with glass minarets reflecting sky and spires whose glitter caught the sun. Far below, the ground was unseen beneath bridges and archways studded with windows, flyovers, walkways, suspended gardens. Airborne vehicles cruised the spaces in between, leaving contrails in their wake that shimmered a little while and then vanished. And occasionally there were creatures like giant birds, with webbed pinions stretching to a vast span and bony beaks and human-sized riders hidden behind masks and goggles. Nathan had always enjoyed these dreams because often he traveled in one of the skimmers, looping the towers and diving under the archways, until he went spinning through a hundred dimensions of the dreamworld and tumbled at last into his own bed, waking exhilarated from the thrill of the ride.

This time, it was different. There was a huge dull sun, just risen, glimpsed moving through the gaps between buildings, climbing ponderously toward the open sky. The topmost towers and minarets had already sprung into glittering life and floated like islands of light above shadowy canyons where the dawn had yet to penetrate. Nathan was gliding through the air, an awareness without substance or being, looking through oval windows into an interlocking maze of rooms, all empty, like a termite mound with no termites. The city was enormous but there appeared to be few people, and those all far away, too far to see clearly, moving singly or in twos and threes, never a crowd. Presently, he found he was drifting beside one of the birds, but from up close it looked more like a reptile, its beak a pointed muzzle, its wings taloned, its long tail tipped with a spike. Its skin looked hard and had a slight gloss on it, as if it was made up of tiny scales, very tight-packed, steel blue in color and sheened with the early sunlight. The rider, too, wore blue, clothed from head to foot in some kind of metallized mesh, his hood close fitting, with a slit for the mouth, a noseguard, and opaque goggles covering the eyeholes. His saddle was very high in the pommel, the reins attached not to a bit but to iron rings that pierced the flesh at the corners of the creature's mouth. Nathan thought it must be very painful, but he noticed the rider used only the lightest touches to steer, barely perceptible to the observer. The creature had an extreme fixity of expression even by animal standards; it took Nathan a little while to realize why. The eyes, set under bony ridges, had neither iris nor pupil: they were blood red from edge to edge, lidless, locked in a perpetual stare.

The flight was very fast, faster than the skimmers, though the wings beat only at intervals; a whisk of the tail acted as a rudder. They came to land very suddenly on a rooftop platform where another hooded figure, this time in a plasticized suit and heavy gauntlets, took the reins while the rider dismounted. The gauntleted man—assuming it was a man—tethered the creature and fed it from a bucket of things that squirmed. Nathan followed the rider to a sort of cylindrical kiosk and stepped through a sliding door into what was plainly an elevator. They descended a short distance and emerged onto a long gallery with a high, coved ceiling and rows of pillars down either side, not straight but warped and twisted into irregular shapes like distorted trees. There were no windows, but a pale glow, like an echo of daylight, came from the ceiling. At the far end they passed into a semicircular room whose curved wall, in contrast to the gallery, was all glass, though shielded in places with translucent screens. There was very little furniture, just a complex unit that might have been a desk and a couple of chairs. The automatic door closed behind them. Beyond the arc of the window, the sun's rays were reaching down into the deep places of the city.

A man stood with his back to them, gazing out. He was taller than the rider by a head, though Nathan had thought the rider exceptionally tall. His silhouette showed wide shoulders, booted feet a little apart, arms presumably folded. He had an aura of power and great stillness. Long after, Nathan would remember this moment, this dream, more vividly than any moment in his life before, but at the time he did not know its significance, nor guess. The rider waited, saying nothing. Eventually, the man turned.

He wore black, with a black hood, but his face was concealed by a mask of something like Perspex, white as alabaster, molded into a semblance of human features. The mouth slit opened between sculpted lips, the nostril holes pierced an aquiline nose, the enlarged eyes were leaf-shaped, protected by bubbles of black glass. Like the rider, like the man on the roof, not an inch of skin was exposed, not even a hair. When he spoke, Nathan understood him; it was only afterward he realized the language was not English.

He said: "Well?"

"It's worse," answered the rider. "Dru didn't want you to know. He's afraid Souza will be cut off."

"It must be. There is no choice." The man's tone was cool rather than cold, all trace of feeling carefully extracted. "We will cut off the whole of Maali, from Ingorut to Khadesh."

"An entire continent?" The horror in the rider's voice was imperfectly suppressed.

"Yes." The white mask expressed neither apology nor regret. "The contamination will spread beyond Souza in months, perhaps weeks. We have to act now. Our Time is running out." And again, with peculiar emphasis: "All of Time is running out."

"Is there any hope?" asked the rider.

Behind the mask, Nathan imagined the man smiled. "Hope is a chimera," he said. "I do not clutch at chimeras. I made my plans long, long ago. There is no hope, but there *are* plans. We will hold to them. Now eat, and rest. You have flown far. Is your xaurian tired?"

"No, sir. He is strong."

"Good. I will summon you later. You will go with the Fifth Phalanx to Maali. You know the coast."

The rider made a brief bow, and withdrew.

The white-masked man moved one hand in a strange gesture, murmuring a word Nathan could not hear. An image appeared in front of him, life-sized, three-dimensional, evidently made of light. It wore a purple cowl and a mask patterned with whorls and lines, and it shivered slightly as though with interference.

"Souza is contaminated," said the white mask, briefly. "Instigate cutoff for Maali."

"The whole of Maali?" said the purple cowl, evidently shocked. His voice crackled, like someone telephoning on a bad line.

"Of course. Send the Fifth Phalanx and one of the senior practors. Raymor will go with them. He knows the terrain."

Purple cowl hesitated, as if considering a protest, but refrained. Then he, too, bowed, vanishing at a gesture from his master.

The man walked toward the window again, resuming his contemplation of the city. Nathan saw him from close up, his chin sunken, the white shapely features gleaming in the daylight, the black bulge of the eye screens revealing nothing. But behind the mask he sensed a mind at work, an inscrutable intelligence, vast and complex, numberless mental circuits interlocking, focused on a single path of thought, a plan, a goal—whatever that goal might be. Nathan had never before imagined such a mind—a mind so powerful that he could *feel* it thinking, could sense the surge and flicker of suppressed emotion, the dreadful urgency beneath the calm of absolute control. Its proximity frightened him and he tried to draw away, pushing at the dream until it began to break up, and he was plunged into a long, dark tunnel of fading sensation. He lost himself in sleep, but when he woke at last the dream was still with him, clear as truth, and the memory of it didn't grow dim.

It was perhaps two weeks before he returned there. He knew it was the same world, the same dream, though the environment had changed. He was with a rider again, possibly Raymor, though now there were many of them, flying in successive V-formations of thirteen, the infrequent wing beats of the xaurians almost exactly in unison. Below, the dull glitter of sunlight moved over a huge expanse of sea, stretching from horizon to horizon. He could see the ripple effect of endless waves, and here and there a dimpling of white as breakers clashed in a volcano of spray. Soon a strip of coast appeared, rushing toward them, growing swiftly. He saw gray cliffs falling sheer to the sea, and beyond, an uneven plateau, treeless and bleak. The phalanx swung left and began to follow the shoreline. On the foremost xaurian he noticed there was a second figure seated behind the rider, dressed in red. What he was doing Nathan didn't know, but his hand moved in a series of intricate gestures, and the air on their shoreward side thickened into a haze, like a veil dividing them from the land. The cliffs were barely visible now, plunging downward to a broad inlet spanned by many bridges and surrounded by a sprawling port. There seemed to be boats on the water, and occasional skimmers wheeling insect-like above. One veered around and came toward them, but the veil grew denser even as it approached, and when it hit the barrier sparks ran along its sides, igniting into flame, and it spiraled down into the ocean like a dying firework. The red figure went on with its ritual: Nathan was close enough now to hear the murmur of a chant. Glancing to seaward, he glimpsed another boat, far outside the barrier. Two xaurians broke away from the outer wing and headed toward it. Nathan couldn't see clearly what happened, but there was a spurt of fire on the boat, and then it had vanished, and the waves rolled on unbroken.

He didn't like the dream now, for all the exhilaration of the flight. He felt as if merely by watching, by being there, he had become a part of it, a mute participant in some terrible misdeed. He tried to pull himself away from the phalanx, and found his thought was falling, dropping like a stone toward the sea. And then his dive slowed to a glide, brushing the wave crests, just above the place where the ship had gone down. There was someone in the water, presumably the last of the crew: he saw the gray hood bobbing up and down. The person had no life belt, no inflatable jacket; he wouldn't last long. The xaurian riders, knowing that, had left him to his fate. Even though the drowning man had no visible face Nathan felt his terror, and the need to help grew inside him, strong as rage, until he thought he would burst with it. He drifted lower, reaching out, feeling the slap of cold water on his skin, seizing the flailing hands with a grip that caught and held. Then they were jerked out of the dream with a violence that made Nathan's stomach turn, landing painfully on a beach of stones. A beach at night, with breakers crumbling on the shingle, and upflung sheets of foam, luminous in the darkness. Nathan released the clasping hands and sensed himself withdrawing, sliding backward into oblivion. The dormitory bell roused him, hours or minutes later. He sat up, conscious of discomfort, and found the sleeves of his pajamas were damp.

That Saturday there was a rugby match against another school. Nathan scored two tries, helping the Ffylde Abbey team to victory, and went home late and on a high. He had been planning to tell Bartlemy about the dreams but somehow, when it came to it, he distrusted his own imagination, and was not yet ready to expose himself to the possibility of disbelief. On Sunday he would see Hazel, though, and confiding in her was second nature to him. (Not George, he decided, without asking himself why. Just Hazel.) In the morning he and Annie sat over a late breakfast, listening to the local news on the radio. A projected housing development, a missing person, the risk of flooding in the area. "A man discovered three days ago on the beach at Pevensey Bay is believed to be an illegal immigrant. He was dressed in waterproof clothing that covered him from head to foot, suggesting he may have swum in from a boat. He speaks no English, and so far his nationality has not been established. Police think it unlikely he was alone and are asking local residents to be on the lookout."

Annie noticed Nathan had stopped eating his cornflakes. "Are you all right?" she inquired.

"Yes. Yes, of course." He resumed his breakfast, but with less enthusiasm. After a minute, he asked: "What will they do with him? Will they—will they put him in prison?"

"The illegal immigrant? I suppose so. Until they work out who he is, and whether to grant him asylum."

"But . . . that's wrong. He's alone. He's desperate. We should help him."

Annie was touched by his concern. "Yes, we should," she said. "The trouble is, people are afraid. They're afraid of strangers, of anybody different. They think immigrants will take their jobs or their homes, even though there aren't that many of them, and newcomers *create* jobs as well as doing them. But fear makes people stupid, and sometimes cruel."

"Could I go and see him?" Nathan demanded abruptly. "The man on the beach?"

Annie looked astonished. "I don't think so," she said. "They wouldn't let you. Maybe you could write."

"Yes, but . . . he doesn't speak English," Nathan reminded her. He gave up on breakfast altogether, and asked to leave the table. He wanted space to think.

"It's impossible," Hazel said that afternoon, in the Den, but she didn't sound sure.

"There are meant to be lots of other universes," Nathan said. "That isn't just in books; Father Clement told us about it, in physics. There are millions of them, some like ours, some different. It's called the multiverse. Supposing, in my dream, I was actually *in* one of them, and somehow I pulled that man out, back into ours?"

"That's ridiculous," Hazel said, curiously daunted. When they were much younger, the two of them had spent a lot of time exploring wardrobes in the hope of making their way into other worlds, but she had outgrown such fantasies now. Or so she told herself, part wistful, part scornful, strangely afraid. She knew Nathan would never lie to her.

"You're talking about *magic*," she said at last. She had no opinion of physics.

"Maybe." Nathan was pensive. "What *is* magic, anyway? According to someone or other, it's just science we don't understand."

"How do we find out more?"

"I don't know. I could ask Uncle Barty: he knows about lots of things. History, and archaeology, and all the sciences. Besides, Mum says his cooking is definitely magical."

Hazel made a snorting noise. "Cooking isn't magic," she said. "Even if that chocolate cake for your last birthday *was* amazing . . . Are there books on it? Magic, not cooking."

Nathan nodded. "They're called grimoires. Mum had some in once. I thought they would be interesting, but they were awfully dull, just about drawing runes and symbols, and picking herbs at the full moon, and boring rituals for calling up demons. There weren't even any sacrifices, let alone stuff about other worlds. They wouldn't be any good to us." There was a long silence, filled with frustrated thought. "What we need," said Nathan, "is a witch. Witches were burned here, hundreds of years ago, in that open space outside the church. Uncle Barty told me about it. I asked him if they were real witches, and he said mostly not—but *mostly* isn't *all*. I read the names: some of them were Carlows, like your great-grandmother. Was she born a Carlow, or did she marry one?"

"Both, I think," Hazel said, frowning. "Dad's always telling Mum her family are inbred. He said Great-Grandma was barmy, and she married her own cousin, which is supposed to make your children mad or sub or something . . . He says she's a witch, too, but I expect that's just an insult."

"We could go and ask her," Nathan suggested tentatively. "She wouldn't mind us asking—would she? It isn't as if witches get burned nowadays."

"She'll mind," Hazel said with conviction. "She's . . . well, you know."

Nathan did know. Effie Carlow's acid tongue and eagle stare did not encourage idle questions. However . . .

"If we can't think of anyone else," he said, "we'll have to ask her. We must ask *someone*."

Back at school, he tried to listen to the news on the Common Room radio as much as possible, but there was nothing further about the man on the beach. He sounded out Father Clement on alternative universes, but the monk said that to his knowledge nobody had ever visited one, though he assumed it would be feasible. In theory. By Friday night when his mother took him home to Eade, Nathan had made up his mind. On Saturday George came around, so it wasn't until Sunday that he told Hazel: "We have to go and see your great-grandmother. There isn't anyone else."

Effie Carlow lived in a cottage on the Chizzledown road about half a mile outside Eade. Built in the Victorian era, weathering had mellowed its facade and climbing plants had overgrown its more commonplace features, rendering it attractive if not picturesque. Too small to be of interest to buyers from London, it had diminutive windows admitting little light into poky rooms and a roof that sagged almost to ground level, while at the rear there was an outbuilding that Effie rented to a local artist as as studio. The walled garden was a miniature wilderness in which weeds and wildflowers predominated.

"We ought to call her first," Nathan had said before they set out.

"She isn't on the phone," said Hazel.

It was about four o'clock when they arrived, a well-chosen hour for a casual visit, or so Nathan hoped. After a nervous exchange of glances with Hazel, he tapped twice with the knocker, noticing belatedly that there was also a doorbell hiding behind a tendril of creeper. After a long wait during which they strained their ears for the sound of approaching feet and heard nothing, the door opened a few inches. "Well?" said Effie Carlow.

"Hello, Great-Grandma," Hazel mumbled, and "We're sorry if we're interrupting," from Nathan, "but there's something we particularly wanted to ask you."

The old woman looked him up and down with her raptor's eye. When he didn't continue, she said impatiently: "So ask me."

"It's about witches," he said, feeling increasingly awkward. "I read in a local history book there were witches burned at the stake here, a long time ago, and some of them were called Carlow. We wanted to know about—about witchcraft, and other worlds, and things, and we wondered if you would be able to help."

There was a change in her expression that he couldn't define, a sort of sharpening, though her glance was always sharp; a subtle adjustment. Then she opened the door wider. "Come in."

They stepped straight into a sitting room crowded with furniture and bric-a-brac. Pictures and bookshelves jostled on the walls, chairs were squashed arm to arm, small tables supported lamps, teacups, ornaments, an old-fashioned wireless. None of the lamps was on and in the gloom they could make out few details, but the overall effect was that of a rummage sale in a phone booth. "Sit down," Effie continued. They sat in adjacent chairs, not quite holding hands, while she made them bitter dark tea with very little milk and added, as an afterthought, a plate of stale cookies. "I've been keeping these for a special guest," she explained. "You can have some, if you like."

"Thank you," Nathan said politely, "but I had a big lunch."

"You can have some."

Impelled by her determination, he took a cookie. Hazel followed suit. She was still surprised they had been invited in and had lapsed into an apprehensive silence, leaving Nathan to do the talking. He attempted to phrase a question but was foiled by the cookie, which was tough and required extensive chewing.

"Why do you want to know about witches?" Effie demanded. "Witches . . . and other worlds and things. But the Carlow witches were of *this* world, until they were burned. What goes on in other worlds no man knows."

"Nathan does," Hazel whispered. Her cookie had proved more disposable.

"And what does Nathan know?"

"I have—these dreams," he said, between swallows. "There's this place—I see different locations, a city, and a shoreline, but I know it's the same place—and there are flying vehicles, like cars without wheels, and people riding on birds that are really reptiles, sort of pterodactyls—and I tried to rescue this man who was drowning, and a few days later I heard something on the news about an illegal immigrant, and I—I knew it was the same man."

"How could you tell?" Effie's manner was brisk.

"They described his clothes. He was in a kind of one-piece suit that covered him all over, with a hood for his face and head. And they said he spoke no English, and they couldn't work out his nationality."

"Inconclusive," Effie said. "An illegal immigrant might well wear a one-piece, a wet suit or something similar, if he had swum ashore. I heard that news item: they said so. As for your dreams—witches know about dreams, I won't deny that, but it sounds to me like you've been watching too many science-fiction films. Concentrate on your homework instead of the television."

"Nathan does well at school," Hazel said bravely.

"Does he? Then why all this nonsense about other worlds?"

"Because it did make sense," Nathan replied, "in my dream. If you didn't believe me, why did you ask us in?"

The old woman leaned forward, cupping her hand around his

face to draw it closer, digging her nails into his cheeks. Her fingers felt all knobbles and bones, but they seemed to be horribly strong. Her fierce eyes stared straight into his. In the poor light he could not tell their color, only that they were dark and had a luster that was not quite human. He fancied she was seeking to look right into his mind, to unpick his thoughts and probe even to his subconscious, but he met stare with stare, trying to remain steadfast, not defiant but unyielding.

At length she released him and sank back in her chair. "So," she said, "a dreamer, a traveler in other worlds. Well, we shall see. Ancestresses of mine were drowned on the ducking stool and burned at the stake, and maybe I have inherited something of their Gift. I can read the future, and sometimes even the present, and only a fool would play cards with me. If there is anything to be seen, Nathan Ward, I will see it. Meanwhile, dream carefully. This tumbling from world to world—if that is what you are doing—is bad for the stomach, and worse for the head. Take care you don't leave your brains behind."

"You *do* believe him," Hazel said, "don't you, Great-Grandma?"

"You are impertinent," Effie snapped. "It is for me to decide whom and what I believe." She rose to her feet and so did the children, conscious they had outstayed their welcome—if indeed they had ever had one. Suddenly, Effie rounded on Hazel, seizing her by the hair, plucking the loose strands off her face. But unlike Nathan, the girl could not meet her gaze, blinking in the grip of something akin to panic. "Remember," her great-grandmother said after a minute or two, "you, too, are a Carlow." The rasp in her voice might have softened, if she had been capable of softness; as it was, Hazel flinched away, twisting her head in the older woman's grasp, averting her eyes. Then Effie let go, and the children were thrust outside. A pileup of cloud was vanquishing the last of the daylight: it seemed as if they had brought the gloom of the cottage with them. They heard the front door shut, not with a *bang* but a *snick*, and began to walk along the roadside.

"Does she have some kind of power," Nathan wondered, "or does she just *think* she has? There's something definitely creepy about her."

Hazel shivered. "Mum says she has the Sight, whatever that means. I remember she knew, the week before, when Uncle Gavin was going to die."

"When was that?"

"Ages ago. Nearly a year. It was while you were at school."

"Was your uncle ill?" Nathan inquired, looking skeptical. "After all, if someone is really ill, it's fairly easy to guess when they're going to die."

"No, he wasn't. It was a—a neurism, or something. Very sudden."

They walked on a while in silence. Nathan was frowning. "What did she mean," he said, "when she told you that, you, too, are a Carlow?"

Hazel didn't reply.

"She thinks you've got power, too, doesn't she? Something you've inherited, like a gene for witchcraft."

"I'm normal," Hazel said abruptly. "I'm normal as normal. I don't want to be like her. Anyway, Mum doesn't have any powers that I know of. If she did, she'd be able to deal with Dad."

"Genes can sometimes skip a generation," Nathan said knowledgeably. "If they're recessive. We learned about that in biology."

"Look, I'm not a witch, okay?" Hazel said, her voice growing deeper as it always did when she was upset. "I don't believe in witches—not even Great-Grandma Effie. I'm just a girl."

"Pity," Nathan remarked. "Being a witch would be cool. We haven't made much progress on other worlds, have we?"

Hazel was silent again, scuffing her feet as she walked. She still seemed to be disturbed by the imputation of witchcraft.

I'll have to ask Uncle Barty, Nathan thought. *But not yet. Not unless I have more dreams.*

But time passed, and though he dreamed of the cup, and woke with the whispers in his ear, he did not revisit the alien world for a long while.

ANNIE, TOO, neither heard nor sensed her unseen pursuers, though as spring mellowed into summer she often walked alone through wood or meadow, half daring the shadows to follow her. She was friendly with Michael, but she didn't go to his house again, troubled by her one afternoon there and its consequences. Rianna was seen in the village, between engagements, and once came into the shop. Annie had noticed her a couple of weeks before on television in a repeat of an old drama, and she was privately taken aback at the contrast between her glamorous onscreen persona and the offscreen reality. Her face was gaunt, almost ugly, the eyes naturally shadowed, the mouth, without lipstick, pale and ill defined. She wore no jewelry, not even a wedding ring. She scanned the shelves with no real interest and then asked for a particular book, but Annie had the impression she was making conversation, checking her out. Maybe Rianna had heard some village gossip, coupling Annie's name with Michael's; but she was fairly sure there had been none—and how would Rianna hear gossip, when she avoided local chitchat and was almost always away?

"I hear you have a son," Rianna said. "Twelve or thirteen?"

"Twelve."

"They say he's very unusual, for a boy of that age."

"I think him special," Annie confirmed with some warmth.

"Part Asian, I understand?"

There was a nuance in her words, Annie believed, and she did her best to suppress a tiny spurt of anger. "Do you?" she said.

If she was hostile, Rianna didn't appear to notice. "Who *was* his father?" she asked. There was a note of boredom in her voice, as if the question was automatic rather than inquisitive, but the narrow eyes were intent. Or so Annie imagined, though in the somber interior of the bookshop it was difficult to be sure.

"He was my husband," she answered, and there was an instant when Rianna appeared to freeze, perhaps recognizing the snub, but it passed, and she turned away and left the shop without further questions.

She seemed more interested in Nathan than in my friendship with Michael, Annie thought, and she found this so baffling that she determined to mention it to Bartlemy, when a suitable opportunity arose.

In the kitchen at Thornyhill, Bartlemy listened to the story in his usual unruffled manner. The cauldron of stock still simmered on the stove; Annie couldn't recall a time when it hadn't been there, and she had a sudden fancy that it was the same as the night she arrived, its contents stirred, sampled, augmented, but never changed, growing richer and more flavorsome over the years. The smell that drifted from beneath the lid still made her mouth water, and a mug of that broth—something Bartlemy doled out only rarely—satisfied hunger and warmed the heart like nothing else. "Do you ever change your stockpot?" she asked him.

"Good stock needs time," he said. "The longer, the better."

"How long?" Annie inquired; but he didn't answer.

"Don't worry about this Rianna Sardou," he said at last. "She's probably just curious."

"Why should she be curious about Nathan?" Annie persisted. "She must know of him through Michael, but . . . why ask about his *father?*"

"It may have been just a shot in the dark. She may be the inquisitive type. Has she ever seen him?"

"I don't know. I don't think so. He likes Michael, so I expect he would've mentioned meeting his wife."

"Mm. Well, no doubt the truth will become evident in due course.

Events—like this stock—take time to mature. You are young, and impatient."

"Not that young," Annie said. "I'm thirty-six."

"How old is Rianna Sardou, do you suppose?"

"Late thirties . . . forty . . . Older than Michael, I think. Why?"

"I just wondered," Bartlemy said.

When she had gone, he sat in the living room with Hoover, drinking sweet tea and gazing into the fire. "Why did I come here?" he asked of no one in particular, but Hoover cocked an ear. "I read the signs, but I have never been one to follow such things. There have been few portents for me, over the years. All I ever wanted to do was heal sickness, and cook. Two sides of the same coin, Rukush. Drugs and potions cure illness, good food makes the body strong, and great food—ah, great food nourishes the soul. I can prepare a dessert that will turn a peasant into a poet, I can soothe the tyrant's rage with soups and sauces, I can roast a sirloin so tender that it would make a proud man humble and an atheist believe in God. That was all the power I ever wanted. But when I saw a fantasy in the smoke I came here, and I waited. And the day Annie knocked on my door I knew that was what I was waiting for. Annie and the child. But still I don't know why. There are always more questions, less answers. I think it is time to draw the curtains shut and make a different fire."

When the last of the logs had burned down he cleaned out the grate and pinned the curtains together against prying eyes. Even so, it was far into the night before he lit a new fire, feeding it not with wood or coal but with bluish crystals that spat and cracked after too long in storage. The flame they emitted was also bluish, and cold looking, and it filled the room with a pale, chill light. Presently, he threw on it some powder that seemed to be damp, turning the flame to smoke, and the room darkened again, and the chimney was closed off so the smoke could not escape, and the eyes of both man and dog grew red from the sting of it. Bartlemy made a gesture, a little like that of the man in Nathan's dream, and the smoke was sucked into a cloud that hovered in one place, and there was a whirling at its heart. Vague colors flickered in its depths like trails of light. Then the whirling steadied, and the colors condensed, and in the midst of the smoke there was a picture.

A cup. It looked medieval or older, with a wide bowl and a short, thick stem entwined in coiling patterns that seemed to shape themselves into runes and hieroglyphs. It was made of opaque glass or polished stone, but it glowed as if endowed with secret life, and appeared to be floating in the green halo of its own light. The thread of a whisper came to Bartlemy's ears from nothing in the room. Then the light vanished and the cup was falling, clattering onto a floor somewhere, rolling back and forth on the arc of its rim. A human hand descended slowly, and picked it up. "The Grimthorn Grail," Bartlemy murmured. "One of a hundred—a thousand—that lay claim to the ancient legend. But it was sold abroad, and lost in the turmoil of war, and the Thorns who failed to care for it are long gone . . ."

The vision of the cup was replaced by a muddle of dim shapes, all unclear, but he thought he could make out a running figure, coming toward him. The image was too dark to see properly but he had an impression of breathlessness and fear, and shadows following, swarming on its heels, and in the quiet of the night there was the sound of whispering, reaching out from the smoke. It seemed to him that it was the same whisper he had heard a few minutes earlier, though louder, and with different words, different purpose. But he couldn't be sure, since the words were indistinguishable, the purpose unrevealed. The picture sombered and was lost, and other images succeeded it, changing swiftly, some distinct, some vague and blurred. A small chapel with a cloaked man going from candle to candle: the lighted taper picked out his profile as he bent his head, the nose outthrust like a broken spar, the lipless fold of the mouth, the eyes sagging between multiple lids. The candles burned with a greasy flame, showing a gargoyle face peering from a stony arch, and a low altar without a cross. Then the scene dissolved into a wood with tangled trees, maybe the Darkwood—then the flash and sparkle of a river in sunshine—a cage or grille, and hands that shook the bars—a wood in springtime, with a brown twig-legged creature lurking in the hollow of a tree—the river again, only this time there was a face beneath the water, and rippled sunlight flowing over it, but he knew it wasn't drowned. Then back to the cloaked man, raising his arm, and a sudden blaze of fire, fire in the chapel, fire in the wood—and lastly, for no reason that Bartlemy could understand, a shingle beach in the drear light of a winter's morning, and the ebb and surge of gray waves, and a man who seemed to have come out of the water, wearing a hood that covered his entire head.

Bartlemy rose from his chair: he had used few crystals, and he assumed the visions were over. "There is a pattern here," he told Hoover, "if only I could see it. Possibly the shadows that hounded Annie are connected to the Grimthorn Grail—but they pursued her *to* this place, not from it, and the Grail has not been here for nearly a century. Who sent them—if they were sent—and how? Such a sending would take power. Josevius Grimthorn is long dead; could his influence live on?"

Hoover made a soft sound in his throat, almost a growl, and Bartlemy, who had bent to unblock the chimney, glanced back into the smoke. It was already thinning, but for a few seconds he saw another image there, too dim to identify, a woman with gray hair in a bun, leaning forward over a shallow basin full of some cloudy liquid, and briefly, very briefly, looking up at the woman, out of the basin, a reflection that he knew was his own face.

For an instant his placidity vanished: he spoke one word, and the smoke was scattered into wisps that fled into every corner of the room. "Careless!" he apostrophized himself. "I do these things so rarely—I never much liked conjuring—but there's no excuse for such a slip." He removed the screen from the flue, and the smoke sneaked out. Then he took a bottle out of a cupboard—a bottle that was grimed with age rather than dirt, like something retrieved from a shipwreck—unstoppered the neck, and poured himself a very small glass, hardly more than a thimbleful. The liquor was almost black and smelled darkly fruity and overpoweringly alcoholic. Bartlemy sat down again to savor it.

Hoover raised his head hopefully.

"No, you can't," said his master. "You know it won't agree with you. Well, well. Euphemia Carlow . . . Where does she fit in, I wonder? Time was when her kind were happy to curdle the milk with a look and cure warts for a farthing, but now . . . the world changes. Still, she must always have known what I am, or guessed. She's no fool, if less wise than she wishes to appear. Let's hope that what she has seen will be a warning to her. Curiosity is no good for either cats or witches."

IN APRIL, Nathan turned thirteen. "You were a spring baby," Annie recalled. "You came with the swallows."

"I thought it was supposed to be a stork," Nathan said with mock innocence.

Annie laughed.

Michael had bought a boat, not an inflatable with an outboard motor but a twenty-six-foot sailboat that he said he would take down to the sea from time to time. He had done quite a bit of sailing when he was younger, he explained, and a boat this size he could handle on his own. For Nathan's birthday he offered to take him, George, and Hazel downriver, weather permitting. Nathan was obviously thrilled at the idea, and Annie suppressed a tiny pang, which she knew to be unworthy, that he preferred an excursion without her. "Why don't you come?" Michael had said, but Annie declined.

"I get seasick."

"On a river?"

"I get seasick on a bouncy castle."

At the last moment Nathan said he would forgo the treat, he wanted to spend a family day after all, but Annie, undeceived, dealt summarily with that. She saw them all off around noon, sweater-clad and life-jacketed for the seagoing part of their trip, and then returned to Thornyhill with Bartlemy. A suitable birthday cake had been prepared, and the sailors had wrapped several slices in foil to take with them, but there was a large section left, and Annie, Bartlemy, and Hoover sat by the fire at teatime (it was not yet too warm for a fire to be unwelcome) and munched their way through a respectable portion of it. Annie talked about Nathan, as she so often did, proud of his academic achievements, but still happier at the person she felt he was growing into. "I'm being boring," she said, catching herself up short. "Boring on about my son."

"What mother doesn't?" Bartlemy smiled. "You know I'm not bored."

"It's at times like this," Annie continued after a few minutes, "birthdays, and family times, that I wonder most about his father. Not—not Daniel, I can't fool myself that he's like Daniel. Maybe in nature, in some ways, but not looks."

"He could be a throwback," Bartlemy said lightly. "You shouldn't worry about it."

"A throwback to what? And I don't worry, that's not the word. I just feel I ought to *know*. One day soon he's going to ask, and I'll have to tell him, but I've no idea *what* I'm going to tell him. Have you . . . thought about it any more?"

"I've thought about it a great deal," Bartlemy said.

"Will you tell me what you've thought?" Annie said a little shyly.

Bartlemy set down his plate with the remainder of a piece of cake. "Very well," he said. "But you must understand this is pure speculation. We may never know the truth."

"I understand."

"We spoke once before of the Gate of Death. It has always been so called because death was supposed to be the only way to open it, but love, so they say, is stronger than death, and it may be that your love opened the Gate—and in a moment lost to memory you passed through, and returned with a child in your womb. Such unexplained pregnancies have happened before: I need hardly mention the most notorious case."

Annie glanced up in bewilderment; then her face cleared. "I *really* don't think Nathan's the new Messiah," she said. "My God, I hope not!"

"I, too . . . but he *is* special. There is a maturity, a strength of character that distinguishes him. He's a teenager now: it will be interesting to see if he displays the wayward behavior usually associated with that age."

"What if he doesn't?" Annie said. "If he doesn't start being rude to me, and having moods, and playing very loud music in his bedroom, and smoking pot and taking E, and treating me as an embarrassment? Is *that* when I should worry?"

She wasn't quite joking, and Bartlemy smiled only a little. "If you want to," he said. "Worrying doesn't achieve anything, but we all do it. If you need to worry that Nathan gives you no real cause for anxiety . . . Exactly. Where were we? You passed the Gate, or may have done, and became pregnant, so you believe, in that moment. *Not* your boyfriend's child: that seems fairly obvious. There are worlds without number beyond the Gate; Powers that rarely touch our lives so nearly. Once in a while, however, those Powers concern themselves with our immediate affairs. Not in my experience, nor that of anyone I know, but it *has* happened. Maybe there is some task to be done, some destiny to fulfill—mind you, I've always had my doubts about Destiny: she's a temperamental lady. I feel Nathan was born for a purpose, though I don't know what it is. Perhaps there is a doom that only he can avert. Time will show. Whatever the truth, it seems clear Nathan has a father from outside this world, a being superior to us, in intellect and quality if not in essence, possibly one of the Powers themselves—anything is possible. You both have enemies, we know that much, enemies on what might be termed a supernatural plane; but a child that unique would attract attention from birth. The circumstances of his conception—the Gate opening for someone still living—would cause ripples that the sensitive might feel. Certainly there is—interest in him, from many sources."

"Now you really are frightening me," Annie said. "Otherworldly beings—Nathan—a mythical task—all this can't be true . . . can it?"

"Someone sent the things that followed you," Bartlemy pointed out. "They may even have slipped into this world after you when the Gate opened: such shadows might do that. But of one thing you can be sure, if you have need of comfort. Whoever fathered Nathan has power of a kind we cannot imagine—the power to break the rules—and such an individual would never leave his son unprotected. Somehow, he will be watching over Nathan. Believe me."

But do I want an alien power watching over my son? Annie asked herself. She finished her cake, and stroked Hoover's rough head, and tried not to feel the future touching her with its shadow.

THE SAILORS had made it to the sea via the little harbor of Grimstone, and enjoyed themselves very much learning how to tack out in the bay, where a brisk wind whipped the waves into scuds. The river journey back took more than two hours, since the Glyde was winding and Michael observed the speed limit, so it was dark before they reached the mooring outside Riverside House. They had left the breeze behind in the bay; it was a clear, still night with a young moon not bright enough to obscure the stars.

"There's the saucepan," Hazel said. "And Orion's belt."

"Do you know your stars?" Michael asked.

"Nathan does."

"Not much," Nathan disclaimed.

"You can navigate by the stars," Michael said, "if you're out at sea. Look, there's the Pole Star, and the Evening Star. They tell you what direction you're going in. It's like a route map up there."

"I thought you had radar," said George.

"Yes, but a good sailor doesn't need it. Not that I'm a good sailor—I don't know the sky well enough."

"Do you know what that star is?" Nathan asked, pointing. "The one just under Orion."

"No idea. I told you, I'm not really an expert. I just remember the easy ones."

"Is that the new star we found last year?" said George. "The one that wasn't on the chart?"

"You found a new star?" Michael was amused. "Well, it's a busy sky up there. Maybe it was an old one that had popped out for a tea break when the chart was drawn up."

Nathan found the opportunity to tread on George's foot. "My star chart's pretty basic," he said.

It was back, the unknown star, hanging above the village; he was almost sure it hadn't been visible farther downriver. He didn't know why, but he wasn't prepared to discuss it with grown-ups yet—not even a grown-up as nice as Michael. It was their star, they had located it, a private star shining over Eade.

"Like the star of Bethlehem," Hazel said later.

"That's silly," George objected. "There's nothing special about Eade. Even if it was the second coming, Jesus would have to be born in the hospital at Crowford, like my cousin Eleanor. That's where the—the maternity unit is. And the Bethlehem star was big and sparkly: the three kings followed it from another country. Ours isn't really noticeable at all. I still think it's a UFO."

"Why would a UFO be interested in Eade?" Hazel retorted scornfully. She thought George was getting much too assertive.

"Why would a star?"

"Shut up arguing," Nathan admonished. Michael rejoined them— he had been locking up the boat—and they cut through the gardens of Riverside House and set off along the lane toward the village. Nathan tried not to keep glancing upward, but sometimes he couldn't help himself, and he half imagined the star was looking back at him, gazing down from its viewpoint in the night like an unwinking eye.

The Luck of the Thorns

Annie wondered a good deal about her conversation with Bartlemy and his theories concerning Nathan's conception. On the one hand she dismissed them as bizarre, on a par with the worst of New Age mysticism, crystal power, geomancy, and the sort of people who talked about former incarnations. On the other, Bartlemy was not that kind of person, and the fold in her memory—the timeless moment locked away—was something *she* felt, dimly now, but still real even after the passage of more than thirteen years. She could recall clearly the deep shock she had experienced, less from Daniel's death than from her own involvement in it, her journey to another place, forgotten but still sensed, forever a part of her, forever changing her. It remained always the most intense event of her life . . . but founded on what? Fantasy—delusion—her imagination overworking in an attempt to blot out the abyss of her loss? No, she decided; in the end, you must trust yourself, because if not yourself, whom can you trust? Besides, she had seen *them,* she had heard their whisperings, and if shadows walked in this world, then anything was possible, in any world. She sat in the bookshop on a quiet afternoon, her fingers slackening on the computer keyboard, revolving these things in her mind, always returning to the same enigma: Nathan's paternity. It was strange how she had accepted it, over the years, rarely troubling herself with speculation. And now . . .

For the first time, Annie found herself trying to go back—and back—into her memory, into the past, into the unopened rooms of her subconscious. She thought she must have been afraid to remember, to even make the attempt, but now it was necessary, it was urgent . . . She pictured the pallor of that hospital room, Daniel lying there, the bruising on his face dark, dark against the whiteness of his skin, white bandages, white pillow . . . Daniel slipping away from her . . . and the sudden opening of his eyes, and the love in them that stabbed her, even now, making a wound that would always be fresh, always raw, as long as her heart beat. She clung to that moment, and shrank from it, because beside it all the other moments of her life were as shadows and half-lights; but this time she knew she must go beyond it, opening up the pain, reaching into death itself. Her fingers slid from the keyboard; her face emptied. There were impressions—colors—a spinning sensation—falling into softness, warmth, touch. There was a love enfolding her, mind and body, filling every pore, eclipsing both heart and thought, absorbing her into its passion and its potency. Daniel's love—it must be Daniel—but Daniel had given much, and taken little, and this was a love that took everything, all that she was, and all that she had, and gave only on its own terms, in its own way. A great gift, a gift that was worth the price, though she paid with her life and her soul . . .

There was a violent jolt, and her head was in her hands, and the world slid back into place. She looked up, and saw the bookshop, and her current screen saver, fish swimming through a coral grove, and the spiraling dust motes caught in a ray of sunshine from a small side window. Gradually her pulse steadied, but she didn't move. After an hour or more, she got up and went to make tea.

When the tea was ready she returned to the table, sat down, sipped, pressed a few keys on the computer, tapped out an e-mail to other dealers about a rare first edition she was trying to obtain for a client. But her thought was elsewhere. She had listened to Bartlemy's theory, but hadn't really digested the implications. Something— *someone*—had taken her, in the instant of Daniel's death, and made her pregnant. She had been invaded and violated, when she was open and vulnerable, when she had offered her whole being, to Daniel, *for* Daniel—but it was not Daniel who had accepted. Some alien power had seized her and used her, drawing a veil in her mind to blind her, leaving her with . . . Nathan. She loved Nathan as much as she had loved Daniel, though differently, but in that moment it didn't matter. A slow-burning anger mounted in her, like no anger she had ever known, a white fire with which she could have torn down the walls between worlds, and stormed across the multiverse to find her ravisher. He had imprinted her with his spirit, but she would tear him out, and take back the life he had riven from her, and the love he had poisoned, and the soul he had left broken or benumbed. Her heart raged until the tea grew cold, and the fire died within her, and the tears came and came and would not stop.

Hazel Bagot found her there, when she came around to borrow a book for school. "What's wrong?" she said, horrified. "Annie, Annie, what's wrong?"

"Nothing," Annie sobbed, struggling for self-control, and Hazel put her arms around her, awkwardly, embarrassed to find an adult weeping with such abandon, though she had seen her mother cry, often and often. Her bracelet caught in Annie's hair, pulling it sharply, so she started with the pain, and Hazel sprang back, stammering an apology, and ran out into the street. And there was

Michael, walking toward her, and she dragged him inside, though he offered little resistance, and left him to do what he could in the way of comfort, while she headed home to brood on the mystery of it, with Annie's hair hooked on her bracelet.

In the shop Annie laid her head against Michael's shoulder, and wept herself to a standstill.

"What is it?" he said. "Can I help?"

"No. Thanks. It's just . . . something a long time ago, something I never understood . . . never realized till now."

"Can you tell me?"

"No. Sorry. It's too . . ."

"Too private?" he suggested.

"Too difficult." She looked up at him, red-eyed, rubbing her nose with the back of her hand, like a child. "Excuse me. I need a tissue. Possibly several."

"I'll get them." He got up. "Where—"

"Toilet paper. In the bathroom. Upstairs on your left. But you shouldn't . . ."

He ran upstairs, returning presently with a roll of toilet paper.

"Thank you," Annie said again, feeling helpless and rather foolish. She blew her nose vigorously, wondering what she could say, unwilling to lie when he was being so kind.

But Michael asked no more questions. "If there's anything I can do . . . ?"

"No, really. I'll be fine now. I'd just like to be alone."

"Sure?" She nodded. He stood looking down at her, and for once the crooked smile wasn't in evidence. "Okay. But I meant what I said. If there's anything I can do, ever, you have only to ask. It sounds melodramatic to say you're alone in the world—I know that's not exactly the case—but you don't have a husband or family, at any rate, not around here. I want you to know you can call on me, anytime."

He does *like me,* Annie thought, and the knowledge warmed her, and unsettled her, more than she would have expected, ruffling what little serenity she had left.

She thought of asking him: *How would Rianna feel about that?* But of course she didn't.

NOT LONG after his birthday Nathan went walking in the woods near Thornyhill. He had left Hoover behind, ostensibly because he wanted to watch for birds and squirrels, but really because he needed some time to himself, to think things over. Hazel had told him about finding his mother in tears, and he had asked Annie what had upset her, but all she would say was that it didn't matter now. "I was crying over spilled milk, and everyone knows that's a waste of energy. What's done is done. It's nothing you need worry about." He didn't want to press her, but instinct told him there was something very wrong, something important, one of many nebulous troubles that threatened to disturb the pattern of his life. The vision of the cup—dreams of another world—the illegal immigrant—Effie Carlow—Michael Addison—the star. He sat down on a log some way from any path, his gaze resting absently on the fluttering of leaf shadows across the woodland floor, primrose clumps around a tree bole, a mist of bluebells stretching away into a green distance. There was no traffic noise from the road, only the song of unseen birds. It was a beautiful scene, restful to the soul, but he was thirteen and his soul was restless. There were so many things he wanted to know . . .

The face was watching him from the crook between branch and tree trunk: he must have been staring at it for some time without seeing it, the way you stare at a puzzle picture until the instant when the hidden image becomes clear. He thought at first that it was an animal, maybe a pine marten—he had always wanted to see a pine marten—but the face, though pointed, was hairless, bark-colored, and thrush-speckled, watching him sideways from a dark slanting eye. He became aware of spindle limbs clinging to the tree trunk, leafy rags of clothing. Even so, it was several minutes before he said, very softly: "Woody?"

The woodwose shrank away, retreating into the shelter of the tree.

"Please don't go! It's me, Nathan. Woody, please . . ."

"Nathan?" It was the slightest of whispers, emanating from behind the oak.

"Yes it is. Really . . ."

"Nathan . . . was little. No bigger than me."

"I grew up," Nathan said. "I couldn't help that. It's what people do. I'm a teenager now."

"You went away." The woodwose was still invisible, only a voice among the leaves.

"I know. I'm sorry. They told me you were imaginary, and I suppose . . . I got to believing them."

"They?" The tip of a long nose reappeared, followed by the gleam of an eye, the twitch of an ear.

"People. My mother. Some of my friends. It wasn't their fault: they didn't know you. It was my fault."

"You've grown too big," Woody said doubtfully. "Too big to talk to."

"I'm the same," Nathan insisted. "Look at me, Woody."

The woodwose studied him, first from one eye, then the other. "You are Nathan," he said at last, "but you are not the same. You are . . . *more*. Perhaps too much . . ."

"It feels that way sometimes," Nathan said. "But you can still talk to me. Honestly you can. Please come out, Woody. Please."

Slowly, tentatively, the woodwose emerged into full view, staying close to the tree, no longer relaxed as he had been with his child playmate but a nervous, distrustful creature, easily startled, poised not to flee but to fade back into the concealment of the wood. "Do you," he murmured, "do you have any—Smarties? You brought some once, I remember, in a tube with a lid on. They were small, and many-colored—all different colors—and they tasted very good."

"I'll bring some next time," Nathan promised. "I'll come again soon. What . . . what have you been doing, all these years?"

But he knew the answer. "Being here," said the woodwose. "Waiting."

"For me?"

"I—yes. You are all I have. You told me so. My parents, my friend." And, after a pause: "What is *imaginary*?"

"It means, I invented you. You came from my mind. Where did you come from, Woody?"

"From your mind," said the woodwose. "I think."

Nathan remembered the man he had pulled from the seas of an-other cosmos, onto the beach at Pevensey Bay. He had no memory of it, but perhaps he had found Woody, too, in a dream, in the woods of some alternative world. It was an uncomfortable idea, though he hadn't yet had time to work out why. The two of them sat for a while, almost the way they used to, though not quite, watching a beetle creeping through the leafmold, and sunspots dancing on a tree trunk, and a tiny bird with a piping call that Nathan would never have seen without his friend to guide him. "Would you look out for anything—different?" Nathan asked at last. "There are things happening now, strange things. I can't explain properly because I don't understand, but I think you should be wary. If you see—oh, I don't know—any-thing unusual, weird . . ."

"Weird?" Woody looked bewildered. There were few words in his vocabulary.

"Odd. Peculiar. *Wrong*." Nathan paused for a minute, struck by a sudden thought. "How do you speak my language, Woody? It isn't natural to you, is it?"

"I must have learned from you," said the woodwose. "I've never spoken to anybody else."

Nathan didn't say any more. He bade his friend goodbye and set off back toward Bartlemy's house. An awful fear was growing in him: that he had brought Woody here, had dreamed him into this world and then abandoned him, and now the woodwose had no other friend, no other place, no other tongue. It was a frightening responsibility, but the wider implications were worse. He had no control over his dreams. What had Effie Carlow said?—*Dream carefully.* Perhaps, if he really had this power, this ability, he might find himself bringing other people here, other creatures, unhappy exiles who could never go home, unless he found a way to dream them back again. The idea was so terrifying it made his mind spin. He forced himself to think rationally, to analyze what it was in his dreaming that had transported the man in the water from world to world—if that was indeed what had happened. There had been the urge to help, to save him—a huge impulse of will. After all, he had only brought back one person—not any of the xaurians or their riders, or the man in the white mask. And maybe some similar impulse had drawn Woody to Thornyhill to be his companion. A selfish impulse, a child's impulse: the desire for a secret friend. "And I couldn't send him back," he reflected, remorsefully, "even if I had the power. I don't remember where he came from." He resolved that he *would* dream carefully from now on, he would suppress all such urges, he wouldn't—he *mustn't*—allow his feelings to dictate his actions.

He wanted to tell Bartlemy—he wanted to tell *someone*—but he feared to be treated as an overimaginative child, diminished by adult skepticism. Somehow, because she was so old, so eccentric, Effie Carlow had been different: he could have endured her scorn, if she had scorned him. But Bartlemy was the person he respected most in the world, knowledgeable and wise, and in his inmost heart Nathan shrank from the very notion of his disbelief.

Even so, the need to confide might have been too much for him, if he had found Bartlemy alone when he returned to Thornyhill. But in the living room he found Rowena Thorn—Mrs. Vanstone, to give her her proper name—drinking tea and talking earnestly about something. She was a long, lean, tweedy sort of woman in her midsixties, with a face that had once been plain until character and humor had left their impress on her features. She was given to serving on committees, organizing charitable events, and riding her friends' horses since she no longer maintained one of her own. In between, she ran an antiques shop in Chizzledown. She greeted Nathan absentmindedly, though she normally found time to inquire after his progress at school, and reverted immediately to the subject under discussion.

"The provenance is clear: they have all the necessary documentation. It *is* the genuine article, I'm sure of it. You've seen our records. That awful little twit Rowland sold it to this Birnbaum chap just before the war—he was a German, too, frightfully bad form if you ask me—and then went and got himself killed, silly business really, survived the Somme and then got run over by a tank or something in the week before the Armistice. Henry died in the flu epidemic and that was more or less the end of the family. My father was only a child at the time, besides being just a cousin, and there was nothing left for him to inherit but debts. My grandmother always said that when we lost the cup we lost our luck, but personally I've never been sure about that. I remember Great-Aunt Verity contended it was our curse, an evil burden the family had a duty to bear. Probably all nonsense, but you never know. The point is, it's ours, and if it really has resurfaced I'm damn well going to get it back."

Nathan, who was becoming interested, helped himself to some elderflower cordial from the kitchen—Bartlemy made his own—and sat down unobtrusively next to Hoover.

"But if Rowland Thorn sold it, as you maintain," Bartlemy was saying, "I don't quite see how you can make a claim. Unless you can manage to buy it back from the present owner?"

"Good Lord no, it's practically priceless. According to what I hear, the British Museum is after it, but it may be too much for their budget. Depends on the other bidders, of course: might go for a song, might run into millions. No: I'm trying another tack. I intend to prove the original sale was actually illegal."

"How will you do that?" Bartlemy asked.

"As you know, old Josevius acquired the cup somewhere back in the Dark Ages. Given to him by the Devil, one story has it; another one says it was an angel."

"I read it was supposed to be a holy relic," Nathan said. He found it curiously difficult to speak of it, as if there were weights on his tongue. Yet he wanted to. He wanted to say: *I found the chapel. I saw the cup.* He couldn't. Hoover, he noticed, merely looked inquiringly at him.

"Depends which story you favor. Didn't know you were interested in my family history, Nathan. Good for you. Too many kids your age only want to play computer games and listen to pop music, far as I can see. History's important. The past belongs to all of us. Where was I?"

"Josevius," Bartlemy prompted.

"Right. Well, he got the cup, somehow or other. Some sources say he made it, but I don't believe that. Never been any craftsmen in our family: we haven't the brains. Anyway, story goes he charged his descendants to hold it in trust—though heaven knows for whom, or what—never to sell it, or lend it, or give it away, or we would lose everything. Should have been kept in the ancient chapel, but that was destroyed, so they had it here, that secret cupboard in the chimney, you'll have found it—"

Nathan's eyes widened. "I didn't know there was a—"

"I did," said Bartlemy. "Yes, I found it. I always wondered what it was for."

"Never saw it myself but my great-aunt spoke of it. Must show me sometime. The cup stayed there for centuries; strangers weren't even allowed to look at it. Lot of odd legends grew up around it, but mostly they stayed in the family. Somewhere along the line it got labeled the Sangreal: couple of historians picked up on that one, said it meant 'Saint Grail,' the Holy Grail, but they got the etymology wrong. The word comes from *sang*, 'blood.' That's French, Nathan, but it's a similar word in a dozen languages. Rumor was, if you were going to die, or some catastrophe was imminent, you'd look in the cup and see it full of blood. Nothing holy about that. It's all been written down, from time to time, by those of my ancestors who *could* read and write. Not a bright lot, the Thorns, I'm afraid. Point is, at some stage in the fifteenth century the issue of selling it must have come up, and one of them made the injunction against it legal. I don't have the document, but there are two separate references to it, one in the diary of a contemporary, the other in the account of an attempted purchase in the Victorian era. The document existed: no question about it. Hopefully it still does. Wondered if you'd mind my having a look for it here?"

"Of course not," Bartlemy said. "But I'm pretty sure I've been through all the papers in the house, and I've never seen such a thing."

"Can I help?" Nathan asked. "It could be in another secret hiding place, like that cupboard you mentioned."

"Could be," said Rowena Thorn. "Any help is welcome. Think it's like an adventure story, do you? *Harry Potter and the Goblet of Fire*, that kind of thing?"

Nathan only smiled in answer. He thought: *Harry Potter has magical powers. His friends have magical powers. Me—I have to dream carefully.* He ached to tell them about the chapel, and his vision there—if it was a vision—but the words would not come. He reflected that real adventures weren't about Hogwarts and Muggles and good guys and bad guys. Real adventures were shadows and confusion and doubt, and a terrifying personal responsibility.

Maybe there's an injunction on my talking of the cup. Not legal, but magical. Or some sort of hypnotism . . .

"Who's got—it—now?" he inquired. "I'm sorry if you've already told Uncle Barty, but I missed that part. Or—or is that private information?"

"Lord no: it's public enough. It's some Austrian chap, father's a count, Graf they call it, grandfather was in the SS. The Birnbaums were a Jewish family, very wealthy, major collectors, paintings, antiques, the lot. The Nazis did for them, of course, and the grandfather—Graf Von Holsten-Pils or whatever he called himself—pocketed most of the loot. After he died the next count seems to have kept a low profile, hoped the stolen goods would pass unnoticed among the rest of the ancestral heirlooms. He had a stroke last year, family fortune's on the wane, son decides to auction off some of the silver. Gets in touch with Sotheby's—not sure why he picked on London, maybe there's a Birnbaum who's been sniffing around back in Germany, maybe he just thinks he'll get more money. Apparently a lot of the stuff is originally English. Anyway, he shows them the cup with the provenance—perhaps he thinks Granddad got it legally—and a chum of mine there gets hold of me. Wanted to check it out, had no idea I might have a claim. Haven't told him, of course. Want to get my hands on that injunction first. Never fire till you can see the whites of their eyes, so my father used to say. Mind you, he was talking about stag hunting, not warfare."

"Is this war, Rowena?" Bartlemy asked mildly. "Do you really believe this cup is the Luck of the Thorns?"

"I'm an antiques dealer," she said. "It's a valuable antique—could be unique—and it was the property of my family. It should be again. Don't know about luck. My father believed—my grandfather believed. I'm a skeptic about most things, but the belief is there: it's in my blood. It always comes down to blood, when you talk about the cup. Supposing it *was* the Grail—if there is such a thing . . ."

"That's the question," said Bartlemy. "The blood of Christ— whoever *he* was . . ." His voice sounded very distant.

Nathan sat like a stock, unable to move. His tongue seemed to stick to the roof of his mouth. He wanted to say something—anything—to cry out and break through the spell or trance, but the harder he tried, the more difficult it became.

"You're a skeptic, like me," Rowena Thorn was saying. "No *evidence* for any Grail, nothing but stories. Great-Aunt Verity said Josevius could have been Joseph of Arimathea, the chap who's supposed to have retrieved the Grail relics and brought them to England. How d'you work that out? said my father. We know Josevius died around A.D. 660—forget the precise date, but it's set down somewhere. If he was around for the Crucifixion he'd have been getting on a bit."

"How does family legend deal with that one?" Bartlemy said.

"Sold his soul to the Devil—told you the Devil came into it— lived for centuries. Even the stories are rubbish, you see. In charge of holy relics one minute, in the pay of Satan the next. None of it stands up."

"What did your great-aunt have to say about it?" Bartlemy wondered. "Do you remember?"

"Said the Grail was evil, not holy. King Arthur and Co. got it wrong. She was a devout Christian: thought it was a pagan thing. Souvenir from the scene of the crime—most terrible crime in history. She thought we had to keep it from doing harm. Went a bit batty in her old age. Still, it made sense to her."

"Has the cup ever been carbon-dated?" Bartlemy said thoughtfully.

"Shouldn't think so. Unless the Grafs had it done. Funnily

enough, my chum at Sotheby's was talking about that. If the cup's two thousand years old, might really be a candidate for the Grail legend. On the other hand, if it was made in the Dark Ages . . ."

"Exactly."

"Doesn't make any odds to me, though. Belongs to the Thorns, whatever it is." An obstinate look settled about her mouth, erasing some of the humor. "Must get it back."

Nathan, finding he could move again, fidgeted in his chair, extending a hand to ruffle Hoover's fur.

"Still want to help me out?" Rowena Thorn asked him. "Not as good as buried treasure, looking for a piece of paper, but it might mean treasure for me. There'd be a reward in it, promise you that . . ."

"It's okay," Nathan said. "I don't want a reward. I'll look anyway."

"Good man. Teach you the right stuff at Ffylde, do they? Better than the comprehensive at Crowford, any day. All they seem to do there is take drugs and beat up the teachers." As Hazel and George were both there, Nathan knew this was an exaggeration, but he didn't say so.

"He gets his principles from his mother," Bartlemy said gently.

Rowena Thorn set down her teacup. "Better be off," she said. "Thanks for everything, Bartlemy. You've always been a good friend."

"You don't mind my living here, do you?" he inquired curiously. "Your ancestral home . . ."

"Good heavens, no. Hardly a mansion, is it? The Thorns never had the money for that. Just inconvenient, hell to maintain—never dared ask you about the plumbing. It isn't as if I ever lived here myself. No sentiment involved."

"You never owned the cup, either," Bartlemy pointed out.

"That's different," she said. "I told you. That's a matter of blood."

At supper that night, Nathan told Annie about the cup of the Thorns—it didn't appear to be a secret—or as much as he was able to tell, without talking about his vision, or the dreams of blood. Hazel was there; George came later. They both absorbed the story with enthusiasm and determined to search for the missing injunction. "D'you think it will be, like, a piece of parchment?" George said. "A scroll or something, yellowing and with spiky writing."

"It's fifteenth century," Nathan said. "I think they had paper in the fifteenth century. When did what's-his-name invent the printing press?"

"Caxton," Annie said, "in the fifteenth century. There was a lot going on then. Would anyone like some ice cream?"

Not surprisingly, everyone did. "Have you ever had a book here as old as that?" Hazel asked when the ice cream had been shared out.

"No. I had a seventeenth-century two-volume history once: that was the oldest. Anything from the fifteenth century would probably be in a museum. Does Rowena have any idea what this document looks like?"

"Don't think so," Nathan said. "We'll just have to go through absolutely everything at Thornyhill."

"If your uncle Barty doesn't mind . . ."

"It could be hidden in a book," Nathan pursued. "Secret papers very often are."

"But—Thornyhill is full of books!" Hazel exclaimed, daunted. "It'll take forever." Suddenly, the prospect of finding a missing document didn't seem half so interesting. "Perhaps Mr. Goodman won't want us rooting around there. He might prefer to do it himself . . ."

"Is there a reward?" George asked.

"Yes," Nathan said, looking rueful, "but I told Mrs. Thorn we wouldn't want it."

"*We* didn't," George and Hazel chimed simultaneously.

"You have to find it first," Annie pointed out. "*Then* you can worry about the reward. Are you sure it's actually at Thornyhill?"

"It must be," Nathan said. "Please don't make things more complicated. Anyway, Mrs. Thorn thought so."

They retreated to the Den to discuss the problem further, until Hazel switched to the subject of a forthcoming party that she wanted Nathan to attend with her. "There's going to be a disco," she said.

"I don't like discos," George offered. "They're stupid."

"You only say that because you're too scared to ask anyone to dance," Hazel said with devastating penetration. "Please come with me, Nathan. Not as—as my boyfriend or anything, just for . . . moral support."

"You—with a boyfriend!" George guffawed.

"No reason why Hazel shouldn't have one, if she wants," Nathan said. "The thing is, next Saturday I was meaning to start searching—"

"Not in the evening," Hazel said. "We could look for the injunction in the afternoon, and *then* go to the party."

"Okay." Nathan was not inspired by discos. He hoped, now that they were teenagers, Hazel wasn't going to start acting too much like a girl—or at any rate, like other girls. "Will there be drugs and people getting beaten up? Only according to Mrs. Thorn, that's what goes on at Crowford Comprehensive. It'll be an awful letdown if it's just dancing."

Hazel giggled. "Jason Wicks got caught trying to sell some E last term," she said. "But it turned out they were his mother's pills for cleaning her contact lenses."

Maybe I could use drugs to control my dreams of the other world, Nathan thought. *Maybe if I took sleeping pills . . .*

But he hadn't had one of those dreams for some time.

His friends left around eleven, and he climbed up to the skylight and sat on the edge, gazing up at the unknown star. He had still been unable to trace it on any chart, and a couple of weeks earlier his astronomy class had spent an hour on top of a tower at Ffylde studying the night sky, but there had been no sign of it. The star was there for *him*, watching him, a single pale eye effortlessly camouflaged among the constellations. He knew he should be afraid, but it was difficult to feel fear when the night was so beautiful, and the star-sparkle so magical: he could almost imagine it was benevolent, the eye of a secret guardian or kindly angel, not merely watching but watching over him, watching out for him, keeping him safe. But why would he need to be kept safe, and from whom—or what? Any why did he feel that it was all connected—the star, the dreams of the otherworld, and the cup of the Thorns—the whispering cup—the Sangreal?

"Nathan!" his mother's voice carried from downstairs. "Bedtime!"

"I'm thirteen," Nathan objected, sliding off the window frame. "I'm too old to have bedtimes."

"You're positively ancient," Annie called, "and you still need your sleep, especially during the term. Come down now."

"Coming."

In bed he drifted comfortably into sleep, at ease despite the problems niggling around the borders of his thought. And then sometime in the night the mists of slumber withdrew, and he was in the light. The light of the other world, a burning sunset with streaks of cyclamen cloud above a puddle of molten gold that spilled along the rim of the sky. He saw it from the top of a tower so high that it must be the tallest in the city; spires and pinnacles glinted far below him, sparking fire from the sunglow; on an adjacent segment of roof he made out two xaurians tethered, tiny at that distance; another wheeled in the gulf of air between. Farther down, he saw the city lights coming on

as dusk deepened, window by window, lamp by lamp, creeping upward out of the shadows until every building was ribbed with beads
of glitter, and the moving flecks of far-off skimmers flashed eyelights
of green and blue and neon pink. Then somehow he was inside the
tower, descending what appeared to be an elevator shaft. He floated
through closed doors along the gallery he had seen before with the
twisted pillars, and into the semicircular room. But now the night outside was altogether dark, and screens covered most of the curving
window. The man in the white mask—ruler, dictator, president,
whatever he was—sat at his desk with his back turned. A woman had
come in. There was something shocking about her appearance, but it
took Nathan a minute to realize what it was.

Her face was naked.

"There may be some lingering daylight," the man said, without
looking around. "You shouldn't walk around unshielded."

"The light is gone." Her voice was cool and differed from that of
the xaurian rider and the purple-cowled hologram in one essential: it
was not subservient. Nathan found himself seeing her in profile and
thought: *She is very beautiful.* Her hair was hidden under a white
headdress, like some kind of wimple; she wore a long white tunic and
trousers, and her skin had the pale golden hue associated in our world
with Orientals. The lines of her cheekbone and jaw reminded him of
pictures he had seen of the head of Nefertiti, though her neck was
longer, slightly too long for an ordinary human, and as she turned
toward him he realized the planes of her face were subtly different,
though it would have been hard to explain in what way. A fraction of
an inch here, a fraction of an inch there, and the whole visage was
somehow distorted, though its beauty remained undiminished. *But
then,* Nathan reflected, *maybe our faces would look that way to her—as
if a fractional adjustment had produced that impression of wrongness, of
something out of kilter.* "Anyway," she went on, "what does it matter?
I do not fear death, not even the sundeath, the Shriveler of all that

lives. The slow hours weary me, and my breath galls. I would welcome Death, if I could find her."

"Don't be in such haste to destroy your beauty," the man said, turning now to gaze at her. "It still gives me pleasure to look on it, and there is little enough cause for pleasure left."

"To be beautiful," she said, "it is necessary to have a world to be beautiful *in*. You wrote a poem once, in the far-off days of youth and hopefulness, saying that creation itself was for my benefit. *The earth, the moons, the sun, the sea/Were made but to embower thee.* Now, the earth is foul, and the sun poisons the sea, and the three moons of Eos turn red. Without creation, without a place to be, I am nothing. You are so clever, Grandir: make me a world to live in."

"I cannot make worlds," he said, "even I, but maybe . . . I can take one. Have patience a while, Halmé, and hide your face from the daylight a little longer. I will find a world for you, I promise."

The woman called Halmé went to the window, sliding one of the screens aside, and Nathan saw she was right: there was a huge moon, not quite full, hanging in the sky, and it was red, and eastward another moon sliver had the same bloodstained hue.

"Close the screen!" said the man. "The moon is too bright. It could be dangerous."

The woman obeyed, but slowly. The more he looked at her, the more beautiful Nathan found her; it was as if his sight was adjusting to her different facial proportions, and now the women of his own world would look forever wrong to him. He watched her leaving: she moved swiftly and very gracefully, the white ends of her wimple fluttering behind her. Halmé was her name, he was certain, but Grandir, he thought, might be a title, like Lord or Excellency. He was thinking about that when the scene changed.

The masked ruler was climbing a stair. The stair moved, like an escalator but in a spiral, twisting around and around inside a cylindrical shaft, and the man was stepping briskly upward, perhaps impatient at its slowness. At the top was a circular chamber with no windows: the architects of this world evidently favored curves in construction. The only light came from a number of clear globes, some smooth-sided, some faceted, which appeared to be suspended in midair, though as Nathan drew closer he saw there were no threads or wires supporting them: they simply floated, motionless or in orbit. A pale radiance came from the heart of each, yet it illuminated nothing in the room save the globes themselves. The man moved to the center of the chamber, where a slightly larger globe with many faces revolved slowly in one place. Lances of light emanated from it, sinking into the darkness, never reaching the walls. The man stretched one hand toward it without actually making contact and murmured a single word: *"Fia!"* A white dazzle flooded the room, so that for an instant Nathan was blinded, even though it was only a dream; then the glare retreated into the globe, and Nathan saw a picture appear above it, as if projected onto the ceiling. At first it was difficult to make out, since he was looking at it from underneath, but then he realized it was a roof—he could see tiles—with a square hole in it, an open skylight, and a boy and a girl emerging into view, staring and pointing, pointing out of the picture, down at the globe. It was a minute or two before he understood. He was seeing himself, himself and Hazel, looking up at a star that didn't belong . . .

He woke much later with the dream still fresh in his mind. It was still dark, and he got up very quietly and stole downstairs to the cupboard between the shelves, and climbed the ladder to the Den, and opened the skylight, and there was the star, only he knew now it wasn't a star, it was a globe that shone both in this world and in the other one, a watching eye for a man whose face was never seen. A guardian angel—a manipulator—a menace. Nathan didn't know, and the only way to find out was to dream on. Or maybe it was all pure fantasy, a story invented by his subconscious mind to explain something he couldn't comprehend. For if it was true, why—why in all the worlds—would a ruler so powerful, so desperate, clearly facing some cosmic catastrophe, be interested in *him*?

He closed the skylight, descended the ladder, went back upstairs to bed. But the question followed him, nagging at his mind, keeping him from sleep: the unimaginable, unanswerable *why*.

NATHAN DIDN'T get a chance to tell Hazel everything for another fortnight. "It'll be easier when the summer vacation starts," he said. "Then we'll have more time together—time to find the missing injunction"—they had barely begun searching—"and time to sort this out."

"Can it be sorted out?" Hazel said doubtfully. It was daylight and the star was invisible, but they had no idea if that meant it couldn't see them. "What are you going to do?"

"I've thought about that. Somehow, I have to find the man on the beach. If they think he's an illegal immigrant I expect he'll be held somewhere. I'll pretend I'm doing a school project on asylum seekers: people always want to help with school projects. Once we've found him, he can answer some of our questions." He had switched from *I* to *we*, Hazel noticed.

She said: "How will you talk to him? He doesn't speak English."

"In my dreams, I speak his language," Nathan said. "Maybe—maybe when I hear it, I'll understand. We'll talk to him somehow. We have to."

"Sign language," Hazel said.

"The first thing is to find him."

With this object in mind, they went to talk to Annie. She was obviously gratified to see them so concerned about the issues of the day, but she wasn't able to help much. "I've got a school project," Nathan said. He didn't like lying to his mother, but he couldn't possibly tell her the truth.

"There's probably some sort of immigration board," she said. "Look it up in the phone book."

Nothing was listed under Immigration, but after Annie had considered the problem further she suggested they try the Home Office. Here, they found a listing for the Immigration and Nationality Directorate, but they couldn't get through. "It's bound to be closed on weekends," Nathan told Hazel. "You'll have to try it during the week. I can't make lots of calls from school."

Hazel looked more doubtful than ever, tugging her hair over her face in the nervous gesture she hadn't yet outgrown. "What'll I say?" she said. "It's a government department. I can't talk to a government department."

In the end Nathan decided to apply to Annie. "If it's a school project," she said, "surely you can call from Ffylde?"

"We're supposed to do it in our own time," Nathan said, feeling uncomfortable. "I just want to know how to contact that man . . ."

"I'll see what I can do," Annie promised.

On Monday morning she drove Nathan back to school, and sat down at the telephone as soon as she returned home. By three o'clock she was frustrated and uncharacteristically furious. The Home Office—"building a safe, just and tolerant society," according to their ad—proved far from helpful. When the Immigration and Nationality Directorate eventually answered the phone, after a succession of busy signals and a long wait with classical music and recorded messages, they refused to give her any information whatsoever. "But it's for my son," Annie said indignantly. "It's a school project. He wants to know how his country works—what we do for refugees and people in trouble." At her insistence, the clerk departed to speak to a superior, picking up the call again after a ten-minute absence to tell Annie that she must write to another department, the Communications Directorate. "Can I speak to your supervisor?" Annie asked. No. "Is there a number I can call at this other place?" Can't give it to you. It's confidential. "I'm a taxpayer," Annie found herself saying in cliché mode (though in fact she paid very little tax due to the smallness of her income). "I pay your wages. I *employ* you. You don't have the right to refuse to answer me." The clerk said in the voice of one accustomed to such tirades that there was no point in blaming her, it wasn't her fault. Annie hung up and dialed Information, which promptly gave her the confidential phone number. The Communications Directorate, however, told her she would need to write to Immigration. She then worked her way through her local MP, the House of Commons, and even Scotland Yard, but no one would fill her in on the procedure for dealing with illegal immigrants, let alone assist her in tracking one down. Finally she abandoned the telephone, made herself coffee, and went on the Internet. Here she found the names of various support groups for asylum seekers operating in the southeast. She wrote down more telephone numbers and decided to return to the attack the next day.

On Tuesday she had better luck. The support groups, unlike the bureaucrats, welcomed interest and were happy to dole out information. Talking to a voluntary organization based in Hastings, she struck gold.

"The man on the beach?" said her contact, a woman named Jillian Squires. "The mystery man? Why does your son want to know about him?"

"Nathan heard the story on the radio," Annie explained. "I'm definitely a biased mum, but still, he's got a very strong sense of social responsibility. When I told him the kind of treatment meted out to immigrants in this country, he got pretty upset." She added shrewdly: "I suspect he suggested the subject for his school project himself. He thinks about things, you see; he doesn't just go away and forget."

"What school's he at?"

"Ffylde Abbey. I'm not well off, but he got a scholarship."

"I know of it. It's got a decent reputation." Jillian Squires seemed to hesitate, then plunged. "Look, I'll tell you what I'll do. I can't give out details about anyone without their permission, obviously, but I'll talk to the man. I've had dealings with him. He's highly intelligent: spoke no English when he got here, but he's learned amazingly fast. If he's willing, I could give him your number, and ask him to get in touch with you."

"That would be wonderful," Annie said gratefully. "But—I thought he would be in prison, or somewhere like that?"

"No. They only put asylum seekers in prison if they've committed a crime. Prison's expensive: the state has to feed them. It's cheaper to leave them on the streets. Anyway, they're only allowed to register as asylum seekers if they claim immediately—and that presupposes they know how the system works."

"If *I* couldn't find that out," Annie said, "how do they?"

"Precisely."

Concluding the call, Annie resolved to scrape something from her weekly housekeeping to send as a donation. Nathan wasn't the only one getting educated, she reflected.

She gave him the news that weekend. "Your man hasn't called yet," she said, "but perhaps he will. We just have to wait. If he doesn't want to talk to you we can't force him: even if that were possible, it wouldn't be fair."

With Bartlemy's permission, Nathan, George, and Hazel spent Saturday searching Thornyhill for the missing document. Nathan's friends were unenthusiastic, but the prospect of Bartlemy's cooking overcame their resistance. He produced homemade cookies with cinnamon and chocolate chips for elevenses, grilled fish for lunch followed by his own wild strawberry ice cream, and iced buns for tea, and in between the three of them tapped the paneling in the hope that it was hollow, and rifled through the attics and some of the murkier closets. Bartlemy didn't show them the secret cupboard in the chimney and Nathan didn't mention it—he had a feeling its very existence was a private matter—but they found another one hidden under some stairs, big enough to conceal a man, and in the attics they unearthed part of a rusty suit of armor, a chest of antique clothing, some tarnished silverware, and a set of porcelain tureens that must once have belonged to a far larger dinner service. Hazel was very taken with a gray fur muff that Bartlemy said was chinchilla, though she knew fur was immoral. ("It's a kind of rat," he explained, which soothed her qualms of conscience but also made the muff appear much less attractive.) They discovered something called an astrolabe—a sort of old-fashioned telescope—and an orrery, which was meant to be a model of the solar system, but Bartlemy remarked that either it was very inaccurate or it was a model of another planetary system altogether. And everywhere there were papers, in large boxes, in small boxes, in chests of drawers, in desks long unopened. Nathan found love letters a hundred years old, tied up with faded ribbon, sepia photographs of simpering Victorian maidens, postcard nudes from the Edwardian era, menus, shopping lists, laundry lists. But there was no sign of the injunction. "Rowena had a hunt downstairs last week," Bartlemy told him. "She must have gone through most of the books, so you needn't bother about them."

"If it isn't at Thornyhill," Nathan said, frowning, "have you any idea where the document might be?"

"Rowena asked me that," Bartlemy said. "I told her to trace the family solicitors from whenever the injunction was last applied, I think she said in the late nineteenth century. Of course, you would find that very mundane. There could be a hiding place in the woods, I suppose, possibly on the site of the old house."

"But no one knows where that is!" Hazel protested.

"You can't expect to have everything easy," Bartlemy said gently.

They left searching the woods for another day and went home,

Hazel carrying the muff, which Bartlemy had given her. "It's okay to wear *old* furs," Nathan said. "It's buying new ones that's wrong."

Back at the bookshop, Annie had bad news for him. "Jillian Squires called," she said. "I'm afraid the man on the beach doesn't want to talk to you. She said he didn't seem to understand about school projects. I'm sorry, darling, but you can't press him, you know. He's homeless, and penniless, and desperate: life must be difficult enough for him. We don't want to make it worse."

Yes, thought Nathan, *life* must *be difficult. He's in the wrong universe, for one thing.*

He said: "Would you mind if I called Mrs. Squires? I won't push her, I promise. I just want to find out . . . how the system works."

"I suppose that would be all right," Annie conceded doubtfully.

That evening when it was dark Nathan climbed up to the skylight to look at the star. He had formed the habit of doing so every night when he was at home. He had borrowed George's binoculars, but they didn't show him anything more. He pictured the dim room with the revolving spheres, and the orb in the center, its many facets coruscating with vanishing light. And then the image on the ceiling—his face, gazing at the star, perhaps right now, this moment—and the white mask tilted upward to study it. It was unbelievable.

But he believed it. Dream and reality meshed too closely for him to deny them. He *had* to talk to the man on the beach, the man from another world . . .

With Annie's permission, he telephoned Jillian Squires in the morning.

"I'm sorry to bother you," he said politely. "Mum told me, the man on the beach wouldn't help, but I wondered—would you say something to him? It's going to sound a bit odd to you, but—but it's *really* important. If he doesn't want to talk to me even then, that's okay. If you would just tell him . . ."

"I don't know what more I can say," Mrs. Squires responded with courtesy but no enthusiasm.

Nathan checked that his mother was out of earshot. "Could you tell him—I'm the person who pulled him out of the sea? Please? That's all."

"Tell him—? How extraordinary. Your mother never mentioned—"

"She doesn't know," Nathan said hastily. "I mean, she wasn't there. I can't—I really can't explain everything now. But *please* would you tell him that?"

"Are you making this up?" Her voice had acquired an edge.

"If I was," Nathan said, "it wouldn't help, would it, because he would know it was made up? He wouldn't want to call me if it wasn't true."

"It's a point," she said. "Very well, I'll tell him. But—"

"Thanks," Nathan said. "Thanks very much," and he hung up as Annie came back into the room.

THERE FOLLOWED a week of school and suspense. Nathan dreamed of the cup, and the snake patterns uncoiling from the rim, and hissing, hissing in his ear. He woke up shaking so badly he felt he had a fever, and was bitterly ashamed of himself for being so much disturbed by a dream. To calm down, he tried to think of places the injunction might be hidden, and whether the man from the sea would agree to talk to him, and what he might say if he did. Finally, he resorted to thinking about the party Hazel wanted him to attend—the party with the disco—and how horrific it would be, perhaps having to dance, with girls huddled into groups giggling, and Jason Wicks, or someone like him, lounging against the wall sneering. By its very unpleasantness, the picture he drew was oddly steadying. Something about the thought of Jason Wicks had a toughening effect on his nerves. He could deal with Jason Wicks. Wicks, and discos, and giggling girls were very much of this world. It was the other worlds of dream and darkness that he couldn't manage so easily.

On Saturday the man telephoned. Annie passed the receiver to Nathan, looking unsure. "He's asking for you," she said.

Nathan took the phone. His heart had begun to thump rather hard, but he kept his voice level. *This is it,* he thought. This was where his imaginings had to pass the reality test. He said: "Hello?"

"Mrs. Squires tell me, you say you pull me from sea." His English, though strangely accented, was amazingly rapid and fluent for someone who must have learned it in a matter of weeks. "I think, that is not possible. How you do this?"

"I don't know exactly," Nathan said, wishing his mother would go away for a few minutes. "I was dreaming, and I saw a man drowning. I had to save him. I grabbed his hands, and sort of—yanked, and there we were."

What are you talking about? Annie mouthed.

Later, Nathan whispered back, wondering what on earth he was going to tell her. On the other end of the line, the immigrant from an alternative universe was saying: "Yes. That is what happened. You came out of air, like angel in old legend. Then you bring me to this place. Why? Cleaner here, some people kind, but society—not modern. Backward."

"I know it must seem strange," Nathan said. "I couldn't help it. We had to come here. This is my place." There was a pause, then he went on: "I have so many things to ask you. Can we meet?"

"Is important . . . yes. You find me, or I find you?"

Uncertain if his mother would allow him to go to Hastings on his own, Nathan suggested a train to Crowford and then a bus, offering to pay for the trip once his new friend arrived. They settled on the following Saturday, and Nathan hung up, trembling slightly. This was a man from another world, someone he had saved, though he didn't know how, and pulled into an involuntary exile, and now, at last, they were going to meet. He would learn about that other world and its masked inhabitants, about the ruler who spied on him, and the winged xaurians, and the talk of contamination, and—

"What was that all about?" Annie demanded.

Nathan was silent for a long minute. "I can't tell you," he said eventually. "I'm sorry. There's something I don't understand yet, and . . . I have to work it out."

"There's more to this immigrant business than a school project, isn't there?"

"Yes. Please don't ask me, Mum. I don't want to lie to you, and I can't tell you the truth."

Annie studied his serious face, and saw the pleading in his eyes. She said in a sudden rush of panic: "You're not doing anything *illegal*, are you? I know these people need help, but you wouldn't—you wouldn't get involved in breaking the law—would you?"

"Of course not. I'm not stupid, Mum. I'll swear it, if you like."

Annie gave a tiny shake of her head, only half relieved. "This man's a stranger to you," she said, "yet you have secrets with him."

"I'll explain when I can," Nathan said. "If I can."

"I ought to stop this right now . . ."

"No! Please . . . I'm not doing anything wrong," he protested, hoping it was true. His activities might not be illegal, but he knew they were questionable. "Please trust me, Mum."

"I trust *you*," Annie said wryly, "but you're too young for me to trust your judgment."

But she made no attempt to prevent his rendezvous with the asylum seeker, and that night she collected him and Hazel from the party at eleven, "because you shouldn't walk home on your own at that hour, even though the village is quite safe," and after they had left Hazel at her home a silence fell between them that neither could break. Nathan was unhappy because he had never been alienated from his mother, and he knew he was hurting her, and Annie saw him turning into a teenager, secretive and hostile, and her heart ached. In bed she couldn't sleep, and she heard him climb up to the Den, but she lacked the will to call him and send him back to his room. A little while later, footsteps on the landing told her he had gone to bed, and she lay wakeful long after, isolated in her separateness, not knowing that Nathan, too, did not sleep.

The Pursuers

The next day they went over to Thornyhill for tea. Nathan left his mother with Bartlemy, hoping she would talk to him, since he knew Bartlemy had a way of making things right. Meanwhile, he took a packet of Smarties and went looking for Woody. As always, it was quiet under the trees, the familiar woodland quiet of birdsong and leaf murmur and the hum of a passing insect. Sunlight speckled the ground, filtering through branches unruffled by any wind. When he had gone some way, he sat down on a convenient log, calling softly: "Woody! Woody!" and waited. The woodwose appeared very quickly; perhaps his long nose had picked up the scent of the Smarties. Nathan offered them to him.

"I like green ones best," Woody volunteered, making a careful selection.

"All the colors taste the same," Nathan pointed out prosaically. "Still, most people have a preference. I like the yellow ones myself."

They sat for a while in Smartie-munching companionship, talk-

ing little. Presently, Nathan began to tell his friend about the cup of
the Thorns, though he still could not speak of the chapel or his vision,
and how they had to find the injunction so Rowena could reclaim her
family heirloom. Woody understood little of this, having had nothing to do with the law in this world or any other, and Nathan's explanation didn't enlighten him, but he was able to assimilate the final
point of the story. "The injunction is probably just a piece of paper,"
Nathan concluded. "If we can find it, Mrs. Thorn can prove that the
cup belongs to her, and get it back. We've had a good look through
the house and it doesn't seem to be there, but Uncle Barty thought it
might be concealed in these woods, maybe on the site of the ancient
home of the Thorns. That was destroyed a long time ago, before
Thornyhill was built—my uncle told me there were other houses,
dwellings he called them, and in the time of Henry the Seventh, or
perhaps it was the Eighth, they built the house the way it is now, sort
of on top. You can still see bits of the old *old* walls, in some of the
rooms. Anyway, there should be the ruins of the original place
around somewhere, under the trees and the leafmold. I thought you
might know where."

"You mean," Woody said, concentrating, "the *first* house was
not—where the house is now?"

"That's right," said Nathan. "Sorry if I sounded muddling. It
would only be a few bits of wall, perhaps not even that. Just lumps in
the ground where the foundations were. I went to see a Roman villa
once and there were no walls, just floors, buried under the soil, and
when they scraped it off they found wonderful pictures in mosaic.
This place might be a bit like that, though I don't know if it's Roman,
and I don't suppose there are any mosaics. The Thorns can trace their
ancestors back to the Saxons or even farther, according to my uncle.
He says there are records of someone called Turnus, which is also
spelt *T-H-Y-R-N-U-S*, in—I think—A.D. 400, and that's meant to be
Thorn latinized, because people often latinized their names in those

days, if they were grand enough. Of course, *Thorn* could be *Thyrnus* anglicized, I suppose."

"I don't do spelling," Woody admitted cautiously. "What is A.D.?"

"It's 'Anno Domini,' the year of Christ's birth. It's how we count time. A.D. was more than two thousand years ago."

"I don't count very well, either," Woody murmured. "I can do up to twenty-three, but—"

"Why twenty-three?"

The woodwose wriggled an assortment of fingers and toes.

"*I* see," Nathan said. He realized Woody was distressed, and added hastily: "It doesn't matter. If we have to count anything, I'll do it. The thing is, you know the woods. I thought you might know of a place where there were odd ridges in the ground, or something like that."

"I know," Woody said. "But I don't go there much. It's in the Darkwood. I don't like it there. The trees grow twisted, as if they are afraid of the sun, and the river changes its course, and at night there are strange creakings and whisperings, and I've seen shadows move where there was no movement to cast a shadow."

"Whisperings?" Nathan said, remembering the snake murmurs in the chapel, which reached even to his dreams. "You mean— voices? What do they say?"

"Nothing," Woody replied. "Nothing I can hear. They just whisper. *Swss—swss—ss*. A hissy sort of sound. No proper words. And once I heard thumping noises, coming from underground."

"Maybe there's a badger's sett," Nathan suggested.

"Not badgers. Smell's wrong. Badgers smell animal, rank, very strong. No animal smells in the Darkwood. More like a tingle than a smell. A tingle in my nose."

"Like a sneeze?"

Woody shook his head decisively. "A different kind of tingle. A

tingle that means something bad, or maybe not bad, something peculiar—like what you said."

"Something weird," Nathan said, recollecting their former conversation.

"I think so." Woody still wasn't sure about the meaning of *weird*.

"Can you take me to this place? There could be secrets buried
there—the injunction, or something else. Something that thumps.
Anyway, we have to see. And it's not dark now; it won't be dark for
ages. We'll be quite safe." He concluded, optimistically: "I'll look
after you."

Woody seemed to accept this, with reservations. "We go there
quickly, and leave quickly," he insisted. "The Darkwood is unfriendly, even to me. Old memories linger there, bad memories."

"The trees remember?" Nathan asked, thinking vaguely of Ents.

"Memories remember," said Woody. "Leaves dying turn to leafmold, trees to wood rot. Always something left. Memories lie thick in
the Darkwood, like the leaves of many seasons. Things can grow
from the memories, as seeds grow from the woodland floor. Bad
memories breed bad spirits."

"I've been to the Darkwood often," Nathan said. "I've never
sensed any danger, not *real* danger." Except in the buried chapel . . .

"You haven't been to this place," Woody said with confidence. "I
would know."

"Let's go quickly then."

Woody took him at his word, flickering ahead between the trees
like something with little more substance than a leaf shadow. When
Nathan was very young, Woody had always led him carefully away
from the garden, holding his hand, helping him if his clothes snagged
on twig or briar; but now he kept well in front of his companion,
pausing only rarely to let him catch up. Several times Nathan had to
call to him to wait. They were far from any path, and as they pene-

trated the Darkwood low branches reached out to trip him; netted stems snarled his ankles. On his previous explorations he had always chosen the most open route, but Woody was undeterred by the undergrowth: his thin body slid through every tangle. As they plunged deeper down the valley the sun went in, or was cut off by a shoulder of hill, and the trees closed over them. In the dimness it grew harder for Nathan to see his guide, unless Woody turned and motioned to him with a quick, nervous gesture. Normally sure-footed, the boy stumbled over tree roots and slithered down sudden steeps in a flurry of dead leaves. Then the woodwose stopped abruptly in the lee of a tree trunk begreened with moss. "We must be careful now," he said, "and quiet."

"Who is there to hear us?" Nathan asked; but Woody did not answer.

They moved forward very cautiously now. The boy made out a ridge in the wood floor, running too straight for nature into a jungle of briar. He tried to follow it, but Woody caught his wrist and pulled him on. They came to another ridge, beyond which the ground fell away for a few feet; peering down, Nathan saw that the short drop was almost sheer, as if it had been shaped by a wall. Or maybe the wall was there still, under leaf and moss and root tendril. "That tree was uprooted in a storm last winter." Woody indicated an upturned bole some way below. "The earth slipped. Lots of earth. Then it was like this."

"I'm going to climb down," Nathan said. "I want to look closer."

"No!" Woody hissed. "You will disturb things. Memories—or worse. We come quickly, go quickly. You promised."

"I must look," Nathan said. "That's what we came for."

He swung his legs over the edge and jumped down. It looked an unlikely spot to find a missing injunction, but he had forgotten about that in the excitement of discovering the place where the first Thorns had lived; an eager curiosity drove him on. He explored the slope with his hands, pushing aside nettle and briar twig, getting scratched and stung. He could feel a network of fine tubers stiffening the soil. Remembering how the chapel had been concealed, he probed in between with his fingers, sensing a loosening in the earth. There was a sound from Woody—a kind of stifled whimper—and he glanced up; but his friend had gone. Something like a zephyr moved across the wood floor toward him, eddying the leaves, shuddering a low-slung branch. The treetops did not even quiver; whatever it was traveled only on the ground, invisible, rippling the undergrowth like a serpent. There was a faint rustling that might have been grass stems rubbing together, but wasn't. Then it swelled to a whisper of many voices, wordless yet filled with unknown words—a whisper that drew swiftly nearer, coiling across the ground, like yet unlike the whisper in the chapel, softer, colder, more deadly . . . Nathan backed away from the earth wall and began to run, down the slope at first and then checking, knowing that was foolish, veering right and uphill again. He didn't look around but the pursuing whisper always seemed to be just behind him, close as his own shadow. He didn't know what had happened to Woody. Cricket and rugby had made him fit but he fell once, setting his foot on a rolling piece of log, and his breath shortened, and even when the whisper failed fear followed him, urging him to panic, blocking out thought and sense. When at last he came to a halt, panting and exhausted, he was back in Thornyhill woods but far from the house, and a distant bend in the road showed through the trees. He looked all around, but there was nothing out of the ordinary, and the birds were singing again, and the sun had returned. He called: "Woody! Woody!" but the woodwose did not reappear. He said: "You were right. I'm sorry," hoping the apology would reach the ears for which it was intended, and set off walking slowly back to the house, keeping parallel with the road, thinking and thinking.

"So Nathan is growing up," Bartlemy said to Annie, over the comfort of tea and exquisite little cookies whose flavor she couldn't identify. "He has secrets. It's a cliché, but he's no longer a child. He's becoming a man, an adult if you prefer, and men keep secrets from their mothers. It's natural. He has asked you to trust him, and I think that's what you should try to do. If there's something going on, something we should know about, we will find out in due course. Forbidding him to meet this stranger won't help. An asylum seeker . . . I wonder now."

"What do you wonder?" Annie inquired. She was feeling insensibly soothed, perhaps by his placid attitude, perhaps by the sweetness of the cookies.

"I was wondering where this stranger comes from. A man on a beach, who has swum in from a boat, only I believe they never traced the boat or found any sign of companions. Illegal immigrants rarely travel singly. Don't press him with questions, but maybe Nathan could be persuaded to bring this man here for a meal. He must be destitute, and he's bound to be hungry."

Annie smiled suddenly. "It's a good idea," she said. "Food is your cureall, isn't it? You use it to work magic, to open hearts and unlock minds. Not a potion, but a cookie"—she took another—"or a mug of broth, or a piece of cake."

"Exactly," said Bartlemy.

And then Hoover looked up, thumping his tail, and they knew Nathan was coming back, and Bartlemy went into the kitchen to find more cookies.

BACK IN the village Nathan went to see Hazel. He needed to talk about what had happened in the Darkwood, he needed a confidante, an ally—in his heart, he knew he needed someone to go back there with him. When he had thrust his hands between the roots, into the crumbling soil of the earth wall, he was sure there had been a hollow space beyond; he even thought he had touched metal, like a rod of iron buried under tree and tuber. He had noted with relief that, as he had hoped, Annie seemed more relaxed with him after her tea with Bartlemy. When he said he was going to see Hazel she started to question him, then stopped short, smiling and saying: "Okay." He smiled back, trusting things were all right again, and went out.

As he approached the Bagots' house he heard raised voices—adult voices, not Hazel's. Her father and Lily. And Effie Carlow. The front door opened and Dave Bagot strode out, carrying a zip bag so full it wouldn't close. He brushed past Nathan, ignoring him, got into his car, and drove off much too fast. Inside, he heard Effie Carlow say: "Good riddance." He knocked tentatively on the still-open door.

Effie's face appeared suddenly from the gloom of the hall, looking more than ever like a predatory bird, beak-nosed and beady-eyed. "So it's you," she said. "Hazel's upstairs, in her room. Of course, in my day a girl didn't invite a boy into her bedroom, not if she wanted to keep her reputation she didn't. But times change. How is it with the dreaming? Been in any new worlds lately?"

"Not lately," Nathan said. From the kitchen, he could hear the sound of weeping—the gentle tears of resignation, not the wild sobs of anger and despair. He felt it was best not to comment on it.

Effie smiled at him, or perhaps merely bared her teeth in a kind of ferocious grin. He went upstairs in search of Hazel.

She stuck her head around the bedroom door and pulled him inside, shutting out any possibility of adult interference. The room was less a bedroom than a lair, the walls layered with pictures and posters, books and CDs stacked on shelf and floor, teen magazines skulking under the bed. There was a desk littered with unfinished homework, a half-eaten bar of chocolate, a bottle of ginger ale, and a portable sound system that pumped out some sort of weird twanging music that Nathan thought might be Indian. Hazel's taste in music was still at the experimental stage: she refused to restrict herself to the accepted trends and was always trying out new genres. It was as if she was searching for a certain type of sound, something that would make her feel a certain way, but she could never quite find it. "What's this?" Nathan asked, picking up a CD case, but Hazel brushed such trivia aside.

"Did you see Dad?"

"He shot past me outside. Has he—"

"He's left. He's really left. He and Mum had a fight, and Great-Grandma Effie came around, and he was yelling at her, too, and I think he hit Mum, and she—Great-Grandma—drove him out with a broomstick. He called her a wicked old witch, and other things, too, four-letter-word things, but he went. I'm so glad. I don't care what anyone says. I'm so glad." She pulled her hair over her face, and pushed her fist in her mouth, and for a moment Nathan thought she was crying.

He said: "Are you okay?"

She nodded but didn't say any more. He put his arm around her, and felt her shuddering.

"He didn't hit you, did he?"

"Not this time. Only the once, with the back of his hand, not a proper hit, just casual. He was drunk. I told you about that." Nathan made an affirmative noise. "Great-Grandma says she's going to stay here for a while. That'll stop him coming back. He's afraid of her."

"Are you?" Nathan asked.

"A bit." He was almost sure she shivered again. "Sometimes. But she's better than Dad. She has to be better than Dad."

They sat for a while listening to the strange twangy music and drank some of the ginger ale, which was flat. When Hazel was calmer Nathan told her about finding the site of the first house of the Thorns, and even about Woody, which she found rather hard to take in—she could deal with other worlds, but semi-human creatures lurking around tree trunks sounded suspiciously like pixies or goblins, and she wasn't having any of that. She said with conscious cynicism that she had long outgrown fairy tales. "You'll understand when you meet him," Nathan assured her. He tried to tell her about the whispering and the phantom pursuit, but that was hardest of all to describe.

"If you didn't see anything," Hazel demanded, "how did you know there was anything there?"

"I saw—movement. Twigs quivering, a disturbance on the ground. It's difficult to explain."

"And you want to go back? D'you really think the missing paper will be there? I mean . . . it doesn't seem awfully likely to me."

"Not the injunction, no," Nathan conceded. "But there's got to be something."

"How do you know?" Hazel asked.

"If there's nothing to hide, why chase me away?"

Hazel could find no argument against this reasoning, though she wasn't happy about it. "All right," she said finally. "I'll go there with you. But *only* if it's a nice, sunny, friendly sort of day. Not if it's all cloudy and—and ominous. Okay?"

"I thought you didn't believe in fairy tales?" Nathan said, feeling sufficiently encouraged to tease her.

"I don't. But I *do* believe in ghost stories. Besides, what happened—whatever it was—frightened you, and you're normally much braver than me."

"When we go back," Nathan said doggedly, "I won't be frightened."

DURING THE week, Bartlemy telephoned Annie. "How would you like a day in London? It'll take your mind off your troubles, real or imagined—stop you worrying about things you can't change."

"That would be lovely," Annie said. "What's brought this on?" She could never recall Bartlemy spending a day in London, or indeed anywhere else, since she had known him.

"Rowena Thorn is off to Sotheby's to take a look at the Grimthorn Grail. She wants me to come with her—moral support—and I thought a day out would do you good."

"The Grimthorn Grail!" Annie exclaimed. "Nathan will be jealous. It's really caught his imagination. I will get to see it, too, won't I?"

"I don't see why not," Bartlemy responded. "If they make a fuss, we can always say you're another expert. Apparently, they've been trying to date it and they've encountered some kind of a problem . . ."

"But I'm not an expert!"

"Of course you are. You have an amazing way with computers, small children, and dogs. We don't have to say what you're an expert *on*."

Annie laughed. Michael Addison, who was in the shop at the time, drinking coffee and leafing through a rare history of the Agricultural Revolution, looked inquiring. After Annie had hung up, she told him of the project.

"I shall have to close for the day," she said.

He grinned. "Shocking. Seriously, the old man's right. You could do with a day off. Playing truant from everything. You worry too much about Nat. He's a good kid."

"I know," she said. "Sometimes, that's what scares me."

"So tell me about the Grimthorn Grail—if it's not a secret?"

They went up to London on Wednesday, leaving the Jowett in Crowford and taking the train. The sun shone, and the city looked its best decked out in the vivid greens of early summer. At Rowena's insistence they took a taxi to Bond Street; Mrs. Thorn had the habits, if not the income, of the privileged, and disdained bus and tube. They were greeted at Sotheby's by her friend Julian Epstein, a fortyish man with badger-striped hair and beard and heavy eyebrows drawn into what appeared to be a permanent frown. He accepted, rather doubtfully, the presence of Bartlemy, hesitated over Annie ("My assistant," Bartlemy said), then gave in. "Any advice is welcome," he said unexpectedly. "This damn cup has everyone baffled. What exactly do you know about its history, Rowena?"

"What I've told you," she said guardedly.

"Have you had it carbon-dated?" Bartlemy inquired.

"Yes," said Epstein, "and no." He led them into a room with strong artificial lighting and no windows, and unlocked a steel cupboard. From inside he produced a box, an ordinary wooden box packed with false straw. "It came in this," he said. "God knows where they'd been keeping it. Took us a day to get it clean." He thrust the straw aside and extricated the cup.

Without really thinking about it, Annie had been anticipating the gleam of gold, even a jewel or two, and its dullness came as something of a disappointment. Rowena took it, turning it in her hands, and an eagerness came into her face that could not be hidden, changing it, making it harder and stronger. Bartlemy wondered if Epstein noticed. "You said, yes *and* no?" he probed gently.

"We tried," Epstein elaborated. "The results were—bizarre. Carbon-dating never fails, but this time . . . They tested it three times, and were told variously that it was a hundred years old, eight thousand years old, and two hundred thousand years old. There appears to be no logical explanation. In addition, we have so far been unable to discover what it is made of. Is there any clue in your family records?"

"Tradition said it was gold," said Rowena. "Or stone." She hadn't taken her eyes off it. "I'd go for stone. Some sort of agate, perhaps. It's definitely not metal. So it didn't want to be dated? Family legend claims it has strange powers. You should be careful how you meddle with legends, Julian."

Epstein looked skeptical. "Are you going to tell me there's a curse?"

Rowena gave a snort, not quite laughter, but made no answer.

"May I see?" Bartlemy requested.

She relinquished the cup slowly, as if with reluctance. He passed his hand over it, his eyes half closing, as though seeing with his fingers, or feeling with senses beyond touch. Observing it more closely, Annie saw it was made of some dark substance, green-tainted, bleared as if with stains so old that they had become a part of its natural patina. The snaky patterns around the rim seemed little more than scratches, worn thin with the scrubbing of centuries. It looked neither valuable nor beautiful, only very ancient, primitive, even crude, holding perhaps some faint echo of forgotten magic, but too remote or too obsolete to have any lingering significance. "Would you like to take a closer look?" Bartlemy said, passing it to Annie—he didn't miss Rowena's quick gesture of interception, abruptly checked.

Annie's fingers closed around the stem. The sudden rush of nausea that swept over her was so violent the world turned black—she felt herself losing hold on consciousness, tried to cry out, let the cup slip from her grasp. Then she fainted.

She came to, moments later, to see Bartlemy's concerned face bent over her. She had been lifted into a chair; his arm was around her shoulders. Julian Epstein peered past him, his natural frown deepened with anxiety. Only Rowena wasn't looking at her: she had picked up the cup, and was staring fixedly into the shallow bowl. "We should get her out of this room," Epstein was saying. "It's airless in here. A touch of claustrophobia . . . ?"

"Possibly," said Bartlemy. "Secure the cup." He threw a quick glance toward Rowena, conveying what might have been a warning.

Epstein turned to Mrs. Thorn; Annie tried to stand up and found she was still sick and shaking. Bartlemy picked her up with surprising ease and carried her from the room.

Afterward, when she was recovering in a comfortable chair by an open window, he asked her what had happened. "I don't know," she said. "I really don't. I touched the goblet, and then—that was it. Sickness. Blackness. I'll be all right in a minute."

He looked at her long and thoughtfully. Presently, Epstein reappeared bringing a glass of water, with Rowena in his train. While Annie sipped from the glass he continued to expand his theory of claustrophobia, almost as if he were trying to convince himself. Mrs. Thorn looked unbelieving.

"Don't start telling me this is more evidence for your family legends," Epstein said to her. "I've never thought of you as the credulous type. You seemed very intrigued by the cup. Are you going to try to buy back the lost heirloom?"

She hesitated, then took the plunge. "No," she said. "I'm going to prove the original sale was illegal."

"How will you do that?"

"There's an injunction in existence dating back to the fifteenth century, specifically forbidding any sale or other disposal of the cup." She didn't mention that she had yet to lay her hands on it.

Epstein's frown lines tightened. "It'll never stand up in court."

"Sorry, Julian," she said, "but it will. Don't want to spoil your fun, but there it is. The Grimthorn Grail's mine—mine and my family's—and I'm taking it back."

The session ended on an unsatisfactory note. Leaving Epstein, presumably to summon lawyers of his own, they went to lunch. But Annie could barely eat, and sat only half listening as Rowena discussed the cup with unconcealed excitement. "It's the genuine article," she said. "No question. I knew it the moment I touched it. Fascinating that business about dates. If it is the *actual* Grail—the real McCoy, Arthur and all—it might have the power to resist scientific analysis. I know: a month ago I'd have said this was baloney, but you heard Julian. No accurate date; they don't even know what it's made of. That's a twenty-four-karat mystery, and in this day and age such mysteries are rare."

"It's certainly interesting," Bartlemy conceded. "There is, as they say, a case to answer."

Rowena turned to Annie. "It was the cup that affected you, wasn't it?" she insisted. "You held it, and you fainted. It was the cup."

"Perhaps," Bartlemy said. "But why? Why Annie?"

"Part of the mystery," Mrs. Thorn declared with evident relish.

Annie, taking no part in the conversation, excused herself and went to the ladies' room. In the mirror, she thought she looked very pale, almost ghostly. As if she had been ill. *Maybe that's it,* she concluded. *Maybe I'm ill. Some sort of summer flu, or migraine, or a brain tumor* . . . She panicked at the idea, resolving to rush to her doctor for a checkup, but in her heart she didn't really believe it. Rowena was right: it was something to do with the cup . . .

Still staring in the mirror, she saw the door opening behind her. A woman glanced in—for an instant their eyes met—and hastily withdrew. Annie spun around, tugged at the door, peered out; but the woman had gone. Nonetheless, Annie knew she couldn't be mistaken. It was Rianna Sardou.

IN THE attic space above the Bagots' house, Effie Carlow had cleared a table for her own use. She was heating something in a blackened saucepan on a small gas-powered camping stove—a thick, dark liquid that bubbled sluggishly. Every so often she would add a few drops from one of a collection of bottles, muttering under her breath as she did so. A pungent smell wafted through the room, overpowering in that confined space. Finding nowhere to waft to, it hung around, stinging Effie's sinuses and making her eyes water. But she seemed indifferent to discomfort. The bracelet lay on the table beside her: a cheap ornament such as teenagers wear, with ragged strands of beads sprouting from an elasticized wristband. Caught among the beads there were still a couple of short curling hairs, light brown in color. Carefully she detached one of them and let it fall into the saucepan. The liquid bubbled on regardless. The smell worsened.

After a few minutes she removed the saucepan from the heat and poured the liquid into a basin to cool. Burned residue adhering to the inside of the pan indicated that during a previous attempt she must have allowed the contents to boil dry. This time she was more diligent, never leaving her experiment for a moment, waiting by the basin, fidgeting in her chair or blowing gently on the dark surface. As the liquid cooled, its consistency changed. It no longer looked thick, becoming instead smooth and shining like black glass. When she thought it was ready she mumbled something—a charm perhaps—bending over the bowl, gazing fixedly into the shallowness of its depths. Her skills were limited, she knew that, but this was the best mirror-magic she had achieved: her former essays had been cloudy, showing images that were few and blurred. She had done better now; she was confident of that. And using the hair would ensure that the spell focused on Annie—Annie whom Hazel had found crying for no cause, who was hiding the truth about Nathan, whatever that truth might be. Hazel had not wanted to confide in her great-grandmother or give her the bracelet, but Effie had learned long ago how to assert control over an unformed mind. Besides, she had told her: "You are a Carlow, not a Bagot. The power is in your blood. One day, I will teach you how to use it."

And now . . . now she stared into the basin and saw shapes developing, not clear and bright as in Bartlemy's spellfire but through a glass darkly, through the looking glass into someone else's life. Annie . . . Annie walking down a lane between dim hedgerows, on the way to Riverside House . . .

IT WAS the day after her trip to London, and she had resolved to ask some of the awkward questions, even if she couldn't get any answers. Michael was in. He greeted her with the twist of his smile and offered coffee. "I'd make it lunch," he said, "but for two things. First, I have to get to town for a three o'clock meeting with my agent, and second, there's nothing in the fridge. That's the problem with living alone a lot: it's easy not to bother with proper meals. I live off snacks. If I buy real food it never gets cooked; it just sits around growing green fur. Very unhealthy."

"For you, or the food?" Annie quipped. She found herself wishing she didn't like Michael quite so much. It made things harder.

"How was your day in the big city?" he inquired. "I should take you up with me sometime, shouldn't I? Or wouldn't you come?"

Annie ignored that. "Actually, I wasn't awfully well," she said, and went on to describe the incident at Sotheby's, while Michael filled a coffeepot and interpolated questions.

"You should go to your doctor," he concluded, looking concerned.

"There's nothing wrong with me, I'm sure of it. I think Rowena was right: it was something to do with the cup. They can't date it; they don't even know what it's made of. Maybe there was some kind of emanation from it—"

"A magical aura?" Michael's tone was sardonic.

"Maybe," Annie said, undeterred. "There are so many strange things in the world—and beyond it. As I've grown older, I've learned . . . you need a very broad mind to take it all in. Magic is the word we use for things we don't understand. Radiation was a magical aura until someone figured it out."

"Fair enough. Are you suggesting the cup of the Grimthorns exudes a new form of radiation? And if so, why didn't it affect anybody else?"

"If I knew," Annie said, "I wouldn't need to speculate. But that wasn't why I wanted to talk to you."

"I hoped you came for the pleasure of my company," Michael said, passing her a cup of coffee.

There was a teasing note in his voice; if she had been a little younger she would have blushed. She was glad to find herself too old for that weakness. "Not entirely," she said, maintaining her poise. "I wanted to ask you . . . I saw Rianna in London."

"That's impossible," Michael responded promptly. "She's on tour in Georgia—Georgia in Russia, not the U.S. state. Forging cultural bonds across the globe: Rianna's into all that. As the play's in English I'm not sure who's going to understand it, but never mind. I thought I'd told you."

"You did," Annie said. "That's why I was so surprised."

He was looking perplexed. "Where did you—"

"We were at lunch. I went to the ladies' room, and while I was looking in the mirror I saw her come in behind me. When she saw me she backed off. I tried to follow her but by the time I opened the door again she'd gone. She wasn't in the restaurant, either."

"You only saw her reflection for a second or two," Michael said. "You could have been mistaken."

"No," Annie said. "She doesn't look like her screen image, but she's distinctive. I saw her; she saw me. That's why she went."

"There's no reason for her to run away from you," Michael pointed out.

"There is if she's supposed to be in Georgia," Annie retorted. "Besides, she's been—odd—with me before. I didn't tell you, but she came into the shop once, and asked me a lot of strange questions."

Michael's face tensed very slightly. "About me?"

"No. About Nathan."

"Nat?" Michael looked honestly bewildered. "Why should Rianna be interested in him?"

"That was one of the things I came to ask you."

Michael had begun to pace about the kitchen; Annie thought she detected something else behind his confusion. "You must have gotten it wrong," he insisted. "Rianna's in Georgia proving her credentials as a citizen of the world. I've had three phone calls from her. She's been complaining about the director—she always does—saying one of her fellow actors is grossly underrated, better than Branagh—she always does—asking me to keep her posted on the mess in the Middle East since she can't get enough news out there . . ."

"Have you—have you been able to phone her?" Annie asked tentatively.

"Of course not. She's moving around too much. She—" He stopped.

"I'm sorry," Annie whispered. "I know it doesn't make sense. But it was her I saw. And that time in the shop, she appeared—oh, intrigued by Nathan. She wanted to know about his father."

"His *father?* God, I keep echoing you like a bloody parrot. I don't get any of this. Rianna and I . . ." He paused, took a deep breath, started again. "I daresay you've guessed. We have a fairly—*disconnected* marriage. We go our separate ways most of the time. When we're together, we get along. Good friends, or so I thought. It was passionate once, but not—not for a while now. Not for a long while. She never wanted a divorce—I give her someone to come home to—and I . . . well, I suppose I just let things chug along. Laziness, you'll tell me. Just like a man." Annie smiled. "I never had a reason to make a change."

"I understand."

"Sorry to bore you with all this. It seemed to be . . . necessary. The thing is, Rianna's got no reason to lie to me about where she is or what she's doing. It's not as if I'm one of those paranoid husbands always checking up on their wives; I never do. If she was in London, she'd tell me. As for Nathan—I mentioned him to her, of course I did. Coming to think of it, she *did* seem rather curious about him, I remarked on it at the time, but I didn't think anything of it. Why should I?"

"Curiouser and curiouser," Annie said.

Michael was silent for a minute, his gaze focused on nothing very much. "She called me the night before last," he resumed eventually. "She wanted the local gossip. She never used to be interested in that kind of stuff—just the big issues—but since we came here . . . I told her about the Grimthorn Grail. I even told her you were going up to town."

"She could have followed us," Annie said, "from Sotheby's. And then she came into the restroom at the restaurant, not realizing I was in there, and rushed off when I recognized her."

"This is ridiculous," Michael said, giving himself a mental shake. "If Rianna had some sinister connection with you in the past, you'd know about it. Unless . . . supposing she knew your husband, before you met him? That might explain her interest in Nat's parentage."

"Just for the record," Annie said, "the man in my life wasn't my husband, and he wasn't Nathan's father, though Nathan doesn't know that. I can't think of any way Daniel could have met someone like Rianna. As for Nathan's real father"—it was her turn to pause and take a breath—"you will just have to take my word for it that it's out of the question that Rianna could ever have known him." And she repeated, not meeting his eyes: "Out of the question."

There was a further silence. Annie wanted to speak, she wanted to look at him, but somehow she couldn't. "I don't want to force your confidence," he said at last, "but I wish you would trust me. It seems to me you're carrying a very heavy burden—alone."

At that, she looked up. "I have Barty."

There was a crease between his brows. "Is he related to you? I've always assumed—"

"No. Just a friend."

"I'm sure he's very kind, but a man who's lived all his life in the village, who's never been anywhere, or done anything . . ."

"He's been somewhere," Annie said with inexplicable conviction. Despite what she knew of his history, she felt suddenly that he must have traveled widely, once upon a time, to know so much, to be who he was.

Michael looked both unconvinced and undecided, but a glance at the clock threw him off his stride. "Damn," he said with restraint. "I must go now. Damn and blast and bugger. We'll talk tomorrow—or the weekend. Don't worry. Whatever there is to sort out, we'll sort it. It's my business now. If Rianna's mixed up in something, I need to know what it is. I must run—I'm going to miss my train." He deposited his mug in the sink, snatched up his jacket and case, and hurried out with Annie in his wake. "I could drop you off on my way to Crowford . . ."

"No need. It's a lovely day. I'd rather walk."

"Till tomorrow then . . ."

He went in such a rush, she realized he had left the kitchen door unlocked. Annie knew she should go back to the shop—she had closed up for a couple of hours—but she lingered, conscious of temptation. If Rianna Sardou was spying on her, she reasoned, then she had a right to spy on Rianna—hadn't she? Anyway, it couldn't hurt just to have a look. She didn't really expect to see anything she hadn't seen before—unless Rianna's tower was unlocked. With a quick glance around, she went back into the house.

Initially, her exploration proved disappointing. Rianna's tower *was* still locked, and naturally she would not pry into Michael's rooms. In their joint bedroom she opened the cupboards, feeling horribly nosy and sly, but found only some items of winter clothing, evidently unneeded at the moment, piles of expensive bed linen, spare pillows, and towels. She thought it strange that there were few personal photographs: it was hardly surprising they had no children, in view of the nature of their marriage, but Michael had once mentioned a married sister, and she was sure he had nephews and nieces. Still, what pictures there were appeared to be studio portraits for publicity or, in Michael's case, dust jacket shots. There were other deficiencies that baffled Annie: no face creams in the main bathroom ("What woman can exist without face cream?"), no cookbooks in the kitchen. Michael didn't seem to be interested in food, but Annie knew that everyone—*everyone*—owned cookbooks, regardless of whether they did any cooking or not. Cookbooks were a style accessory, and Rianna, for all her country jeans, was a creature of style. There was a full-length lambskin coat in the wardrobe that must have cost a four-figure sum, and in London her reflection had been wearing a loose-fitting khaki top, off one shoulder, which undoubtedly boasted a designer label. Defeated by the locked door of Bluebeard's Chamber, Annie prowled around upstairs again, forgetting her inhibitions in frustration. Where did detectives look, when they conducted searches? Trash cans, wastebaskets . . . other kinds of bins. Idly, she lifted the lid on the laundry basket. There were the inevitable socks and underpants, a crumpled shirt, a glimpse of khaki underneath. Suddenly alert, Annie thrust the shirt aside. To her surprise, it felt slightly damp. And underneath it was the khaki top Rianna had been wearing the previous day, the top that had been in her thought moments earlier. She picked it up, to look closer, to be certain. It was wet.

She's here, Annie thought. *Michael lied to me* . . . But she didn't believe he'd lied. If Rianna was around, and he knew it, he would have had a cover story; that would have been simple enough. He wouldn't have come out with some spiel about Georgia unless he thought it was true. Besides, his confusion and doubt had been genuine; she was sure of that. So how did the top get in the laundry basket? Perhaps Rianna was here, and he didn't know. Annie looked around warily, but the house both looked and felt utterly empty, and though she listened with ears on the stretch not a board creaked. In such an old building, the quiet was almost unnatural. There should have been the chunder of vintage plumbing, the groan of a door shifting in a draft, the rustle of air in the chimneys. Of course, Rianna could be in the locked tower, living there secretly, but surely Michael would be aware of her. And why was the top *wet*? What did wet clothing suggest? Rain? It hadn't rained for a couple of days. Water, anyway. *Water* . . .

Annie ran downstairs and out into the garden. The boat was tied up to a small wooden platform built along the riverbank; she could see the mast protruding above a thicket of shrubs. Rianna could live on the boat, Annie thought, without Michael knowing, at least for a few days. And the top got wet because she fell in or something . . . She made her way cautiously down to the river, taking care to remain screened by the bushes. Peeping around a rhododendron, she saw that the yacht looked deserted; but after all, Rianna would probably be away during the day. Eventually, she emerged from behind the shrub and stepped onto the jetty. She tried to peer through the cabin windows but couldn't see any sign of life. Summoning all her courage, and taking a firm grip on the rigging, she jumped aboard. The deck tilted alarmingly, making her ever-sensitive stomach give a responding jolt. Doing her best to steady both herself and the boat she scrambled around the available deck space, clinging to boom and halyard, squinting through the low windows in the hope of seeing a cup or plate on the table, a half-eaten sandwich, a bottle of mineral water. But no Marie-Celestian traces were visible; if Rianna was staying there, she had been scrupulously tidy. Turning back to the platform, Annie saw that her exertions had caused the boat to drift a little farther out. The gap wasn't very wide, but she was already feeling queasy. She hesitated, steeled herself, and leapt for the riverbank.

She landed on the very edge of the platform, missed her footing, and grabbed at the mooring post as one leg slipped into the water. For an instant the touch of the river felt like a clammy hand around her ankle. Then she pulled herself up onto the planks, panting with relief, and stood up. A cloud had slid over the sun, and when she turned around the surface of the Glyde had darkened. And near the bank something was happening.

The river seemed to be whirling upward into a waterspout, though there was no corresponding cloud column thrusting down to meet it. A thickening rope of water grew in front of her, swaying slightly like a blind snake groping for its prey. Now it was two feet high—four feet—five . . . The whirling slowed; there was just a pillar of water, suspended in midair, its base rooted in the Glyde. Annie was reminded of a photograph that freezes the splashback from a diver, but the pillar wasn't motionless: it rippled and quivered, drawing more water into itself, gradually acquiring shape and meaning. The top rounded into a head; shoulders spread outward; hips swelled. Its fluid substance began to solidify and color poured into its translucency: the whiteness of skin, the streaming darkness of hair, a ribbon-like garment that wrapped its long limbs in a watery shimmer. Already the face was recognizable, though it looked far paler, more exotic, less human. "Rianna . . . ," Annie whispered. Her voice seemed to be squeezed in her throat. The figure floated toward the bank, its feet still in the river. Boneless arms detached themselves from the main body and reached toward her . . .

Belatedly, panic kicked in. Annie took to her heels. She knew it was coming after her—she heard the squelchy tread of its feet on the boards. Glancing back, she saw it stumble or slither, as if uncertain of its balance on land; but it was growing more solid every second, and she ran on, not daring to look again. As she entered the lane the cloud shadow deepened: something seemed to be crawling under the hedgerows, and the grasses moved without any wind. Her horror redoubled. *They* were there, waiting for her, hemming her in, and the thing that looked like Rianna Sardou was on her tail, and she had no way forward, no way back. Only the center of the lane was clear, though *they* crowded her on either side. Hesitation would be fatal. She sprinted straight down the middle, looking neither to right nor left, running, running for her life . . . And somehow at the end of the lane she was still running, and the hedgerows were empty of anything but hedge, and when she ventured to look around there was nothing there, nothing at all. No ripple of pursuing movement, no entity made of river water. Presently, the sun came out again, and the bright afternoon was back, but she knew the nightmare hadn't really gone away, only slipped into the shadows.

She went back to the shop—she felt safer in the shop—and telephoned Bartlemy, but he was out. She made herself some tea, with sugar for the shock, and sat by the phone again, calling and calling, until Bartlemy answered at last.

AT SCHOOL Nathan dreamed of the other world again. A brief incursion, but it frightened him in a way the earlier dreams had not. He was sitting behind a rider on the back of a xaurian, one of three flying a patrol along an unfamiliar coastline. He knew it was a patrol because his rider spoke briefly into some kind of unseen communicator, possibly inside the mask; Nathan heard another voice close to the ear making an automatic response. It was just after sunset: a green glow was fading swiftly above the horizon and one of the three moons had risen directly ahead, while the faint rind of another was visible to their left. The brighter of the moons flung a reddish glitter across the sea, pockmarking the vast gloom of the water. On their right the shore looked uninhabited: no lights showed to indicate house or town, only the whiteness of foam frills around jutting headlands, and occasional strips of beach shining copper in the moongleam. He wondered if the rider in front of him was Raymor, but he had no way of telling. There seemed to be no immediate danger of his drawing anyone back into his own world, so he concentrated on his surroundings and the excitement of the flight, absorbing impressions, trying to learn all he could. Presently he found he could feel the wind rushing over him, cool but not cold, and the skin of the xaurian against his legs, harder than leather and with the smooth finish of fish or snakeskin. The second xaurian was flying a little behind him and to the side; the third, a little farther back. The moon shone red in their red eyes, so they glowed like bulbs of blood.

Suddenly, he saw the neighboring rider turn his head, staring fixedly at the space where he was sitting. He heard a voice from the communicator, no longer automatic: "Raymor! Ray! There's something behind you . . ." Raymor lifted his mount above the other two, describing a swift loop to scan the empty air. "No!" came the cry, increasingly urgent. "Not behind us, behind *you*. On your xaurian. It looks like a shadow. Maybe a poor-quality holocast, but—very dim. Can you see?"

Raymor twisted in the saddle; the third rider had broken the formation to draw near and point. Nathan was terrified. He had always been invisible before, except in the moment when he pulled the man out of the sea. But now, in his eagerness to experience this world, to be part of it, his thought was beginning to take on a physical form, and he didn't know how to stop it. He struggled to make himself fade, to eliminate the sensations he had reached for moments earlier, but he couldn't. Raymor had hooked the reins around the pommel and stretched out a gauntleted hand toward the incubus, though he could obviously make out little in the dark. Freed from restraint, the xaurian's flight tilted. Raymor's flailing arm encountered something that was neither shadow nor substance, and Nathan felt himself knocked sideways. His grip slipped on the xaurian's flank and with a wordless cry he plunged down into the dark . . .

He woke immediately, the fear still fresh in him. He was giddy from the fall and the dormitory reeled around him; it took a while to settle down. He lay thinking and thinking, unable to sleep, trying not to panic. He had always been a mere spectator in the alien universe; now he was becoming a player. Perhaps it was his own fault, because he had sought involvement: he had rescued the drowning man; he had wanted to feel the wind and the touch of the reptile's skin. But he knew, whatever he was doing, he had little or no control over it. Supposing he materialized completely, would he be trapped in that world, in his dream, striving in vain to awaken or return? And what would become of his body *here*? Would he be dead, or in a coma? And when he was there, would the so-called contamination affect him, without mask or protective clothing? He imagined himself going to bed in a wet suit and goggles, and laughed at the idea, which made him feel better, but not much.

By morning he had come to no real decisions, except that he must see the immigrant—it was Thursday, but he could hardly contain his impatience for another forty-eight hours—and somehow, he had to stop dreaming. He was unusually inattentive in class and yawned so much one teacher sent him to the sickroom. "I couldn't sleep last night," he told Brother James. "I have trouble sometimes. Perhaps . . . perhaps I could have some sleeping pills?"

"Nonsense!" snorted the monk. "Don't need drugs at your age.

Get out on the cricket pitch—get plenty of fresh air and exercise. That'll do the trick. You've obviously been cooped up too long with your studies. I'll speak to your housemaster about it."

Nathan said, "Thank you," but he wasn't comforted. He didn't think cricket would solve his problems at all.

"THERE ARE many kinds of water spirit," Bartlemy told Annie, sitting in her tiny living room that night while she drank the hot chocolate he had made for her. He had used certain ingredients brought from his own kitchen; what they were she didn't know, but she felt much calmer. "There are naiads, nymphs, nixes, kelpies—loreleis, selkies, sirens—though the last two prefer the sea. But I'm inclined to think that this was something different. It's clearly able to assume a human form, which requires considerable power, and a convincing form at that. It seems to have convinced Michael, unless he's involved in some way." He didn't mention the being he had seen in the spell-fire, submerged in water but not drowned, yet it was on his mind. Some things were coming together at last.

"I don't *think* so," Annie said cautiously. "But—but—you—don't seem to be very—well, astonished. You *believe* me. I wouldn't believe me, if I were you. At least, I'd find it difficult."

"Why shouldn't I believe you?" said Bartlemy. "You've always been completely truthful. As it is, I have some knowledge of these things."

"I've begun to realize that," Annie said. "Maybe . . . I've known all along. What—what knowledge, exactly?"

"That would take a long time to answer. For the present, you must just accept that I *know*. It's more important to concentrate on what is happening here. Plainly, there is a real Rianna Sardou whose image has been borrowed by this creature, though where she is now—"

"Touring in Georgia," Annie supplied promptly.

"Possibly. It would be helpful if we could be sure. Taking the form of another being is the most difficult kind of sympathetic magic. It generally requires the participation of the original, willing or otherwise, or some significant token from them."

"Like a glove or a lock of hair?" Annie suggested.

"That might not be adequate," Bartlemy said. "More . . . a severed hand, or an eye, or some other organ from which the image can be built up." Annie choked over her chocolate. "But let's not take fright prematurely. Until we know what spirit is involved, we can't guess of what it might be capable. Or indeed what purpose it may have."

"Nathan," Annie said instantly, blanching. "It asked about Nathan. I can't let him come back here. He'll have to stay at school—or with friends."

"Don't overreact," said Bartlemy. "We know nothing for certain."

"You keep saying that, or something like it," Annie said with a wan attempt at humor.

"Because it's true. We can, however, make a few deductions. As I said, I believe Nathan has a powerful father, who *may* be looking after him. Someone is clearly looking after you."

"What do you mean? I was chased by a—a sort of water zombie, and then by *them* . . ."

Bartlemy steepled his fingers. "And none of them caught up. Doesn't that provide us with food for thought? You said Rianna ran swiftly, and she was close behind you. Supposing *they* appeared, not to join the chase, but to cut her off? I have been wondering about these phantom furies of yours. You thought they followed you here, but actually they *drove* you."

"But why?" Annie queried, puzzled and unconvinced.

"To bring you to me. I could protect you, and the boy. I have some highly specialized talents. And someone thought you needed that type of protection."

"But you're saying that *they*—these shadow beings, whatever they are—they're *helping* us? I can't accept that. If they were part of some force for good, surely they wouldn't be so terrifying?"

"I didn't say they were good," Bartlemy temporized. "But they may have helped, once or twice. When they pursued you down the lane, after your first visit to Michael, they could have been trying to keep you away from the water spirit. Anyway, how do you define *good*, or differentiate it from evil? Even human nature is never black and white. Our moral stance depends so much on upbringing, on the precepts of our society, on thinly veiled self-interest. And for the werefolk—those who are less, or more, than human—morality as we understand it simply doesn't exist."

"Are you saying *you* don't believe in good and evil?" Annie asked very quietly. "Because if you are—"

"Not at all. I'm merely pointing out that other beings do not judge as we do."

"That's a matter for them," Annie said. "If I don't make my own judgments, who will? Even if I'm wrong, I have to go by what *I* believe, don't I?"

He took her hand with an oddly melancholic smile. "You are wiser than I," he said after a pause. "I knew someone like you, once before, someone I loved very dearly. Sometimes, I see a look on your face, a turn of your head . . ."

"What happened to her?"

"She died. But it wasn't sad, not for her. Only for me, and the others who mourned her. She did something that she believed in. There was a great sickness, and she was a skilled healer, so she went to help, but the plague caught up with her in the end."

"Plague?" Annie murmured.

"That may be the reason why I have tried to acquire something of her skill, since she departed. Medicine and food are both about physical well-being. Heal the body, nourish the soul." The faint sad smile flickered across his face again. "It would have amused her, to hear me talk this way. She was one of those people who never noticed what she ate, even if I cooked it. My Ailean . . . Ah well, it was all a long time ago."

"How long?" Annie said in a whisper. She felt she stood upon the edge of something, of a great discovery, in that moment of recollection and gentle grief. The revelation was coming of a truth she had long sensed without actually knowing it . . .

"Oh, seven hundred years or so," he said. "A long time."

Annie clasped his hand in silence. She didn't doubt him; she knew him too well for that. But for the first time she accepted, not only that there were other worlds beyond this one, but that the world she lived in was not as it appeared. Barriers crumpled in her mind, and her imagination reached out, and she was excited, and humbled, and very much afraid.

The Man
on the
Beach

Michael didn't return until Saturday. Annie felt a strangeness on seeing him, knowing the truth, finding herself unable to tell him. How could she say that there was a creature walking around in the form of his wife—a creature with whom he had perhaps shared board and bed—who was really a thing of magic and menace, spun from river water, perhaps altogether evil? She couldn't say it. He would think her mad or deluded, and when he saw Rianna next might mention the matter, and then who knew what she would do. Ignorance kept him safe. Yet he was already troubled—she saw the uncertainty in his face, and knew an impulse to smooth the worry from his forehead, and kiss the smile back onto his mouth, an impulse she had not known before anxiety touched him. She told herself it was just an impulse, a natural urge to offer comfort, and pushed it sternly away.

"I meant to see you yesterday," he said. "I'm sorry. I stayed the night in London. I wanted to find a way to reach Rianna. Her agent definitely believes she's in Georgia, but he has no means of contacting her or anyone in the company. They seem to have gone beyond the ken of mobile phones. A primitive place, Georgia. I got hold of the mother of one of the other actors, and the boyfriend of another, but they're in the same boat as me: they just wait for occasional calls. I'm sure you're wrong about seeing her. I really can't imagine why she should lie."

"But you're worried," Annie said. Had he seen Rianna's top in the laundry basket? Of course not—or if he had, it would mean nothing to him. Men didn't notice anything to do with clothes.

"No—no, I'm not. Well, not much. Just confused. Any danger of coffee?"

She made it, while Michael seemed to be hesitating, teetering on the verge of some perilous plunge. "Where's the man of the house?" he asked, evidently playing for time. "Shouldn't he be around this morning?"

"Nathan's out with his friends," Annie said. Actually, she knew, Nathan was out with a stranger, the unknown asylum seeker, but she didn't feel ready to discuss all that now. Besides, no doubt his friends came into it somewhere.

"I was wondering," Michael said, plunging, "about his father . . . You said something, before I left. You said he *wasn't* the man in your life . . . ?"

"No," Annie said. "Daniel died. Nathan was the result of a—I suppose you could call it a one-night stand, just after. I didn't even know the man." She lifted her chin, looking out of the kitchen window. In some obscure way she felt this was part of her penance, for the crime she hadn't committed, for surrendering, for letting it happen. "Are you shocked?"

"Of course not." He moved closer—she felt it—and laid a tentative hand on her shoulder. "We all do things—when we're upset, when we're hurt, when we're grieving—that are out of character.

You'd lost the man you loved. You needed . . . consolation. Was that how it was?"

"In a way," Annie said.

The kettle boiled, and she made the coffee. Michael didn't try to touch her again. "Human lives are a mess," she said, "aren't they?" *And inhuman lives.*

"Tell me about it," said Michael.

"Incidentally"—she struggled to resume casual conversation— "I've been checking some old stock lately, and I've come across a couple of books that might interest you. I'm always unearthing stuff in this place—stuff I hadn't cataloged, some that's been here since before I came. It's a bottomless pit of bookdom."

"All right," he conceded, "let's talk about books."

NATHAN WAS waiting at the bus stop on the edge of the village. He had had an uncomfortable scene with Hazel, not quite a quarrel, because she wanted to come with him, and he felt he had to see the man on his own, at least for the first time. "Two of us might alarm him," he suggested.

"He's a grown-up," Hazel said shortly. "He's not going to be frightened by two kids."

"Not frightened, but . . . put off. Anyway, you have to divert George. We can't tell him all this, not yet, anyway. Please, Hazel."

"I don't want to hang out with George. He's geeky."

"That's unkind, and untrue. Hazel . . ."

In the end she agreed, but reluctantly. And now Nathan was waiting for the bus from Crowford, knowing it wouldn't be on time, because buses never were, and shaking inwardly as the wait stretched out and the morning grew longer and longer. When the bus finally appeared, he thought the tension was almost unbearable. This was where dream became reality, where the other world came home. A woman got off with a shopping basket, someone he vaguely knew, so he forced himself to smile and say hello, then a young mother with toddler and stroller. *Will I recognize him?* Nathan wondered. *I've never seen his face. How will I know . . . ?* A man was approaching the exit with a stumbling stride, a very tall man. "This Eade?" he asked the driver.

"That's right."

And there he was. The man on the beach. The immigrant from another universe. Nathan's first thought was that he was a *very* tall man. He had realized in his dreams that the inhabitants of that alternative cosmos were taller than average, but seeing one of them in the flesh brought it home to him. The exile must have been seven feet high, broad-shouldered but very lean, dressed in garments no doubt assembled from a secondhand shop: a flapping raincoat, trousers that didn't quite cover his ankles, a rugby shirt striped in blue and maroon. The clothes seemed only to accentuate his differentness; Nathan was reminded of Dr. Who in some old episodes that George's brother had on video. His skin was sallow and dark, ocher not brown, and his face showed proportions similar to those of the woman Halmé, though it was striking rather than beautiful. His jaw curved down from high cheekbones to the narrow jut of the chin; his hair was long and black and wild; his eyes glinted in cadaverous sockets, the irises deeply purple and bright as if lit from within. You could see he was special, Nathan thought; everyone must see that. It explained the attitude of Jillian Squires: she, too, had seen and respected his uniqueness. As the bright eyes sought him out he extended his hand. "I'm Nathan Ward."

The exile didn't take Nathan's hand; perhaps he was not yet familiar with the gesture. "I remember you," he said.

"Will you tell me your name?" Nathan asked.

"I am Errek Moy Rhindon. Here they call me Eric. Eric Rhindon."

Man and boy studied each other, curiosity matched with curiosity. Nathan hoped he wasn't being impolite. It was difficult to subscribe to the manners of another world when you didn't know what they were. "Thank you very much for coming."

Eric nodded, accepting the courtesy as his due. "Maybe I must thank you for saving me," he said. "But this world strange to me. Is hard to adapt. Your society have decline from noble past, I think."

"You mean, ancient Greece?" Nathan hazarded. "Or Egypt?" They had begun to walk along as they talked. Nathan was heading for a café where there were several quiet corners suitable for private conversation.

"Egypt? Greece?" Eric shrugged. "They are other planets?"

"Countries. On this planet. Part of our—noble past."

"No! I mean, great civilization in space. Advanced *technology*." He pronounced the word with care. Evidently it was a recent acquisition. "Also much force. Like in my world. Force very strong there. Not strong here now. All used up."

"What kind of force?" Nathan was baffled.

"Energy. Special energy. Like electrics, but special. Controlled by mind, hand, words. May the force be with you."

Nathan laughed. "You mean magic," he said. "We don't have any magic here. Just in stories."

"Stories must be true. I have seen films, this week, at Mrs. Squires's house, about the noble past. *A long time ago in a galaxy far, far away* . . . This cannot be a lie. To lie is a crime." He stopped abruptly, and stared at Nathan. "Do they lie in your world?"

"Not lies," Nathan said, fumbling for the right words. "Stories. Made-up stories, for fun. Are there no stories in your world?"

Eric was scowling with a mixture of concentration and bewilderment. "Stories *must* be true. To make up, is wrong. Evil. Lies corrupt."

"In our world," Nathan said, "we differentiate between lies and stories. If we know a story is made up, then it doesn't matter. It's good. We learn from stories. Don't you do that in your world?"

"No," Eric said curtly.

They walked on. "You watched *Star Wars*?" Nathan inquired cautiously.

"History," Eric said. "I thought—is history. I thought I learn about this world. I understand the force."

"Me, too," Nathan said. "Without made-up stories, I wouldn't understand. There's magic in your world—I saw that, I understood, because of made-up stories about magic, in this world. Do you see?"

Eric thought about it for a while. Then he nodded.

"You're very clever," Nathan said diffidently. "You understand things very quickly. And you've learned our language in no time at all. You must have been very important in your world. A scientist or something?"

Eric smiled, and shrugged. "I was not important," he said. "I was not . . . *scientist*." He obviously didn't know the word. "Once, I was fisherman. But fish died as air grew thin. Special layer of air, protecting from sun. We destroyed it, let in sundeath. Force poisoned. Sea poisoned. Not many fish now. Only monsters. I work in factory, make food to taste of fish, but not real."

"So you do have made-up things," Nathan said. "You have made-up food. Your food is a lie."

"You are wise," Eric declared. "Made-up food bad."

"You said, the force was poisoned. Is that what they meant when they talked of the contamination?" Eric looked uncomprehending, and Nathan strove to recollect his dreams, and the sound of the language. "*Unvarhu-sag?*"

"Yes! *Unvarhu-sag*. Force poisoned. What word you say? Contamination. I will remember."

They had reached the café, which did vegetarian lunches. It was early for lunch, but Nathan decided that didn't matter. "Come and have some real food," he said, glad he hadn't chosen anything like a McDonald's—not that there was one in Eade. They sat down at a corner table and Nathan ordered baked potatoes with cheese and a salad. He hoped that would be real enough.

"What exactly *is* the contamination?" he asked Eric. "What were they doing when they closed off Maali?"

"*Unvarhu-sag* is . . . poisoning. People sick, animals, birds—few left after air grow thin, but contamination take them. In time trees, plants die, too. All die. It begin long ago"—he gave a wry smile—"in galaxy far, far away. Powerful men use force to destroy, in war. Create bad force, evil, poison. Like dark side, but . . . illness. Illness of everything. Galaxy cut off with good force, but all force same power, same energy. In the end, bad corrupt good. Where is force, is contamination. It spread through universe. First, we poison with *technology,* make air thin, water unclean, but that is slow, slow, many thousand years to destroy one planet. Contamination quicker. Maali cut off, maybe gone in two, three seasons. Nothing can do. All die. All die . . ."

"You had family," Nathan said, realizing. "A wife, children . . ."

"No children. In my world, we use force to live long. Force inside us, make us strong, not much sick, never old. Only contamination kill. But long life mean, no children. Force change you."

"The force—magic—makes you sterile?"

"Sterile." Once again, Nathan saw him committing a word to memory. "Yes. No children now for many hundred years."

"None?"

"None." Suddenly, Eric's face lightened. "Many children here. Is good to see children. Your world younger, cleaner. *You* save me—a child save me. In old legend, angels are children. Legends made up— is crime to make up story now, against law, but legend very old, before crime, before law. I think—you are right. We learn from made-up story, perhaps more than from history." He repeated, emphatically: "You are wise."

Nathan didn't feel at all wise, but he pushed away his embarrassment. When you were talking to someone from another universe, there were bound to be misunderstandings. Their baked potatoes arrived; Eric sniffed enthusiastically. "I have this before," he explained. "In hostel." He forked up a lavish mouthful. "Taste better here."

"This is a good place," Nathan said, meaning the café. "Do you live in the hostel?"

"No. I go for meals, sometimes. Also to Mrs. Squires and her friends, kind people. But I like to sleep under sky, to be free. In my world, dangerous to stay outside too long, even at night. Moons reflect sunrays." There was a pause while he concentrated on eating. "They say, I am asylum seeker. Must apply to government to stay, or go back. But I think, they cannot send me back." He grinned wolfishly through the baked potato. "But you say, no force here except in made-up story. This not true. You bring me here. The force is strong in *you*. There is force in every world. Like electrics, like gravity. Is part of life."

"Not here," Nathan said positively. "I don't *know* how I brought you here. I dream about your world, but I can't control what happens in my dream, or what I do." He thought about the last dream, when they could see him, or almost see him, and shivered. "It frightens me."

Eric nodded sagely. "To have power is fearful," he said. "Is good you know that. You learn control, in time."

"There's no one to teach me," Nathan said. "Not in this world." He continued, awkwardly: "Are you angry about being here? On the telephone, you said you found our society backward. I know it must seem sort of primitive to you; I've seen enough of your world to realize that. Would you like—if I could do it—would you want to go home?"

"Of course not. I go home, I die. Many good things here. I like to sleep under sky, to see children. My world very far away now, like long ago. Memory old, not sharp, not bad pain. Much to learn here, to fill my mind. I grow accustomed very soon." He added, after an intermission with salad and more potato: "Food good. No real food in my world now. I like real food."

"I think," Nathan said, "my mother suggested—I should take you to see Uncle Barty. He's the wisest person I know. We should tell him the truth about you." Nobody meeting Eric, he thought, could possibly doubt him. He wondered what Jillian Squires had really made of the exile. "Besides, he's the best cook in the whole world."

"I always tell truth," Eric said. "But people believe I come from another country, not another world. There is place called Maali here?"

"In Africa," Nathan affirmed. "I hadn't thought of that. Mali. It's nearly the same name. Like Errek and Eric. I suppose . . . names could be similar in all worlds." He found himself inventing addresses like Paris, Narnia, and Timbuktu, Tatooine. That sounded reasonable, but what if you tried it with Manchester, or Worthing? Worthing, Naboo, for instance?

"This *Uncle Barty*, he is good friend?"

"He's not really my uncle," Nathan said. Perhaps Eric didn't know what *uncle* meant, but he didn't feel up to explaining it now, particularly since it wasn't relevant. "But he is a *great* friend, and a truly wonderful cook. He'll give you more real food than you can eat."

"When we go see him?"

They finished their meal, and Nathan paid from the allowance he now received in honor of being thirteen. "Children have pocket money," Annie had said. "Teenagers have an allowance." He left the café with Eric and headed out of the village to Thornyhill. People stared to see them together: the dark, serious boy and the man with his height and his wild hair and his purple eyes. Many who had commented occasionally on Nathan's strangeness—"Too polite—too quiet—never teases smaller children—never yells at adults"—saw further evidence of it in his eccentric companion. Jason Wicks, slouching around a corner with a friend—Jason had practiced slouching so much he was getting very good at it—shouted an insult that its target didn't even hear, and relapsed into a savage mutter.

"You don't like that kid, do you?" said Jason's friend, astutely. "We ought to deal with him."

"I will."

"Who's the weirdo?"

"Nathan's the weirdo." He embellished the phrase with ugly adjectives. "The other bloke's just some tramp." He continued, with rare perception: "Probably one of those illegal immigrants. Dad says they sneak over here, sponge off the state, take our jobs . . ."

"Your dad's been on the dole for years."

"Goes to show then, dunnit?"

Beyond the village, Nathan was trying to clear his backlog of questions, but there were too many for one day, one talk, and he didn't want Eric to feel under pressure, and he didn't know where to begin, or when to stop. He returned over and over to the subject of the contamination. "You mean, it's poisoned your entire galaxy?"

"Many galaxies. Too many to count. I tell you, whole universe poisoned." Eric's eyes seemed to darken at the thought. "My planet in last galaxy. Maybe a few other planets survive, but not right for life. No air. My planet—Eos—good place, then air grow thin, sundeath come. Now, contamination. Last people run to Eos, nowhere else left to go. Government set up in Ynd."

"Ynd? Is that the city?"

"Continent. City is called Arkatron. Grandir live there."

"Please tell me about the Grandir," Nathan said.

"Emperor. President. No word here. Like prime minister, but

more important. Ruler of whole world." Eric was evidently thinking hard, trying to clarify his meaning, but his stride didn't slacken. "Once, Grandir rule galaxies—thousand thousand galaxies." He didn't know the terms for the higher numbers, Nathan guessed. "Now, just one planet, maybe just one continent."

"Is the Grandir a title, like emperor, or a name?" Nathan wanted to know.

"Title. Like prime minister, like—queen. Name not used. Perhaps by family; no one else."

"How long has this Grandir ruled?"

Eric shrugged. "Before contamination. Much before. Five thousand years, ten . . . Force is strong with him. Power give long life. Is good for ruler—he learn much wisdom, many things. They say, he has plan to save us, ancient plan from long ago, but not ready yet. Hope plan ready soon, or nobody left to save."

"I wish I could help," Nathan said, "but I don't think I could dream everyone here."

"Would be wrong," Eric said thoughtfully. "Too many of us for small planet. Backward here. My people take over. Not good for you."

"Are all the people in your world as clever as you?" Nathan asked. "It's amazing how fast you've learned our language."

"No. I am stupid. I learn slow, slow, and speak very bad. English easy, not too many words. My language more difficult."

"In the dreams," Nathan remarked, "I understand it. Would you say something, to see if I understand now?"

Eric obliged, glancing around at the woods they were entering as he spoke. Nathan found he *could* follow his speech, though it was far harder than in dreams, as though the atmosphere of this world fogged his thinking, and when he tried to answer his tongue stumbled over the simplest phrases.

"You have accent of Ynd," Eric said, "accent of the city. I think you dream much there."

"Yes."

The woods were deepening on either side as they made their way toward Thornyhill. It was a sunlit afternoon with a few skimming clouds, their shadows flying swiftly over the ground. As always there was movement everywhere: the dancing of light and shade, leaf and wind. Nathan looked for Woody, feeling he was there, but could not see him. And suddenly there seemed to be too much movement—a shimmer over the road, a twisting of the path that wound away beneath the trees, a shifting of the leafmold where no feet were seen to tread. Eric stiffened and stared, his eyes widening until white showed all around the purple irises. Nathan took his arm and felt the tensing of muscles beneath his clothes, a rigidity that he realized was that of fear.

"We go back," Eric said. "Now. *Now.*"

It's like at the site of the lost house, Nathan thought. *A wind coming after us, just aboveground—a wind with footsteps in it . . .*

"What is it?" he demanded, though there was no reason Eric should know.

"Gnomon," the exile said. He had swung around and they were walking quickly back toward the village, looking behind every few seconds, along the empty road. The grasses on the shoulder trembled and bent; seeds scattered from a dandelion head.

"Shouldn't we run?" Nathan whispered.

"No. They run faster. We walk, they walk. I hope." Eric's dark ocher complexion had faded to sallow.

"What's a gnomon? Is it from your world?"

"They. Always many. Have shape sometimes, but not solid. No flesh. Move between worlds. Also called Ozmosees: in old legend they are servants of Oz, king of underworld. Story untrue, illegal, but maybe some truth, very small truth. Someone control them, send them here. Send them for *me.*"

"How would anyone know you're here?"

They were walking quicker now, and still quicker. The ripple of movement kept pace with them.

"Maybe riders see I not drown. See you. Tell Grandir. Tell *some-one*."

"But . . . I've seen them before," Nathan said. "Before you came."

A car whizzed past; on the shoulder, the grasses froze; Eric stopped abruptly. "Then maybe," he said, "they come for you."

He seized Nathan's hand and began to walk much faster, so the boy had to run to keep up. "What happens—if they catch us?" he panted, but Eric didn't answer. And then they were out of the woods, and into broad fields, and wide spaces of sunlight, and only a natural breeze ruffled the grass behind them.

Eric released Nathan's hand with an air of bewilderment. "I fear for you," he said. "Adult must protect child, yes? I not remember, but I do it. *Imris*. Older than memory."

"Instinct," Nathan supplied, finding he knew the word.

"Much here I not understand. Chance you save me, but your power not chance. Is like Ozmosees, to dream into other world—but you sometime solid there, real; gnomon never solid. And gnomons from my world, but follow *you* . . ." He thought for a minute. His thought had a visible intensity; his brow contracted, his eye color fluctuated; Nathan could almost see the flickering of circuits inside his head. "I stay," he announced at last. "You save me; I save you. Is balance. I watch and learn. In my world, special herb keep off gnomons. *Sylpherim*. Smell very strong, very bad. Gnomons not solid, all senses: smell, hearing, sight. Made of senses. Not endure too strong smell, very high noise, bright bright light. Maybe I find same herb here. I search."

"What happens," Nathan reiterated, "if the gnomons catch someone?"

"Go inside him, eat his mind, bring madness . . ." He laid his big hand on Nathan's forehead. "Not you," he said. "I help." Then he turned and strode off at great speed into the fields.

Nathan didn't try to follow. He walked slowly back to the village, trying to digest everything Eric had told him, struggling to resist the creeping onset of fear. *The gnomons aren't after me,* he told himself, *wherever they come from.* Their whispers had accompanied his vision of the Grail; they haunted Thornyhill woods and the lost home of the Thorns; the woodwose had seen them there, too, without him. Something drew them to this place, something to do with traditions and stories that the Thorns themselves didn't fully understand. *The answer is in the stories,* Nathan decided with a flash of illumination—but the tales were garbled, forgotten with the passage of centuries, only fragments written down. And what could the Grimthorn Grail have to do with the ruler of a dying world, hemmed in on the last surviving planet, brooding on some secret plan that might never come to fruition?

He needed to talk to Hazel. If he talked things through, maybe they would be clearer.

Maybe not.

ANNIE AND Michael were looking at books. "I think this box comes from Thornyhill," she said. "There are so many books there: Barty started this business by clearing some out. I found this the other day, in one of the cupboards. It's probably been there since before I came. I must have put some stuff on top of it and forgotten about it. It's very easy to overlook things here. Too many books, too many cupboards, too many nooks and crannies where all sorts of objects can go and hide."

"And yet it's a small house," Michael remarked.

"Larger inside," Annie said darkly.

"I suppose Bartlemy's a collector himself?"

"I don't know. He doesn't spend all his time going to sales or auctions, like Rowena Thorn. I get special books for him sometimes, if he asks me, or if I hear of one I think will interest him. I suppose . . . he's an *incidental* collector. He just goes through life picking up bits and pieces on the way."

"Like the rest of us, in fact," Michael grinned. "He seems to have picked up quite a lot. How old is he?"

Annie smiled to herself. "I've always been too polite to ask."

They found a social history of the Georgian era that Michael said he wanted, and a couple of novels by Mrs. Henry Wood that he said he couldn't resist. He insisted on paying her over the odds—none of the books was valuable—and went away with an adjuration to call him if she needed company or a confidant. And for the first time, he gave her a farewell kiss, a peck on the cheek that was somehow not quite casual, leaving her disconcerted, and slightly flustered, and vaguely pleased, though she was not yet ready to tell herself why. Villagers in Eade did not kiss, and while the citified newcomers hugged, gushed, and darlinged one another in the fashionable manner, Annie had always drawn back from such contact, finding it faintly insincere. But Michael, though she was sure he could kiss and darling with the best of them, wasn't insincere—or not with her. After he had gone she sat for several minutes in an agreeable haze that passed for thought, returning to reality on the reflection that if Rianna Sardou was actually the manifestation of a malevolent water spirit, it was hardly necessary to have scruples about her. Of course, the real Rianna must be somewhere—comatose, dead, imprisoned, or in Georgia . . .

She tried to shake off fruitless speculation and looked down at the book in her hand, which turned out to be an early cookbook. She must restore it to Bartlemy: it would surely be one he wouldn't wish to lose. She began to leaf through it, noting detailed recipes in printed copperplate, with references to marchpane and poupetons and Gâteau Mellifleur, and line drawings to illustrate the results. There were even a few color plates, protected with sheets of tissue paper, showing still-life paintings of sumptuous dishes. It was as she turned the page to one of these that a piece of paper slipped out and flapped its way to the floor. Annie bent to retrieve it, assuming it was part of the book, but she saw her mistake almost immediately. It was hand-written, not printed, and had nothing to do with cooking. She stared at it for a moment then closed the book and jumped to her feet. A hasty thumb through her address book and then she was on the phone.

"Rowena? Is that you? It's Annie Ward. I think I've found your injunction."

Rowena Thorn arrived within the hour, trailing her solicitor like a poodle on a leash. "This is it," the solicitor confirmed, studying the document. "It's not the original—at a guess that disintegrated, if it was drawn up as long ago as you say—this is an update, made in the nineteenth century, but it's perfectly valid. Now we've really got a chance to prove that the sale of the cup was illegal."

"And I found it," Annie said. "It doesn't seem fair. The children searched so hard, and I didn't look at all."

"You get the reward," said Rowena. "Five hundred pounds. Sorry it's not more, but I intend to keep the cup, not sell it, so it isn't going to bring in any money. I'll do something for your boy and his friends, too. Chocolates? Or maybe we could all go out for a slap-up meal."

"That would be terrific," Annie said. "But I don't want the money—"

"Nonsense! Everyone wants money, unless they're mad or brain-less, and you're a bright girl. You take it and have done with. You'll spend it on your son no doubt, mothers always do, but he's a good lad and hasn't had much spoiling. Don't refuse me—I owe you for this, more than money. I'm the rightful owner of the cup—knew it as soon as I saw it. I'd give my soul to get it back."

"You shouldn't say such things," Annie said, with a sudden shiver. "I know you didn't mean it seriously, but—"

"I meant it all right," Rowena said.

IN THE evening Nathan brought Hazel and George to supper, and they asked eagerly for the story of Annie's find, and discussed at length what would happen next, and whether Rowena Thorn really would be able to recover the Grail. "It'll be up to the courts to decide," George said wisely. He had recently decided he wanted to be a barrister, after watching a courtroom drama on television, and was doing his best to adopt suitable language and turns of phrase.

"If the injunction says the cup mustn't be sold, then they'll *have* to give it back to Mrs. Thorn, won't they?" Hazel said.

"I don't suppose it'll be that straightforward," Annie responded. "Legal matters never are. Even if they accept that the sale was invalid, there might be the issue of proving Rowena's own entitlement."

"She's a Thorn," George said, forgetting his barristerly manner. "Everyone knows that. There aren't any others."

"I don't see that," Hazel objected with a sudden frown. "There are bound to be distant cousins and things: all families have those. I'm a Thorn, in a way. Great-Grandma's a Carlow, and they're descended from the Thorns. There could be lots of semi-Thorns, spread all over the place."

"Are *you* going to put in a claim for the cup?" George demanded flippantly.

"You're very quiet," Annie said to Nathan, who had taken little part in the discussion. "How did it go with your immigrant friend?"

Nathan, though glad about the discovery of the injunction, had had other things on his mind. "Eric," he said absently. "His name's Eric."

"Did you take him to see Uncle Barty?"

"No. No, not yet. I will, though. He needs lots of good food. He's an amazing person. He's learned to speak English so fast, and his eyes are purple, deep purple, like violets, and he . . . he likes *Star Wars*."

"He sounds cool," Hazel said, her eyes narrowing under her hair. They hadn't had a chance to talk privately yet.

"He's the coolest person I ever met," Nathan said.

Later, when Hazel and George had gone home, Annie tried to draw him out on the subject, with little success.

"Did he tell you where he's from?"

"We talked about it," Nathan said guardedly. And, because Annie looked expectant: "Mali. That's what he said."

"Mali in Africa?"

"I suppose so. Unless there's another one somewhere. He . . . he wasn't clear."

"I thought you said he spoke very good English," Annie said, a little too sharply. "Anyway, I never heard of people from Mali having purple eyes."

But to this Nathan made no reply at all.

He knew he would dream of the other world that night. Meeting Eric had made it seem much more real, much closer; he almost felt that if he tried, he could enter it while awake, in a daydream not a dream, but the idea alarmed him—it was as if he was losing his hold on his own world—and didn't try. He drifted into a sleep that was brief and shallow, and then he was awake again, he was there, in the city. Arkatron. He knew its name now. Arkatron, city of Ynd. He was instantly conscious of being more solid than before, more visible; he struggled to think himself back into a state of disembodied awareness, but he couldn't do it. He was in the long gallery with the twisted pillars: the artificial light made him feel very exposed. Looking down at himself, he saw he was wearing pajamas, and it occurred to him that in the future he would have to start sleeping in his clothes. He felt very unconfident about wandering around an unknown universe in his nightwear. Of course, there were precedents—the children in *Peter Pan*, Arthur Dent in *Hitchhiker*—but in a world where fiction was outlawed nobody would know them.

He moved along the gallery, darting from pillar to pillar, ready to hide at any time. At the far end, the door to the Grandir's chamber opened and he emerged, white-masked as ever, accompanied by the purple-cowled man Nathan had seen previously in hologram. The woman Halmé walked a little behind them; she, too, wore a mask, a delicate etching of her own face in some dark substance that glittered subtly under the light. Her garments this time were a pale lilac and a section of her wimple was wound around her neck, shielding her throat. But he knew it was her: the mask must have been modeled on her features, and her poise, the grace of her movements were unmistakable. The two men didn't glance his way, but as she passed the pillar that concealed him she turned for a second and looked back.

Nathan followed them as well as he could, frustrated by the difficulty of keeping out of sight. They met few other people, and those always stopped when they saw the Grandir, standing motionless, presumably out of respect, until he had moved on. This gave Nathan a moment to get under cover, or such cover as he could find, slipping around a corner or into a doorway. They passed down many corridors, curving and intersecting like the passages in a maze, and moving staircases that swung around at the touch of a button, so you could alight in a number of different places. Halmé did not look around again, but Nathan wondered if she was aware of him. She walked always behind the men, not out of humility, he was certain, but because her thought was elsewhere, and their murmured exchanges did not interest her. And then they went through a sliding door into a cylindrical cell that he knew was an elevator, and he dared not follow. He was too clearly defined; they would see him; he could only wait, half frantic at the suspense, until the elevator returned. There was no illuminated panel to indicate its progress, no buttons that he could perceive, but presently the door reopened, and the elevator was back, empty. He stepped inside.

The door closed and the elevator began to descend immediately, though he had touched nothing. Its motion was smooth and very fast: even in that dream state his stomach seemed to be left behind. He remembered he had been in an elevator in an earlier dream, but then he must have been too insubstantial to react to it; the more solid he became, the more he responded to his surroundings. A terrible fear grew in him that the time would come when he was completely solid, and then he would be unable to wake up, but he tried to suppress it: he had fears enough to deal with for now. When the door slid back again, at the bottom of the shaft, he almost expected to find someone waiting for him. But the passage was vacant, and a single door at the end showed him the only way his quarries could have gone. There was lettering on the door, in the language of Eos. In his mind it translated as PRIVATE—NO UNAUTHORIZED ENTRY. There was little light down here and he felt as if he must be underground, in some dim subbasement below the city. The gloom gave him confidence: here at least he had a reasonable chance of passing unremarked. He touched the door, pressing gingerly. To his surprise, it opened at once.

He found himself entering a long room that reminded him of a laboratory in a film, the kind where they did experiments on animals. There were boxes and cages along the right-hand wall, most of which appeared to be unoccupied; along the left was a range of screens and storage units. The space in between was entirely taken up by workbenches stacked with bizarre scientific equipment: odd-shaped retorts connected with convoluted glass tubing, sealed metal containers, things that might be futuristic microscopes, or telescopes, or other kinds of scopes. The area was poorly lit for a laboratory, and the Grandir and his two companions, at the far end, had evidently not noticed the opening of the door. Cautiously, Nathan began to move toward them, peering into the cages on his right as he went. As he had already noted, most of them were empty, but one was heaving with locust-like insects whose bodies shone with a faint, evil phosphorescence, while in another a gigantic black rat bared wicked teeth at him. Strangest of all, in a third there was a cat that seemed at one moment to be lying dead and at the next, savagely alive, clawing at the sides of its prison. The Grandir, Halmé, and purple-cowl were staring at a much larger cage at the very end of the room. Nathan slipped under an adjacent workbench and crept as close as he dared.

"I thought there were none left," said purple-cowl. "They were wiped out a thousand years ago."

"Not all," said the Grandir. "I saved a few—just a few—and bred from them."

"But . . . is this prison secure?"

"Of course. You need have no fear. The glass has been infused with threads of iron, too fine for the naked eye to see them. They cannot tolerate it."

"Iron?" queried purple-cowl. "I didn't know that."

"It used to be common knowledge, in the days when such knowledge was necessary," the Grandir said. "It emits a magnetic field that can kill them. There are disadvantages to being equipped with hypersenses. They can become all but invisible, and pass through solid objects, but they react to stimuli that would not affect us."

"I remember now. The scent of a particular herb, the right sound level . . ."

Nathan crawled forward on hands and knees until he could see into the cage. He knew what was there now, but they looked different in this world. Almost solid, except if they moved, when their substance seemed to blur, becoming briefly fluid. They resembled monkeys, or so he thought at first, save that they were hairless, and there was a webbing beneath their arms that extended into wings, not perhaps adequate for flight but designed to skim short distances. Their eyes were enormous, too large even for nocturnal primates, milky globes with a slitted pupil that shrank or dilated with every variation of light, and their faces were squashed into tiny triangles with no brow and little mouth, only distended nostrils in a flattened nose and outthrust ears that moved and twitched constantly. Their skin was dark, of some noncolor just short of black, and it had no sheen, no visible texture: it was as matte as shadow. There were maybe thirty or forty of them, some motionless on branch-like perches, others climbing over one another, heaving like the locusts, their bodies appearing to dissolve and blend into a single swell of movement. Nathan found that the more he stared at them, the more he found them both fascinating and horrible.

"The cage is soundproofed," the Grandir said, "for their own protection, and as you see, I do not allow strong light in here. They dislike even ordinary daylight, though they are not affected by the sundeath."

"They were made illegal," purple-cowl said. "You ratified the law."

"Naturally. They are very dangerous. In the wrong hands, they could do great harm. As it is, I do not use them . . . here."

"It is true then? They can pass through the dimensions?"

"They can pass not merely between dimensions—that is a child's trick—but between universes. All they need is an opening, a weakening of the barrier, and a reference point. These things can be engineered. Of course, not all have that ability—the genotype is unpredictable—but I have destroyed those that are of no use to me."

The purple cowl was silent for a minute, evidently absorbing the implications. "How do you control them?" he asked. "Can they be trained?"

"They respond to powerful thought waves," the Grandir explained. "There are certain spells and rituals, some of them forbid-

den, that magnify the brain's telepathic faculty, and enable the practor to control and dominate lesser minds. These creatures have hardly
any mind at all—just enough for my purposes. Once subjugated, they
will obey my every thought, regardless of distance or location. I can
even entrance myself and see—or hear—through their senses. They
are my eyes and ears in another world."

For the first time, Halmé spoke. She had been gazing for a long
time into the cage, apparently paying little attention to the discussion.
"They are disgusting," she said.

"They are useful," said the Grandir. Nathan had a feeling he was
correcting her. "I find I even have a certain affection for them, as people in ancient days had for their pets. They are as werenature made
them. And if we do manage to escape our doom, believe me, it will be
in part—in a small part—due to them. You should not condemn them
because they are not beautiful."

She did not answer, but detached her mask and crouched down,
pressing her naked face close to the glass. Gazing and gazing.

"Don't do that!" the Grandir said sharply, but though he reached
out, he refrained from pulling her away. "These are half trained.
Your face might impress them. They could become attached to you—
imprinted with your image. That would be very dangerous. I have always been careful to attach them to an inanimate object or specific
location."

The cup, Nathan thought. The Grimthorn Grail. He didn't know
why or how, but he was sure of it.

Slowly, almost reluctantly, Halmé drew away and replaced her
mask. Purple-cowl made a sudden movement; he had obviously been
staring at her exposed face—Nathan could sense his intentness and
his shock. An unmasked face must *be* a shock, he realized, in this
world of masks and cowls. And perhaps, even here, her beauty was
something special, the stuff of legend, spoken of but never seen, a
jewel hidden in a secret vault. He thought of the beauties of his own

world, seen continuously on television, in newspapers, in magazines, and they seemed to him shallow, creatures of plastic and celluloid, cosmetics and artifice. Here was mystery, the beauty of myth and fairy tale, the face of Helen. He recalled reading the lines somewhere: *Was this the face that launched a thousand ships, And burned the topless towers of Illium?* He had never really understood how towers could be topless, but there was a magic in the words, and he could imagine them applied to Halmé. For her, the Grandir might indeed seek to tear down the barriers between the worlds and make another Eden, a paradise beyond contamination.

As he watched her, the laboratory darkened, and he felt himself fading—thinning—dissolving back into sleep. It was a curiously slow process, as if he was unwilling to leave, and when he woke in his own room it troubled him, because he sensed that like the gnomons he was becoming attached, not to a single place or an object but to a world, a state of being, that was not native to him. For all its troubles this alternative cosmos both excited and intrigued him, and with every dream, every materialization, he found it harder to let go.

"WE NEED iron," he told Hazel, the next day. George was out with his family and they were alone. "I thought of the poker by the fire, but it looks like brass, and our cutlery's stainless steel: I don't know how much iron there is in it."

"Why iron?" Hazel demanded.

He explained about the gnomons, and his dream.

"It's like in the old days," Hazel said unexpectedly. "Great-Grandma told me, people used to have iron to ward off bad spirits— wicked fairies—things like that. Uncle Dicky—he's the builder—he was doing a renovation once, and he said he found all this iron stuff buried under the front door."

"What stuff?" Nathan asked. "I can't find anything that's made of iron."

"I don't know. Tools and things. Great-Grandma said people used horseshoes. She still has a couple: she brought them with her. There's one on her bedroom door and one outside the attic where she . . . she goes sometimes. She likes to be private there."

There was a short, significant silence. "Could you get them?" Nathan said at last. "Borrow them, I mean. Not steal. We'd put them back."

"I could try. But now your mum's found the injunction, do you really need to go back to that place?"

"I was driven away," Nathan said. "That's reason enough. Let's see if your great-grandma's out."

In fact, Effie had gone back to her cottage, presumably to pick up something, and borrowing the horseshoes presented no problem. She must have hung them outdoors at some stage, for they were worn from weather and much handling, all sharp edges eroded, misshapen loops pierced with holes where the nails had once gone. It looked as if she had had them for a very long time. Nathan and Hazel took one each and tried putting them in their pockets, but the pockets weren't big enough. So at Nathan's suggestion they got some string, threaded it through one of the nail holes, and hung them around their necks. They felt awkward and cumbersome, but it was easier than having to carry them. Then they set off for Thornyhill. "I'll have to persuade Woody to show us the way again," Nathan said. "He'll be a bit shy of you—he's shy of me now—so you'll have to let me talk to him alone, just to begin with. And I think we should take Hoover. Extra protection."

"He's the soppiest dog on the planet," Hazel said. She liked Hoover, but she was in a mood to be scornful. This was an adventure where Nathan, even more than usual, seemed to be way ahead of her, and close though they were she didn't enjoy the feeling of always tagging along behind. "He looks like Scooby-Doo."

"So he's going to be good at dealing with magic."

"I don't believe in magic," Hazel insisted. "It's just Great-Grandma muttering to herself, trying to frighten people. Other universes—that's different. That's science." And, after a pause: "What happened with the asylum seeker?"

"Eric," Nathan said. "Eric Rhindon. He's the most extraordinary person."

He told her everything, or everything he could remember, while they walked. At Thornyhill, they scrounged sandwiches off Bartlemy "for a picnic," summoned Hoover to accompany them, and set off into the woods. Leaving the dog with Hazel, Nathan went on ahead to find Woody. Persuading the woodwose to accept his friend was less difficult than he had anticipated.

"I know her," Woody said. "She climbs trees and just sits there for hours, very still, almost as still as me. Like an animal. She used to come here a lot. Not so much now." He added, greatly daring: "I liked her."

Of course, thought Nathan. *It's the same as picking up language from me. He's picked up my likes and dislikes, too.*

But Woody was less comfortable about Hoover. "The dog? He used to hunt for me, when you were little, trying to sniff me out. I'm afraid of him."

"He won't hurt you," Nathan promised. "I expect, when I was a baby, he was just being protective. He doesn't look it, but he's a very protective dog. That's why we're taking him along now. He'll protect you, too."

Woody took some convincing—the idea of returning to the site of the former house terrified him—but eventually he agreed. "You mustn't let the dog see me," he said, evidently torn between his various fears. "You see me—the girl can see me—but not *him*. Otherwise he'll hunt me down."

"All right," Nathan said.

Rejoining the others, he instructed Hoover accordingly. "He won't understand you, stupid," Hazel said, but when Woody approached, the dog kept his head down and his ears flattened, gazing pointedly at the ground. Woody eyed him nervously, sparing only a brief glance for Hazel.

"What *is* he really?" she whispered to Nathan as they followed him through the trees.

"I don't know. I think perhaps—he came from another world, too. I might have brought him here, like Eric, only when I was very young."

Hazel said nothing. She knew Nathan's dreampower troubled him deeply, but she couldn't help being a little envious. She had no power of any kind. It was wonderful—it made her feel special— being his friend, but sometimes she wanted more.

The woods were the deep green of summer, sun-mottled, rippling with birdsong and insect hum. There were wildflowers here and there: pink campion, purple nightshade, white deadnettle, yellow aconite. "Yellow is a warning," Hazel said unexpectedly. "Great-Grandma told me. Even buttercups are poisonous to some animals." As they entered the Darkwood the shoulder of the hill cut off the sun for a few minutes, and there seemed to be less green, more rotten wood, old leaves, moss-grown stumps of trees long fallen. As always, the birds fell silent; a cloud of midges billowed toward them. Farther down the slope Hazel's white T-shirt was suddenly alive, coated with winged ants. Nathan called Woody to a halt and brushed them off, but they still swarmed around her, ignoring Nathan's darker clothing, and they wouldn't leave her alone until the little troop had covered some distance. They reached their destination unawares, while

Nathan was still looking for familiar landmarks. Afterward, he wondered if the trees had moved, just a little way, or if the place looked different because it was earlier in the day, and later in the season, and woodland can change with every month, every hour. There was more sunlight, and the ridges in the ground looked slight and insignificant. He came to the drop and prepared to scramble down.

"Last time, we stayed too long," Woody said. "I go now. If you stay, you have to deal with bad memories, bad spirits."

"We can deal with them," Nathan said. "We have iron."

Woody came close, stretching out a brown finger as Nathan extracted the horseshoe from under his sweatshirt. But the woodwose flinched away from it, as if he, too, were adversely affected. "Iron is strong," he said and flickered around, vanishing into the treescape in an instant.

"Can we find the way back?" Hazel asked.

"Hoover can," said Nathan. "Anyway, the wood isn't large. Get your horseshoe out and hold on to it."

Hazel did so, glancing fearfully over her shoulder. Nathan slid down the short drop and began to feel between the root filaments, scrabbling at the earth with his fingers, realizing too late that he should have brought a trowel. Presently, as before, his hand encountered metal. It occurred to him that it could be iron, and he wondered if that was chance, or whether it was there to keep the whisperers away. He cleared some of the soil, until he could see bars, embedded in stone, and beyond, he was certain, a darkness that wasn't more soil but space.

"Nathan." Hazel had been on her knees, peering down, watching him, but now she was standing, looking the other way. Hoover's hackles rose; his lip lifted; the low unfamiliar growl rumbled in his throat. And there was the deadly breeze, curving toward them, ruffling last year's leaves, nudging hanging bough and jutting twig. The murmur came with it, sibilant and soft, filling their heads with words they didn't want to understand.

"Keep Hoover close to you!" Nathan adjured. "Hold the horse-shoe out!"

The ripple of motion came to within a couple of yards before it stopped. Nathan had hoped they would be driven off, panicked into flight, but instead they circled, angrily—he could feel the anger—stirring the leaf litter, whispering with many voices. He remembered the tiny mouth slits, and pictured them moving in a language they themselves couldn't comprehend, parroting a memory of some ancient impression, an echo of someone else's thought. "You'll have to hold them off," he told Hazel. "I need to dig."

"I don't like this," she said.

"They won't come too close to the iron."

"I *really* don't like this." She was pale, clutching the scruff of Hoover's neck, not to restrain him but for reassurance.

Nathan returned to scraping at the soil. It seemed to take ages. Human hands, he concluded, were not designed for digging, possibly because at an early stage in the evolutionary process we had come up with tools. Hazel kept saying "Hurry," and Hoover's muted growl persisted, and the gnomons circled and whispered, a menace seen only as a shiver in the air, a shudder in the leaves. To the right of the barred window Nathan found something that he thought might be a door, a very small door under a crumbling lintel. The wood was blackened and rotten: he could thrust his hand through it. As he had suspected, there was a space beyond, a cell perhaps, a long-forgotten dungeon buried for centuries under earth and root, exposed now by the fall of a tree and his own excavations. In his excitement, he could almost ignore the threat of the gnomons. He tried to clear the soil even faster, wrenching at the deadwood.

"There's something here," he said to Hazel. "Some kind of prison cell . . ."

The pervasive whisper surged abruptly, so that for a minute he hesitated—and in that minute he heard another sound. A scraping, pounding, wood-tearing sound. Even as he had dug down to get in, someone *inside* the cell was digging to get out—someone or some-*thing*. Nathan drew back, and the spinning gnomons wheeled away from the iron about his neck. He climbed back up the drop to Hazel and Hoover: the dog turned his attention to whatever was emerging from underground. He barked twice, in a quick, imperative way. Nathan was remembering what Woody had told him about hearing a thumping from under the earth. "Maybe this wasn't such a good idea," he said.

There was a sudden explosion of loose soil and wood flakes, and a shape shot out of the hollow beneath. They saw it only briefly, but it looked human, or nearly so, about four feet high, covered with bris-tling hair, or perhaps some of that was its clothes. The head swiveled for a second to look at them, and Nathan glimpsed a face so smoth-ered in beard and whiskers that little skin was exposed. The eyes were squeezed to dark slots against the impact of daylight. Then the figure turned and bolted with extraordinary speed into the depths of the wood. The gnomons gathered themselves together and streamed after it.

"That can't have happened," Hazel said at last. "I mean, no one could be buried there, and then still be alive. It just isn't possible."

"I hope he'll be all right," Nathan said. "Whoever—or what-ever—he is."

"What do we do now?"

"Go home, I suppose." After the excitement, there was a sense of anticlimax. Their breathing had shortened with the tension, but now they relaxed. Hoover flopped one ear and cocked the other, waiting for orders.

"Home is good," Hazel said.

Iron and Water

Nathan and Hazel went back to his house for tea and talked things over in the Den. It was only when she got home that Hazel realized she had left the horseshoes behind. *It can't matter*, she told herself; *Great-Grandma won't notice.* She could go back but she had homework to do: Annie was the sort of person who insisted weekend homework should be done on Friday night or Saturday morning, but Lily Bagot, though loving, was less particular, and now that she no longer had Nathan's encouragement Hazel usually left it till Sunday night. She was sitting at her desk, her back to the door, writing—or trying to write—a history essay, with her Walkman on and earphones pumping Lemon Jelly direct to her brain, so she never heard the sound of an entrance. Then a hand seized the nape of her neck, and someone ripped the earphones away. She was twisted around in her chair, and Effie Carlow's face was thrust close to hers. At that range it seemed to be all hooked nose and wicked eyes. Hazel's start of fright and surprise subsided, leaving just the fright.

"Thief!" said her great-grandmother. "Where are they? What have you done with them?"

"We just borrowed them," Hazel gasped, abandoning any idea of pleading ignorance. "I was going to put them back, honestly. I forgot. I'm sorry . . ."

"What did you want them for?"

"We needed iron," Hazel said. Her heart was thumping uncomfortably, even more than it had that afternoon. "For—for protection."

"Against what?"

"Things." Hazel tried to think of a satisfactory lie, and couldn't. She had always found it all but impossible to lie to her great-grandmother. "Sort of—ghosts. At least, not ghosts exactly, but . . . Nathan says they're called gnomons. They come from . . ."

"From another world?" The menace of the face withdrew a little; a thin smile slid across Effie's mouth. "Well, well. Young Nathan *has* been careless, hasn't he? I warned him about that. I need to know more. You'll have to get me some more tokens, from his mother and from him. I've used the last of Annie's hairs."

"It was you, wasn't it? Nathan said she fainted, in London. You did that!"

"It was an error. Anyway, *you* did it. You brought me the hair. Clever girl."

"I didn't mean to," Hazel protested, almost beseeching. "The bracelet—it got caught, it was an accident—and you took it. I didn't know what you were going to do."

"Well, you know now," Effie snapped. "Get me some more. You can take them from her hairbrush, when you go over there. And something from the boy. No more excuses. It's important. Ask him to cut you off a lock. I need a strong connection."

"Why should I ask him that?" Hazel demanded. "It's silly."

"Say you want to wear it next to your heart," Effie mocked.

"I couldn't possibly. We're *friends*. He'd think—"

"Never mind what he thinks. Just do it."

"I shan't see him till next weekend," Hazel pointed out desperately.

"Go around there tomorrow—get something from his room. A shoe—no, a sock—something worn next to the skin. Something good for a charm."

"I don't believe in magic."

"Then it won't matter, will it?" The old woman sat down on the bed, watching her. Her great-granddaughter found her suddenly terrible: the strength in her thin body, the grip of that gnarled hand, the soul-piercing stare of those black eyes under their hooded folds. She dominated the room, indifferent to teenage clutter, making it no longer Hazel's private lair but a dubious retreat, easily invaded and taken over. Since she had moved in her dark, sly personality seemed to pervade the whole house, filling it with new shadows and subtle fears. It was better with Dad, Hazel thought; at least she knew where she was with him. It would be best if they both went away . . .

"Magic exists in this other world of Nathan's, doesn't it? He visits it by magic—brings magical creatures back here. You believe that?"

"I suppose so. It's different." She remembered what Nathan had told her about Eric. "Magic is a—a force there, like electricity. It's *real*. Magic here is just—superstition." For all her terrors, her mouth set obstinately.

Effie laughed, showing uneven teeth. "Superstition! Oh yes, superstition has its uses: I've used it often and often. But magic is real here, too, my child. Our world has its own werecreatures, its own dimensions of the imagination. And some of us are born with the power—the Gift—to do things that others cannot, to live out a longer life span. Do you know how old I am?" She leaned forward, her expression both taunting and threatening. "You call me great-grandmother, but so did your mother when she was a girl, and *her* mother, and another before her. People forget, you see. I *make* them forget. A word—a spell—and I am just old Effie Carlow, no one knows quite how old but it doesn't matter, because *old* covers everything. If I were young they would suspect, but the old are always with you. Who notices or cares how long they go on?"

"I don't want to hear!" Hazel put her hands over her ears but the crone plucked them away effortlessly with her dreadful wiry strength. "I don't believe you! I don't want to *know*!"

"You have no choice. The Gift is in your blood. One day you'll be an old woman like me, clutching at power, mazing each generation of your family and neighbors so they won't recall quite how long you've been around. One day . . . You see, magic here has always been a furtive, hole-in-the-corner business. Even Josevius Grimthorn—he was a Roman to begin with, so they say, or at any rate he came with the Romans, built his house down in the valley, Roman-fashion, before the Darkwood came—he had great power, great skill, he lived nearly seven hundred years, but he had to hide his true nature in a muddle of myths and conflicting stories. He was my ancestor, and yours. But this world of Nathan's—I know it. I know it in my water. Magic is everywhere there, you say. As common as electricity. If I could reach that power source, draw on it . . ." Her face sharpened, glittered with inner fire. "Don't you see? I might be young again. No more playing at old age, no more muttered charms in locked attics while the shadow of the Gate draws ever closer. I could be forever renewed, like the moon, and live a thousand years . . . I must learn more. Get me the tokens. Tomorrow. And bring back my horseshoes. I, too, require protection. Iron is a safeguard against many things."

"I—I'll try," Hazel found herself saying. "I can't promise . . ."

Effie's hand shot out again, grasping her face, crushing flesh against bone. "You will succeed," she said. "For both of us."

HAZEL PLAYED truant from her last lesson the following afternoon and went around to the bookshop, awaiting a moment when Annie was busy to let herself into the house. "I left something behind," she called out. Annie relayed an acknowledgment and Hazel raced up to her bedroom, finding her hairbrush on the dressing table, pulling out a hank of hair and stuffing it into her pocket. It wasn't very much hair—Annie's curls were short and fine and rarely needed the attentions of a brush—but she told herself it would have to do. Then she went to Nathan's room, looking around in confusion for an item that would meet Effie's requirements, settling on an old sweatshirt of his that she had borrowed once or twice. When Annie came in she was so flustered she forgot about the horseshoes, mumbled an excuse, and ran off. Annie stared after her, reflecting sadly that teenage-itis appeared to be afflicting not only her son but his friends as well.

Back at her own home, Hazel went upstairs and tapped on the attic door. When nobody answered she knocked again, waited a moment, then tried the handle. It wasn't locked—Effie must have left in a hurry, she decided. Cautiously, she pushed it open and went in.

It was the first time she had been there since her great-grandmother moved in, and she saw immediately that storage boxes and rubbish had been piled up on the side and a space cleared for use, with a table and chair, the stove gas, bottles, dried herbs, a porcelain basin. She went to place the hank of hair in the middle of the table, with the sweatshirt, which she folded carefully as though trying to make it appear more presentable; she hadn't noticed it was straight out of the wash, rinsed of any trace of its wearer, and would therefore be useless for spy-charms. Then she began to examine the other objects, picking up the bunches of herbs, unscrewing the tops from the bottles and sniffing the contents, wrinkling her nose at the results. The basin was half full of water—rather murky water, with green specks floating in it that might have been algae, the corpse of a tiny insect, and a thin brownish deposit on the bottom like sand or mud. Hazel wondered if it had come from the river. It seemed very strange that her great-grandmother should have a basin of river water in the attic; she guessed it must be for some kind of charm, but what kind she couldn't imagine. In her mind, she always preferred to say *charm*, not spell, since a charm was somehow less magical, more whimsical, something that could be attributed to the quirky behavior of a half-mad old woman, an act with no real power, no serious implications. Hazel glanced around for clues, uncertain, having no idea what to look for, finding nothing. Then she was drawn back to the basin, peering down at it. She felt a tingle crawl down her spine. The water had begun to move, rippled as though by a current; the residue on the bottom was stirred, clouding it over. Perhaps that was why the basin appeared suddenly much deeper. The cloudiness darkened, changing to water shadows shot with green: a pale shape gleamed through it. An oval shape, like a face. It emerged slowly, with shifting features, constantly remolding itself. For a few seconds she thought it looked like that actress, Michael Addison's wife, with the funny name—Rianna, Rianna Sardou. But it altered again, becoming the white bloodless face of the drowned, its lips notched with tooth points, huge eyes bulging against closed lids. Hazel was shaking all over. She tried to draw back, but the eyes opened—eyes with no whites, dark as midnight, deep as the ocean. Hazel was caught and held.

"Who are you?" The lips didn't move; the voice was inside her head. A voice with surges in it, like wave rhythms, cold as the sea.

"Hazel."

"The old woman sent you to me?"

"N-no. I came in here to leave something for her. Then I saw the basin . . ."

"So you called me."

"No!"

"Then perhaps . . . you responded to a call. There is power in you, unawakened, a coral bud closed tight, waiting for the tide to change. You are very young. The woman is old, old and stale: her heart has rotted. Cunning has twisted her mind into strange byways. Your mind is clear and clean. I would see you more closely."

The water swirled and churned; some splashed over the rim of the basin. Hazel saw that the head was rising—the curve of the crown loomed out of the wave ring—wet hair clung like weed to the scalp. But in the upheaval the mesmeric stare was broken. Hazel jerked backward, upsetting a bottle, knocking against the corner of a box. The sharp edge stabbed into her thigh with a pain that did much to clear her thoughts. She stumbled toward the door, falling over her own feet, slamming it behind her as she escaped. She ran down to her room and shut herself in, wedging a chair under the door handle, huddling on the bed to recover. But the alien presence was in her house, and she could not feel safe.

In the attic the head rose out of the basin and the water swirl subsided, lapping about its neck. It turned this way and that, surveying the empty room. Then its gaze came to rest on the door, and it smiled.

ANNIE FOUND herself something of a local heroine after the discovery of the injunction. The regional newspapers had started to latch on to the story, producing scrappy and largely inaccurate histories of the cup focusing strongly on its association with Grail legend. The *Crowford Gazette* and the *Mid-Sussex Times* sent reporters to Eade, both of whom showed up in due course at the bookshop, followed by a freelancer affiliated to the *Independent*, on the trail of a possible feature. Rowena, courting publicity as part of her campaign, arrived to join the party, and Annie made coffee for all and sundry and posed for photographs at her side. The injunction had been lodged with a lawyer but Rowena had thoughtfully provided herself with a photocopy for the two of them to flourish at the cameras. "Quite a little adventure for you," commented the Londoner from the *Indy*. "I expect it's pretty quiet down here most of the time. Or do you have elegant village murders for the local old-lady-hood to solve?"

Annie's mind glanced off toward Rianna Sardou, and what she had lately learned about Bartlemy. "A body a day," she said.

Rowena gave a bark of laughter. "Miss Marple knew her stuff," she said. "You'd be surprised what goes on in a village."

Annie was thinking of this exchange the next day when the stranger came in. Village life not being what it was in Miss Marple's day, strangers were not unusual in Eade: tourists on the antiques trail, city dwellers ruralizing with ex-London friends, people from neighboring towns in search of a picnic spot by the river. But this man was definitely a stranger with a capital *S*. He was seven feet tall, and his eyes gleamed purple in the alien contours of his face. Annie guessed at once who he must be but it was Eric who spoke first, placing his hands on her worktable and staring intently at her. "You are mother of Nathan Ward," he said. It sounded like an accusation, and for a moment she was afraid Nathan had upset his visitor after all.

"I'm sorry if you didn't want to talk to him. He really didn't mean to bother anyone."

"Bother? Is no bother. I like to talk to him. He is fine boy."

"Thank you," Annie said, pleased but disconcerted.

"He not look like you. I think—child must look like parent, yes? Or—is different here?"

"Children don't always look like their parents," Annie said, puzzled by the last comment. "Nathan must be . . . a throwback. How do you mean, it's different here? Different from Mali?"

"Many things different here," Eric said. "Nathan tell about me?"

"A little. He didn't mention your name."

"I am Eric Rhindon. You——?"

"Annie. Pull up a chair. Would you like some coffee?" She wasn't an inveterate coffee drinker herself, but it had become a reflex with any guest.

"Is good coffee or bad coffee? In Maali, we drink *kharva*, always taste same. In your world, coffee never same."

My world? Annie thought. *My world?* She said: "It's good coffee. I promise."

She went into the kitchen to put the kettle on. When she returned with the coffeepot, Eric was studying the books. *Studying*, she felt, was the right term. He frowned at the words in a collection of poetry with burning concentration. "Why do lines stop before edge of page?" he inquired. "I not understand. I not read your language well."

"I gather you spoke no English at all when you arrived," Annie said. "I think you've made the most incredible progress. You're always hearing of some genius who's learned a language in six weeks, but I never before met anyone who really did. These are poems, that's all." And, seeing his baffled expression: "Like songs, but without music." The word *poem* must be one he had not come across before.

"We have songs," he said, "but lines go all way to end. What use song without music?"

"I'll show you," Annie said, taking the book from him. This was the most bizarre conversation she had had in a season of bizarre conversations, but she was finding it stimulating. She understood why Nathan was so impressed with Eric. For all his strangeness, she couldn't help warming to him.

The book was an anthology, and she began to read from the first poem she saw, which happened to be Elizabeth Barrett Browning's tale of Pan inventing his pipes. The poem is all rhyme and rhythm, and the words make their own music, and as she read she saw Eric tilt his head on one side, and the color in his eyes brightened to a glitter.

> *"This is the way," laughed the great god Pan*
> *(Laughed while he sat by the river),*
> *"The only way, since the gods began*
> *To make sweet music, they could succeed."*
> *Then, dropping his mouth to a hole in the reed,*
> *He blew in power by the river.*
>
> *Sweet, sweet, sweet, O Pan!*
> *Piercing sweet by the river!*
> *Blinding sweet, O great god Pan!*
> *The sun on the hill forgot to die*
> *And the lilies revived, and the dragonfly*
> *Came back to dream on the river.*
>
> *Yet half a beast is the great god Pan,*
> *To laugh as he sits by the river,*
> *Making a poet out of a man.*
> *The true gods sigh for the cost and pain—*
> *For the reed which grows never more again*
> *As a reed with the reeds in the river.*

There was a short silence when she had finished. "How can music stop sun?" Eric asked. "And *true gods* . . . ? Gods are not true. Only in old legend. God is Man made big. This world very strange. Stories that lie, songs without music, lines that not go to end of page."

"Have some coffee," Annie said.

He accepted both milk and sugar and pronounced the coffee

good. "I like poem," he decided eventually. "Is kind of spell, yes? Very potent. Poem control force?"

"Force?" Annie was lost again.

Eric leaned forward, suddenly somber. "You need spell," he said. "Many spells. I come to tell you, Nathan in great danger. But you not worry. I help him."

"What danger?" Annie said. "Why?" She had her own fears about Nathan, but she couldn't understand why this stranger should share them.

"Gnomon," Eric said. "Gnomon from my world. They follow him in wood. They are not solid, unseen, very bad. They move through worlds. But you not worry. You take care of him, and I find something to help."

"What are gnomons?" Annie asked, but there was a hollow note in her voice.

"I tell you. Unseen, bring madness. I come to warn you. Tell Nathan, stay in daylight. Not go to woods at night."

"He won't," Annie said. There was a chill around her heart.

Them . . .

Eric finished his coffee quickly, though it was hot. "Like to buy book," he said. "But I have not much money. Only for food."

"I could get you something to eat . . ."

"Not now. Must go. Search woods for *sylpherim*."

Annie had no idea what *sylpherim* was, but she sensed his urgency. "Have it," she said, handing him the book.

He shook his head. "No money."

"A present."

Suddenly he smiled, a great sweep of a smile lighting up his face. "People here very kind. Thank you." He gave a nod, almost like a bow. "May the force be with you." Then he was gone.

"Good heavens," Annie said to herself, inadequately. And then:

"Force? He was talking about . . . magic. How much magic is there in Mali, I wonder?" But she knew now he didn't come from Mali. Not Mali in Africa, anyway. *We must take him to Bartlemy,* she decided. *He knows things. He knows about* them . . .

She reran his words of warning in her mind, and tried not to be afraid.

ROWENA THORN was in the back room of her antiques shop in Chizzledown when she heard the clang of the bell on the door. Her assistant was at lunch so she came out herself, relaxing with arms akimbo while the prospective customer had a chance to look around. Antiques shops are normally dim and cluttered but Rowena had gone for a different look, with pine flooring, pale walls, an emphasis on space and light. It made it much easier to keep an eye on things. Dimness and clutter were relegated to the storeroom. Her visitor, however, barely glanced at the various items displayed alluringly around him. "I am looking for Mrs. Thorn," he said. He had a slight accent, possibly German.

"I'm Mrs. Thorn," she said.

"My name is Dieter Von Humboldt. Your friend at Sotheby's may perhaps have mentioned me."

She nodded, straightening up, rising—physically and mentally—to the challenge. "You're the Graf, Graf Von Humboldt. Your grandfather's the one who acquired my cup. Under pretty unsavory circumstances—still, that's hardly your fault."

Her tone did not suggest forgiveness, and the visitor's "Thank you" was stiff and automatic. She guessed he was somewhere in his thirties, though it was difficult to be sure: he was the sort of man who looked middle-aged from twenty-five but never really changed. His hair was receding like a neap tide from the wide expanse of his forehead, expensive glasses shrank his eyes, his mouth was both thin and—at that juncture—tight-lipped. For the rest, his shoulders were rather broad, his tailoring conservative. Except for the accent, his English was virtually perfect.

"I am told you are making a claim for ownership of the cup. Is that so?"

"Must know it is. Been in several newspapers."

"I do not always believe what I read in the papers," Von Humboldt explained punctiliously. "I hope you will forgive me for arriving like this, without writing or telephoning first. I wished to meet you, to understand your position."

"All quite straightforward," Rowena said. "The cup belonged to my family for centuries—perhaps millennia. At some point there was an injunction drawn up forbidding its sale. Got lost down the years, but it's in my hands now. Proves the original sale was illegal. Don't know about your grandfather's rights of ownership—not my business—but the chap he got it from shouldn't have had it anyway. Any of that family popped up to claim it, too?"

"Unfortunately, yes. There were some cousins who went to America; their representatives have been in touch with me. I do not blame them, you understand, nor you: of course not. Nor am I certain what are the rights and wrongs of the case. Your ancestor may have acted illegally in selling the cup, but the buyer must have been in ignorance of the injunction and could hardly be held responsible. Then there are the moral issues. By modern standards my grandfather acted wrongly, yet he had the principles of his time. He saw the cup as legitimate spoils of war. The idea is not yet outmoded: I infer the Americans expect to enrich themselves rebuilding Iraq, for example."

"No need to justify your grandfather to me." Rowena shrugged. "Might have to do so in court, though."

"That is the crux of the matter," Von Humboldt said. "A court case could be long and costly for everyone involved. I was hoping we might find a way to resolve the conflict without that."

"What way?" Rowena asked bluntly. Privately, she was quite sure that no such avenue could be found, since she at least would settle for nothing less than possession of the cup, but she was willing to listen to him for now.

"There are various possibilities." The Graf became deliberately vague. "Much depends—forgive me—on the strength of your claim, and that of this Alex Birnbaum. We need to be frank with each other, to pool information." Rowena allowed herself a cynical smile. Noting it, he moved on briskly. "However, I might be prepared to offer, let us say, a division of the spoils. The cup could be sold, and those of us who have the greatest right to it could share the profits."

"Generous," Rowena said. " 'Fraid you've missed the point. I don't want the cup sold. Not interested in profits. It's a family heirloom, and I want it back. Haven't the funds to buy it, and wouldn't if I had. Belongs to me. You wanted frankness; I'm being frank. Nowhere to go but court."

"I see." She sensed he was not convinced. "Well, I will be staying around for a while. There is a very pleasant little hotel here, and I should like to see the locality from which the cup originated. I believe there are many interesting stories about it. Perhaps, even though you will not do business with me, we could have lunch, and you would tell me some of them?"

"Perhaps." Rowena was unencouraging.

"I hope we will speak further," he said. He turned to leave—then hesitated. "There are many things about this matter that I do not comprehend, but at this moment there is one in particular."

Rowena said "Yes?" interrogatively, because it was clearly expected of her.

"You have many beautiful things in this shop, which you are ready, presumably eager, to sell. The cup is not especially beautiful, and since the failed attempt at carbon-dating its antiquity must be called into question. Whatever legends may be attached to it, they can have no basis in fact. You strike me as an intelligent, hard-nosed woman, not given to sentimentality. Yet you only wish to possess this thing, for its own sake, without regard to value or potential profit. I find that extraordinary." His tone was politely skeptical.

Rowena made a sound half laugh, half snort. "Think I'm faking it? Try me."

"I will," said Von Humboldt. When she volunteered nothing further, he left.

THAT WEEK Nathan had a dream that he thought must be set in a different world from that of Eos, though whether in the same universe or another he couldn't tell. Once again, he was incorporeal, a mere awareness floating in space. Below him stretched an expanse of sea so vast he thought either the world in question must be flat or the planet far bigger than earth. The water was a wonderful deep blue—it looked much bluer than any sea he remembered—with a string of tiny islands scattered across it, their colors blurred with distance into a brownish neutrality, given brilliance by the light of that enormous day. Because of course the sky, too, was impossibly huge: the sun, falling from its zenith, seemed to have a long, long way to go before it would reach the horizon. Clouds were building up to block its route, great towers of cumulus, top-heavy with rain. Their shadow came crawling toward the islands, darkening the sea to indigo. White wave wrinkles indicated the new restlessness of the waters. The sun, struggling toward evening, sent a few long rays through a cleft in the cloud wall, throwing a path of glitter across the sea shadow, touching the nearest island with green. Nathan was much lower now, and he glimpsed the contouring of cultivation, clusters of what might be houses, the outthrust jetty of a miniature harbor. Then the clouds rose to smother the last light, and the colors went out. There was a crack of thunder so loud it might have been the crashing of world against world. Lightning zigzagged across the sky-roof and stabbed earthward with many prongs. Nathan was descending fast, and even though he had no substance everything became suddenly very alarming.

The sea went mad. Waves arose like rolling cliffs and heaving mountains; the writhing column of a waterspout flowed upward into a connecting arm of cloud. Chasms opened that seemed to reach into the depths of the ocean, and creatures from a lightless realm flickered briefly into view. Tentacles seethed, electricity crackled along the arc of a spine or the flourish of a gigantic fin. And there were other things in the tumult, human shapes that were not quite human, things half seen and half guessed—beings made of darkness and cloud swirl, of sea spume and black water. Night fell, and there was only chaos and noise. And somewhere in the midst of the storm Nathan's awareness still hung on, shivering, if thought can shiver, overwhelmed by the power and horror of the elements.

He didn't know how long the dream lasted. Ages later, or so it seemed, the world was quiet again, and the clouds must have lifted and thinned, for a line of dawn spread along the sea's rim, and a slow pallor seeped into that world, turning it to monochrome. The water was calm now, the sky veiled. There was no sign of the night's violence.

But the islands had gone.

At first Nathan thought he might have moved, and the island chain would be somewhere else, but when he looked around he saw the flotsam, rocking gently on the swell, and he knew he was still in the same place. Uprooted trees, with mud still clotting their tubers, floating mounds of rubbish, smaller items that it was best not to look at too closely, though they might have been nothing significant. But the islands themselves had vanished for good, devoured by the storm's fury and the sea's hunger. The cloud veil drew back and the rising sun appeared, its light reaching out across the endless waters. And somehow

Nathan knew that in all that world there was no longer even a tiny patch of land remaining, not a single rock standing out from the waves. The ocean ruled unchecked. The last seabirds wheeled and keened over the flotsam, soon to die. There was no other lament.

Nathan sensed that what had happened was not the result of scientific pollution or magical contamination; the tempest had come from the sea itself, from the rage of elements that hated Man. And now the entire planet was a desert of water where only fish might live, and the spirits of wave and darkness reigned alone.

He woke with the dawn, long before his schoolmates, and lay unsleeping while the aftermath of fear ebbed from his mind.

Later that day, Annie called him.

"Are you all right?"

"Of course I'm all right," he said, surprised. "Why shouldn't I be?" If he had reasons not to be, surely his mother wasn't privy to any of them.

"Your friend came to see me. Eric Rhindon. He says you're in danger." She added, by way of palliative: "I like him very much."

"So do I. Mum . . . don't worry. He's just overreacting to something. He isn't used to this country. He was being persecuted, you know."

"This country," Annie said, "or this world?"

Nathan evaded a direct answer. Clearly, explanations lay ahead—long, tangled complex explanations that might well not be believed—but he would plunge into that quagmire when he came to it. His present problem was to focus on schoolwork when all his thought was elsewhere.

Back home on Friday evening he used homework and tiredness to dodge discussion. On Saturday he got up at eight-thirty, breakfasted in haste, and went to the local hardware store. He had to wait, as it didn't open till nine. Once inside, he told the assistant he needed something made of iron. "Proper iron, not some kind of alloy," he said. "It's for a school project." Everyone always seemed to accept that.

The assistant summoned the manager, who was intrigued. "Of course, in the old days we'd have been an ironmonger's," he said, pointing to a faded notice demoted to a wall at the back of the shop. "Everything was made of iron then. Now—you're quite right, it's all some alloy, or stainless steel, or Teflon"—he tapped a saucepan—"or plastic. Very up to date—they invented some of this stuff designing rockets—but it doesn't wear like iron. What exactly is this project about?"

Nathan improvised on lines suggested by the manager's conversation, and explained he needed some examples of iron in use today. "All I've got is a couple of old horseshoes, and they're only borrowed."

"This is what you want." The manager showed his range of mock-antique door furniture, handles, knockers, numbers, all painted black. Nathan bought a selection of numbers for himself, Hazel, Eric, and his mother: he knew he was going to have to start telling Annie everything soon, and he wanted her, too, to be properly protected. It didn't occur to him to buy one for Bartlemy; if he had thought about it, he would have realized that he sensed the old man required no protection. The numbers cost a lot of money, and he knew he would have to tell Annie whatever happened, if only to get his allowance supplemented. He stuffed his purchases in his rucksack, all except the seven that he had chosen for his own: he put that in his pocket. Then he set off through the village to look for Eric.

They met at the edge of the woods. "You not come here," Eric said. "Is not safe, not in night or day. No *sylpherim*. Stay with your mother."

"It's okay," Nathan said. "I've got protection." He produced the number four. "This is for you. It's iron. I had another dream, and your ruler, the Grandir, was talking about it. Something about iron's magnetic field being too strong for gnomons. We know a bit about that even in this world: people used to use it to ward off evil spirits."

"Stupid!" Eric exclaimed, evidently in self-blame. "Me—stupid. Is in old legend, but I forget. I begin to learn. Much truth in untrue stories." He accepted the iron reverently, as if it was a great gift. "Thank you for this."

"Have you been all right?" Nathan asked. "I know you said you liked sleeping out, and the weather's pretty warm, but what about food and stuff?"

"I go to café where you take me," Eric said. "Chop wood, dig garden. They give me food."

"Good," said Nathan. "But I think we should go and see Uncle Barty now. The gnomons won't be able to stop us this time."

"In dream," Eric said as they walked, "what else you learn?"

"I think the Grandir may be controlling the gnomons, even across the worlds. I'm practically certain he sent them here. Do you know . . . who is the woman with him? Is she his wife? Her name is Halmé."

"You have seen her?" Nathan mmed an affirmation. "They say she is most beautiful of women. His sister, and his wife."

Nathan absorbed this thoughtfully. "In this world," he said after a pause, "we don't allow that. It's called incest. It's against the law. I think actually it's because the genes are too similar, so it can be dangerous for the children."

"No children," said Eric. "There is old rumor they try, long ago, before sterile begin, but no children come. Force strong in their family. Children perhaps more powerful. Incest common in my world, in strong family. You see . . . Halmé? You see her face?"

"Yes," said Nathan. "You're right. She *is* the most beautiful of women."

"Your mother beautiful also," Eric suggested.

Nathan glanced up at him, suddenly smiling. "Yes she is," he said. Halmé's beauty was that of Helen, a queen of ancient legend, a goddess—but Annie's beauty was something closer to the earth, nearer the heart, less perfect, less breathtaking, but not less touching. *A beauty that shines from inside,* he thought, and he remembered how Halmé was weary of her endless life, and her dying world, and how little she seemed to care for anything. For all her swan neck, and the poise of her head, and the artwork of her bones, there was nothing inside her that shone anymore.

As they drew nearer to Thornyhill the familiar ripple came snaking through the leaves, and the whispers began. Even with the iron in his pocket, Nathan knew the eternal clutch of fear in his stomach, but he clasped the number tightly, and held it out, and Eric did the same, and *they* retreated. Not far, never far, and the pressure of their rage and their reluctance was like a tangible barrier, but Nathan and Eric kept going. When they reached the path to the house the gnomons suddenly melted away, their nothingness vanishing into the quiet of the wood.

"You are very brave," Eric declared. "They follow you, but you have no fear."

"They aren't following me," Nathan said. "And I've been to Thornyhill often enough without any interference. They just don't want me to bring you here."

"Why not?" Eric demanded in bewilderment.

"I don't know. But anything they don't want me to do, I'm doing."

He knocked on the door, wondering what he would say, how he would explain to Bartlemy about the uninvited guest. But when the door opened there was no need for explanations. There was no need to say anything at all.

"I've been expecting you," Bartlemy said. "Come on in. Breakfast is ready."

"I've PREPARED a room for you," Bartlemy told the visitor after they had eaten. Eric had devoured scrambled eggs, bacon, mushrooms, toast, and marmalade like a hungry wolf; Nathan, his appetite impaired less by the cereal he had had earlier than inner tension, managed only some toast.

"But—Eric likes to sleep out," he said hastily, and then stopped, knowing he sounded ungrateful.

"That's fine," Bartlemy said, addressing the exile. "The bed is there if you want it."

"You are kind," Eric said gravely. "There is much kindness here. But maybe I bring trouble." He glanced at Nathan for guidance. "I not want to bring trouble for you."

"No trouble comes to this house," Bartlemy said with quiet assurance.

"There are things we should tell you," Nathan began.

"If you wish." As with Annie, years before, Bartlemy's manner was unhurried and incurious.

"Eric comes from another world!" Nathan blurted out.

"So I assumed. Most unusual." Bartlemy inclined his head courteously in Eric's direction. "I don't think I ever met anyone from another world before. Your English is excellent."

"I learn too slow. Must read more. Read poetry now: lines that stop before end of page. Mother of Nathan give me book."

"There are many books here for you to read," Bartlemy said.

"We're not joking!" Nathan protested, on the edge of frustration and fury.

Bartlemy gave him a look so serious that his anger died in an instant. "Nor I," he said. "What I would like to know is how Eric got here. There is only one way between the worlds that I am aware of, and Death alone opens that Gate. So say the Ultimate Laws. But even those laws are made to be broken, so it seems. I gather you arrived on the beach at Pevensey Bay. Do you know how it happened?"

Nathan had never heard Bartlemy talk in that way before, and for a moment the world seemed to be suddenly fluid, mutating into a different reality. But of course it was not the world, it was himself, growing, changing, making room for new concepts, broader visions. He said before Eric could answer: "It was me. My fault. I have these dreams of other worlds—*his* world—and he was drowning, and I tried to save him. I didn't mean to, but I brought him here. I know it was awfully irresponsible—I concentrate very hard now, when I dream, so as not to do it again—but if I'd left him, he would have died."

"Is true," Eric confirmed. "In my world, I am dead."

"That old trick," Bartlemy said. "The cat in the box is both alive and dead. Well, well. But *dreams* . . . I have known many strange things to happen in dreams." He looked thoughtful but not particularly surprised.

"There's a star that watches me," Nathan went on, "above our house. Only it isn't a star, it's a crystal globe, and it's in both worlds, I've seen it in dreams, and *he's* using it, spying on me."

"Hmm. Not crystal. It could be a globe of interdimensional space, bound by magic. I have heard of such things. Images would pass through it from world to world."

Nathan rushed on, eager to tell more, yet still reeling inwardly. Bartlemy's acceptance of everything made it all somehow both more real and more terrible, because he had always been a comfort figure, a normal adult in a normal universe—and now he, too, was forever altered. But there would be time enough to deal with the implications later. "There are these creatures," he said, "they're called gnomons, they come from Eric's world, too. They're invisible here, only not quite, and they've been following us, and if they catch you they get inside your head and drive you mad. We have to carry iron: they're afraid of it."

"I think I've seen them," Bartlemy said, "if you can see something that's invisible."

"When?"

"The first night your mother came here. You were a baby in a sling around her neck. These—creatures—seemed to be pursuing you both, but I am less sure now. Their purpose, I believe, was to drive her here, where she would find sanctuary. They may be evil, but their acts are not always so. Anyway, this house is a refuge from all such invaders. The door handles and hinges are of iron, and the window lattices. Iron is an ancient ward against bad spirits."

"You seem to know everything," Nathan said, increasingly baffled. "And I worried about telling you. I thought you wouldn't believe me."

"Your uncle is wise man," Eric declared. "He know what is truth, what is lies."

"I don't know enough," Bartlemy said. "Perhaps you would start at the beginning."

Nathan complied, describing his dreams and parallel events in this world, trying to remember everything up to the release of the prisoner in the Darkwood and his other dream that week of the islands swallowed in the storm. Everything but that first vision of the Grail, which he couldn't discuss. "The gnomons may have sent Mum to you all those years ago," he concluded doubtfully, "but they definitely tried to prevent me bringing Eric here today, and freeing that person—whoever—whatever he was—last weekend."

"Do you know where he went?" Bartlemy asked.

"He just ran. He could have gone anywhere."

"Maybe I should prepare a room for him, too."

He rose to collect the plates, but Nathan jumped up to forestall him. Eric followed them into the kitchen, trailed by Hoover, who had clearly detected an element of difference in the newcomer's smell. Bartlemy washed while Nathan dried, and Eric moved around the room, examining bottles of vinegar and oil, pots of homemade preserves, bunches of herbs.

"A little while ago," Nathan said, "you mentioned *magic* as if—as if it was something quite normal."

"Oh, it's not *normal*," Bartlemy responded. "If there's such a thing as normality. But that's too large a subject for now. I need some time to think about all this. You needn't worry about your friend: I'll take care of him."

He was interrupted by a cry from Eric. He had lifted a sealed jar containing a sprig of some dried herb and was smiling a smile of triumph. *"Sylpherim!"* he exclaimed. "Is same—or almost same—as in my world." He tried to unscrew the top, but Bartlemy stopped him with a hand on his arm.

"Best not in here."

"Yes. Yes, you are right. Too strong . . ."

"What do we call it here?" Nathan inquired, peering into the jar.

"Silphium," Bartlemy replied. "I grew it in my herb garden, under glass. Otherwise the smell might be a little . . . overpowering."

"I never heard of it before," Nathan said. "Is it very rare?" Annie had often commented that Bartlemy had many rare herbs in both kitchen and garden.

"It's extinct," Bartlemy said.

NATHAN LEFT after lunch, his mind so full of new ideas, new understandings, new questions, he thought they must be spilling out of his ears. "What on earth am I going to tell Mum?" he asked Bartlemy.

"What do you want to tell her?"

"The truth, of course, but . . ."

"Then do it."

He was trying to work out how to begin when he ran into Hazel. He was conscious of a pang of guilt: he had excluded her, without meaning to, from too much that was important. But at least filling her in wouldn't be difficult.

"Where've you been?" she demanded. "I've been looking for you all over. Your mum said you rushed off early somewhere—she thought you were with me."

"Sorry. I had to take Eric to Uncle Barty. I knew he'd be safe there. Is something wrong?"

"It's Great-Grandma." Hazel's expression was at once worried and shut in, the look he knew from her reserved, up-the-tree moods. "She's disappeared. She went into the attic on Monday—I saw her— and she never came out."

"Knock on the door."

"No, stupid. I mean, we did. Mum and I. We broke the lock and went in, but she *wasn't there*. She never came out, but she wasn't there. She isn't at her cottage. She's just—gone."

"She's awfully eccentric," Nathan offered doubtfully. He had a feeling there was something more, something Hazel wasn't telling him, lending an edge of panic to her anxiety. "She's bound to turn up."

Hazel jerked her head impatiently and tugged her hair over her eyes. "Something's happened to her," she insisted. "Something bad."

"Why should anything bad happen to Effie? I know we asked her about other worlds that time but she isn't involved. She doesn't know anything about . . . anything. She's the kind of old lady who's been around forever and will probably go on being around forever." Hazel flicked him a curious glance between strands of hair. "She's as tough as . . . oh, I don't know. Something old and tough."

"You don't understand," Hazel said. "She's been doing things—charms—in the attic. Charms for watching people. Magic."

"But you don't believe—"

"I don't *want* to believe, stupid. I don't want it to be true! I don't mind the other-world stuff, that's science, but magic—if it's real, it has no rules, it's dangerous . . . But Great-Grandma thinks she's a witch, she thinks she's old—a hundred, two hundred—she says she has power. She's been mixing with stuff—and I think it's backfired on her."

"What haven't you told me?" Nathan demanded.

He could see her withdrawing from him, into one of her moods, behind the tangle of her hair. "There's a lot you don't tell me," she said.

"We need to talk."

An Inspector Calls

Two dogs found the body wedged under the riverbank, early on Sunday morning. Their owner, an elderly villager who disapproved of cell phones, walked briskly back along the Glyde to the nearest house, which happened to be Riverside. Michael called the police and returned with the man to the spot where the dogs had been left on guard. Uniforms arrived, followed by CID, and there was an unpleasant interlude while those who were ordered to do so got wet and the body arrived on the bank and was zipped into a plastic bag. "Well, she's dead," the police doctor said brightly. "A good few days, I'd say. Probably drowned. In her mid, late sixties, pretty fit from the look of her. Accident, at a guess. Fell in—hit her head—caught in the weed. Autopsy should tell us more."

Michael and the dog owner were asked if they minded taking a look for possible identification.

"I'm sure I recognize her," Michael said. "Yes . . . I've seen her around. The local witch, I always thought."

"It's old Missus Carlow," confirmed the villager. "Pretty old she was, too. Been around as long as I can remember. Can't really take it in, her dying. Not like this, any road. She wasn't the type."

"Was she getting a bit dithery?" the police constable inquired.

"Not she. Sharp as anything, she was. Not the sort to slip in the river and get herself drowned."

"D'you know her next of kin?"

In due course two officers paid a call on Lily Bagot, the dog owner dropped in on the pub and let fall a few cryptic utterances, and Michael knocked on Annie's door in search of coffee and a sympathetic ear.

"Stupid to be shaken up," he said, sitting at the back of the bookshop, closed for Sunday, cupping the coffee mug between his hands. "All the same . . . I haven't seen too many dead bodies, and none like that. My mother looked peaceful, my grandfather empty, like a waxwork. But Mrs. Carlow—there was an expression on her face—rage, fear, horror, any combination. Her eyes wide open and the weed hanging over them. Sorry: sounds such a cliché. *She died with an expression of unspeakable horror on her face.* I know you think it's a big adventure, Nat. That's your age."

"It's horrible," Annie said quietly. The previous evening Nathan had started to tell her about Eric, dreams, other worlds, and she had listened and accepted, adding her own experience of the gnomons. But she had said nothing about Rianna Sardou or the thing from the river, and now the drowning struck her as more than ordinarily unpleasant. There was too much water about.

"She was Hazel's great-grandma," Nathan said. "I ought to go see her."

"Nathan—!"

"Hazel, I mean. Don't worry, Mum. I'm not turning into a ghoul."

"It's natural you'd be interested," Michael said. "I expect you'd like it to be murder, but I'm afraid it was just an accident. The rage and horror was probably because she fell in the river, and found herself caught in the weed. That would be enough to horrify anyone."

"Hazel must have been fond of her," Annie said. "She'd been staying with the Bagots for a while, hadn't she?"

"Since Hazel's dad left," Nathan replied. "Hazel's a bit afraid of her—I mean, she was—but so was he."

"I said she looked like a witch," Michael remarked.

Nathan went around to the Bagots' house as soon as he could. Lily let him in; she wasn't crying, but she looked frightened. "She thinks Dad'll come back," Hazel explained. "She's scared. I don't think she was fond of Great-Grandma—she couldn't be, 'cos Great-Grandma wasn't fond of *her*, she wasn't fond of anyone—but she protected us. Now there's nobody."

"There's the police," Nathan suggested. Hazel grimaced. "Mum'll help. About your great-grandma—d'you want to say *I told you so?*"

"I told you so."

In Hazel's room, he gave her back the horseshoes. She sat on the bed, holding one of them, stroking the coarse metal with a single finger. "It's too late," she said. "We should never have taken them. She needed the iron, too. Something got through . . ." She hadn't told him about the face in the basin, and the head emerging into the room. That had been too grotesque, too unnatural—no mumbled charm but a reality that defied belief. She refused to think about it, let alone discuss it, but it filled her mind, squashing all other thoughts into the corners. She tried to convince herself that Effie's death really might have been accidental, but it was difficult when horrible ideas were crowding into her head. It was hard to keep hold of a failing reality with only the corners of her mind. In the end she put on some music that sounded Eastern, with a twangy instrument that she said was a sitar, and they drank Coke because there was no ginger ale, and talked little, but she was glad he was there.

After Nathan had gone she went back to the attic. Nothing had been done about the broken lock, and the door swung loose. She had a feeling it ought to be fixed—an attic should have a lock—but she didn't know what to do about it. There was no point in mentioning it to her mother right now. Inside, everything was as they had found it when—with the assistance of a muscular neighbor—they broke in. The herbs and bottles on the table, the smell—very faint now—that didn't belong in an attic, an outdoor smell, a river smell, the shards of the broken basin on the floor. Hazel didn't pick them up; she didn't want to touch them. She had a trash bag with her and she crammed in all the stuff on the table, quickly and carelessly; the bottles clattered as she carried them downstairs. She had intended to throw them away but her mother was in the kitchen talking to someone and she didn't want to answer questions about what was going in the garbage. In the end she hid the bag under her bed and left it there.

Later, Lily talked about Effie's age (a gray area), and how she must have slipped, and what a tragedy it was for someone who was still so fit and had more than her fair share of marbles. Hazel gnawed on her frustration and a lingering sense of guilt, and said nothing.

It wasn't until Wednesday that the detectives came to Riverside House. Michael opened the door to an inspector from the CID and a uniformed sergeant who identified themselves politely, presented warrant cards, and requested a brief word. The sergeant, a woman, was black, burly, and six feet tall; the inspector was about the same height but much slimmer, with a narrow, intent face that looked both pale and dark, hard eyes, and a secretive mouth. His name was Pobjoy. It didn't suit him. He declined coffee for both of them in the voice of one who would decline any such offer as a matter of principle.

"The inquest is next week, isn't it?" Michael said. "I was told my attendance wouldn't be required."

"No, sir. We only need evidence from the man who found the body. We just wanted to confirm a few small points."

Michael studied the officer consideringly, absorbing the significance of his rank and plainclothes status. "There's nothing suspicious about the death, is there?"

"You think there might be?"

"Well—no," Michael responded, slightly nonplussed. "Old woman walking by the river, presumably after dark, falls in, drowns . . . It's an unhappy accident but surely nothing more."

"What makes you so sure she was walking after dark?" the inspector said.

"Easier to miss your footing, I suppose. Unless she had bad eyesight."

"Her eyesight was excellent."

"Maybe she had an attack of dizziness," Michael speculated. "She must have been getting on a bit. She was a great-grandmother, I gather."

"The autopsy confirmed she was exceptionally fit for her age," the inspector said noncommittally. "Whatever that was."

"Don't you know?"

"There is no record of her birth, and her relatives seem to be—uncertain—about it. Did you see her walking along the riverbank on a regular basis? Living here, you must know everyone who uses this route."

"Not really," Michael said. "Our strip of the bank's private. People walk farther up—that way—and the path isn't good, so it doesn't get used as much as you would expect. I've seen the old boy with the dog a few times, but I don't ever recall seeing Mrs. Carlow before. In the village, yes, but not by the river. What exactly are you getting at, Inspector?"

But Pobjoy wasn't giving anything away. "Merely trying to establish the facts. The lady was strong and healthy, and in full possession of her faculties. She also had a reputation for being extremely acute. If she was in the habit of strolling along by the river we thought you might know; otherwise it seems an unlikely thing for her to do. You said yourself, the path isn't popular. And she had no dog."

"Did she fall or was she pushed?" Michael asked. "Is that the idea?"

"There is no evidence of foul play," Pobjoy said repressively. "But we would like to know if you saw anyone frequenting the area in the days preceding the discovery of the body."

"Acting suspiciously? I don't think so."

The inspector proceeded to take Michael through every encounter of that week, no matter how trivial. The postman, a courier with a consignment of books, a delivery from Sainsbury's in Crowford, a couple of schoolboys fishing without a permit, another dog walker. "And your wife?" Pobjoy concluded. "I'm afraid we'll need to talk to her as well. When do you expect her back?"

"In a month or so," Michael said. "She's in Georgia." This time it was the policeman's turn to look nonplussed. "She's an actress. She's been on tour for a while. I doubt if she could tell you anything useful; she doesn't spend much time here."

Pobjoy threw him a swift, hard look, curiously devoid of expression. "I see," he said, in a tone that made Michael wonder exactly what he saw. "That will be all for now, but I may need to come back to you." He offered no thanks, departing on a curt nod, leaving Michael thoughtful and vaguely disquieted.

Outside, Sergeant Hale asked: "Well, sir? Do you really think there's something wrong?"

The inspector shrugged. "Maybe." Evidently he wasn't prepared to discuss the matter. As they headed back to the village where they had left the car, he said: "I'll meet you in the pub in half an hour or so. I want to take a look around. Get yourself some lunch."

The sergeant set off pubward and Pobjoy wandered down the High Street, apparently aimless, dropping in on the deli to buy some cheese, observing Lily Bagot, whom he had not yet interviewed, without telling her who he was. While he was there Annie came in, exchanged a friendly word, bought half a dozen eggs. When she left he watched where she went, and after a few minutes he followed her into the bookshop.

He leafed through a volume of military history—a subject in which he was genuinely interested—and murmured a couple of preliminary courtesies before identifying himself. Clearly she wasn't the type to offer casual gossip about the Bagots, so he had nothing to lose by putting his inquiries on a semi-official footing.

"What's wrong?" she said. "Surely . . . surely Mrs. Carlow's death was just an accident. Why should anyone harm her?"

"That's what I was wondering," he said. He let the remark hang, sensing the trace element of doubt in her voice and knowing the value of silence with a possible witness; but Annie didn't react. She looked almost fragile, he decided, with her sensitive mouth, her soft eyes, the filmy halo of her hair—a gentle creature whose warmth of heart showed in her face. But there was strength under the softness, and evidently a capacity for reserve. "I get the impression she was a sharp old lady," he resumed. "No one gains financially from her death, as far as I can tell, but she might have made enemies."

"She could be outspoken," Annie conceded.

"So she must have upset people."

"Not particularly. You know how it is: everyone makes allowances for the very old and the very young. They can get away with all kinds of cheek. I expect Effie traded on that. She tended to say what she thought, but nobody really minded. It wasn't as if she was a gossip or a scandalmonger, always stirring up trouble. Actually, she kept herself to herself most of the time. Until . . ."

"Until she moved in with Mrs. Bagot?" Pobjoy suggested.

"That was just a temporary measure. Lily's broken up with her husband; she needs support. Effie just came to help."

"And how did the husband feel about that?"

"I'm afraid I don't know." Annie met his eyes full on. "Why don't you ask him?"

"I expect I shall."

He tried a few more inquiries, but without eliciting any interesting results, bought the book he had been studying, and left, a little reluctantly. A nice woman, he thought, and crime rarely brought him in contact with nice women. He had recently moved from Hastings, which had a major drug culture and all the depressing fallout that invariably accompanies it. His marriage had fallen by the wayside some years earlier, the pressures of his job taking too heavy a toll on his home life. A notorious failure on his watch—the fault, in fact, of an arrogant colleague who had planted evidence, leading to repercussions that had affected him—had led to his removal to the relative backwater of Crowford. There was little serious crime in the area and only the occasional murder, usually domestic in origin. Fellow coppers had raised eyebrows at his interest in the death of Effie Carlow, but despite the scandal in his past he had a reputation as a talented detective and his superiors had allowed him the leeway to investigate. He couldn't define precisely what he thought was wrong in the case, just a collection of niggling details that didn't fit in. There was the curious statement of Lily Bagot and her daughter that Effie had shut herself in the attic and never emerged, for instance. And now the possible hostility of Dave Bagot. He rang the CID office and got someone to check the man's record. Two convictions for drunk and disorderly, one for driving under the influence. Plus an assault charge that had been dropped for lack of evidence. All of which, though far from conclusive, at least suggested further lines of inquiry.

And then there was the question of the anonymous letter.

AT THORNYHILL, Eric was improving his English by reading the newspapers. He had done his quota of work at the café but had accepted a small cash payment instead of lunch, since Bartlemy had managed to imbue him with the idea that it was an offense against local custom to eat out when you were staying somewhere as a guest. He had slept out only once so far, lured indoors by the comfort of the bed and the restful atmosphere of the house. In the evening he and Bartlemy talked about poetry, and politics, and the alternative world that had been his home, but his host studiously avoided any discussion of Nathan's dreams. The newspapers had been Bartlemy's suggestion; he had returned from shopping at Sainsbury's in Crowford with an armful of the quality press. Reading one of the multiple supplements, Eric gave an exclamation in his own language. Hoover, who had been watching him with the air of a schoolmaster surveying a promising pupil, pricked his ears and gave a short bark.

"What is it?" Bartlemy asked, emerging from the kitchen.

"This." Eric had evidently paled: his dark skin had a greenish tinge. He indicated a lengthy feature illustrated with two photographs. One showed Annie and Rowena Thorn wielding a piece of paper in the bookshop; the other, printed "by special permission of Sotheby's," was the Grimthorn Grail.

"Yes, that's Annie," Bartlemy confirmed. "Not a bad picture—for a newspaper shot."

"She's famous?" Eric queried, looking inexplicably troubled.

"Good heavens, no. It's just because she found a missing document that may prove Rowena's right to reclaim that cup. It used to be the property of her family."

"Not possible." Eric made a graphic gesture of dismissal. He gestured frequently and with energy, Bartlemy noticed, perhaps to compensate for his still-imperfect grasp of the language. "Cup is from my world. Must not be here."

"Are you sure?"

"I cannot mistake. I never see it—it is too important, you would say, holy?—but I see many pictures. Is first of three. Everyone know of them. Part of religion."

"I thought you didn't believe in God?" Bartlemy murmured.

Eric struggled to explain himself. "Religion is not God. Religion is spirit, faith. There is word you use here, in church—*salvation*. We are not many now, people of my world—even Eos die soon—but we believe will be saved. Maybe just one man, one woman, but they will not be sterile, will have children again, our world will continue. Salvation."

"And this cup is part of that?" Bartlemy pursued.

"Very important, special, holy. First of three. Cannot be *here*. Is kept in safety, in secret place, guarded by monster from ancient time, until is needed."

"What do you mean, *first of three*?"

"Three things. Cup, sword, crown. Belong together. All holy. Cup of stone, sword of *stroar*, crown of iron. Make Great Spell to save us."

"Sword of *straw*?" Bartlemy echoed.

"*Stroar,*" Eric repeated. "Is special metal in my world. Very strong, make sharp edge, sharp point. I not know name here. Maybe not exist on earth."

"I see. The stone, too, would be different—perhaps just slight molecular differences, but it would defeat analysis. And the age . . . from another universe, another time, impossible to date. That would

explain the anomalies. Although iron seems to be iron everywhere."
He fell silent for a moment, pondering. Eric returned to his contemplation of the newspaper, as agitated as a Catholic might be to find the Shroud of Turin on Mars. "So what is this Great Spell?" Bartlemy asked at last.

"Is deep mystery," Eric said. "If we know, our world is saved; but no one knows. Maybe Grandir find out. People say, first Grandir make three, long long ago, a million years our time. Cup is sometimes full of blood, sword moves without hand to hold, crown has many powers—I not know them. *His* crown, *his* blood, sword that kill *him*. True story so old, much confusion now. Is forbidden to discuss, because people may invent, lie. Religion must not lie."

"That's a novel idea," Bartlemy remarked. "What was the first Grandir's name?"

"Great secret," Eric said. "Grandir's name always secret. I think, name in language of force, has power."

"Yes . . . names have power, language has power, especially the language of magic. I wonder . . ."

"How is this here?" Eric reverted to his former plea. "Is wrong, bad. If cup here, my world cannot be saved. No hope left. Who steal it? Who bring it here? Perhaps Nathan dream—"

"*No.*" Bartlemy spoke with unaccustomed sharpness. "There may be a connection, but not that. Anyway, this cup has been here for centuries. Possibly our world is where it was sent for safekeeping, the secret place you mentioned. The ancient monster could be just a blind, a focus for gossip, a distraction for thieves. It's an old ruse: you build a vault to challenge and confuse people, and hide your treasure under the bed."

"Cup is kept under bed?" Eric was horrified.

"Don't worry, I was speaking metaphorically. At the moment, I promise you, it's secure. We must arrange for you to see it. The photograph is pretty clear, but we need to be sure. If you *could* see it, would you know definitely if it was from your world? There are many cups and chalices similar to this."

"I know it," Eric insisted. "Patterns there—there—holy, have much power. How can it be here? I think, *I* am here for chance. Others dream like Nathan?"

"I doubt it," Bartlemy said. "There is obviously some link between our worlds that goes a long way back. It may be chance that Nathan brought you here, but it isn't chance that makes him dream. I need you to tell me everything you can remember about the cup—and the other items. In our world the cup is also supposed to be one of several relics—three or four, legend is unclear. Another is a spear, which might be transposed into a sword; I don't know about the crown. Stories have always centered on the cup. Here, too, it is said to have held the blood of someone holy. There seem to be parallels between the traditions in your world and ours that cannot be coincidence. Do you give the cup a name, or is that secret, too?"

"*Sangreal,*" Eric said. "That is *sangré,* blood, and *grala,* cup, bowl. Is word in language of force."

"It sounds," Bartlemy said, "like the language we use here for strong magics, which is in turn a source for many other languages. Your world may be far more advanced than ours—advanced enough to be on the verge of annihilation—but there are plainly many basic similarities. Right, let's have the story from the beginning. It isn't forbidden to discuss it here."

Eric told him all he could, but he knew little more than the scanty details he had already provided. The first Grandir had been a ruler of great power and holiness, treacherously murdered by his best friend—an ending he himself had foreseen, though why he had done nothing to avoid it was not clear. In some versions the killer was his own son, or his sister-wife. He had prophesied that eventually mortals would misuse the magic that abounded in their universe, and it would turn into a poison that would destroy them. But he had created a spell that might yet save them, a spell that was embodied in the cup, the sword, the crown: the cup that had held his blood, the sword that slew him, the crown he had worn in life—yet he was slain before he could reveal what it was. Why? asked Bartlemy, gently practical. It seemed a particularly ill-timed assassination. Eric shrugged and gestured, looked both tragic and doubtful. It was fate, doom, a grim inevitability. Or maybe it had been written down, in a document since lost, or whispered in someone's ear and passed on, down the ages, to each chosen listener, until the moment came when they would speak the words aloud. But the moment had come, and no one had spoken. Why should the cup be hoarded in an alien world, by those who did not know its value? Were the sword and the crown here, too, or scattered throughout assorted universes? They must be recovered, and returned to Eos, and then maybe the spell would be completed.

"Perhaps that is why Nathan bring me here, though he not know it. Is pattern, destiny. Cup not safe here. Must be watched, guarded."

Bartlemy remembered Nathan's reference to the star shining only on Eade.

"Someone's watching," he said.

"ARE YOU—are you quite all right at the moment?" It was Edmund Gable who spoke, one of Nathan's classmates and the boy who occupied the bed next to him in the dormitory. They both played on the cricket team and had been good friends almost from the beginning.

"Of course I am," Nathan said. Ned looked anxious and unsure, a state of mind that wasn't normal for him. "Why?"

"You don't seem to be concentrating in class lately—only a B in chemistry, and—"

Nathan grinned. "You sound like Brother Bunsen." This was

their nickname for Mr. Bunyan, the chemistry teacher. "Chemistry isn't my subject. Of the sciences, I prefer physics and biology, you know that."

"You used to be on top in all of them. Something's wrong—something weird. I woke up last night and looked at you, and you looked sort of—dim."

"Thanks! I'm supposed to look clever in my sleep?"

"Not that kind of dim. I mean—blurred. Like you weren't quite there."

Nathan's heart jolted so violently it was a minute before he could speak. "You must have imagined it. I expect you were dreaming or something. Anyway, how could you see? It was dark."

"Early dawn," said Ned. "There was light enough to see by. Honestly. And I *didn't* imagine it. You were almost—transparent. Like a ghost."

"Well, I'm here now," Nathan said. "Solid as anything. Feel." He held out his arm. "If I were a ghost I'd be dead, wouldn't I? Not about to thrash you at cricket practice this afternoon."

He brushed the incident aside as best he could, and Ned didn't refer to it again, but Nathan was horribly frightened.

Until Ned spoke to him, he had completely forgotten his dream. How many other dreams might he have forgotten? Was there information he ought to know, mislaid in his subconscious? And what might he have done on all those lost voyages? Supposing he dreamed every night? He tried to rein in speculation, tempering his panic with what he hoped was common sense. After all, he remembered the dream now. And surely whatever power it was that let such dreams happen, it wouldn't cheat him by blanking them out.

The evidence of dematerialization was more disturbing. Presumably, the more real he became in the dream, the less real was the body he left behind him. As he seemed to become increasingly solid every time, and he could find no way of stopping the process, he began to wonder what would happen if he disappeared completely from the bed in which he slept. Would he ever be able to get back? Instinct told him that his body acted as a kind of anchor, pulling his spirit home; even in alternative universes they were never entirely separate. But if his physical being vanished from this world, perhaps his spirit would be unable to find the way back. He would have to discuss it with his uncle Barty. Somehow, he felt sure, the old man would know what to do. Or if he didn't feel sure, at least he felt hopeful. The relief of having an adult to turn to rushed over him like a sudden warmth, and he headed for his next lesson, French, in a more optimistic frame of mind.

Even so, French didn't hold his attention. His thought drifted, back into the now remembered dream. He was back in the chamber at the top of the tower, where the pale globes rotated slowly, suspended in midair, emitting a light that went nowhere. The Grandir moved around the room, studying first one, then another, his footsteps virtually soundless on the dark floor. Because the light illuminated so little, Nathan could only see him when he drew close to a globe, then the white mask would glimmer into being as though equally suspended, while his somber garments made his torso all but invisible. Nathan himself had no trouble finding concealment; all he had to do was keep well away from the spheres. What had Bartlemy called them? Globes of interdimensional space, bound by magic . . .

The Grandir approached one of the peripheral spheres, spoke the word he had used before, a word not in the common language of Eos. *"Fia!"* Nathan trusted the subsequent flash blinded the man as effectively as it did him; otherwise, if the Grandir had looked in the right direction, he must have been revealed. But the ruler was concentrating on the ceiling. A circular image had appeared, inverted; Nathan guessed it was sea. There was just a breadth of dark blue with a thin strip of sky along the bottom, curving slightly as it was refracted by the sphere. He wondered if it was the ocean he had seen in another dream.

The Grandir obliterated the image with another word and moved on. A different sphere, a different scene. A tumbled mass of reddish rock with what looked like the entrance to a cave, a high-tech cave with sliding doors emblazoned with a sun symbol in bronze. Nathan was reminded irresistibly of *Thunderbirds*, but when the doors opened a figure emerged, far smaller than he anticipated, changing the whole scale of the scene into something huge and magnificent, though it was difficult to appreciate it upside down. The figure wore futuristic clothes of a dull rainbow sheen and seemed to have a shaven head, but he thought it might be a woman. It descended a flight of steps set among the rocks and was lost to view. The Grandir watched for a few minutes while nothing happened. A featherless bird, like a xaurian, dropped out of the yellow sky and snatched at a snake, which stretched its jaws in threat, a spiked ruff extending around its neck. But the Grandir did not wait for the outcome, and the image flicked out.

Several more scenes followed. There was a world of snow where shaggy beings shuffled around, insulated from the cold by a pelt of fur that might be their clothing or their hide. An enormous creature like a mammoth hove into view, surmounted by a carved seat where three more of the shaggies perched precariously. Then there was something that resembled a medieval village, with worn thatch on the roofs and smoking chimneys and a young woman in padded leather trousers whose hair was an extraordinary apricot gold. Then a woodland scene that for some reason made him uncomfortable, a woodland in autumn—but an autumn richer than any he had ever imagined, where the leaves were yellow and flame red and crimson and magenta, and vividly spotted fungi swelled from every tree bole. Other visions unfolded in succession: a desert with riders mounted on two-legged reptilian animals winding across it in a long defile; a city on top of a cliff, where bridges and buildings extruded from the rock as if they were part of it; a forest of giant mushrooms, their ragged caps overhanging a house or temple with scarlet pillars and curling roofs. Lastly there was a wide green lake, mirror-smooth and bordered with spiked bulrushes twenty feet high, and beside it a purple-clad man sat on a flat stone in what might be meditation, still as a tree.

These are other worlds, Nathan thought, awe mingling with a strange excitement. *The globes are like peepholes in the very fabric of space and time, and I can see through into different realities, different states of being. And these are just a few. There must be thousands of them, millions, perhaps billions, many of them far more alien and bizarre. There could be places where the world is flat, or the sea is pink, or the most intelligent life form is a talking rabbit. Infinity has room for everything.* And *everything* seemed to him suddenly such a big word; he had never known how big, a huge word, encompassing realms beyond imagination, and galaxies beyond counting, and creatures of every size and shape and form. His mind could not stretch far enough to take it in.

He looked around and saw, almost with relief, that he was still in the circular chamber, and the multiworld visions had gone, and there were only the spheres turning slowly, and the rays of light that never reached the walls. The Grandir was in the center now, his hands encircling the largest globe, not touching but apparently locating a particular facet. The brilliance flared, and an image appeared above him. Not the bookshop this time but a section of riverbank. It must be near Michael's house, where they'd found Effie Carlow. A woman was walking along the path, a dark-haired woman whose face Nathan glimpsed only briefly. He saw the jut of prominent cheekbones, the downward sweep of brooding eyebrows. He was sure he knew her, but it took him a few seconds to remember. Rianna Sardou, the actress and TV star, Michael's absentee wife. He wondered why she was back, now of all times, and what it meant, seeing her walk along that stretch of river—if indeed it meant anything at all. She had a perfect right to come back if she wished to, he told himself; after all, she lived there.

As she went past, the long grasses beside the path parted, and a face peered out. A swarthy, warty face half covered in hair, the narrow eyes netted with wrinkles, the expression both sly and somehow desperate. Nathan had seen that face only once before, and then just for an instant, but he recognized it immediately. The prisoner in the Darkwood. He started, twisting his head, trying to see better, but the dream had begun to slip away, and the picture vanished. There was a moment when the white mask seemed to rotate slowly among the globes, as though seeking him out, then sleep engulfed him again.

He emerged from his recollections to find the class had fallen silent and the teacher was eyeing him expectantly. A page of French prose was open in front of him. With only a little prompting, he began to translate.

DAVE BAGOT turned up at the house on Thursday evening. Hazel, listening at the kitchen door, heard him say to her mother: "Now the old witch has gone you'll take me back, won't you? Kicking me out wasn't your idea. It was all her. She hated men. Evil old hag."

"She's dead," Lily said listlessly.

"Can't say I'm sorry. I know, I know, she was your grandmother, but—"

"I don't want you back. I don't want you to come back at all."

"Don't be so fucking silly. You're my *wife*, this is my *home*, I've got a right to be here. You can't turn me out." More four-letter words followed, and shouting, and eventually the sound of a blow. *He gets to that part much sooner these days*, Hazel thought. Her mind whizzed around, wondering what to do, who to turn to. If only that police detective were still around—but he hadn't proved much use after all. She slipped out, hearing her mother sob, feeling a tug at her insides that made it hard to go. But she must get help.

It was just after eight when she arrived at the bookshop, rattling the knocker, clutching at Annie when she opened the door. "Nathan said, come to you," she explained. "No—you mustn't go back there. Dad's too strong. Find someone. Call someone."

They found Michael, on his way to the pub for a quick pint. Seeing him, Annie thought for a confused moment that he looked like the answer to a prayer, her knight in shining armor—then she remembered that Dave Bagot was a big man, heavily built, where Michael was thin and whippy, and suddenly she was afraid for him, and terrified for Lily, and all the mixed-up fears made her behave stupidly, stammering and clasping his arm. "Call the police," he said tersely. "No—don't come with me. Just show me the way."

But they went with him, of course, while Annie called the police on her cell phone, hearing the shiver of panic as she spoke. "Please c-come. Come quickly."

At the Bagots' house the front door was open the way Hazel had left it. Michael went in, and they heard his voice raised, sharp and cold and unfamiliar—a scuffling sound—a thump—a fall. "Wait," Annie told Hazel, and rushed in. They were in the kitchen. There was a chair upset, and broken crockery on the floor—Lily had been washing up—and she was crouching by the wall with her hands trying to cover her face. Michael was struggling to his feet with blood running from his nose, but Dave Bagot hit him again before he could stand up, and again, calling him interfering, a busybody, and the usual foul names. Annie screamed at him to stop, but he paid no attention—she made a grab for him but he knocked her aside. Then she saw the saucepan on the drainboard, the kind of heavy-duty saucepan that could also go in the oven, and she picked it up with both hands, and swung it, bringing it crashing down on his head. And then he was crumpled up on the floor—as much as his substantial figure could crumple—and Michael's face was all blood and anger and amazement, and Lily uncurled herself, forgetting her damaged face. Annie stared down at what she had done, totally horrified.

"Maybe I've killed him . . ."

"No such luck," Michael said grimly, and suddenly he hugged her. "You star. You *star*."

"You're bleeding on me," Annie said. "Let me clean you up."

"I'll get something," Lily offered. Her face was bruised but not bloodied and she seemed to be pulling herself together.

"I wasn't much use," Michael said ruefully, "was I?"

"You were wonderful," Annie whispered. "Should we try to revive him?"

"No."

Then Hazel came in with a neighbor, and about ten minutes later uniformed police arrived, and there were cups of tea, and offers of help, and Lily was adjured to call her lawyer about an injunction, and Dave Bagot came to himself with a severe headache to find he was being bundled into a police car and taken away. "Is he being arrested?" Hazel asked one of the officers.

"Not at the moment, unless your mother decides to press charges. But CID want to question him about the death of the old woman, and a night in the cells won't hurt."

"It was brilliant," Hazel told Nathan the next evening. "I don't care if he *is* my dad. It was totally brilliant. I think your mum is the bravest person in the world."

Nathan grinned, bursting with suppressed pride. "I like her, too."

He added presently: "I wish I hadn't missed it. I don't suppose I could have done anything, but—"

"You didn't need to. Your mum did it."

"School's fine, but boarding is a pain. With all this stuff happening, I ought to be here. Thank God vacation starts soon." Because he was at a private school, his term finished well before Hazel's.

"The best part is, the police think he might have pushed Great-Grandma in the river."

"Are you sure?"

"It's obvious," Hazel said. "That's what they meant by *holding him for questioning*, or whatever they call it."

"But he didn't do it—did he?"

"Of course not. It was something she . . . called up, conjured . . . something not—not human. I wanted the police to come, I hoped they would find out things, but then I realized it was no good. I never thought of them arresting Dad. It's really neat."

"But what if he goes to prison?"

"I hope he does," Hazel said. There was a note of defiance in her voice, and Nathan didn't push it any farther.

Later, he asked his mother about it. "Do the police really think Hazel's dad shoved Effie Carlow in the river?"

"I don't know," Annie said. "They haven't told me."

"Do *you* think so?"

She sighed. At heart, she wished she did. "No. That would take planning—sneaking after her, catching her unawares, picking the right spot to do it. His violence is always impulsive, not planned. I hate the way he behaves, that goes without saying, but there's a big difference between hitting someone in anger and killing someone in cold blood. I'm sure Effie's death was just an accident."

There was a pause, loaded with thoughts unspoken.

"Well anyway," Nathan said, "you hit him with a saucepan. That was just—wow."

Annie couldn't help smiling at the glow in his eyes. After recent misunderstandings, and despite burgeoning problems, suddenly life felt good. "Michael was amazing," she said. "It was brave of him to tackle Dave Bagot. Dave's much bigger than he is."

"Yes, but you did for him," Nathan said. She gave him a squeeze, and noticed how tall he was getting, taller than her now. "Have you seen Eric?"

"Not lately, but we're going to Thornyhill on Sunday. Uncle Barty says we've something important to discuss."

That night before he went to bed, he climbed up to the skylight to look at the star. He hadn't done it for a while, things had been so busy, and there had been such a lot to think about. Sometimes it seemed to him that his head was becoming so crowded, soon his thoughts, maybe even his dreams, would start spilling out of his ears and eyes, taking shape around him. But then, perhaps they already had. There was Eric—and there was the star. It looked very ordinary and star-like, except that it didn't twinkle: it was just a steady white pinpoint of radiance. What else had it seen? he wondered. The prisoner from the Darkwood, who had evidently escaped the gnomons, and was hanging around for some secret purpose . . . the death of Effie Carlow . . . Hazel knew something, he was certain, something she wasn't telling him, but maybe, like in books, it was something she didn't know she knew, or didn't think was important. And then he let go of his thoughts, because they were too many for him, and gazed at the stars of his own world, arranged in their grand familiar design, spelling out stories and mysteries for soothsayers, luring astroscientists into the wilderness of space. There were nights when the vastness of the universe oppressed him, but this time it seemed to him that the constellations were like signposts, and the routes were well known, somewhere in his spirit, and all of it—every nebula, every galaxy— was home. His stars, his place, his world. He gave the intruder one last hard look, and scrambled down from the Den, and went to bed.

"MAGIC," BARTLEMY was saying after lunch, "is part of what we think of as the spiritual plane. You will see if you take a quick look at history that mankind, as a species, tends toward overenthusiasm. We latch on to one big idea and try to use it to cover everything. Whatever it is, it has to be the only truth, the explanation for every single detail, every niggle, every hiccup in reality. First it was religion, then science. Right now, we are trying to cut our world to fit the scientific laws. But there is a dimension of the spirit that exists apart from those laws—there are elementals everywhere, mostly in an incorporeal state, and they express themselves through what we call magic. Humans originally had no such powers, but power was given to them, or to some—never mind how, the theory is too long for now—and that power is known as the Gift. It has spread genetically, so these days there is probably a little of it in all of us. In its most extreme form, it can include intensive telepathic and telekinetic abilities, spellbinding, separation of spirit from body, influence over or partial control of other minds. If developed, it can lead to longevity, though beyond the normal life span this is usually accompanied by sterility. If overused, it will corrupt the user, and turn to madness. But owing to our present penchant for science, extreme magic is not widely used here. Perhaps that is fortunate."

"But it is in Eric's world," Nathan said.

"Evidently. Such power may be native to humans there. What is clear is that so much—er—force has been generated that it is, so to speak, floating around loose, like electric storms: hence the contamination. Uncontrolled magic is very dangerous, in any world. I'm not sure how it could be poisoned in the way Eric describes, possibly by the misuse of an exceptionally potent spell. The people there are plainly so imbued with power that they habitually live for thousands of years and no longer have children. Someone like Eric, indeed, uses his power *only* to live: he has nothing left for anything else. In this world, with no extraneous magic to draw on, that ability may wane. I have explained to him that he can expect to age here."

"Is no matter," Eric said. "I have thought much on this, read much poetry. Life is maybe more beautiful, if it does not reach end of page."

Annie met his eyes as he spoke, and found them very bright, not knowing that brightness was mirrored in her own.

"How do you know all this?" Nathan asked. "Do you—have you—"

"I have the Gift in a small way. I rarely use it. I have seen what it can do to people. I only ever wanted to heal—heal the body to heal the spirit—and cook beautiful food. The right food, too, is good for the soul, or so I believe."

"Is fine idea," Eric said, full of lunch. There was general agreement.

"How—how old are you?" Nathan inquired tentatively, studying his friend with new perception.

"Dear me, don't you know that's not a polite question? Old enough. I have seen many things, both real and unreal. But this is the first time I have had anything to do with matters beyond this entire universe. I am working on theory here; I have no personal experience. This time, Nathan, you are the expert."

"I don't want to be," Nathan said, with a shiver.

"From what Eric tells me, the Grimthorn Grail is an artifact from his world, which seems to have been placed here for a purpose, possibly safekeeping. I would like Eric to examine the cup before we are certain, but he seems to be very positive about it." Eric assented vigorously. "I think—this may tie in with Nathan's dream journeys, but I have no idea why."

"Do you have these dreams all the time?" Annie asked her son, a little shyly.

"No. I don't know. I might forget. I've been worrying . . ." He related the incident that week, and his fears about his hold on this reality. It did nothing to ease his mind when Bartlemy listened in silence, his normally comfortable face very serious.

"What about sleeping pills?" Annie suggested. "Might they prevent the dreams?"

"I wondered about that," Nathan said.

"Not a good idea. We don't know how long this problem will last, and Nathan needs to be in control. I can only say that I believe in due course he will *learn* what to do. We must have faith in whatever fates there may be to take care of him. There are, however, certain precautions that *can* be taken." He turned to Nathan. "There is a preparation of herbs that must be kept in the bedroom—don't worry, the aroma is quite strong but not unpleasant—and an oil of the same, which I will give you to anoint your hands and face before sleeping. The herbs have a powerful attraction for the spirit world, and may help your spirit find its way home, if it strays. We will also draw the Mark of Agares, the Rune of Finding, on your wall, and you must inscribe it in indelible ink on your arm or chest, renewing it whenever it begins to fade. But how effective such things will be across the barriers of space and time I do not know."

"You're not very encouraging," Nathan said, hoping he sounded brave, and realizing he didn't. He had been privately sure Bartlemy would have a solution.

"Then take courage. Have faith. This ability has been given to you for a reason. I don't think you will be allowed to get lost."

"I hope you're right," Nathan said doubtfully, but he felt a very little reassured. Absently, he ruffled Hoover's head. The dog was sitting at his feet, chin on his lap, large brown eyes raised to his face. "I wish I could take you with me. It would be good to have company."

"Perhaps you could dream him with you," Annie said idly.

"That could be dangerous," Bartlemy said. "Don't try. We don't know the full scope of your power. You could take someone with you and be unable to bring them back. I'm fond of Hoover; we've been together a long time."

Annie said she was joking and Nathan thought of asking how long, but refrained.

"What about the death of Effie Carlow?" Annie inquired a little later. "Was it really an accident? People don't often drown in the Glyde."

"You said you thought it *was*," Nathan reminded her.

She made no answer, remembering all too vividly the thing from the river that had turned into Rianna Sardou. She was still reluctant to tell Nathan about that, feeling in some obscure way that knowing would only increase his danger, and she had no intention of discussing with him the secret of his conception, though she knew Bartlemy wanted her to. But that was too deep a matter, too personal, a wound that could not be touched.

"This woman who die," Eric asked, "she was bad person?"

"Oh no," said Bartlemy. "Just a small-time witch with a little power, not enough to achieve anything, but enough perhaps to poke and pry, and get herself into trouble."

"Hazel said Effie told her she was two hundred years old," Nathan volunteered. "I thought she was a bit batty, but . . . did she have the Gift?"

"In a way. She had certainly been around for some time. The villagers didn't notice—she was clever enough for that—but I did. She didn't trouble me. She was something of an anachronism, a country witch of a former century, living more on her reputation than her deeds. She was clearly curious about Nathan, and maybe about the cup, but whether curiosity killed the cat or not we may never know."

"They released Dave Bagot," Annie said. "I heard this morning. But he could be rearrested. Inspector Pobjoy seems pretty suspicious of him."

"Pobjoy?" Nathan echoed. "What a name! Is he fat and pompous?"

"No," Annie said. "Thin and pompless. The taciturn type who

says nothing and waits for you to incriminate yourself. You could imagine him staying quiet for so long, you'd confess just to break the silence."

"Pobjoy." Bartlemy, too, was ruminating on the name. "I've heard that before. His father, maybe . . . no, grandfather . . ."

"When?" asked Annie.

And: "Where?" Nathan.

"In the war." It was strange to hear him refer to it like that, as if he had been from another generation—but then, they reflected, he was. A generation outside time.

He didn't seem disposed to continue, and Nathan, conscious of cliché, inquired: "What did you do—in the war?"

"What I always do." Bartlemy smiled faintly. "I cooked."

THE OBJECT of this casual speculation sat in the living room of his house, ignoring the radio that chattered in the background, surveying a piece of evidence that he knew he shouldn't have brought home with him. But so far he was the only person to take the case seriously, and no one would call him to account. His house felt very empty despite its smallness, quiet with his own intent quietness, its décor in neither good taste nor bad. He wasn't interested in it, and it showed. For him, it wasn't a house, just a place to sleep and sometimes eat, when he remembered meals. Part of a take-out dinner grew cold on the table at his side. Had he been asked, he couldn't even have told an interrogator the color of the curtains.

But he had absorbed everything about the letter. Handwritten in block capitals with a thick-tipped felt pen that, if the writer had any sense, would have been thrown away immediately afterward. The effect was intended to be characterless, but there was a certain roundedness about the lettering that reminded him of the increasingly rare communications he received from the ten-year-old daughter whom he hardly saw. The pen was red—symbolizing blood?—the paper the kind used in a photocopier. Easy enough for a child to obtain, probably from school. He was sure the writer was a child. "Effie Carlow didn't die naturally. She was killed." Saying the same thing twice—a childish mistake, or an ill-educated adult.

There was only one child connected with the case. An officer had noted she looked pleased when they took Dave Bagot away. Had she written the letter because she really believed he had murdered her great-grandmother, or simply to make trouble for him? If the former, she might have filial reservations; if the latter, why not name him?

But the letter never mentioned a killer, only the fact of the killing. The letter never mentioned a person at all . . .

Sing a
Song of
Sixpence

O n the following Sunday, Rowena Thorn had invited Annie,
the children, and Bartlemy out to lunch to celebrate finding
the injunction. Bartlemy had declined; he rarely went out locally, preferring to keep a low profile, but he suggested they might take Eric instead. Somehow Michael joined the party as well—Annie wasn't
quite sure how, only that she found herself inviting him—and they all
went to one of the local pubs, the Happy Huntsman near Chizzledown, which had a particularly good restaurant.

"That man just said something about *in his world*," George whispered to Nathan as they arrived. "Is he nuts?"

"It's his English," Nathan said, improvising furiously. "He means
his *country*."

Annie, meanwhile, had already told Michael and Rowena: "Eric's
a little eccentric. He thinks he's from another world. But he isn't mad
or anything—actually, he's frightfully intelligent—I expect it's just
the shock of finding himself here. He doesn't talk about his escape,

but I gather it was pretty traumatic." Which, she felt, was perfectly true—in a way.

They sat down around a large table and ordered lavishly. Rowena insisted on champagne; the children were restricted to Coke. "Couldn't we pretend we're fourteen?" George said hopefully. "You're allowed alcohol in a pub at fourteen, provided you don't buy it. And I have wine with Mum and Dad sometimes."

"You've given me wine at home, Mum," Nathan put in. "*And* beer."

"Yes, but this is a restaurant, and I'm responsible for all of you," Annie said. "So it's Coke."

Hazel made no contribution; she was always at her gruffest with people she didn't know well, and she found both Eric and Rowena, in their different ways, rather overpowering. Nathan was rather startled to note how easily Mrs. Thorn got on with the exile, after a certain initial restraint. They seemed to be talking about poetry. The anthology Annie had given Eric contained many classics: Kipling, Yeats, *Invictus, The Highwayman*, apparently all old favorites with Rowena. When they moved on to the subject of the cup two of their auditors grew nervous, but they needn't have worried.

"Been in my family for so long we've lost count of the centuries," Rowena was saying. "Very old family. Goes back to the Romans, or so my grandfather claimed. Thyrnus was the name then—if there really is a connection. Can't think of anyone else who can even try to trace their ancestors back that far. Wouldn't mean much to you, of course, coming from where you do. Africa, isn't it?"

"Eos," said Eric. "My family also old. My mother three thousand now."

Fortunately, Rowena decided he hadn't understood her, and reverted to the matter of the Grail. "Point is, the cup's a sacred charge. The Luck of the Thorns—or our curse. Not too clear which—but we have to look after it. Knew that as soon as I saw it. Never really believed all that stuff before, but when I touched it, held it . . . Should never have been sold, d'you see?"

"Sold?" Eric looked appalled. "Is terrible. *Sangreal* is holy object, has power to save world. Your family must protect it. You, me, we must get it back. Is our sacred task. Force bring us together for this."

"Not sure about force," Rowena smiled. "Still, all help's welcome. Didn't know they had Grail legends in Africa. Although I've heard they go in for Saint George in Egypt."

"The Grail legend gets around," Nathan said, sotto voce.

They were at the dessert stage—in the children's case involving Banoffi pie, treacle tart, and ice cream—when a man who had been eating alone at another table came over to them. "Hope I'm not intruding," he said with a slight American accent, "but I couldn't help overhearing . . . Forgive me"—he turned to Rowena—"but I think you must be Mrs. Thorn."

Rowena assumed the aloof expression with which earlier Thorns had outfaced impertinence from the peasantry. She thought she could guess the man's identity already. "Yes," she said curtly. "And you are?"

"Alex Birnbaum." Suspicion confirmed. He had frizzy hair that stuck out and a clever, agreeable face, which, however, did nothing to endear him to Rowena. "I was wondering if we could have a talk sometime."

She shrugged. "Shouldn't think there's much point. Don't have a negotiating position." She added, for the benefit of the rest of the table: "This is another one who's after the Grail. Place is crawling with 'em."

"Your family bought it from Roland Thorn?" Annie said encouragingly. She knew from Rowena's manner that she shouldn't offer encouragement, but she felt sorry for the man.

"That's right. I understand you claim the sale was illegal, but

Joseph—he was my mother's great-uncle—didn't know that. I don't want the cup back, Mrs. Thorn, I assure you. All I want is some kind of compensation from the Von Humboldts—some acknowledgment of remorse for what they did. Joseph Birnbaum had an amazing collection of art treasures. They took everything, and he and his wife, his children, his grandchildren all died in Dachau. It's a common enough story, but that doesn't make it any better. My mother was a child: they sent her to the U.S. with friends. She was one of the lucky ones. As for the treasures, there's no doubt the Von Humboldts are still sitting on much of Joseph's collection."

"A bad business," Rowena said, "but I don't see what I can do about it. My only interest is in recovering the cup. If that's not what you're after, why are you here?"

"To track down Dieter Von Humboldt. This affair has brought him out into the open; beforehand, the Von Humboldts denied all knowledge of Joseph's collection. They've kept it out of sight since the end of the war. Believe me, Mrs. Thorn, I don't want money—at least, not from you."

"Everyone wants money," Rowena said with an echo of the Graf's cynicism.

"What *do* you want from her, then?" Michael said.

"To ask about the cup. My mother had a disturbing experience as a child in Germany; it made a great impression on her. It's become our family ghost story."

"What happened?" Annie asked.

"Well . . . it was a few days before she was due to leave. She remembers Abel—the family friend who took care of her—she remembers him begging Joseph to come, too, with the rest of the family, but he brushed aside Abel's fears. He still thought he had enough influence to be secure. He was showing my mother some of his things, including the cup. She says that when she looked in it, it was full of blood. She was so frightened she knocked it onto the floor, and the blood spilled over the carpet, and soaked in, and disappeared. She took it as a warning, a sign of Joseph's imminent death. But she was only a child—about ten at the time—and he dismissed her terrors, even as he had dismissed Abel's advice. And so he died . . ."

Nathan, thinking of his own secret vision, felt a coldness around his heart. He told himself that it was a long time since he had seen it, and no one close to him had died, so whatever the vision portended, it couldn't be that.

"Many see blood in cup," Eric was saying matter-of-factly. "Is natural. Holy relic"—he had picked up the word from Bartlemy—"have many powers."

"As it happens," Rowena admitted, "Thorn family tradition says seeing the cup full of blood *is* a death warning. Never heard of a specific case before, though. Here—better sit down. Have some coffee. No trying to pester me for a deal, mind."

Alex Birnbaum hesitated, demurred, and finally succumbed, pulling up a chair between Rowena and Annie and talking mainly to the latter.

"Did your mum get the reward?" George asked Nathan, under his breath. "You know—for finding the injunction."

"No idea," Nathan said. "Maybe this is it."

"Bet she turned it down," said George. "My mum says she's awfully unworldly." His tone was at once critical and faintly apologetic.

"Yes, she is," Nathan assented with pride.

On his other side, Hazel whispered into his ear: "How come Eric knows so much about the cup?"

"Tell you later," Nathan whispered back, thinking that he had a lot to tell, about Bartlemy, and magic, and how his mother knew—and wondering if Hazel would have trouble dealing with it all. It was only much later that it occurred to him how strange it was, that he himself could accept the widening of his world—his *worlds*—so easily. It was as if, on some subconscious level, he had always been aware that his own universe was full of undiscovered secrets—that Bartlemy, in his quiet way, was someone unique and special, as enduring as hill and wood—that beyond the science he was taught there was a dimension that could not be measured by physical laws. The hardest thing, for some reason, was coming to terms with his mother's attitude. Her comprehension of the magical plane, her acceptance of it, was too far outside the range of normal parental behavior. Had he thought about it a little more, he would have realized that it turned her from being simply a mother into a person, and he was still young enough to find that unsettling.

The grown-ups ordered more drinks in order to toast Annie for finding the injunction, and Michael for tackling Dave Bagot, and Annie again for her resourcefulness with the saucepan. George took a gulp of Michael's whiskey and turned bright pink, and Eric, who was going through an experimental stage with alcohol, sampled a Kahlúa that he offered to share with Hazel, thus earning her deep, if largely silent, gratitude. The celebration ended on a lighthearted note, and they headed home in various taxis feeling mellow and well fed, any private doubts or fears temporarily set aside.

AT HOME Nathan had drawn the Mark of Agares on a piece of paper, which he taped to the wall above his bed; he also drew it on the inside of his arm below the wrist, in indelible felt pen. For school, he tucked a card with the rune on it under his mattress. Ned Gable, noticing the sigil on his arm, thought it was a tattoo and was suitably envious, while the games master told him to wash it off; Nathan didn't mention that he couldn't. Bartlemy had made up the herbal mixture that he promised, but it smelled too pungent to take it to Ffylde. It was the last week of term, and once vacation was under way he would be able to concentrate on sorting out his problems—if they could be sorted out—without the distraction of education. Hazel, being at a public school, had another fortnight to go, but after that they would be able to spend time together, and solve the mystery of Effie's death, and the prisoner from the Darkwood, and the gnomons, and the Grimthorn Grail, and . . .

He fell asleep on Monday night with ideas whirring around in his head, and when he opened his eyes he was somewhere else.

Not somewhere he expected to be. There was no curved architecture, no panorama of the city with its many-colored lights and its skimmers and xaurians swooping and wheeling as if in a complex aerial ballet. Wherever he was, it was completely dark. He seemed to be lying on ground rather than floor: it felt hard and lumpy and rather gritty. His own body was quite solid; parts of the ground dug into it. He stood up, and began cautiously to move around, touching something that was unmistakably rock. A rock wall. *I'm in a cave,* he deduced. There had to be a way out. The air was fresh, not stale. If he could work out where the draft came from . . . But there wasn't really a draft, just a nuance in the atmosphere, the hint of a change. Following it, he found himself progressing down a sort of passage. The rocks drew close on either side—now the walls were barely a yard apart—but when he reached up he couldn't touch the roof. He was twisted this way and that in the narrowing space, peering with dilated eyes into the unresponsive blackness. Another turn of the passage—and another—and suddenly he could see something.

Not very much, but something. A crooked slit, tapering to a point far above him, blue against the dark. The deep velvet blue of a night unstained by any artificial light. High up between encroaching walls of rock, a single star shone. He wriggled through the slot—it would have been too narrow for adults, unless they were very slim—and out into the night. He couldn't see very much in the star glimmer, but he was aware of a slope dropping away from him, of a vast empty landscape stretching out to some remote horizon. The air was cold and dry; overhead, the stars soared upward in unfamiliar constellations, some huge and bright and near, others in distant clusters like glittering trails of dust. He didn't see any moon at first, but presently one hove into view, around a shoulder of rock to his right, a pinkish half-moon, fraying at the edges, dimming the stars in its vicinity. He thought: *That's one of the moons of Eos, I'm almost certain . . .* But he didn't know where on Eos he might be, and there was little point in starting to walk somewhere when he had no idea in which direction he should go. In any case he could see enough of the terrain to tell that it was very rugged, humped into low ridges and pitted with star shadows; walking could be hazardous in the dark. He decided to stay close to the cave and wait for morning. It was a fortunate decision.

Afterward, he wondered what would have happened if he had moved. Would he have woken with the sunrise—or never woken at all? His dreams always seemed to have a purpose, even if he wasn't sure what it was, and formerly he had felt in some way protected—at least until his materialization became more solid. But with this dream he realized he was on his own, vulnerable to dangers he didn't understand. He was being transported into an alien world without guidance or aid, swept blindly toward some hidden precipice. In that moment the knowledge terrified him even more than the fear that he might not get back.

The dawn came slowly, paling the sky to the east (he assumed it was east), fading the pink half-moon to a feather-like translucency. Morning twilight reached across the emptiness, showing him a desert of sand and rock, ribbed with the wave patterns of some prehistoric ocean, veined with river swirls long gone dry. A double line of boulders snaked up the slope toward him; the ground there was particularly uneven, rearing into knife-edged crests and swollen into bumps and mounds. When the sun's arc finally lifted over the horizon, color spilled across the world: the sand was a pale terra-cotta, the rocks cream, furrowed with gray, torn or eroded here and there to reveal a core of sky blue, or blood orange, or raw-beef red. For a second he was entranced with the terrible, harsh beauty of it; then he was aware of pain. Sudden, blazing pain. Where the dawn touched his hand he saw it reddening, beginning to blister. He could feel his face doing the same. He bolted back to the slot and wriggled into the welcome shadow of the cave. The pain eased, but only a little, and then the relief set in, as he thought of how it would have been if the sun had found him exposed on that shelterless landscape, shoeless and pajama-clad . . .

He could peer out through the slot, though the naked light stung his eyes. He saw what he thought were birds circling, very high up, perhaps vultures. As they flew lower he realized they were xaurians, but not like the ones he had seen in the city. These were riderless, maybe a little smaller, and their colors varied: many were dark gray or black, some blotched and spotted, one white. *The xaurians they ride are domesticated,* he thought; *they've been specially bred. These are wild ones.* Interest diverted him from the pain of his burned skin. He wondered what they found to eat, out here in the desert.

One dropped suddenly, wings and body streamlining into an arrow. Whatever it had seen, it missed, but shortly after it stooped again, rising this time with a snake in its hind claws that writhed like a whip, trying to bite. Nathan remembered Eric had said there were few creatures that could resist the growing levels of pollution, but he supposed that if you could survive in the desert, you could survive anything. He shrank back into the cave for a while, closing his eyes to rest them. When he looked again there were xaurians approaching in a V-formation of three. They had riders. A patrol.

The wild reptiles veered away from them but only to a safe distance, where they spiraled slowly, watching the intruders. The patrol dipped low—"They're coming in to land," Nathan murmured with a rush of anxiety. They had to be aiming for the cave—there was nowhere else—but the entrance should be too narrow to admit them. Close up, he saw they looked different from other patrols, black-clad, with scarlet insignias on their foreheads. It came to him that they were some illicit group, raiders or terrorists from a subversive organization. He tried to memorize the scarlet emblem, an intricate design set in a circle, but although he knew he would recognize it if he saw it again he didn't think he would be able to draw it. The foremost rider drifted to the ground near the top of the slope and dismounted, glancing warily around. Even though he was used to seeing the hoods Nathan found the figure peculiarly sinister, with its black-goggled stare and the shapeless mesh hiding every feature. There was something in its stance, a sort of hot-wired alertness, a slimness of the shoulders, a suggestion of poise. He thought it might be a woman. Not a woman like Halmé, with a face of magic and legend, but a lithe, athletic creature, deadly as a tigress.

He thought: *She's thin enough to get through the cave entrance . . .*

The other two hovered but didn't land. The rider began to climb the last of the slope while the xaurian waited, untethered. Suddenly it rose on a wing beat, beak open in a scream. Nathan saw the ground twitch: the twin lines of boulders began to heave upward. The earthbound rider stumbled. Of the two who were airborne, one swung off into an ascending curve; the other plunged down to rescue his companion. What happened next left Nathan almost too amazed for fear.

There was a deep rumble—not the crack of rending stone, more like a growl in the belly of the earth—and a huge section of the hillside simply broke away, hoisting itself as though forced by subterranean pressures. Sand billowed in clouds around it; the humps and boulders tilted but didn't fall. A crevasse split open to reveal a gleam of black surrounded with smoky bronze. There was an instant of confusion, and then Nathan understood what he was seeing. The monster had been lying on the slope, its hide the color and texture of the desert, blending with it, becoming a part of the sandscape, vast and invisible. If he had strayed a few yards farther, he would have stood on it. The flattened skull was perhaps forty feet across, surmounted by a double ridge of bone; the spines continued down its neck and along the spreading mass of its body, also somewhat flattened like that of certain desert-dwelling lizards that Nathan had seen on nature programs. Somewhere below, the remote coil of its tail rasped over the ground, raising more dust clouds. Nearer, jagged rocks uncrooked into elbow joints; a splayed foot shifted, making the cave vibrate. The fallen rider was trying to get up, balanced unsteadily on the head. Above her another rider descended, his xaurian thrashing the air, its wings dwarfed by the monster beneath. Claws seized the woman's arms—Nathan was quite sure it was a woman—and lifted her, but she wasn't weightless, and the xaurian strained to gain height. The riderless reptile was also in flight, wheeling around them. Still higher up, against the sun, the third xaurian was being watched by its wild cousins. There was a stab of flame from some unidentifiable weapon, and they sheered off. The woman kept her head. Dangling in midair, with a piece of the desert rearing toward her, she managed a call, hoarse but imperative—repeated it, more clearly—and her mount swerved to dip beneath her.

But the monster was not so easily balked. Encumbered by its own weight, slow from long slumber, still it was starting to awaken fully, its movements accelerating. The great head swung around; the jaws parted, displaying triple rows of haphazard teeth. A long, deep blue tongue unraveled, thick as a conveyer belt, wrapping itself around the lowest xaurian, plucking it from the air like an insect. There was a snap as the maw closed, the crunch of teeth biting through bone. A flailing wing tip went limp and was swallowed up. The second rider tugged on the reins, exhorting his beast with word and spell, and gradually it began to pull away, struggling skyward with its burden. The behemoth gulped the last of its meal, belched foul air—Nathan pinched his nose—and turned in search of the next.

That was when the third rider returned. Nathan, watching in an agony of helplessness and horror, had almost forgotten him. He dived into the monster's line of vision, skimming the knobbled land-scape of its skull, sweeping the crevasse of one eye with an outthrust pinion. He must have punctured the surface, for a bubble of white fluid appeared, blurring its gleam, and red welled within the white. With an alarming burst of speed the head twisted, snatching at this new prey—but the smaller reptile was too quick and too agile, swerving out of range and looping around for another pass. Again it dived, aiming for the other eye . . . Nathan saw the rider point with what must be a kind of gun. But there was a brain somewhere in the giant skull, and the monster learned from its mistakes. The eyelid snapped shut—the flame-flash sparked harmlessly off its hide. The head jerked back, and the tongue was unleashed in a movement too swift for sight to follow. For an instant Nathan saw rider and mount strug-gling in a blue coil of muscle, then they were sucked into the vast gape of its maw.

It took longer over its meal this time, grinding at the morsel as if something about it was too tough or stringy to be effortlessly pulver-ized. When the jaws parted so the tongue could explore every cranny, Nathan saw fragments of black mesh caught between its teeth. He felt sick.

The last of the invaders were farther away by now, but not far enough. The xaurian had landed so the woman could climb up behind her rescuer, and had then taken off again, flying more comfortably with the extra load transferred from its claws to its back. But it was gaining height too slowly, and the monster, its hunger whetted rather than sated, was alert and fast. Its whole body swiveled, the sagging belly grinding rock into dust, feet pounding the earth so the desert trembled. A sandstorm swirled in its wake. Nathan found he was pleading or praying: "No! No! Please no . . ." The neck extended, the enormous mouth unclosed . . .

And then the wild xaurians came, zooming out of the sky, homing in on the lunging head. The white one led them, and the lashing of their wings forced both eyes to close, and the blind muzzle swayed to and fro, snapping at air. Whatever hatred they might have felt for their domesticated kin, evidently it had been undermined by the sight of the two xaurians being eaten. They knew their adversary, and they could maneuver far quicker than their larger cousins. They swarmed around the skull, beating it with their leathern pinions, clawing at every exposed glint of eye, the inside of a nostril, the shallow indentation of an ear. The blue tongue flicked out, probing, but without vision it could not snare them. The ridden xaurian gradually drew away, its flight labored, the rescued woman, sitting behind the saddle, holding tight to her companion. Nathan was almost sure they were going to make it.

But the desert sun was growing dim, and the dream was slipping away. He tried to hang on, desperate to be certain of their escape, to catch the last moments of the xaurian attack, but it was no good. The darkness of the cave poured into his mind, filling it from edge to edge, and when it receded it was daylight in his own world.

"Where were you last night?" Ned Gable asked.

"What?"

"I woke in the night, and you weren't there."

"You should do something about your sleeping problem," Nathan said, ignoring the coldness that trickled down his spine. "You're always waking in the night and imagining things. Anyway, if I really wasn't there, I must have been in the bathroom."

"Okay," said his friend. "If that's all you want to tell me. But if you've got a cloak of invisibility, you might share it with me."

"I wish." Nathan grinned.

"How come your face is burned?"

"Oh . . ." Nathan touched his cheek, which felt very tender. "Must've been yesterday. Tennis."

"I thought brown skin didn't get sunburned," Ned said.

"Depends on the sun."

BACK HOME, Annie was surprised to receive a visit from Alex Birnbaum, who wanted to take her out to lunch. She suspected he was after information about Rowena, but in fact he talked about painting and sculpture, sounding like someone who knew his stuff, and about himself, sounding like every other man she had ever met. But it was a pleasant meal and she enjoyed herself, returning to the shop with an inward tweak of guilt, because she didn't feel she *should* be enjoying herself quite so often. They had pulled a dead body from the river, and an exile from another world was living at Thornyhill, and Nathan was in danger. This was no time to start having fun.

Later that afternoon Inspector Pobjoy dropped in. Seeing him, Annie remembered the journalist from the *Indy* who had made a joke about village murders solved by old ladies. Only in this case, it was the old lady who was dead.

"How are your investigations progressing?" she asked politely.

The inspector was leafing through a book. In itself, this was not unusual; after all, it was a bookshop. But Annie was increasingly conscious that many of her customers had only a superficial interest in buying books.

Insofar as he allowed himself normal expressions, Pobjoy looked startled at being questioned so directly. "There is . . . progress," he said cagily. "Have you heard anything that might have a bearing on the case?"

"No," Annie said baldly, throwing in a smile for good measure. She had had two or three glasses of wine with lunch and was feeling slightly light-headed. "I heard you released Dave Bagot. I must say, I don't think pushing his grandmother-in-law into the river is quite his style."

"The evidence is inconclusive."

"D'you really believe it was murder?" Annie persisted. "Is there any conclusive evidence for that?"

"Let's say—there are a few pointers," he amended. And, on an impulse: "We received an anonymous letter stating very specifically that Mrs. Carlow's death wasn't natural. Have you any idea who might have sent it?"

"An anonymous letter . . . good God, no." Annie was genuinely taken aback. Whatever she had been expecting, it wasn't that. "Don't you think it could have been just someone out to make trouble?"

"It's always a possibility. After all, there has been trouble . . . for Dave Bagot, to start with." He was feeling his way, but her reaction wasn't what he'd anticipated.

"You mean, I hit him over the head with a saucepan." She grinned mischievously. "I daresay that counts as trouble."

"I didn't know that." His face lightened with the beginnings of a smile. "I heard there was a scene and you were involved, but not . . . um . . . the details. Good for you. Of course, we don't like to encourage the public to resort to violence, but . . ."

"Of course." For a moment, there was a spark of camaraderie between them. *I really mustn't drink at lunchtime,* Annie thought.

She went on: "Incidentally, there's a friend of mine who thinks he may have known one of your relatives. Bartlemy Goodman. He lives out at Thornyhill, in the woods. I don't suppose you've been to see him."

"Which of my relatives did he meet?" His manner was cooling down again.

"Well," Annie said, pulling herself together, "it wasn't Bartlemy, of course, he's not old enough. It would have been—his father, and your grandfather, I think he said. In the war. It could be coincidence—but *Pobjoy* isn't a common name, is it?"

He gave a noncommittal grunt.

"Did you hate it when you were a boy?" Annie asked gently.

He shrugged. "What's in a name? And—for the record—I ask the questions."

This time, he left without buying a book.

THE INSPECTOR interviewed Hazel in the presence of her mother, as required by law, with Sergeant Hale in the background for good measure. Hazel, almost completely hidden behind the tangle of her hair, was at her quietest. She felt both overawed by the presence of the police and resentful of that awe, nagged by guilt about her father—which she also resented—and frightened about the authorship of the letter. But writing a letter wasn't a crime—was it?—and anyhow, they had no way of finding out it was her.

Pobjoy placed the letter on the table in front of her. "Did you write this?"

Lily Bagot stared at it in bewilderment. "Of course she didn't. She would never do such a thing. I can't think why you're making this fuss over Great-Grandma's death—it was just an accident."

"I thought she was your *grandmother*?" The inspector seized on the discrepancy immediately.

"Yes. Sorry. My grandmother, Hazel's great-grandmother . . ." Lily pressed a hand to her forehead in an effort to sort out the muddle of her thoughts. "I'm getting mixed up. Anyway, whoever wrote that letter, it wasn't Hazel. And it's a lie."

"Please let your daughter answer for herself."

Hazel sat with her lips clamped together, lest a stray word escape and incriminate her. She wished there were a tree at hand for her to climb.

"Did you write this letter?"

She allowed herself a quick shake of the head. "Tell him no," Lily prompted, but Hazel still didn't speak.

"Our experts say this is the handwriting of a child."

There was an appreciable pause. "I'm not a child," Hazel said.

"No crime has been committed as yet," the inspector pursued. "But the letter writer could be found guilty of wasting police time, if she has some information about Mrs. Carlow's death that she is deliberately withholding."

"I told you, my daughter didn't write—"

"Please, Mrs. Bagot. Hazel, *do* you know something?"

"Not really." How could she tell him what she knew? He'd laugh in her face, which would be worse than threats. "I know it wasn't an accident, that's all. She went to the attic and locked herself in and never came out. I'd have heard her: my room's underneath. I always heard her before."

"So you wrote the letter?"

"Mm." It was almost an admission.

"But she must have come out of the attic," Pobjoy said carefully, "in order to get to the river."

Hazel relapsed into silence.

"Would you like something to drink?"

"Bacardi and Coke." She had never had one, but it sounded like a good idea.

"Just Coke," said Pobjoy, nodding at Sergeant Hale. There was Coke in the kitchen. The sergeant brought it to her, poured it into a glass.

"She must have left the attic," the inspector reiterated, "to get into the river."

Hazel mumbled something into the Coke.

"What?"

"The basin was broken."

"Yes," said Pobjoy. "There was a broken basin in the attic. Are you saying—she might have been drowned in the basin, not the river?"

Hazel gave a half nod. *It's true,* she thought. A bit of the truth. The basin, and the river. He would never manage the whole truth.

Lily, like the inspector, was following the clue in a different direction. "That's nonsense. She doesn't know what she's saying. You're bullying her . . ."

"We can check the broken shards for fingerprints," Pobjoy was saying. Instinct told him they were on to something, though he wasn't sure what. As the girl had said, her room was underneath the attic. She must have overheard an argument—a struggle—not knowing what it meant, not till it was too late, afraid to accuse someone close to her. "Who else had a key to the attic?"

"Nobody," Lily said. "My grandmother took the only key."

"There may have been a copy you didn't know about—in your husband's possession, for instance."

"You don't understand," Lily persisted. "Gran came to stay here when—when my husband moved out. She took the key then. It was unplanned. Dave couldn't have known she would do that—he had no idea he might need a copy made. If—if he had meant to hurt her, which he didn't."

"They didn't get along, did they?" said Pobjoy. Her argument had been garbled, but he took the point. Every time he thought a clue was leading him somewhere, the trail petered out. Beneath his surface inscrutability, he was beginning to be annoyed.

"Gran didn't get along with most people," Lily said. "She was— she could be a difficult person."

"*Why* did she take the attic key?" Pobjoy demanded. "What did she want to do there?"

Lily merely looked baffled, but he saw the sudden tension in Hazel's expression, behind the disorder of her hair.

"She liked her privacy," Lily said, though she didn't look convinced about it. "She wanted a place to be . . . alone."

"What do you think?" he asked Hazel.

Hazel achieved a gesture between a twitch and a shrug, which got the interrogation exactly nowhere.

"I know you're keeping something from me," Pobjoy said in what was, for him, a gentle manner. "Why did you write the letter? Did you want justice for your great-grandmother? Or revenge on her killer?"

Hazel was looking down at her hands. This time, she didn't even manage a gesture.

"Who are you protecting?"

He didn't expect an answer, but he got one, in the suddenly deep voice that she used when she was nervous or upset. "Nobody."

"Then why won't you tell me what you know?"

She lifted her head, pushing her hair aside, and for the first time she met his eyes. "You wouldn't believe me," she said.

ROWENA HAD employed Eric to do a few odd jobs for her in the shop in Chizzledown that week. He had never seen a screwdriver and thought a hammer was an antiquated religious symbol, but, as always, he learned fast, and his strength matched his size, making him invaluable when it came to heavy lifting. Two young men arriving with a vanload of furniture Rowena had bought at an auction found themselves effortlessly upstaged by a giant of a man who looked like a cross between a gypsy and a tramp, spoke bad English, and had to be at least twice their age (the actual arithmetic they would have found rather hard to take). But somehow, Rowena noticed, Eric always seemed to win friends. After much moving of furniture, and coffee and sandwiches, the youths evidently decided in favor of Eric's eccentricities. With Rowena, he spent his spare time scanning old books or poring over pictures of the cup. "Of course you cannot date," he explained. "*Sangreal* from my world. Time in my world different from yours. Stone different, too."

He's a little barmy, Rowena thought. *But it's an explanation—of sorts.* She knew nothing of particle physics, but everyone was aware that alternative universes were supposed to be a scientific fact. And there was his evident belief in magic as if it was a natural form of energy, like radiation or kinetics. All nonsense, of course: she knew it was nonsense, her father and grandfather would have known it was nonsense. But then, her father and grandfather would have thought the cell phone and the microchip nonsense, and she herself had always dismissed the legends surrounding the cup of the Thorns—until lately.

"We need to arrange for you to see the Grail," she told Eric, remembering Annie's reaction to the cup—or at least, what she assumed was a reaction to the cup. If he saw it, if he touched it, there might be a sign. She would *know*.

She called Julian Epstein, but the looming court case had made Sotheby's wary and unwilling to cut her any more slack.

On the Friday, Dieter Von Humboldt came into the shop again.

"Have some tea," said Rowena, allowing a trace of brisk friendliness to color her approach. "Been hoping for a chance to talk to you."

"So you have been thinking about my proposition?"

"Ran into that chap Birnbaum the other day. Seems determined to get his pound of flesh—or pound of something, anyway. Says he wants justice, not money. Think it was justice." She led him into the back room and offered him a chair.

"So," he said, "you want the cup, I want money, he wants justice. It will be interesting trying to work out a three-way split."

"That emotional stuff about the death of his family will go down well with the court," Rowena said, watching Von Humboldt narrowly. "I'm just the relic of an old family—outmoded class system and all that—you're the grandson of a Nazi. Sorry to be blunt, but there it is. He'll get the sympathy vote."

"I felt your rush into legal action was—a little hasty." She could sense he was pleased at what he thought of as her weakening, but he held back, waiting for her to put her cards on the table. Like all frank, matter-of-fact people who rarely choose to be devious, Rowena was very good at it when she did. She had no intention of showing her hand. Let him guess—and guess wrong.

"I was thinking of a meeting," she said. "Informal. Couple of witnesses but no lawyers. Got to have the right location. Birnbaum's impressed by the history of the cup, so let's use it. Family home's been sold years ago, but I know the chap who owns it. He'd let us meet there. Make Birnbaum feel he's trying to destroy a tradition. He won't want that. He's the romantic type."

"That would benefit you," Von Humboldt pointed out, "but not me."

"We'd have to deal on the side. He won't give an inch to you; he might to me."

"You are unscrupulous," the Austrian said. He sounded slightly shocked.

"The cup belongs to my family. I want something out of this."

"Something . . . I see. Yet you said all you wanted was the cup itself." Von Humboldt accepted a mug of tea, but didn't drink.

"As things stand, not much chance of that. Could have fought you in the courts, harder with Birnbaum. For him, we need to deal out of court."

"And with Birnbaum out of the way, you will return to legal means to fight me?"

She permitted herself a quick, tight grin. "Nice one. No: if we make a bargain, that's it. Not suggesting anything in a hurry, though. Just a meeting to start the ball rolling. Doesn't commit anyone to anything, does it? Wasn't that what you wanted?"

"As you say."

"One more thing: the Grail should be there."

"No." His tone was flat.

"Why the fuss? Have all the security you want. No one'll nick it—it's unsalable without provenance. That's why Sotheby's contacted me in the first place. Carbon-dating didn't work; if I say it's a fake you probably won't get a buyer. Not at the price you want, anyway. Need it there if we're going to meet. Atmosphere."

"Mrs. Thorn, *I* am not a romantic. You won't get around me like that." Von Humboldt was looking puzzled.

"Know that."

"Why then?"

"Told you. Atmosphere." She waited a minute, then affected to drop her guard. "Want to see it back where it belongs, just once. Then, if I have to let it go . . ." She shrugged.

He didn't entirely believe her, but she knew he was curious—and he didn't want to wait for slow legal machinery to grind into action.

"I'll discuss the matter with Sotheby's," he said.

FOR NATHAN, the advent of summer vacation didn't bring the usual feeling of unalloyed bliss. Instead, there was relief, because the distraction of school was removed and he could focus on other matters, a faintly uncomfortable fizz of excitement, and the leading edge of fear. He put out tracksuit bottoms and a sweatshirt to sleep in—he was fed up with universe-hopping in pajamas—anointed himself with Bartlemy's herbal mixture, and proceeded to sleep without dreams, or at least none of any significance.

Saturday was spent with Hazel and George, who were, as always, deeply envious of his early release. "How come people who pay for education get less of it?" George wanted to know.

"Mum doesn't pay. I'm on a scholarship."

"You know what I mean."

That evening Annie said she had to go and see Bartlemy for a couple of hours. "Will you be all right on your own?"

" 'Course. Anyhow, Hazel will stay. She's been grilled by the cops: she needs lots of moral support."

"Are you okay?" Annie asked her.

Hazel nodded. She'd told Nathan about writing the letter, but no one else.

"I'll put a pizza in the oven. Mushroom and mozzarella or pepperoni?"

They opted for pepperoni. "What're you going to see Uncle Barty about?" Nathan asked. It was unusual for her to go without inviting him.

"Private talk," Annie said. Bartlemy had been emphatic that she should come alone. "Grown-up stuff." And, mentally crossing her fingers: "Probably about money."

Nathan said nothing, but he didn't believe her.

Annie arrived at Thornyhill to find Bartlemy alone; Eric had gone to have supper with Rowena Thorn. "She's up to something," Bartlemy said, taking Annie into the kitchen. "Apparently, she's trying to persuade the owner to allow the Grail to be brought here for a couple of days. She wants Eric to get a look at it. She seems to have taken quite a shine to him."

"Everyone does," Annie said with a smile. "Perhaps she believes he really *does* come from another world."

"Perhaps." Because she was walking, not driving, he presented her with a glass of elderflower champagne that packed the punch of vintage Krug. "I'm afraid we're not eating till later. I have a little research I want to do first, and I need you with me, in case there's anyone—or any*thing*—you recognize."

"What sort of research? And why all the secrecy?"

"You'll see."

In the drawing room he had pushed back the furniture and rolled up the Oriental rugs. The curtains were drawn, shutting out the long, light evening. "I would prefer to wait for dark," he said, "but it would make us very late." He crouched down by the fireplace, striking a match; Annie thought what was on the hearth wasn't coal. The lumps appeared to be pallid and angular, like chunks of crystal. Presently, they began to burn with a bluish flame that looked wan in the veiled daylight.

"What are you doing?" she asked him, and there was a note of fear or doubt in her voice.

"Something I haven't done in a long, long while. I was never very good at it; my heart wasn't in it, as they say. But I had the Gift, so I was taught all the tricks of the trade. I rarely use them. Cooking has always been magic enough for me." Hoover padded at his side as he began to sprinkle powder from a flask around the perimeter of a wide circle. A mark on the floor, faint as a shadow, indicated that this had been done before.

Annie said: "Is this—magic?"

"Oh yes. One of the oldest spells. Quite powerful, really, but don't worry. As long as the boundary is correctly sealed nothing can leave the circle." Still using the powder, he drew four strange runes beyond the rim. When not talking to her, he murmured something under his breath, words she couldn't hear properly or, hearing, couldn't understand. "I'll do the talking. You can sit here. It's best if you stay in the chair. On no account try to cross the perimeter."

Annie sat down, clutching her glass. "Are you—are you going to call up the dead?"

"Good Lord, no. Waste of time, in most cases. Spirits who have passed the Gate cannot return. Of course, some don't, and the re-cently deceased often hang around for a bit—unfinished business and all that. I suppose we could try . . . well, we'll see. In due course."

"Can you summon people from another world?"

"No. That would take unimaginable power. The circle is just for this world. It's a way of getting in touch with spirits who don't usually talk to Man. Or people who don't want to. Once called to the circle, you see, they have to answer your questions truthfully. At least, that's the theory of it. They have to say something, anyway. And even lies and distortions can be informative, if you read them right. Personally, I don't know that it will be useful and I don't really like doing it, but we need all the information we can get." Suddenly, he turned to her with his most calming smile. "Don't be upset by anything you see. Or hear. Spirits are a lot like people: they like to talk big and act tough. And they resent being summoned, of course. It's rather like the genie of the lamp, you know. You rub, he has to appear. I've often thought he must have been regularly annoyed about that."

"I never saw it that way," Annie murmured.

He postioned himself at the circle's edge, one hand on Hoover's head. She had the feeling the dog, too, had been here before. Bartlemy spoke a single word—she thought it was *"Fiumé!"*—and a spark ran around the perimeter, igniting the powder to a flame that flared and sank. Then both the runes and the boundary burned with a barely visible flicker. In darkness the effect would have been far more dramatic, but for Annie it was the banality of it—the fact that darkness and drama were not essential—that she found deeply disturbing. This was a spell, it was potent, it was *real*, perhaps even dangerous—and yet it was also ordinary. As much a part of Bartlemy's routine as preparing a complex dish he hadn't tried for a while, with ingredients that might have gone off in the interim.

Hoover sat down looking unusually alert, both ears cocked. Bartlemy started to speak in an unfamiliar language, a language that sounded cold and strange even in his soft voice, changing it, changing *him*. At the heart of the circle there was a thickening in the air—a mistiness—a blur. Then a shape. A woman—a woman who looked pale and insubstantial, as if drifting in and out of reality. She seemed to be seated—there was a suggestion of chair beneath her—and held something in her hands as if it was very precious, something small and round. She was all monochrome save for a red veil that covered her face.

"Greeting, Ragnlech," Bartlemy said politely, in English. "You are welcome."

"What do you seek of us?" The voice from behind the veil was faint as the wind sighing far off, and full of echoes.

"Knowledge. A seeress sees many things, both present and past. I need to know what the sisterhood have seen."

The woman lifted the veil. Her face looked curiously unstable, sometimes young and unlined, sometimes withered with years. The skull gleamed through the dim covering of her flesh. Her eye sockets were empty. When she raised her hands, holding the little ball, Annie closed her own eyes for a second.

Only for a second. Now the Eye was in place, in the left-hand socket. It looked far more solid than the face around it, glowing as if lit from within, fixing some point beyond the circle with a monstrous stare.

"What would you have us see?" asked the seeress.

"The vessel called the Grimthorn Grail. I would know how it came into the world, and for what purpose. Also something of its making, if possible."

"Its making is hidden from us, and its purpose. One Josevius Grimthorn brought it here, more than thirteen hundred years ago, from another place. A place outside the dimensions of this world. How he did this we cannot tell. There was great magic involved, but it is unfamiliar to us."

"If not its purpose, can you tell me of its power?"

"Its aura is very bright." The Eye shone brilliantly for an instant, then Ragnlech blinked once, and a tear ran down the shadow of her face. It looked like blood. "It hurts us. We cannot look at it. Its power is great. It can wipe the memory of those who should not see it, or bind the tongue. It has protectors, beings—entities—not of this world. They are invisible here, or nearly so. They speak words without thought, make footsteps without feet. They were sent with the cup."

"Sent . . . Who sent them?"

"We cannot see. There are spells here . . . beyond our ken. It is perilous for us to pierce the shield. We will not do it."

"I wouldn't ask you to put yourself in peril. Ragnlech . . ."

But the woman had already faded from view.

"I could recall her," Bartlemy said, half to himself. "However . . . This is obviously a matter beyond the vision of the seers. It's probably useless, but we'll try elsewhere." He reverted to the alien language, the words hissing on the air like a music of knife blades.

Another figure materialized in the circle, a man, very tall and all but naked, far more solid than the seeress. His body appeared to be made of braided muscle; antlers sprang from the thick snarl of his hair. His face was all long bones and savagery, the way a stag might look if it were predatory and human enough to be psychopathic.

"What is the word in the Wood, wild one?" Bartlemy asked.

"The Wood is shrinking. There is no word anymore." The great head tossed, stag-like. "Why do you call me?"

"There is a matter noised abroad—a little matter or great, I know not. It is called the Grimthorn Grail. I thought *you* might know more."

"The Wood here keeps its secrets, even from me," the man said sharply. "But I heard something—or dreamed something. It is all the same. I heard of a world where trees dominate, and a stag can run all day without crossing a path or scenting a hunter. A world without men. The Grail opens the Gate to that world, or so they say. Maybe to all worlds. But I would not meddle with it. It is protected."

"By whom?"

"If I knew that, I would be less prudent. But you cannot challenge the foe you cannot see. That is a foolishness I leave to Man."

"There is much in what you say," sighed Bartlemy.

The antlered man faded, to be replaced by an old crone who was, Annie thought in mingled pity and horror, the ugliest creature she had ever seen. She was half bald, and a single tooth protruded like a tusk over the lipless verge of her mouth. Her eyes were screwed so tightly they were almost shut; her voice emerged in a mumble. Bartlemy looked at her for a long moment and then dismissed her unquestioned.

"That one has grown too old and sleepy to know anything anymore. Soon, I think, she will fall into the ultimate slumber, and nothing will wake her. Once she was powerful indeed; she was Hexaté, the queen of midnight and sacrifice. But she drank too deep of whatever it was they were drinking—some potion, or raw wine, or blood—and now her brain has rotted. I wish I could say it was a tragedy. Ah well . . ."

He began another conjuration. As he spoke, Annie thought she heard a noise from behind her, a quiet *snick* like the lifting of the latch on the door. She saw Hoover, too, prick up his ears. When they turned, the door to the kitchen was open, but she wasn't sure it had ever been closed—Bartlemy didn't normally close it—and anyway, doors in Thornyhill, like in many old houses, tended to open and shut of their own free will, nudged by a draft or a shifting of ancient joists. Certainly there was no one there that she could see. Hoover stared for a minute, ears twitching, then he turned his attention back to the ritual.

At the hub of the circle a slight form developed slowly. It had fair curls of the shade usually called flaxen—though Annie wasn't sure what color flax was really meant to be—a slender, androgynous body, and a pale, heart-shaped face with a faintly wistful mouth. It troubled Annie that although she decided the child looked about ten, she couldn't make up her mind about its sex. She compromised by thinking of it as *he* without actually concluding it was a boy. It seemed to be the epitome of innocence and purity—until she saw its eyes.

Its eyes were old.

"Eriost," said Bartlemy. "Greeting."

"*You* were never one for these games," the child remarked. "What changes?"

"Not you," said Bartlemy. "Werefolk do not change."

"I am not werefolk! I am a spirit, ancient and powerful, prominent in the hierarchy. What do you want of me, fat one?"

"News of the cup called the Sangreal, or Grimthorn Grail. What do you know of its power or its purpose?"

"It is a pretty toy," the child said. "Everyone wants it. They say it comes from another world and can open the Gate itself. Maybe that's true, maybe it isn't. But *everyone* wants to find out."

"It's been around for centuries," Bartlemy said thoughtfully. "Why all the interest *now*?"

"Its time is coming," said the child. "Whenever that is. Nobody knows exactly, but they can *feel*. There is a shifting in the pattern, a coming-together of things. It will be soon."

"How soon?"

"There will be signs and portents. There always are." The child laughed, a laugh like a chime of silver bells. "The mouse runs."

"The mouse—?"

The child began to sing in a clear, choirboy voice that was also somehow mocking:

Hickory dickory dock
the mouse runs up the clock
the clock strikes ONE—
the mouse is gone—
hickory . . . dickory . . . DOCK!

"Very doom-laden," Bartlemy said politely. "You seem to be well informed. Truly has it been said: *There is a chiel amang ye takin' notes.* The other Old Ones knew far less—or are not telling. Perhaps you have heard something of a certain water spirit who is also taking an interest in these affairs."

"A water spirit?" With one of the quick-change moods of childhood, the small face grew suddenly serious. "There are no spirits in the waters anymore. The last mermaid died long ago. They hung her bier with weed, and closed her eyes with shells, and the crabs she used to hunt had their revenge on her. Still, they say that in the deepest, darkest places, far from the reach of Man . . ."

"The river here is neither deep nor dark," said Bartlemy. "But something stirs in the water."

The child was silent a moment, then began to chant:

"Cloud on the sunset
wave on the tide
fish from the deep sea
swim up the Glyde.

Reed in the river pool
weed in the stream
one there a-sleeping
too deep to dream.

Eyes in the mirror
dark as the room;
eyes in the water
deep as the tomb.

Feet tread the river
hands pluck the tide;

death from the deep sea
swims up the Glyde.

Bartlemy pondered for a few seconds. Then he asked: "Do you know its name?"

"Maybe—maybe not. Maybe it has no name. What need for names, in the dark of the ocean?"

"Nonetheless, it has come out of the dark," Bartlemy said. "It would not have done so unless it had been called, and to be called there must be a name."

But the child had lost interest, as children do, switching from unnatural maturity to distorted juvenilia. It began to sing a slightly lewd version of some nursery doggerel.

Sing a song of sixpence
a pocket full of rye,
go and catch a maidenhead
to bake in a pie.

When the pie is opened
the head begins to bleed.
Isn't that a dainty dish
where somebody can feed?

The horrible verse restarted, the tone at once gleeful and derisive, then gradually faded out as Bartlemy murmured a dismissal. The child became a wisp of fog from which eyes gleamed briefly; then it vanished.

Annie said: "What was that?"

"A spirit. Don't judge by appearances: it's very old, not wise perhaps but *knowing*. It has told us a good deal—if it spoke the truth. Your water spirit comes from the sea, probably from the depths of the ocean. Things have hung on there, in the dark where men cannot go. Humanity has overrun the planet—some spirits adapt, and batten on mortal weakness, on superstition and greed and despair. Others retreat to the wild, lonely places and hide there, in the heart of desert or jungle. And there is no place wilder and lonelier than the deeps of the sea. They say the Great Sea Serpent still sleeps there, its coils wound so tight around the world they have carved the Marianas trench. There are squid larger than ships, and strange creatures left over from the age of dinosaurs, and the lost lair of the Kraken. Also a few gods and goddesses of the ancient world whose worship has long been abandoned. I could call one or two, if the circle would hold, and they have not forgotten who they once were. As it is, you cannot call a spirit without a name."

"You want to summon that—thing—here?" Annie said.

"We ought to see it. That's why I asked you to attend this conjuration. I need you to identify what we see." He gave her the familiar smile of reassurance, though in this case she was not much reassured. "*Know your enemy,* the saying goes. Don't be afraid. The circle will contain it."

"But you said you can't summon it without using its name?" Annie said hopefully.

"That's the rule. So I shall have to do what all wizards do at such times."

"What's that?"

"Cheat."

He resumed the incantation, but this time she heard a name she recognized. *Rianna. Rianna Sardou.*

"It is a name this spirit has worn and maybe still wears," said Bartlemy. "It cannot lightly be cast off. When it comes—if it comes—don't speak. Watch."

It came. In the circle the mist congealed, becoming a wavering column not unlike the one Annie had seen rising from the river. In the same way it gradually assumed a form and face, like and unlike Rianna. Its hair streamed as weed in the current, and its long robe rippled ceaselessly in many folds, and the ground beneath it seemed to move like water.

It said: "I told you I will decide when to contact you. I must not be called like this. And don't use the woman's name. It forces me into her image." The voice was Rianna's, but there was an echo behind it of something else.

"Which name would you have me use?" Bartlemy inquired softly.

Annie thought the spirit couldn't see clearly beyond the perimeter, but evidently it could hear.

"Who are you?"

"One who called you."

"You have no right! I am not to be called by any stray wizard who can draw a circle! Release me!"

Bartlemy persisted, ignoring its anger. "What is your interest in the boy Nathan?"

"You cannot question me!"

"What do you know of the Grimthorn Grail?"

"What do *you* know? The Grail is the lock; the boy—may be the key. The Gate can be opened. We thought it was shut forever, save to the mortal dead, but it *can* be opened. You are another, aren't you? Another petty human who calls yourself Gifted, grasping at the chance of power. You don't know what power means. Let me but open the Gate, and I will show you power. Do you know how strong I am, even now? Your little circle cannot hold *me*—" It flung back its head, raising its arms, dissolving into water that fountained upward like a geyser, smashing against the ceiling, spraying the room. Annie's scream was cut off as a vicious jet caught her full in the face.

Bartlemy spoke a single word, not loud but very clear, unmistakably a Command. His hand thrust outward in a gesture of repudiation. The water jet shrank back into a fluid pillar that dwindled, bubbled, and was gone. Outside the perimeter, steam rose from sodden floor and furniture, clothing and hair, and streamed back into the circle, vanishing in upon itself as if swallowed by the air. Annie was panting for breath. Hoover started to shake himself, but his fur was already dry.

"Well," said Bartlemy, "I think that will do for tonight. A little more action than I had expected. Was that the spirit you saw?"

"Yes. It thought you were someone else, didn't it? To begin with, anyway. So . . . someone else has summoned it?"

"That I already suspected. The question is who." While he talked, Bartlemy stretched out his hand, palm downward. The flickering circle was extinguished. The room went very dark, and Annie realized night had fallen, unnoticed, beyond the curtained windows. Bartlemy switched on the lights and began to mop up the residual powder.

"Effie Carlow?" Annie asked.

"Possibly."

"Except that she's dead, and the child hinted that the water spirit drowned her, but it still thought *someone* was calling it."

"Exactly."

Bartlemy took a bottle from a cupboard and poured a little of the contents into a glass. It was of a red so dark it was black, and it smelled strongly of fruit, and even more strongly of alcohol. He handed it to Annie, who sipped cautiously. Unaccustomed color flooded her cheeks. "In a minute we'll have something to eat, then I'll call a taxi to take you home."

Much later, when she had gone, he sat in an armchair by candlelight—he liked candlelight, it was restful—gazing through the curtains, now half open, catching a glimmer of the wandering moon.

"It responded to the name of Rianna Sardou," he remarked, probably to Hoover, since no one else was listening. "But Rianna herself should be the first to answer to her name. Unless she cannot . . ."

Sturm und Drang

Nathan pulled the back door closed behind them but didn't run the risk of dropping the latch: the sound it made was too distinctive, even among a host of other noises. The latch on the drawing room door had almost been a risk too far. And then they had lurked in the kitchen, peering out only when Bartlemy and Annie were sufficiently engrossed not to notice. Hoover, loyally, hadn't barked or even thumped his tail. Now they crept through the garden and into the woods, too stunned by what they had seen to be wary of the darkness or any potential danger. When they reached the road, the shadows slunk after them, but they were carrying their modern talismans of iron and the ripple in the night was content merely to follow.

"He's a wizard," Hazel said when they were some distance from the house. "A real wizard. Your uncle Barty. Or maybe a warlock."

"He can't be a warlock. He's too fat. Whoever heard of a fat warlock?"

"He's a w-wizard," Hazel repeated, her tongue falling over the words as if they constituted a verbal obstacle race.

"Your great-grandmother was a witch," Nathan pointed out.

"Yes, but . . . not like that. Just charms, and whispered curses; small-time stuff. Not like *that* . . ."

"Anyhow, you don't believe in magic."

"Do I have a choice?" Hazel muttered.

They walked on for a while without speaking. Behind them, the shadows played at grandmother's footsteps on the empty road, falling silent when Nathan looked back. "*They're* there," he said. "The gnomons." They felt the fear reaching out to them, but it could not take hold on their minds: they had too many other things to trouble them. They walked a little faster; that was all.

When they were clear of the trees Hazel said: "What was all that about Michael's wife, and your mum recognizing that spirit thing?" She still didn't want to discuss her own encounter with the head in the basin.

"Mum's not telling me everything," Nathan said, disquieted. But then, he wasn't telling her everything, either.

"They never do," Hazel said wisely. "My mum never tells me *anything*."

"Your mum hasn't been running into malignant water demons," Nathan retorted.

"She might of. I told you, she never tells me—"

But Nathan wasn't attending. "*Why* didn't she tell me? Does she still think I need protecting? I can look after myself in *other worlds* . . ."

"That's why you've got that weird sunburn," Hazel remarked dampingly.

"All right—I make mistakes. To tell you the truth, the whole business scares the life out of me. But there's no point in anyone trying to protect me 'cos they can't. I've gone beyond that. She should at least trust me."

Hazel didn't know what to say to that, but Nathan didn't seem to require an answer: he was too busy brooding. They had walked some distance farther when she said, abruptly: "What's that?"

"What's what?"

"That."

The wood had finished but they were still a fair way from the first houses. There was a sudden scuffling in the hedgerow, a shaking of grasses, a twitching of briars. Something was in there, hidden by the leaf tangle and the matted stems. Something bigger than a gnomon and far more solid. The grasses parted: for an instant, a face peeped out, barely visible in the darkness; but they knew who it must be.

"The prisoner!" Hazel hissed in a savage whisper. "He's spying on us."

"He's spying on *someone*," Nathan amended. He moved toward the hedgerow with a purposeful air, though he himself had no idea what his purpose might be. The face vanished. The leaf tangle quivered once, and was still.

Nathan said, "That's got rid of that," as if he had merely been intent on frightening the creature, but privately he was worried. It should have run, not stayed in the vicinity of its long imprisonment, watching people it didn't even know. And . . . why had it been imprisoned, and by whom? For that matter, when? No answers were likely to materialize in the near future, and he turned back to Hazel, eager now to get home, suddenly hungry. It seemed a long time since the pizza they had eaten earlier.

Hazel went back to her own home late, and Annie returned even later, when Nathan was in bed with a book. They said good night, but nothing more. Annie was very tired but lay sleepless for a long while, going over the events of the evening in her mind. Nathan tumbled immediately into oblivion, plagued by the more normal kind of dream, waking periodically in the small, dark hours as though his subconscious mind needed to check on him, afraid of where he might go.

THE FOLLOWING week the inquest on Effie Carlow finally took place, bringing in a verdict of Accidental Death, and Inspector Pobjoy was assigned to another case.

"I know you're keen on this business of the old lady," said the assistant chief constable, "but from the sound of it you're never going to be able to prove anything, even if her relatives *did* give her a push. If we managed to get a conviction on circumstantial evidence, some clever lawyer would come along and overturn it ten minutes later."

"The girl knows more than she's saying," Pobjoy insisted. "She hinted Mrs. Carlow was killed in the attic and dumped in the river later. If I had a forensic team to go over the place with a fine-tooth comb . . ."

"Sorry. We can't spare any more resources on this one. The robbery at Haverleigh Hall is a bigger priority. They took half a million in Georgian silver and antique jewelry, and a load of paintings including a Constable and a dubious Titian. Probably a commission, and from the way they knocked out the alarm system they're very professional."

"Sir Richard Wykeham, isn't it?" said Pobjoy. "Knighted two years ago for services to the country—that is, getting very rich. Arms, wasn't it?"

"I see you've already done your homework," the ACC said drily. "Wykeham's an important man. I personally don't like him—don't know anyone who does—but he has a lot of influence. With a capital *I*."

"Which makes him much *more* important than some nameless old lady from an obscure village who had nothing," Pobjoy commented.

"You know the realities," the ACC said. "It's not as though

you're getting anywhere. Even if you get a statement out of the girl pointing the finger at one of her parents, the evidence of minors never holds up well in court. Look at the Damilola Taylor cock-up. And I can't really see any kid being prepared to convict her mum or dad."

Pobjoy nearly said *Your boys not yet in their teens, sir?* but refrained.

"Get onto the Haverleigh Hall case," the ACC concluded. "We won't get Sir Richard's stuff back for him but at least we can nab the boys who did it, preferably before they clean out anyone else. Yes, I know you want to stick with your potential murder but you'll have to drop it. Money talks, we both know that."

"Does its evidence stand up in court?" Pobjoy inquired.

"Oh yes," sighed the ACC. "Usually in a wig and gown."

Since Hazel and George hadn't gotten out of school yet, the beginning of vacation found Nathan left much to his own devices. He caught the bus into Chizzledown and went to see Eric, who was still working for Rowena Thorn. They walked to the foot of the down that gave the village its name and picnicked on sandwiches provided by Annie. On the slope above them was a huge symbol carved into the chalk, less famous than the horses and giants seen elsewhere since it was simply a pattern and no one knew what it was meant to be. It consisted of a line bisected by an arc and set within a circle. "In my world," Eric said unexpectedly, "is ancient symbol of great magic."

"What does it mean?" Nathan demanded excitedly.

Eric achieved one of his magnificent shrugs. "Who knows? Is deep mystery."

Nathan's brief excitement waned. "It could be a coincidence," he said. What with *Star Wars*, and the force, and the spellpower of poetry, he felt that almost everything meant something special to Eric.

"What is—coincidence?" the exile asked.

When that had been explained, with difficulty and at length, Nathan told him about his latest dream: the cave, the desert, the monster, the unsuccessful tomb raiders, and the wild xaurians. Eric was both enthused and disturbed. "Is right place," he decided. "Must be. *Sangreal*, sword, crown hide there. You not see?"

"It was pitch dark in the cave," Nathan said. "I couldn't see anything. Do you know who the raiders were?"

Eric hesitated. "Maybe just thieves," he said at last. "But—maybe not. There is group—you would say, revolters?—they say Grandir do nothing to save us, let all die except few who are chosen, keep spell of first Grandir till end. Revolters might try to steal treasures, to do spell."

Nathan said: "Could they?"

"No. Nobody can do spell. Secret is lost. But maybe they guess. Is illegal, but I think many try, if they have opportunity."

Nathan mmed an affirmation. "What have they got to lose?"

"Law is strict," Eric offered. "Many put in prison."

Nathan gave him another sandwich, and they moved on to the subject of the xaurians. "Their skin very tough," Eric explained. "Protect against sundeath. Also special lid over eye, always closed but—invisible . . ."

"Transparent?" Nathan deduced.

"They see through it. *Transparent*. I will remember." He always did, Nathan noticed. Any new word had to be committed to memory only once. "Long ago, men catch wild xaurians, change genes, make them bigger, stronger, but to obey. Some wild ones still there, though many die. Not lots of animals for them to hunt now."

"Why would the wild ones help men?" Nathan asked.

"Very intelligent," Eric suggested doubtfully. "Like dolphin here."

Nathan wondered how he had heard about dolphins. "Is helping men a sign of intelligence?" he said. Of course, dolphins had been known to rescue drowning sailors, so maybe it was a good analogy.

They finished their lunch, and he made his way back to Eade. In the shop he found Michael, who asked him if he would like to come out on the boat one day—"Yes, *please!*"—and then left him to his mother's company. "What were you and Uncle Barty up to last night?" Nathan inquired, as innocently as he could manage. He didn't want to deceive her; nor did he want her to deceive him. He had felt guilty about sneaking out to spy on her the previous evening, but with the dreams increasingly taking over his life he thought he needed to know everything—especially those things adults didn't want him to know.

"Just supper," Annie said, equally ill at ease with deceit. "Talk."

"About me?"

"No." After all, that was mostly true. "You are not the only subject of discussion in my life, you know. We talked of—money matters. The running of the shop. That sort of thing."

"You've never had private meetings about that before," said Nathan.

"I expect we did. You just didn't notice."

She isn't going to tell me, he thought. *I need to know—but she won't tell. Should I say I was there?*

I wonder if I ought to tell him? Annie agonized. *He's involved in all this. But he's so young, so young . . . I want to keep him out, keep him safe, at least until he's older. The more he knows, the more he'll want to know—until in the end he'll ask about his father . . .*

She said nothing.

So did he.

That night, he knew he would dream. Not the idle dreams of the roving mind but the dreams of the soul, dreams of the other world. This time, he was aware of things before the dream started—of a stomach-churning sensation of falling, plunging into a tunnel of black whirling space. Clouds of dark matter spun around him, stars that seemed tiny (but somehow he knew they were huge) streamed past, shattering into firedust on the invisible shoals of Time. Every so often planets heaved into his orbit, bellying with oceans and continents, wreathed in weather systems. When he emerged from the tunnel there was a blinding light, a vast sun outdazzling the lesser stars. He shut his eyes. Then he was on solid ground, and he opened them to find himself staring at the rim of a desktop. The Grandir's desk in the semicircular office. He was crouching behind it, conspicuously solid, while a few feet away the Grandir stood with his back to him, receiving a report from a figure in hologram.

The holocast (he was sure that was the correct term) wore a curious flat-topped headdress, and its black mask had bubbles of yellow glass over the eye slits, giving it a slightly evil look. Its coverall outfit was also black, of some sleek, glossy material rather like leather, with padded gauntlets banded with metal on the knuckles and what might have been a weapon strapped to the shoulder. Its stance was rigid, clearly military.

"He came originally from Ingorut," the holocast was saying. "He gives his name as Derzhin Zamork, which checks out on the computer, but our records were scrambled after that last piece of sabotage and the genoprint could be faked. Since the continent was cut off, we have no way of checking."

"It doesn't matter," said the Grandir. "His name is not important. He is a neo-salvationist: that's all we need to know. What information has he given you about the organization?"

"Not much, sir. These people work in cells, virtually isolated from other operatives, to protect the group in this very eventuality. He doesn't even know who supplied him with data and gave him orders."

"Standard procedure." The tone was indifferent. "I would have done it that way myself, when I was young and imaginative. These people are moderately intelligent. Did you find the implant?"

There was a pause—a hesitation—as if the holocast had been taken by surprise. "I—yes, sir. It was on the spinal cord, at the base of the skull. But . . ."

The Grandir didn't repeat the *but*. He merely waited.

"We are unable to process it. Sir. It has been designed to activate only when surrounded by living tissue—his tissue. If we had a telepathic scanner—"

"We do not. Such equipment is rare, as you well know. The last one was on Quorus: it was lost when the planet was cut off. What dosage of truth serum have you been using?"

"Up to point seven, sir. His body seems to have a natural resistance, possibly induced by an activating spell." This time the pause stretched out much longer. "Would you like to interrogate him yourself, sir?"

"No. What about the woman?"

"She has been—more difficult. Her resistance level is even higher, and there are the same problems with an implant. She wouldn't even tell us her name, though we were able to obtain that from Zamork. He calls her Kwanji Ley. He says she was trained as a third-level practor."

"That explains much. She could have learned the location of the cave by magic. The knowledge is shielded, but such spells can be unraveled. Very well. No further questioning is needed. They have been careful to know nothing of their manipulators. Place them in Deep Confinement."

"For how long?" asked the holocast.

"Indefinitely."

It's the two I saw in the desert, Nathan thought. *That's who they're talking about. They escaped the monster but were arrested back in Arkatron.*

The holocast was fading and he closed his eyes, willing himself to accompany it, focusing on his memory of the two raiders. For a few moments—which seemed interminable—nothing happened. He heard the footsteps of the Grandir moving away, and opened his eyes again to see the ruler standing by the window, gazing out of the gap between two screens. *In a second he'll turn around,* Nathan thought. *He'll come back to the desk. There's no other cover here and I can't get out. He'll find me* . . .

Darkness took him so swiftly he wasn't aware of it. Yet once again the emerging was slow, though without the cosmic effects. He was struggling against a muffling blanket of oblivion, fighting for consciousness, for sensation, for self. Every time he thought he was waking another layer of sleep would engulf him, pressing him down into the abyss. At last after a final effort he broke through the veil, thin as a shadow, and found himself in the light.

Not the dazzling light of the Eosian sun but a soft pallor that seemed at first to have no source, no boundaries, no form. Gradually, his surroundings acquired definition, and he saw he was in a cylindrical room without windows or doors, the curving walls and circular floor all of a matte, creamy white smoothness. The height of the chamber was more than twice its diameter, and the ceiling appeared to be made of opaque glass, with a broad pillar depending from the center, glossy as marble, and black. He was sitting with his back to it. He heard a voice somewhere behind him, the voice of the yellow-eyed holocast. "You are now in Deep Confinement, in Pit S00437C. The period of your incarceration has not been determined. That is all."

There was the sound of a step, the faint *swoosh* of a sliding door.

The pillar lifted off the floor and retreated upward, vanishing through an aperture in the glass ceiling, which then closed. Nathan turned around.

The woman was there, leaning against the wall, one leg bent, the other stretched out in front of her. His first thought was how relaxed she looked. She had risked mortal danger to obtain the secrets of the cave, had failed and all but died, and now she was thrown into prison for an unspecified term—yet she looked at peace, or at least at ease. It was warm in the Pit and her sleeveless, coat-like garment hung open; she wore nothing else. Her body was lean and very muscular for a woman, and it did not seem to curve in and out like the women of his own world: her hips, as far as he could judge, were very straight, and her breasts barely swelled from her chest. She could see him—in that space, there was nowhere to hide—but she appeared untroubled by either his presence or her own near nakedness. Her face was not beautiful, he was sure, even by the standards of Eos: it was all curves and angles, lines and bones, with a purple luster in the eyes that reminded him of Eric, only his were far lighter, the color of amethyst. It was a face that seemed to be designed for quickness of expression, for eagerness and fire, but now her inward dial was set for repose, and she studied him without a flicker of curiosity or a flutter of emotion.

She said: "I thought I would be alone here. I was told, you are always alone in the Pits. Forever alone: wasn't that the idea? Are you an illusion they have sent me—a holocast—or the result of that last injection?"

"No one sent me," he said. "I'm real. At least, I think I am. I'm real in my world; I might not be real here."

She didn't try to make sense of this. He realized later, thinking of what she must have endured, that she was beyond sense: the most she could manage was calm. She was determined to have no hope, no fear, no weakness that her jailers could take hold of.

"You are very small," she said presently.

"I'm thirteen. I haven't finished growing."

There was a long, long pause.

"You're a child? I thought—there were no more children. I have never seen a child. Why did they send you to me?"

"I told you, no one sent me," he reiterated. This was his first conversation with anyone in his dreams, he thought, and she didn't believe in him. Well, that was fair enough. "I dreamed myself here. It's something I can do; I don't know how or why. I come from another world."

"All the worlds are gone," she said. *"Unvarhu-sag."*

"No: I mean, another universe. Beyond the Gate." He didn't know if this concept would have any meaning for her. "I saw you in the desert, when you escaped the lizard-monster. I was watching from the cave. What did you go to find there? Was it the Sangreal?"

"Questions," she sighed. "I knew there would be questions. For an illusion, you know, you really are very good. The fine detail is quite perfect. I can't imagine you'll tell me how they do it?"

"Nobody did it," he persisted. "I was just born, the normal way: I was born and I grew. Please try to believe me. Look, the cup isn't in the cave: that's a blind. It's in my world. Someone put it there, probably for safekeeping, though we're not sure. Why were you after it? If you'd managed to get it, what would you have done with it? If the cup *is* part of a spell to save your world, we need to know how it works. Please—"

She didn't answer. Her mouth was very serious, a somber line, but the trace of a smile lifted the corners. "If you are real," she said, "show me. Touch me."

He hadn't thought of that, and it was so simple. He came over to her, reached his hand out toward hers. "May I?" It seemed important to ask, in this world of masks and coveralls, where he had never seen people touch one another. Eric, he recalled, was always diffident about physical contact.

Kwanji Ley nodded.

He laid his hand over hers. There was a quiver in her fingers—he felt it—like an electrical response. She said: "They cannot do this." And then: "They have scrambled my mind. It must be a spell. The Grandir is very powerful—more powerful than we had guessed. I have protection, but it isn't strong enough. *I* am not strong enough . . ." Her voice failed, dwindling to something close to a whisper, terrible in one formerly so composed. He didn't know if she was talking to herself or to him.

"You *are* strong," he told her, terrified at what he had done. "I can see that. You're very strong. There's really nothing wrong with you: it's me. I'm—I don't know, a freak I suppose. I dream, and I'm here. At first, I was just thought, invisible, but now I get more solid all the time. Please tell me about the cup. I'll wake up soon, and then I'll be gone, so—"

"If you're real," she said, "you can't possibly go. We're in Deep Confinement. There is no way out. Nobody has ever escaped from the Pits."

"You still don't understand. For me, this is a dream. I'll just— vanish . . ."

Suddenly, Kwanji seized his arm—her other hand brushed over his face, exploring his features like a blind woman. "You feel too solid to vanish," she said, "or my touch lies. You are no werecreature: your eyes are human. Magic cannot do this. Who is controlling you?"

"*No one.*" He was vehement, desperate. He could feel the darkness rushing toward him, tingling in his feet, rising in his mind. At any moment it would reclaim him.

"I think you believe it," she said. "They have fooled you, too. There is *always* someone in control . . ."

And then it was over. He had a last vision of her face, lips parting in astonishment, before it faded—broke up—and he was wrenched away, out of light, out of thought, out of that whole world . . .

He woke in his bed at home, cold with sweat, starting up to see the beginning of dawn lightening the curtains. He was saying her name—*Kwanji*—urging, pleading with the empty room.

"THE GRAIL is coming home," Bartlemy said. "On Saturday, to be precise. I gather our friend Julian Epstein is not happy. It will be transported in a sealed van, with guards—"

"Armed?" Nathan asked eagerly. They were sitting in the bookshop, Bartlemy and Annie on the available chairs, Nathan on the edge of the table.

"I really don't know," Bartlemy admitted. "They're bringing it to Thornyhill, where the—er—principal disputants will gather. Rowena Thorn, the Graf Von Humboldt, and Alex Birnbaum. Also myself and Eric."

"We should be there," Nathan said. "We're as involved as they are."

"Yes, but they don't know that, and I have no intention of attempting to tell them," Bartlemy said reasonably.

"Why is Von Humboldt doing this?" Annie asked. "What does he hope to gain?"

"There are wheels within wheels," Bartlemy explained. "Rowena, I infer, has convinced him that under these conditions she can persuade Birnbaum to waive his claim. He has a great respect for the cup's historical background, the Luck of the Thorns and so on. If he thinks he is ceding it to Rowena, he will be prepared to back down."

"It's true," Annie said. "He might."

"You've seen more of him than we have. Anyway, Von Humboldt believes it's worth a try. Rowena has allowed him to think that once Birnbaum is out of the running she will countenance a sale and a division of the spoils. He wants to avoid a long, messy, and expensive court case at any price."

"That's understandable," Annie said. "But what *is* Rowena up to? She'd never agree to sell the cup—would she? She couldn't—seriously—be planning . . . ? No."

"Robbery?" Bartlemy smiled. "I don't think so. I gather what she really wants is to get Eric to have a look at it. She's been very impressed by him. People usually are. Whether she's come to accept that he's from another world I can't say, but she's no fool, and she must realize he isn't mad. She wants him to see it—she wants it to be in situ. She's gone to considerable lengths to organize it. I must admit, I had no idea she was capable of such duplicity. People are constantly surprising me—it's really very reassuring."

"At your age," Annie said with a furtive smile, "I should imagine there are few surprises left."

"That's where you're wrong," said Bartlemy. "The longer I live, the more I realize that *no one* is ever predictable. Just when you think you've got people worked out, they do something extraordinary. Human nature has amazing depths—and shallows, of course. Whatever Freud may say, there are no rules of human behavior."

"Surely your genes dictate who you are," Annie interpolated.

"Genes don't dictate," Bartlemy responded. "You can be trapped by your heredity—or you can live up to it—or you can rise above it. You make yourself. How can genes make a poet out of a monkey who came down from the trees? I have told you about magic, of the powers of the Gifted few, but the true magic is in the soul of Man."

"Men can do terrible things," Nathan said, thinking of the Pits.

"And wonderful ones. They are two sides of the same coin. The darkness and the light is in all of us. We make ourselves into who we are. We choose."

"What about environmental factors?" said Annie.

Their conversation wandered down psychoanalytical byways, while Nathan slipped into his own thoughts. These were mostly concerned with the back door at Thornyhill, and Hoover's reliability as a guard dog who would never bark at a friend . . .

NATHAN HOPED he would dream again about Kwanji Ley that week, but he had another dream about the sea, in the world where all land had been devoured, and one about a beautiful country that resembled his childhood image of Narnia. There were green hills and mossy rocks and streams that plashed (whatever plashing was), and woods even lovelier and somehow *woodier* than Thornyhill, with thickets of dogrose and honeysuckle, and a red squirrel flickering through the leaves, and birds singing whose names he didn't know. Night came, with a giant moon seen through a lacework of twig and branch, and an owl cruising on silent wings. And then suddenly there was Fear. The moonlight was crawling with it; the woodland floor heaved upward into a wave. *They* were there, the Ozmosees—even there, in that beautiful wild place. He had no iron on him, no protection. He ran like a mad thing, pursued by the nightmare, until he stumbled over a tree root and went hurtling down—and down—into the black depths of undisturbed sleep.

Afterward, when he thought about the dream, he wondered if that was the place where he had found Woody, on some long-forgotten voyage of his childhood. It was a while since he had seen his friend, and one afternoon he went into the woods alone, equipped with a gift of Smarties, and they sat and talked together under the trees, though he didn't mention the dream. He told Woody about the coming of the Grail, and his own plans for Saturday. He wanted many eyes watching when the time came.

"I will watch," said Woody. "But others watch also."

"You mean the gnomons?" Nathan frowned. "I think—they are

bound to the cup. I don't know what they'll do. They can't enter Thornyhill: there's too much iron, and silphium in the herb garden, and I expect Bartlemy could manage the light and sound effects, too."

"I was thinking of the dwarf," said Woody.

"What dwarf?" But as he spoke, he knew.

"The one you released from the ground. The prisoner."

"We can't worry about him as well," Nathan said. But the worry remained, niggling at the edges of his mind, and he couldn't shake it off.

At the bookshop, Alex Birnbaum came in to talk about the cup, and invited Annie for a drink. Michael arrived in time to hear her polite acceptance. "Your admirer," he said lightly, when Alex had gone.

Annie was conscious of an agreeable warmth about the heart. "He's nice," she said. "I like him." She wasn't cruel, but she was female, and Michael was still a married man.

"I was hoping you'd have dinner with me," he said. "Friday." It was the first time he'd asked her to dinner, and his tone was uncertain.

"Nathan—"

"Nat can look after himself."

She smiled, a little shyly. "All right."

But on Friday morning, Rianna Sardou came home.

MICHAEL TELEPHONED to tell her, sounding both embarrassed and apologetic. "The Georgia tour was cut short—political unrest or something; too near Chechnya for comfort I expect. Maybe we could do dinner next week. She'll be in London reading for a new production of *Macbeth*."

Which role? Annie wondered. *Banquo's ghost?* And which Rianna had actually "come home"—the real one, or the spirit who wore her face? In addition, the idea of dining with Michael on the quiet, when his wife—or someone who might be his wife—was around, troubled her conscience.

"It can't have been her you saw in London," Michael added. "She's been in Georgia all the time. I fished."

Annie said something noncommittal and hung up. After a minute's reflection, she tried Bartlemy's number, but he was out, probably finalizing arrangements with Rowena Thorn. When Nathan came in to lunch, he found his mother distracted. She told him Michael had canceled, but not why, and she had never gotten around to describing the horror from the river. She was picturing it, going to the tower to sleep (did it sleep?)—worse still, sharing a bed with Michael.

She had to know.

Michael had told her he would be out that afternoon; he was involved in a special project at the university run during the vacation for nonstudents. Around three, with one of Nathan's door numbers in her pocket—though she didn't know if iron would be any use against the water spirit—she closed the shop and walked around to Riverside House.

It looked very quiet, sleeping in the sunshine, neither ominous nor welcoming, both picturesque and bland. It occurred to her that unlike most village houses in the pith of the afternoon it didn't actually appear to sleep, it had too little personality—it was more like a show house than a real home, all façade and interior décor, no heart. She rang the doorbell and waited, her pulse thumping, listening for the sounds of an approach.

She heard nothing. No footsteps, no fiddling with handle or lock—nothing. The door jerked abruptly open, and Rianna was there.

For a second—less than a second—Annie wasn't certain. It looked like a woman, flesh-and-blood, jeans-and-sweater, bare feet with painted nails, dark hair swept up in a butterfly clip with long strands escaping down her neck. She knew a pang of guilt—if it was a woman—because a woman could be wronged, and hurt, whatever Michael had said about the state of their marriage. And then she looked into the eyes, and knew. There was a blackness there beyond iris or pupil, the dark of the ocean depths where no light has ever been since life began. And no human feet could approach so noiselessly on such a quiet day—bare feet, where surely a normal person would have worn sandals, bare feet that had left faint damp prints on the rug behind her . . .

Annie felt her face whiten, knew she had betrayed herself. It was all she could do not to run. But her voice, when she found it, was steady enough. "I was looking for Michael. I've come across a book I think would interest him, a history of Victorian London. Is he in?"

"No," said the thing, baldly. Perhaps it didn't comprehend the significance of her pale cheek; perhaps, even after the chase, it thought she could be deceived. "I'll tell him you called."

And then, in an altered tone: "How is your son?"

There was no threat in the question; rather a suppressed fever, a kind of greed. Annie felt an unexpected surge of anger, scattering her fears—the ancient, primitive rage of a mother protecting her child. She remembered Bartlemy's gesture of dismissal when the spirit had appeared in the circle, the single word of Command. She forgot that she had no Gift, no power. She flung out her hand, cried: *"Envarré!"* The thing that was Rianna Sardou seemed to flinch—but only seemed. It wavered, its substance changing, dissolving into a form of roiling water that reached out to seize her. She tried to resist, but her throat was held in a grip as strong as the currents of the sea, and fluid fingers streamed into nose and mouth, and water rushed into her lungs . . .

She came to, choking, vomiting a fountain onto the planks of the jetty. She was lying by the river, soaking wet and shivering, and Michael was bending over her with an expression of relief on his face, having evidently applied artificial respiration. "What happened?" he said, giving her no time to answer. "I found you here—in the river. I heard a cry, and then I found you—I thought you were dead—I thought you were dead . . ." His concern was so evident, a warmth flooded through her that almost stopped the shivers. "Thank God I came back."

"Why—"

"I'd forgotten a load of essays. No point in going without them. Thank all the gods . . ."

He carried her up to the house, saw that she could undress herself, provided her with bathrobe, blanket, hot sweet tea. "I don't know where Rianna's gone," he said. "I thought she was around this afternoon. What were you doing here? What *happened*?"

Annie faltered. She couldn't lie anymore—he was in danger—but he would never believe the truth. She would have to compromise. "I c-came to see Rianna," she stammered. "I wanted to ask her—about that time in London. I was so sure it was her. I thought if I asked her—if I saw how she reacted—I would know. She opened the door—her manner was very strange. Everything went black. I don't even remember being near the river. She lunged at me—and everything went black . . ." She hated deceiving him, even by omission, but she could think of nothing else to say. As it was, he looked at her in absolute bewilderment.

"Rianna—are you saying—*Rianna* attacked you? But—she can't have done. Not *Rianna*. She doesn't care about me, not like that. We've slept in separate beds for years. Even if she *was* jealous, she'd be dramatic, she'd make scenes, but she's not *violent*. She couldn't . . . What did she say?"

Annie answered without thinking: *"How is your son?"*

"What?"

"She said: *How is your son?* Michael . . . this wasn't—this isn't about you. I can't say—I don't know any more. But it's not about you."

Michael stared at her, shock and concern slowly evaporating from his face, to be replaced by the contemplative expression of a scholar scanning some inscrutable antique text. When he spoke, his voice had acquired a new edge. "So what is it about?"

SHE DIDN'T tell him, she couldn't, not without evidence to convince him of the impossible. He didn't press her. She had nearly died—she was obviously shaken—he took her home, saw she was all right, insisted on informing her doctor. If there was a shade of withdrawal in his attitude, only the most sensitive antennae would have picked it up—but Annie's were very sensitive. He knew she hadn't told him everything, he couldn't believe ill of Rianna: all that was clear enough. Her only consolation was that Nathan didn't come in till later, so she didn't have to go through any complicated explanations with him. She would tell Bartlemy . . . when an opportunity offered. That evening she cooked supper, and Nathan went to the video shop to rent a movie, returning with a dark sci-fi thriller that did nothing to cheer her up. She slept badly and woke late, to find a note on the kitchen table from her son saying he had already breakfasted and gone out. Panic struck: he could be near the river, pursued by a watery succubus with eyes that opened on the abyss. She phoned Bartlemy, pouring out her fears, but he seemed to think there was no immediate threat to Nathan, and told her sternly in future not to go looking for trouble. "Good thing Michael was there. Nice timing, coming back like that."

"He knows I'm lying to him," Annie said awkwardly.

"Never mind. Women always lie to men: it's part of the fun."

Annie knew he only meant to lighten her worries, but she didn't think it was fun at all.

Bartlemy returned to the preparation of a midday meal that would have induced conviviality between members of Hamas and Mossad, had they ever been persuaded to share it—though he was slightly less confident about the claimants to the Grimthorn Grail. Alex Birnbaum arrived shortly before noon, followed by Rowena and Eric. They assumed Dieter Von Humboldt was traveling with his property.

It had been decided in the end that the cup would come down from London by car, since a secure van would draw too much attention to it. The car in question was Julian Epstein's BMW, driven by Julian himself, with a guard in the front seat and another in the back, handcuffed to a strongbox containing the Grail. Nathan would have been gratified to learn that both were armed. It drew up outside Thornyhill around one, at Bartlemy's directions reversing up the grassy track where he parked his Jowett Javelin. The guards were invited inside, but Julian insisted that one remain by the front door. In the drawing room Bartlemy served a choice of sherry, whiskey, gin and tonic.

"Where's the Graf?" Mrs. Thorn demanded without preamble as the newcomers entered.

"We thought he was with you," said Epstein.

"Well, he isn't. *We* thought he'd be with *you*."

"Perhaps he's delayed," Bartlemy murmured, though he considered it unlikely.

Hoover was sniffing the guard unenthusiastically, fixing his concealed holster with a whiskery stare. "He any good as a watchdog?" the man inquired.

"I wouldn't know," said Bartlemy. "I've never asked him."

Hoover gave a short, somehow pointed bark, "almost as if he understood," the guard told his wife later. He sat down, clutching the strongbox, and man and dog eyed each other in mutual suspicion.

"Let's get on with it then," Rowena said briskly. For all her business-like manner, Bartlemy could feel the knuckles of her determination underneath.

"Not till the owner gets here," Epstein responded. "Who is this man?"

"Sorry. Remiss of me. Eric Rhindon—Julian Epstein. Eric works for me. Think he might be able to help us learn more about the cup. Bit of an authority on these things."

Epstein glanced from Eric to Bartlemy. "Everyone you know is an authority," he murmured.

"Not surprising, in my line of work," Rowena breezed. "Come on, Julian. Von Humboldt's fault if he's late. No point in holding things up. The cup's here: we may as well take a look at it. Then we can start talking."

But Epstein was adamant. "I cannot open the box without Von Humboldt's express permission."

"Surely he has already given it," Bartlemy said, pouring a soothing sherry. "He would hardly have organized this meeting and arranged for the cup to be brought here if he hadn't intended it to be seen."

Rowena opened her mouth to agree and shut it again when Bartlemy, moving across the room, paused to give her shoulder a meaningful squeeze. Julian declined the sherry—"I'm driving"—and then accepted when his host suggested one of the guards should drive back. The guard drank fruit juice, manfully. Eric, in pursuit of new experiences, graduated from sherry to whiskey. The alcoholic drinks of his world were clearly as limited as the food, though fortunately his capacity appeared to be up to the challenge.

By two o'clock, when Von Humboldt still hadn't arrived, Bartlemy proposed starting lunch. Epstein tried Von Humboldt's

cell phone without success, and reluctantly agreed. Everyone re-
paired to the dining room, including the guard, who ate with the
strongbox in his lap. It was a day of clammy heat and lowering
cloud, when the air seemed to be squashed between earth and sky,
and the old house offered a welcome haven of cool. Exquisite food
and chilled wine did much to relax the ill-assorted party: the guard,
mellowed by atmosphere if not wine, became indiscreet about former clients, Epstein teetered on the verge of admitting his dislike of
the Graf and revived his old friendship with Rowena, and Eric
struck up a new friendship with Birnbaum. Bartlemy took a picnic
outside to the guard at the door and kindly stayed to chat, admiring
photos of a leather-clad boyfriend and three whippets before returning to the group indoors. It was only when silence fell that they
were conscious of tension, not among themselves, not anymore, but
beyond, creeping in from the woods, prickling at the walls of the
house. In the sudden quiet Hoover padded to the window and put
his forepaws on the sill, gazing out with ears cocked. "What is it,
boy?" Bartlemy asked.

The dog turned to him with an expression so intelligent that even
Epstein was startled. "Perhaps we should return to the drawing room
for coffee," Bartlemy said, and though it sounded like a suggestion,
they knew it wasn't. Everybody moved at once, with neither comment nor protest.

"Where on earth is Von Humboldt?" Epstein said, after trying
his cell phone again. "Could he have had an accident?"

"Whatever's happened," said Bartlemy, "it seems plain he isn't
coming. Now you have to decide what to do."

All eyes were on the representative of Sotheby's. "I should like
to see it," Alex averred. "My mother said it was accursed, and now—
there's something in the air—I could almost believe her."

"It was our burden," said Rowena, "and our luck. Ill luck to all
others who lay hand on it."

"Is a great treasure, a sacred thing," Eric supplied. "If is here, is here in trust."

Epstein nodded to the guard. "We'll open it," he said.

THE CLOUDS were darkening as Nathan and Hazel approached the path, not piling up but hanging down, great swags of cumulus bellying low over the woods. It was still very hot, and the air around the house seemed to tingle, as if it had pins and needles. There was a soft growl of thunder far off. "They're here," Nathan said as a familiar shiver of movement passed over the ground, cutting them off from Thornyhill. His gaze followed the ripple, and he imagined the gnomons were paying no attention to them; instead, they appeared to be circling the house, keeping their distance, restrained by some other power, by the proximity of iron or silphium. The children held out their numbers—"Our lucky numbers," Hazel said—and broke through, easily eluding the eye of the guard, then made their way around the back, avoiding the windows, and took shelter in the herb garden. Nathan reconnoitered the kitchen door.

"Can we get in?" Hazel whispered when he returned.

"Not yet. Uncle Barty keeps going in and out, getting food or something. We'll have to wait."

"I think it's going to rain."

It was an understatement. Two or three fat drops struck their heads, and then the clouds started to liquefy, streaming earthward with all the blinding vigor of a monsoon. Thunder blotted out Nathan's next remark, but he grabbed Hazel's arm and tugged her into the lee of the wall, where the broad eaves offered a little cover. Lightning ripped across the sky, so that for an instant both garden and wood were spotlit, and they could see branches sagging under the onslaught of the rain, stems broken, leaves pummeled into the ground.

More thunder rattled their eardrums, and the lightning followed immediately—Hazel saw a flickering lance earth itself only yards away, blackening the grass with a hiss audible even beneath the roar of the storm. She wondered if the gnomons would endure it or scatter; under these conditions, the subtle indicators of their presence were impossible to make out. Already the two children were wet to the skin. Hazel's hair, always in her eyes, was plastered in rats' tails across her face. "We're doing no good here!" she yelled in Nathan's ear. "We should go." But they didn't leave the protection of the eaves until the rain eased. Another lightning flash must have struck an electric cable; in the adjacent kitchen window, the lights went out. Although it was day, the afternoon was suddenly very dark. There was a movement behind the bean plants, not the gnomons—something bigger, more substantial. Even as they froze, a small figure shot past them into the house.

Inside, four people were brooding over the cup when the storm started, their intent faces so focused on the object before them that they barely registered the deepening gloom, the first thunder roll. For a second, in the poor light, each face seemed to wear the same expression of hunger, and the same fanatic gleam danced from eye to eye. Then Alex drew back, perhaps disappointed that the result of his search wasn't gaudier or more glamorous, Epstein recovered his professional detachment, and the illusion was broken. Only Rowena and Eric remained poring over the cup. "Is the one," Eric said. "The treasure of treasures." His normally resonant voice was hushed; Rowena thought she saw tears on his cheek.

Bartlemy, anticipating the side effects of the storm, had gone to fetch candles. The guard relaxed on a chair, still shackled to the empty box; his colleague had retreated inside the front door, with Hoover crouching watchfully at his side.

"What is it made of?" Rowena asked the exile.

"Stone. Is greenstone of Eos, much used in old days. Not common now. Jewels are *aeson*, have great value, but not important. Only *Sangreal* important."

"He *knows* about it?" muttered Epstein, sotto voce.

"Is the Grail valuable, where you come from?" Rowena persisted.

Eric managed a gesture at once vague and emphatic. "Has—no value. Too sacred."

"Priceless," said Rowena. "I see."

And then the lights went out. *Something* rushed into the room with the violence of a small tornado, bringing with it an indescribable smell, a reek not quite animal, not quite human. Rowena grabbed for the cup; Eric hesitated, unwilling to relinquish it; Epstein and Birnbaum joined the fray. The guard tried to lunge, forgetting his handcuff, and smashed his elbow on the box. Hands scrabbled on the prize, though no one was sure, in the dimness, which belonged to whom. "I've got it!—You've got it?—Who's got it?—*What's that?*" The cup slipped through too many fingers, dropped—but never hit the ground. Feet fled toward the kitchen. Something no one had seen clearly was gone as fast as it came. Bartlemy returned with a candelabra. The sudden light showed a tangle of hands, snatching at nothing. Nothing.

Eric swore in his own language, Epstein sat down too quickly, almost missing the chair, Alex said: "My God." Rowena produced a string of expletives they had never heard her use before. "Follow," Bartlemy said. Hoover bounded from the room.

Outside, Nathan and Hazel saw the thief emerge clasping the trophy to his chest. They took one look at each other and set off in pursuit, regardless of the rain. But they skidded on wet leaves and could barely see, whereas their quarry moved quickly, apparently untroubled by the weather. In moments he was out of what little sight they had. Then Hoover overtook them, loping ahead, picking up the rank smell that even the storm could not eradicate. Soon he, too, was lost to view, but the erratic sound of barking kept them on the trail. The rain slackened, and they began to run faster. Hazel stumbled several times; her hands were muddied where she had flung them out to break her fall. Nathan was more sure-footed, but his T-shirt was smeared green from hindering branches and his jeans were slimed to the knee. Their pace accelerated—too late they realized why, as the slope grew steeper and they both slid some distance, Hazel landing up to her waist in brambles and leafmold. As she scrambled to her feet, her language almost rivaled Rowena's. "Come on," Nathan said. "We can't stop now." She followed on his heels, or as near his heels as she could manage, dogged more than eager; her enthusiasm for adventure had gotten lost in the mud and the rain. But Nathan, more careful now, was moving as rapidly as he dared. Hoover's hindquarters appeared some way ahead, tail draggled but still waving. Suddenly, he halted, head down. There was no sign of their quarry. But even before he got there, Nathan knew where the thief had gone. He dropped to the ground and jumped down through the hole into the chapel.

The dwarf was at the far end, thrusting the Grail into the alcove where Nathan had seen it in the vision. He began to chant—no, to gabble—words in a strange tongue, the tongue Bartlemy had used to summon spirits to the circle. It might even have been the same one the Grandir had used to conjure images from the magical globes. The dwarf's voice was harsh and cracked, as if long unused. Nathan ran forward, trying to reach the cup, but the dwarf grabbed him and they fell to the ground, half wrestling, half punching, neither gaining any advantage. Behind him he heard Hazel call out; Hoover was growling his rare, deep growl, but he didn't come down. The green nimbus surrounded the cup; whispers came from every corner of the ruin. Somehow Nathan broke free, tried to stand—his opponent head-butted him in the chest, hurling him backward, driving the breath from his lungs. The whispering died; when Nathan looked again, the alcove was empty. The cup had gone.

The dwarf emitted a sound that might have been a cackle, leapt for the hole with demonic agility, and disappeared. Nathan caught Hazel's startled cry, Hoover's angry howl. He clambered out more slowly, slithering on the wet earth, while Hazel struggled to get a grip on his arms. Hoover had abandoned the pursuit and waited for them, wagging encouragement. "Where's the Grail?" Hazel demanded when he finally emerged. "He didn't have it. I thought you—"

"He sent it back," Nathan said. The sky was clearing, and in the growing light the three of them looked sodden, dirty, and defeated. "He sent it back to the other world. It isn't safe there, I know it isn't. It's meant to be here, till they need it. I don't know if it's good or evil, but we were supposed to look after it, and we failed."

"How do you know?" Hazel asked.

"I'm not sure. I just—*know*."

They didn't say any more. Somberly they climbed back up the hill, Hoover in the lead. The rain had stopped altogether and the wood began to steam, pale strands of vapor rising from the leafmold and drifting upward. The trees faded to branching shapes of gray, their foliage all but drained of green. Mist-ghosts floated a little way above the ground, or coiled around trunk and bole. Nathan watched for any hint of the gnomons: a disturbance in the mist, a shudder of twig and leaf; but the wood was still, almost unnaturally so. They hadn't left the valley, and there were no birds. High above he glimpsed the specter of the sun, its white face shining wanly through the fog.

Hoover stopped just short of the crest of the hill, the fur bristling on his nape. He padded a few yards to the right, investigating something humped on the ground, colorless in the mist. Then he raised his head, looking at Nathan. The boy went over to him; Hazel came after, inexplicably reluctant. She couldn't see what they were staring at until she drew nearer, but then suddenly the veil thinned, and the hump acquired form and meaning. The lack of color was a suit, a gray suit, incongruous in those surroundings. The back was uppermost, the face—fortunately—half buried in leaf litter, the arms outstretched as if to prevent a fall. The fingers dug into the soil as if he had clawed at the ground in some final spasm. Nathan had squatted down beside him; he turned a curiously blank face up to hers. "I think he's dead," he said, and his voice, too, was blank, wiped of all emotion. "He's very cold."

Hazel swallowed, wanting not to look, unable to tear her eyes away. The man's hair was sleeked against his head, but in one place it seemed to be matted with dark stuff that might have been dried blood. He was facing downhill. "Who is he?" she said.

"Don't know. But I think we should get the police."

"Again," Hazel said.

On Robbery and Murder

Inspector Pobjoy was in conference with the Assistant Chief Constable. Again. "His name is Dieter Von Humboldt. He was a Graf, which is some sort of German count. Sorry, Austrian."

"They're all Huns," the ACC said vaguely, abandoning any attempt at political correctness.

"He owned the cup, known as the Grimthorn Grail. His grandfather acquired it when he was in the SS, and now Von Humboldt was planning to sell it. Birnbaum—a descendant of the Jewish collector who had it before—he'd made a claim for it, so had Rowena Thorn. They'd arranged a big meeting to try to settle the matter out of court, and for some reason the cup had to be there. Von Humboldt didn't show, but the chap from Sotheby's let them take a look at it. I suppose everyone wanted to be sure it was the real thing, though why they didn't do so in London—"

"Somebody up to something?"

"Probably, but who, or what, isn't clear. Nobody could've arranged the storm. The lights went out, and someone rushed in through the back door and snatched the cup. According to witnesses, it was either a hairy dwarf or a monkey." His tone was darkly skeptical.

" 'Murders in the Rue Morgue,' " said the ACC, brightening.

"The two kids were outside, evidently trying to sneak a look at the proceedings," Pobjoy continued. He hadn't read Edgar Allan Poe. "They gave chase, but the thief got away. On their way back, they came across the body. I've interviewed them separately: they tell the same story, and it fits. We can be fairly confident about some of the times. The meteorological office says the storm started at four twenty-three. Goodman called us as soon as the kids got back to the house, that was five thirty-nine exactly. We haven't had the autopsy results yet, but off the record they say Von Humboldt was dead before lunch, say between eleven and one."

"Could he have been killed by the thief before the robbery?"

"Possibly, but why? If you're going to pinch the cup, you don't need to kill the owner. If you've killed the owner, presumably you don't need to pinch the cup—although I'm not sure what killing the owner would achieve."

"Who does the damn thing belong to now?" the ACC asked.

"There's a younger brother. He's flying over to identify the body. Not that there's any doubt."

"All right. Let's forget the robbery for a minute. What's the motive for murder?"

"It puts a stop to the sale for a while," Pobjoy said. "Muddies already muddy waters. It *might* have facilitated the theft. It might have been part of another plan to get the cup that was never carried through. There's been a certain amount of publicity about it. Epstein—the chap from Sotheby's—says serious collectors are interested. Some of them might not be legit."

"A commission?" sighed the ACC.

"Could be. But I have to tell you, Epstein doesn't think so. There are still questions over the cup's authenticity. Apparently, it hasn't been possible to date it or even specify what it's made of. Whether interest would have hardened depended on further analysis."

"It's valuable, isn't it?"

"Somewhere between priceless and worthless, Epstein says." Pobjoy didn't show bewilderment because he never did, but the quirks of the antiques business were beyond his ken.

"That's helpful," the ACC grunted. "What is it with this place? A sleepy little village that hasn't had a crime rate for a decade, and suddenly they've got robbery and murder all in one day." There was a silence—the kind of silence that is heavy with things unsaid. "Don't tell me: let me guess. You're still harping on the death of the old woman. You think that fits in somewhere."

"You said it, sir," Pobjoy responded pointedly. "No crime worth mentioning for a decade. A few petty thefts, a couple of break-ins at the bigger houses in the vicinity, a bit of drunk-and-disorderly and the usual domestic violence—Dave Bagot, for instance—but no questionable corpses. And now we have two. I don't believe in coincidence."

"The drowning was accidental. Don't make things complicated."

"It was a curiously timed accident. And Mrs. Carlow's great-granddaughter was one of the kids who found Von Humboldt. It's a link."

"You said she wrote the letter," said the ACC, dredging the fact from an overcrowded memory. "Do you suspect her?"

"No. But these people are all connected. Eade's a small place. Birnbaum and Von Humboldt had both been in the area for a while. As far as I can gather, they were fishing; Birnbaum admits he wanted some background on the cup. Von Humboldt was trying to persuade

Mrs. Thorn to negotiate—and it seems he succeeded. Bringing the cup from London was her condition."

"Could she have set up the robbery?" the ACC asked.

"If she did," said Pobjoy, "she's a bloody good actress. When I spoke to her I could feel the anger coming off her in waves. Besides, according to her lawyer, she had a pretty good case for getting it legally."

"So who's our prime suspect?"

"For the robbery, or the murder?" Pobjoy inquired with a rare note of humor.

"Either. Both. Bugger it."

"Well, aside from the issue of the cup, Birnbaum's got a grudge against the Von Humboldts. His great-uncle's family died in a concentration camp, and the Graf in the SS swiped their art collection. That gives him a strong motive, and his alibi's doubtful. He's staying in a pub in Chizzledown—the Happy Huntsman. They think he went out after eleven, but they're not sure. He arrived at Thornyhill shortly before twelve. Could have met Von Humboldt on the way, chased him into the wood, and killed him."

"And the robbery? Oh, yes, the dwarf—or monkey. Nice one. Anyone else in the frame?"

"There was another man present, some sort of asylum seeker, presumably an illegal, but thank God that's not our department. He's been doing a bit of work for Mrs. Thorn, she says unpaid, but I daresay that's because he's got no permits. I've been checking him out, but there isn't much to find. He's supposed to be from Africa somewhere, but he looks like a mix. Unusual type. Came ashore at Pevensey Bay, some support group in Hastings helped him out. Calls himself Eric Rhindon. I spoke to him only briefly."

"Damn these bloody foreigners. Need an interpreter?"

"No, sir. His English is a bit peculiar, but he's fluent."

There was a pause. "What about the chap who called us—Goodman? Living in a house that used to belong to the Thorns, pally with Mrs. Thorn, presiding over the peace talks. Sounds like a busybody. What do we know about him?"

"Not enough," said the inspector.

NATHAN AND Hazel were well ahead of the police. They were having supper in the room behind the bookshop, two days later, discussing the matter for the umpteenth time. Annie encouraged them, believing it was sound therapy for them to talk out any traumatic reaction. She sensed Hazel was particularly upset.

"He *must* have been killed by the same person who drowned Mrs. Carlow," Nathan said, "but I don't quite see how it fits in. She was a witch who was interested in the Grail—he was the owner—the two murders *have* to be connected, but . . . The dwarf might have attacked Von Humboldt, thinking he had the cup on him, but not your great-gran. We know she—" He stopped. He still hadn't told Annie they had seen Bartlemy draw the circle, and he wasn't meant to know about the water spirit.

But Annie was following her own train of thought. "Was he wet?"

"Von Humboldt? Of course. It had been raining."

Hazel, too, had thoughts of her own. "He was hit on the head," she said. "We saw the blood." There was a shudder in her voice, even though they'd been through it before. "That was what killed him."

"The dwarf couldn't have done that," Nathan announced abruptly, an arrested look on his face.

"Why not?"

"Too short."

"He could have been up a tree," Hazel said.

Woody might know, Nathan was thinking. *He sees everything that goes on around Thornyhill, and I* did *ask him to keep a lookout. I must go and talk to him.*

"Anyway," Annie said, reverting to a grievance already thoroughly aired, "you shouldn't have been there. If you hadn't been spying on the meeting, you wouldn't have fallen over the body. You had no business—"

"It *was* our business," Nathan reiterated, also for the umpteenth time. "Hazel's great-grandmother was killed first, and I'm the one who keeps dreaming of other worlds. We're involved. On a need-to-know basis, we need to know everything."

"I hate it when you get smart," Annie sighed.

"George wants to go to the wood to look for clues," Nathan pursued, "but I said we should leave that to the police." He evidently felt he was being generous, trusting Pobjoy with the investigation. "They've got the area cordoned off anyway."

"George is a twit," Hazel muttered, feeling an obscure need to pick on someone, even if he wasn't there.

"And, " Nathan resumed, "if we hadn't spied on the meeting, we wouldn't have been able to chase the dwarf, and we wouldn't have known what he did with the Grail. Uncle Barty was pretty pleased with us."

"Running after criminals is *dangerous.*" Annie's voice lacked conviction, and she knew it. Everything that was happening right now was dangerous, and there was nothing she could do to stop it.

She produced strawberries and cream and noted that Nathan's appetite, at least, was unimpaired. "Try not to worry about it," she said to Hazel, feeling inadequate and clumsy. "I know it's distressing when you first see a dead body, but . . . it's just like old clothes. Castoffs. The spirit leaves behind what it doesn't need anymore."

"His spirit didn't have much choice, did it?" said Nathan.

Later that night he climbed up to the skylight and looked at the star. Did its range reach as far as the woods? he wondered. Had that pale mask looked down from another world and seen, perhaps with indifference, the killer of Dieter Von Humboldt? The star that wasn't a star twinkled on noncommittally, insofar as it could be said to twinkle. Nathan went to bed eagerly, hoping to dream—of the chamber of crystals, and the aerial view of this world, of Kwanji Ley in Deep Confinement, in a white cylindrical pit—but hope cheated him, and he only slept.

THE NEXT morning Pobjoy went to Thornyhill to talk to Bartlemy. He didn't take Belinda Hale since he wanted to keep the conversation informal. He hadn't called to say he was coming, but his host seemed unsurprised, proffering coffee and cookies as if he had been expecting a visitor. To the inspector, a cookie was something that came out of a package, tasting like slightly sweetened sand. He had never eaten cookies like these. Interviewees sometimes offered him alcohol, which he always refused, in case it affected his judgment; it hadn't occurred to him that his detachment could be undermined by a cookie. Until now. As it was, it occurred to him for perhaps a few seconds, until the cookie took hold and his taste buds succumbed to its blandishments.

"I was wondering," he said, "if you could fill me in on a few things." He was going to add that it was merely a matter of routine, but then remembered that line had been done to death in detective fiction and no one believed it anymore.

"What kind of things?"

"Starting with the robbery, whose idea was it to bring the cup down from London, and why here? If the various claimants wanted to meet on neutral territory, what was wrong with a hotel room? This house isn't secure—they found that out the hard way—and you weren't involved in the business except in an advisory capacity. So—why here?"

"It was Mrs. Thorn's idea," Bartlemy explained. "I assumed she would have told you. This house, as I think you know, once belonged to her family; it was the home of the Grail. She wanted, I imagine, to impress Birnbaum and Von Humboldt with the whole tradition of Thorn ownership—to get the weight of history on her side. It worked with Birnbaum. I never met Von Humboldt, but from what I've heard I doubt if it would have had the same effect on him."

"And that was why the cup was brought here? So Birnbaum would see it in its setting, be overcome with remorse for daring to aspire to it, and back off?"

"Nicely put." Bartlemy smiled, and nudged the plate of cookies toward his guest. "Mrs. Thorn, I believe, used that argument with Von Humboldt to persuade him to bring the cup here. But I suspect her real motives were more complex. She feels very strongly that by selling it, her ancestors failed in some way, and it's up to her to put things right. A question of family honor, you might say. Returning the cup to its original home, if only for an afternoon, was a significant step. A gesture showing her commitment to the cause." He didn't mention Eric's role in the affair. The introduction of an alternative universe into the case would only complicate matters.

Pobjoy thought: *That* sounds *like pseudo-psychological nonsense* . . . But the cookies had softened his normal hard-edged clarity of mind, and he didn't dispute it.

He asked: "Could she have engineered the robbery?"

"I suppose so—any of them could—but I don't think it's likely. Mrs. Thorn is in a strong position to reclaim the cup legally. If it was found in her possession *illegally,* I should imagine that position would be seriously affected. Remember, she doesn't want to sell it, so if she had it, she'd keep it."

"Unless she lied about her attitude."

"She didn't lie," Bartlemy said with quiet certainty, and Pobjoy found himself accepting that.

"Who else knew the cup was being brought here?"

"The people at Sotheby's, obviously—but you'll have checked that out. I don't know if Birnbaum or Von Humboldt told anyone else. I only discussed it with Annie Ward, who stands to me in the relation of a niece, and it would be ludicrous to suspect her."

"Yes," Pobjoy agreed, with a warmth that surprised him. "It *would*."

"The children knew because children always do," Bartlemy pursued, "but I don't think word got around the village. Annie might have mentioned it to Michael Addison: he's a friend of hers, and a historian, so the subject would be of interest to him. You've met him, I believe. But remember, the value of the cup is still in doubt, so it must have been stolen for what it *is*, not for what it's worth. That severely limits the range of possibilities."

"What about this dwarf?" Pobjoy demanded. "Did you see it?"

"No—I was out of the room. But there was a storm, the lights went out, it was unnaturally dark in here. I expect people's imaginations were on overtime."

Although that was what Pobjoy had been thinking himself, he felt an irrational urge to argue. "What about the children?" he said. "Could it have been one of them?"

"You've met them," Bartlemy said. "They're teenagers. Hazel isn't tall, but she's far too tall for a dwarf, and Nathan's growing by the hour. Besides, they would've been recognized."

In a Halloween mask? Pobjoy wondered, but he didn't say it. The idea had come to him in the small hours, and he thought it might fit, with the robbery if not the murder. The children would probably have believed they were helping Rowena Thorn. In his experience, crime and teenagers went together like bacon and eggs. If it hadn't been for the cookie effect, he would have pressed on with the subject. But . . .

"An unusual name, Pobjoy," Bartlemy was saying. "There can't be many of them."

A joke of a name, the inspector reflected. They had tried to make a joke of *him,* mocking him, caricaturing. From his earliest school-days, his personality had tightened and hardened against his name, until the joke was no longer funny, and people forgot it.

"My father mentioned a Pobjoy," Bartlemy went on, in a tone of gentle reminiscence. "In the war."

"My grandfather was in the SOE," the inspector said, caught off guard. He remembered belatedly that Annie had said something about a connection.

"Yes," said Bartlemy. "That would be him. Working with the re-sistance, just before the invasion. They gave him a medal of some kind, didn't they?"

"I still have it."

"He was a brave man. I saw—a photgraph—once. You have a look of him, in a certain light."

"What did your father do?" Pobjoy asked, thrown completely off course.

"Oh . . . he was a cook. He'd been in France some time, off and on: the home of great cuisine. He spoke French like a native, as they say. He was working for a rather high-profile Nazi during the occupa-tion: that's how he met your grandfather."

"He was in Intelligence, too?"

"Good heavens, no. Nothing so dramatic. Walter Pobjoy was a hero. My father was just a cook. He passed on tidbits, from time to time. Culinary tidbits. And . . . recipes, so to speak. He made himself useful: that was all."

"Cooking runs in the family, doesn't it?" said Pobjoy, giving up on robbery and murder, at least for the moment.

Bartlemy smiled his placid smile. "All sorts of things run in fam-ilies," he said. "Did they call you Walter, after your grandfather?"

"It's my middle name," the inspector admitted. "James Walter Pobjoy." He wanted to say *Call me James,* but caution, reserve, inhibition got in the way. After all, Bartlemy was a witness, a potential suspect . . .

"It's a pleasure to meet the grandson of so distinguished a man," Bartlemy said.

"We were an army family," Pobjoy found himself saying. "My father, too—he was killed in Ireland, when I was very young—and then the money ran out, and I was sent to a state comprehensive instead of Marlborough and Sandhurst, and I wanted a new direction. So I joined the police." He broke off abruptly, shocked to find himself in the midst of revelation.

"Have another cookie," said Bartlemy.

When his visitor had gone the old man sat for a while without moving, lost in thought. Hoover, who had been a mute witness to the preceding interview, scrounged the last cookie and waited hopefully. "So he suspects the children," Bartlemy said. "I should have anticipated that. But he can prove nothing without evidence, and the evidence, as we know, is out of reach." His mind dwelled on the dwarf, trying to fit him into the pattern. There were two kinds of dwarfs, he knew: those who are merely small humans, and the true dwarf race, who are werefolk. The latter tended to be hairier, less humanoid, exceptionally strong for their size, preferring to live underground, with the indefinite life span of the werekind and the ability to do without sustenance for long periods. The fragmentary stories of Josevius Grimthorn often credited him with an assistant—a hunchback, or a goblin, or, of course, a dwarf. But there was no hint as to why that assistant should have been imprisoned, or why he might wish to return the Grimthorn Grail to its place of origin. Still, true dwarfs, Bartlemy was aware, were by nature obsessive, brooding on one idea sometimes for centuries, usually connected with treasure. A lost jewel, a cursed hoard—whose curse was often aggravated by dwarfish mischief—a ring with obscure powers. And dwarfs, like most werefolk, inclined neither to evil nor to good, but their vindictive nature, and an inbuilt resentment of the taller races, made them more easily drawn to the dark side, and influenced by evil men.

"Our friend the inspector must look for his clues in the wood, and unpick them in the forensic laboratory," Bartlemy remarked. "But we have our own ways of searching. It is time to light the spell-fire and look in the smoke for glimpses of the past. And it may tell us nothing, Rukush: magic is always unpredictable. Then we will have to summon a seeress, who will complain that we didn't ask the right questions last time, and tell us, no doubt, that the past is veiled, and she is forbidden to gaze back so far. I would so much rather stick to cooking." He added, idly: "I liked the inspector, though. Rather more intense than his grandfather. A man who will get hold of the wrong idea and hang on to it with the persistence of a dwarf . . . but I liked him. What do you think?"

Hoover put his head on one side and thumped his tail.

NATHAN WAS in the woods, searching. He had avoided the police cordon, concentrating initially on the area between the house and the valley, then moving into the Darkwood, calling softly as he went: "Woody! Woody!" Twigs snapped, leaves crunched, midges swarmed, but of the woodwose there was no sign. He would have liked to have brought Hoover, but he was afraid the presence of the dog would deter his friend. *He must have seen something,* Nathan thought. *He sees everything in the woods. Perhaps he ran away, because he was frightened. He saw the murderer, maybe he saw the murder itself, and now he's hiding somewhere, shivering and alone . . . I must find him.*

And, as an afterthought: *If what he'd seen was just a man, an ordinary human killer, he wouldn't go on being afraid, would he? He'd come out now, and talk to me. But the killer wasn't ordinary, wasn't human, and so he's still hiding . . .*

Nathan called and called, whispering encouragement, but no one came, and eventually he went home, anxious and frustrated.

Woody was still on his mind when he went to bed, and slipped over the borders of sleep without speculating on whether he might dream. And so, of course, he dreamed.

Once again, he *felt* the transition: the whirling tunnel, on a collision course with stars and planets, the sudden plunge into blinding light. And then—reality. A different reality. He was leaning against a wall, a curving wall, in a pale hollow place. The Pit. In front of him, Kwanji Ley sat staring at him with widening eyes. She was altered, he thought, in some indefinable way—thinner, edgier, more tense. Time must have passed—*how much time?* At first, perhaps, the Pit had offered a kind of relief, the respite after interrogation, but now her sense of peace had gone and she was fighting, uselessly, with no visible enemy, no focus for her resistance, no witness to her struggle—fighting the terrible sameness, the nothing closing in on her, holding her like a fly in amber—fighting the creeping onset of despair. The fight had worn her down; her face was all bones now, bones and shadows, though in that diffuse light it was difficult to see where the shadows were supposed to lie, or what was casting them. Maybe they were shadows under her skin, in her soul.

She said: "Who are you?" Her voice, too, was altered. It was the voice of someone who hasn't spoken to another human being in a long while.

"My name's Nathan." It sounded very similar to the way he would have said it in English, except that the *th* had become *t,* and in his mind he knew it would be spelled *Naithan.*

"Why did you come back? *How* did you come back? You're real—I know you're real. There's been no one else. No holocasts, no visions, no wereghosts sent to trap me. Touch me. *Please.*"

He took her hands, and her grip was tight and strong. Like a man dangling from a cliff edge, clutching at a tree root to save himself . . .

"I'm real. I told you, I dreamed my way here. Because I wanted to."

"Why did you take so long?"

"I'm sorry. It wasn't long for me. Just a few days. But I don't have control over it. The dreams come when they will."

She said "Aaaah," and released his hands, but her gaze still held him.

"Will you tell me about the cup?" he asked at last. "I know it's part of a spell, but they say even the Grandir doesn't know it, or not all of it . . . but if you were trying to steal it, you must have some idea how the spell works . . ."

"If you're from another world," she said, scorn and disappointment in her face, "how do you know this?"

He told her about some of his other dreams, and about time, and when he had finished the scorn was gone, and there was a glitter in her eyes like twilight on a purple sea.

"You saved him," she said, talking of Eric. "You pulled him out of the sea, out of this world—into yours."

"Yes." He knew what was coming.

"Then you can do it with *me*. Not to your world—just *out*, somewhere here, anywhere. Get me out, and I'll tell you what you want to know. You can do it—you said so. *Get me out!*" She caught his hands again—her face looked feverish, lit from within with a phantom glow, the freakish gleam of desperation, panic, returning hope, recurring fear.

"I'll try," Nathan said unhappily, "but it may not work, and if it does, it's dangerous. I can't guarantee to keep you in this world; you could end up in any universe, anywhere."

"The power is in your mind," said Kwanji Ley. "Use it. *Think*."

"I'll try," he repeated. "But you must talk to me first. When I pull you out of here—*if* I do—I'll probably lose track of you. I did with Eric; it took me ages to trace him. I need to know about the Grail now."

"So it's a trick." She sat back, the light dying out of her gaze.

"No."

"Then prove it."

"I *can't*. I would if I could, but—you just have to believe me. Or not. It's up to you."

She breathed deeply, and stared at him, *into* him, with eyes that sought to read his mind—but failed. He was still a child in years, and a child's thoughts are on the wrong wavelength for adult telepathy. Eventually she said: "What the hell. I don't suppose I can tell you anything that the Grandir doesn't know already. It's just—there are things I am *not* meant to know. Do you understand?"

"I'm not sure."

"Well . . . where to start? I'm a third-level practor. This means I have certain magical skills and I was originally licensed to use them for the authorities. But my grandfather was a first-level practor, a mage of the Upper Chamber with knowledge of the Hidden Magics. He was eight thousand years old and died recently, caught in the contamination, though I believe his death was engineered by agents of the government. Before he died he knew he was out of favor—he disagreed with present policies—and he told me certain things. Are you following me?"

"Things you're not meant to know?"

"Yes. He said the Sangreal and two other objects were made by the first Grandir for the performance of a Great Spell. The first Grandir could see into the future—or maybe he just took a guess, knowing human nature and how it works—anyway, he anticipated a time when our universe would be heading for destruction, and we would have to escape or die. So he took one of the Great Spells, and adapted it, making the cup, the sword, and the crown to be symbols that, when brought together with the proper ceremonies, become the lever to open the barrier between worlds. The cup is the feminine principle, the sword is the masculine, and the crown is the circle that binds."

"What is a Great Spell?" Nathan asked.

"They are the deepest of the Hidden Magics, the most potent. It is said there are only seven in all the worlds. They must always have the three basic constituents: the masculine, the feminine, and the element of binding. They require an enormous amount of power, far more than any one man—any normal man—can wield, and the fallout can be catastrophic. According to my grandfather, secret records show that a Great Spell was performed several millennia ago that resulted in the deaths of all concerned except the then Grandir and caused an entire galaxy to implode and disappear into a black hole."

"What was it *for*?" Nathan said. "What did they intend to achieve?"

"We don't know. Something . . . big. World changing."

"And nobody noticed what—"

"It was thousands of years ago. I wasn't there. Look, the theory is that it was a Great Spell that produced the magical inversion that caused the contamination. It would have to be a Great Spell to turn magic to evil, to make it work against the practors—and if it was done wrong, or carelessly, then the spin-off might well be the poisoning of magic everywhere. That's how Great Spells work. They can go *very* wrong—end-of-the-world wrong. Clear?"

"Yes," said Nathan. "Sort of. You mean, you wanted to steal the cup—and the other things—to do the spell yourself. But how could you, if you don't know what it is, and you haven't the power, and if it goes wrong, it's the end of the world?"

"It's the end of the world anyway," Kwanji said. "There are powerful people in our movement, secret sympathizers—I don't know their names, I don't know their status, but they are working to learn the spell. We may even have people close to the Grandir: I can't say. We don't allow any one individual to know too much. My job was to obtain the symbols. I failed. But if you get me out of here . . . Maybe I should go to your world, find the Grail there, and bring it back. If your power is all you claim, you can help me."

"I don't *claim* anything," Nathan protested. "My power, as you call it, is erratic. I told you. But the cup isn't in my world anymore: someone sent it back here. I think it's probably in the cave again."

Kwanji brightened again. "Then take me to it!"

But Nathan was pursuing his own thoughts. "I don't understand about the Grandir. If he knew the spell he'd do it, wouldn't he? I've seen him up close, in my dreams—he's ruthless, but he wants to save the people, to save the rest of this world. I'm sure of it. He has the power, and he's got some kind of a plan, even if it isn't ready yet . . ."

"He's afraid to act," she said dismissively. "Or maybe he's just afraid to fail. He's been around a long time, longer than anyone can remember: his powers may be weakening. No one knows. He tells his councilors little and everyone else nothing. He might have a plan, yes, but it'll be a plan just for *him*, him and his bridesister, his precious Halmé. He might have kept the Grail in your world because he wanted to open the barrier from there, without a Great Spell—to open it just enough for two people to slip through."

"If that was what he wanted, he'd have done it already," Nathan retorted with a confidence he couldn't explain.

"Have you seen her?" Kwanji demanded, with an abrupt change of subject. "In your dreams—have you seen Halmé?"

"Yes."

"Is she—?"

"She's beautiful. Yes." Halmé the legend, the unseen face of Helen. He saw a trace of something like awe in Kwanji's expression, foreign to her nature—until she banished it.

"They say her father kept her hidden for a hundred years, for fear that her beauty would drive men mad," she said. "Anyone who set eyes on her was immediately executed."

"*Really?*" Nathan was startled. "That's ridiculous. I mean— overreaction! She's beautiful, but—she's a woman. Like you. An ordinary woman."

"Maybe it was just a rumor," Kwanji said, and the hint of a smile softened her mouth. "Still, you are indeed a child—an alien. You don't understand what beauty means."

"It doesn't mean killing," Nathan said positively.

Kwanji gave a complicated shiver, as though throwing off some clinging foulness. "We've talked enough," she declared. "It's time to go. You must dream now. Dream me out of here—dream me to the Sangreal."

"I *am* dreaming," Nathan said. He took her hands, and this time it was *his* clasp that was tight. He tried to recapture the urgency he'd felt when he rescued Eric, the surge of his inner will, but there was only a faltering, and the certainty of failure. He closed his eyes, picturing the desert beyond the cave, concentrating on Kwanji's handclasp, on her need—reaching for the uprush of the dark. For a long minute he thought nothing was happening—and then it had already happened, the world had turned, he could no longer feel the floor of the Pit beneath him. He opened his eyes again, even as her fingers slipped through his, and he saw the desert night stretching in every direction, and the predawn pallor spilling slowly along the horizon. A dozen thoughts flashed through his mind at once—the giant lizard-monster, the distance to the cave, the sundeath that was coming inexorably with the advent of day. She had no mask, no protective clothing, only the inadequate garment of her imprisonment. He tried to shout: No! *No!*—he tried to hold on to her. But the darkness was too strong for him. He was sucked away, out of that world, out of consciousness, into a gulf of sleep . . .

When he woke, it was morning. Morning in this world. The thread of sky between the curtains was gray. Thought was already there in his waking mind, jerking him upright, filling him with a terrible awareness. He'd dumped her there—out in the desert, with the monster and the sundeath. She had no chance. She might dodge the monster, but not the sun. The cave had been far away. She would die—because of him. "I must get back," he said out loud. "I *must*." But no one answered, and sleep was far away. He was back in his own world at the whim of some erratic fate, and there was nothing he could do about it. In his frustration he tore down the Mark of Agares where it was pinned on the wall. Then he went into the bathroom and scrubbed furiously at the rune on his arm, until it was almost obliterated. Perhaps without the Mark to hold him he would be able to get back—but when he lay down again and closed his eyes there was only the beat of his heart, and the shapes of vanished light on the back of his eyelids.

INSPECTOR POBJOY stared in bewilderment at the autopsy results. "This isn't possible," he said to the assistant pathologist, who had been ordered to convey the bad news. "It *has* to be murder. Think of the blow to his head. It has to be . . ."

"Not necessarily." The pathologist tried to look deprecating, but succeeded only in looking smug. "There were plenty of low branches in the wood. He pushes one away from him, it springs back, catches him on the side of the skull—there may have been blood traces, though it'd be hard to find anything after the storm—the branch knocks him out. His face is pressed into the leafmold—nose and mouth fill with mud—he asphyxiates."

"It says he *drowned*."

"It was raining."

"No one drowns in the rain! Do you take me for an idiot?"

"Look, there was water in his lungs. The rain may have caused a small flood; at ground level, it wouldn't need to be much. If his face was covered for long enough . . ."

Pobjoy made an impatient gesture.

"You can't argue with the facts," said the pathologist. Smugly.

Pobjoy looked as if he could, and would, argue with any facts they wished to provide. He dismissed the pathologist before another body was added to the roster and sat studying the autopsy report and brooding savagely. He had two people who had (allegedly) drowned, under circumstances that were in one case merely suspicious, while in the other definitely bizarre. Surely it was impossible to drown in a wood? Could the corpse have been moved after death? Improbable, according to the report. Of course, when you have eliminated the impossible, whatever remains, no matter how improbable, *must* be the truth. God, he hated Sherlock Holmes. A man who had oozed smugness—a cokehead—a conspiracy theorist with paranoid tendencies. The trouble was, this whole case reeked of Sherlock Holmes–ness. A quiet village, a stolen chalice, two people who had—against all the odds—died naturally. And a dwarf. No doubt there was some fiendish supercriminal behind it all, with uncanny powers of disguise and a penchant for drowning his victims even if there was no water at hand . . .

He jerked his mind back to reality and tried to focus on more credible options.

"I SEEM to have missed all the excitement," said Michael. "Rianna and I spent the weekend near Oxford—an old friend of mine was having a barbecue. It rained there, too. Funny thing: you can have the best summer for a decade and if you organize a barbecue it'll *always* rain."

"Your alibi?" asked Rowena. She had dropped in to talk things over with Annie and found Michael there, ostensibly on the same errand.

"I don't want an alibi," Michael said with a faint grimace. "I wanted to be where the action was."

"Too much action," said Rowena. "One dead body and a major theft. Police are bloody useless. Trying to tell me I imagined things! There's enough going on now without anyone throwing in imagination. Didn't see the thief too clearly—dark in there when the lights went out—but he was short, quick, and hairy. *Really* short—like four feet. Not a performing animal, no chance. Moved like a person. Had to be a dwarf."

"Why should a dwarf steal the Grimthorn Grail?" Annie said. She was talking on autopilot, her thoughts elsewhere. Rianna Sardou was in London—or at least something that looked like Rianna Sardou *might* be in London. Michael hadn't renewed his dinner invitation, but he was here.

"Don't know," said Rowena. "Whole thing's a complete mystery. Tell you this much, though: I'm going to get it back. Got my ear to the ground already. Anyone tries to fence it, I'll know. Got a lot of contacts in the trade."

"Surely it would be impossible to sell?" Michael said. "Its main value must be as a historical artifact. That would mean a very specific market."

Rowena made a gloomy noise, possibly affirmation. "Eric's got some strange ideas about it," she remarked. "Alternative realities and all that. Explains a few things, but . . . Good man, though. Trustworthy. Wherever he's from." She flicked Annie a sharp look, but her hostess missed it. "Anyway," she concluded, "I'll be off now. Got calls to make. If you think of anything—"

"I'll be in touch," Annie assured her.

She was left with Michael.

"Actually," he said, "I didn't really come to talk about all that. I know it's a bit of a thrill—the kids must have had a ball, chasing the thief, and getting covered in mud, and stumbling over a body—not such a great idea, that last one, I hope they weren't upset—"

"Nathan's okay," Annie said.

"It's not as though they knew him, thank God—where was I? Oh—hedging. I came to talk about something else."

Annie looked a question.

"Rianna. I tried to ask her what happened, the other afternoon, but she denied even seeing you. And her clothes—the clothes she was wearing when I left—they were on the bedroom floor, and they were *wet*. She's acting very odd lately—I can't put my finger on it—but she's not herself. Last weekend my friends asked if she'd been ill. It's as if she's had some sort of a personality change. There are illnesses that take you like that, brain tumors, that kind of thing. I suggested she might see a doctor but she flared up. Annie, I don't know what to do. It isn't the best marriage in the world, but if she's going to be ill I must stick by her."

"Yes," Annie said, since something was clearly expected of her.

"Of course, it could be purely mental—schizophrenia, for instance. It *can* develop later in life, though it usually starts in adolescence. If she's evolving a dual personality . . ."

You could say so, Annie thought.

"Oh bugger," Michael said, his mouth wry. "I'm making a mess of this. Look, I wanted to say . . . Whatever happens with Rianna, I want to see you. I was still hoping we could do dinner . . . this week? I'm sorry: this all sounds so irrational. I'm saying in the same breath that I'm worried about my wife and I want to be with you. You must think me such a cad."

"No," said Annie. She was feeling very short of words.

"If she is going mad, maybe I could lock her in the attic, go all dark and brooding, and you and I could . . . Sorry. Sorry. I sound flip and shallow. It's just that I'm upset. I always act flip when I'm upset. About dinner—"

And at that moment—of course—the shop door opened.

This time it was Inspector Pobjoy, with Belinda Hale in his wake and an official expression on his face. Annie's pang of irritation evaporated into nebulous anxiety.

"Where's your son?" Pobjoy asked without preamble, paying no attention to Michael.

"He went into the woods—walking. He's not much of a one for computer games and things—fortunately. He likes to get out. The other kids aren't on vacation yet, so . . ."

"Why do you want to know?" Michael demanded. He had gotten to his feet, and his attitude was a shade protective, with a hint of challenge.

"I'm afraid that's my business," said the inspector. "I'd like a word with you alone, Mrs. Ward."

"I'm staying," Michael said flatly. And to Annie: "I don't like the look of this. You may need some advice. I can fix you up with a lawyer if necessary."

"Are you going to arrest me?" Annie said, baffled and almost laughing.

"No, Mrs. Ward. Just a few questions."

"Sit down," she said, looking around at a shortage of chairs. "I mean—question away."

Chairless, the inspector proceeded. "Your son and his friends helped in the search for Mrs. Thorn's missing injunction, didn't they? The one you found?"

"Yes."

"I expect they were very keen. It was a bit of an adventure, right? They got *involved*."

"Er . . . yes."

"They're good kids," Michael said sharply. "No criminal tendencies. Especially Nat."

"I daresay they were fairly partisan," Pobjoy pursued in a fairly relaxed manner. "They knew Mrs. Thorn—they supported her. They wanted her to have the cup—of course they did. It was a family heirloom: the Luck of the Thorns. They must have found it all rather romantic. When they heard the Grail was being brought to Thornyhill, naturally they wanted to see it. They hid outside the house to spy on the meeting."

"What are you suggesting?" Michael snapped. Annie laid a hand on his arm, restraining him, though he had hardly moved. She, too, was standing, staring at the policeman. Her face was very pale.

Pobjoy continued remorselessly. "The cup was stolen, according to witnesses, by a mystery dwarf. I don't believe in mystery dwarfs. I think it was just a short person. Maybe a child."

"Nat's tall for his age," Michael said instantly.

"Taller than me," Annie said softly. Horrible doubts were fomenting at the back of her brain.

"The girl isn't," Pobjoy rejoined. "She's on the small side—five feet or less. She could have worn a mask. Something left over from Halloween, or a costume party. It's the kind of thing a kid would have. The lights went out, and she seized her opportunity. Got the cup, and they ran off into the woods. Then they hid it somewhere, intending to come back and claim they'd chased the real thief."

"Bollocks," Michael said. "Utter bollocks from start to finish."

"I don't suppose they thought it was wrong," Pobjoy went on, ignoring him. "They thought the cup was Mrs. Thorn's by right, and they were stealing it for *her*. They probably plan to give it to her as soon as the fuss has died down. I expect they see themselves as heroes, *rescuing* the cup from the bad guys."

"Nathan's not that naïve." Annie spoke at last, conscious of a growing certainty. "Anyway, he would never, *ever* let Hazel take the risk. He's not bossy, but he's the leader among his friends, the dominant one. He wouldn't allow anyone, least of all Hazel, to take the dangerous role. He just wouldn't. Even if his morals got twisted up the way you suggest, he'd always insist on doing the risky part himself. And he's much too tall for a dwarf."

"I hate to spoil a good idea," Michael added sarcastically, "but so's Hazel. Rowena Thorn was in here earlier. She said specifically that the thief couldn't have been more than four feet tall."

"People get confused in the dark," said Pobjoy. "I prefer the obvious explanation. Contrary to popular fiction, it's usually true."

"Do you think they murdered the Graf as well?" Annie asked quietly.

"According to the autopsy report"—Pobjoy almost sighed—"his death was an accident."

"Accident?" Michael and Annie demanded in chorus.

"They seem to think he could've been struck by a rebounding branch, knocked out with his face in the leaf litter, and drowned in mud and rainwater."

"Drowned . . . ," Annie echoed, in a whisper.

"There are too many people getting drowned around here lately," Michael said in a suddenly shaken voice.

"But . . ." Annie's face changed as a thought struck her. "I understood he died around lunchtime. That's what you said before. It didn't start to rain until much later."

Pobjoy swore to himself. She was right, and he hadn't spotted it. The path lab had conveniently forgotten—or failed to check—what time the rain started. And before that, the ground would have been dry as a bone.

"When your son comes back, Mrs. Ward," he said, "I'd like to talk to him. Please call me at this number." He handed her a card. "And don't worry too much about what the children did. They're underage, and although the act was criminal, the motives weren't. Once they've returned the cup, I'm sure the court will take a lenient view."

"They don't have the cup to return," Annie said when the police had gone. "I *know*."

"Me, too," said Michael. "We need a lawyer."

"I must warn Lily," Annie said. And: "Thank you. Thank you for standing by me. Us."

"I'll always stand by you," Michael said. His tone was abrupt and almost cold, free from sentiment. She looked up at him with the hint of a question in her face.

His arms went around her as though of their own volition, and he kissed her—not a quick peck on the cheek but a real kiss, opening her mouth with his. But the moment of intimacy was swift, and swiftly over. He drew back, looking as shaken as she felt. "Sorry. Sorry. I shouldn't have . . . *Very* bad timing. I'll sort out the lawyer, I promise. Call you tomorrow." And then he went, letting the door slam behind him, leaving her in such a state of emotional upheaval she almost forgot to phone Lily Bagot.

The Grail
Quest

Hazel and Lily were taken to the police station in Crowford for a formal interview. Pobjoy wanted answers, and he judged the official surroundings might prove sufficiently daunting to inspire them. Deep down inside, he had a nagging feeling he could be on a losing streak, but the circumstantial evidence was damning, and his hunches had gotten him exactly nowhere. He had believed the children's story at first, but bitter experience had taught him to distrust belief. There had been the insurance fraudster who claimed he was in France when his business premises burned down, the stepfather who wept crocodile tears for a murdered teenager, the pedophile teacher who declared his only interest was in education. True, he hadn't actually *believed* any of them, but he might have done, if he had been more credulous, if they had been well-behaved thirteen-year-olds who had managed to sneak under the barbed-wire fence of his instincts. You thought you had seen it all, he reflected, and then something worse came along. Still, their motives had been good . . .

"You wanted to help Mrs. Thorn, didn't you?" he said. "That's why you looked for the injunction."

Hazel made a tiny sound that might have been: "Mm."

"And then you were afraid it wouldn't do the trick. D'you have a friend who knows about the law?"

Hazel thought of George's legal ambitions, but decided that didn't qualify. She said, a little louder: "No."

"You heard they were bringing the cup to Thornyhill, so you and Nathan decided to spy on the meeting. You must have been pretty excited about it."

It wasn't a question, and Hazel saw no need to answer it. She shut her mouth very tightly, trying not to be afraid, wishing Nathan were here. He would've known what to say.

"Were you excited?"

She shrugged.

"But you were interested enough to go to Thornyhill, and hide outside the house. Were you hoping to sneak in when no one was looking, and see what was going on?"

Another shrug. But she was tugging at her hair, pulling it over her face, always a sign of nerves.

"They were just naturally curious," Lily said. "They'd heard a lot about the cup. It was just an adventure to them."

"I'm sure it was," said Pobjoy. "You must have been disappointed when you didn't find the injunction. I expect you and Nathan talked about how wonderful it would be if you could get the cup, and give it back to Mrs. Thorn. Didn't you, Hazel? *Didn't you?*"

"No."

"So what *did* you talk about then? Tell me."

Other worlds, Hazel thought. *Dreampower.* She didn't answer.

"What—did—you—talk—about?" Pobjoy repeated.

"Stuff. Music. School. You know."

"But not the cup of the Thorns?"

"Not much."

"Not *much*." It was too small an admission to be of value, but he did his best to build on it. "Not much, but enough. You thought of the Graf Von Humboldt and the people from Sotheby's as the bad guys, didn't you? You thought the cup was rightfully the property of Mrs. Thorn. You waited in the storm, hoping for an opportunity, and then the lights went out. Do you recognize this?" He held up a rubbery green thing with rat's-tail hair hanging down on either side.

"It's my witch mask," Hazel said, taken by surprise. "I had it for Halloween, two years ago. What about it?"

"You can't take that," Lily said. "You couldn't—you didn't have a search warrant. I know you have to have a search warrant."

"It was in the garbage can," Pobjoy said. "We don't need a warrant for that. At a guess, you were the one who threw it out, just before we got there."

Lily turned from the inspector to her daughter in evident panic, looking both guilty and confused. Annie had told her about the inspector's insinuations, and she had found the mask in Hazel's room before she returned from school and determined to dispose of it. "I want a lawyer," she said.

"If you insist. It will mean keeping you both here for some time while we obtain one."

"What about the mask?" Hazel hadn't been primed. "Why is it important?"

"Witnesses to the theft described someone *short*, almost a dwarf, with lots of hair"—he glanced at Hazel's untidy mop—"the face unclear. How tall are you, Hazel?"

As the sense of what he said sank in, she went white, then red. White with shock, red with anger. "There *was* a dwarf," she said. "He was nearly a foot shorter than me. We saw him—we chased him. I haven't bothered with that stupid mask in ages. Ask the other people—ask Mr. Goodman, Mrs. Thorn. It was a *dwarf*."

"Mr. Goodman wasn't in the room at the time of the theft," Pobjoy said. "Of the others, both Alex Birnbaum and Julian Epstein concede that the thief could have been a child." The concessions had been reluctant, but he didn't mention that.

"I'm nearly five feet," Hazel confessed; it was clearly a sore point. "It's not that tall, but it's too tall for a dwarf. He was *really short*, I told you—"

"You tell lies sometimes, don't you? You sent us an anonymous letter about your great-grandmother's death. That was a lie, wasn't it?" He didn't really think so, he just wanted to keep her off balance, talking too much, admitting things. "Mrs. Carlow died naturally; you just wanted to make trouble. For your father, perhaps? You thought if he went to prison he wouldn't hurt your mother anymore. Was that it?"

"No—it wasn't that—it wasn't him—"

"And now you're lying about this. I'm sure it was all in a good cause—right? You weren't stealing the cup, you were saving it. Planning to restore it to its rightful owner."

"No—"

"Stop!" Lily cried. "Stop *now*. I want a lawyer. I don't care how long it takes. You can't bully her anymore. You're not allowed to talk to her until the lawyer comes. I can say that, can't I?" She sounded both resolute and uncertain.

"I didn't do anything," Hazel persisted. "I didn't take the cup. Nathan will tell you—"

"I expect it was Nathan's idea," Pobjoy suggested, giving them both an out. "He pushed you into it, didn't he?"

Hazel gave him a look so scornful he was jolted. "*Nathan?* Nathan would never do *anything* wrong. He's not like that. And he doesn't push people into things. You're stupid. Nathan's . . . different. He would never steal in a million years."

And the worst of it is, Pobjoy thought, beating a temporary retreat, *I believe her.*

NATHAN HAD been searching for Woody again, still without success. It was nearly six when he got home, and Annie looked both anxious and impatient. "Hazel's been arrested," she said.

"*What?*"

Annie launched into a disjointed explanation. "They may not have actually arrested her but I saw them drive off in a police car with her and Lily. They want to talk to you, too. They think you took the Grail. If you have any idea where it is—"

"Do *you* think I took it?" he demanded, picking up on the implication immediately.

"Of course not. But if we could get it back I'm sure they'd drop the whole thing."

"What about the murder?"

"They've convinced themselves it was an accident," Annie explained. "Never mind about the murder. It's the cup . . . I ought to call the inspector. He said he wanted to see you at once."

"*No.* Please, Mum. I can get the cup if you just give me time. I'm almost certain I know where it is. The dwarf sent it back into the other world . . ."

"Worlds tend to be big places," Annie pointed out. "Where would you look?"

"It was kept in a cave before it was here, or so they said. I'm sure it's back there. It's the logical place. If I could get it—return it to Sotheby's—they'd let Hazel go, wouldn't they? There wouldn't be a crime anymore."

"I think that would depend on how Sotheby's and the Graf's family felt about it," Annie said doubtfully. "And the police, of course. Oh dear. If you bring it back, they'll *definitely* think you took it."

"Doesn't matter," Nathan said. "Let them think."

He had started upstairs as he spoke. Annie called after him: "What are you going to do?"

"Sleep!" came the answer.

He had never been able to sleep—or dream—to order, but now he must, *he must*. He thought of Hazel in a gray-walled room, shrinking into a chair while faceless policemen hurled accusations at her. It wasn't a relaxing image. That was no good: he must find the place in his mind, the weak spot, the chink through which his awareness escaped when it moved from Here to There. The falling darkness spotted with stars and whirling with planets. He reached not out but inward, all the way in, deep into himself. There seemed to be great spaces in his head, as if its inside were far bigger than its outside, and shadows lay darkly over the crevasses of the subconscious, and somewhere up above there was a white light shining into him, its rays streaming down like a visitation from God. And *then* he found what he was looking for, on the far left—he didn't know if he could see it or feel it, but it was there behind his eye, a patch of something that didn't belong. He thought it was bluish, though it was hard to be sure, and filled with snowflecks that winked in and out of existence like interference on a TV screen. He pulled with his mind, drawing all his being inward, pouring himself into that blob of otherness. Instantly, he dreamed.

There may have been sleep: he felt as if he emerged not from a waking state but from brief yet bottomless oblivion. He spun down the tunnel, trying to decide if the planets and galaxies were the same or different ones. He thought it might be a wormhole, if a wormhole could connect not just different points in space but spaces in different worlds. A planet hove past him that was red with boiling gases; storms the size of continents slipped beneath his feet—if his consciousness had feet. Giant rings rushed toward him—then there was something in front of him like a wall, a cold dead surface pitted with craters, like a bad case of global acne. But it flicked away, and everything speeded up, and sound was a dim throbbing roar, as of a vast wind far off, but he had a strange feeling that if you could slow it down, there might be music in it. Then came the dazzle of light, so his eyes closed, and a kind of silent, whole-body *thud* as he collided with atmosphere, destination, his own being.

He opened his eyes and looked around. He felt more solid than he ever had—he sensed the difference at once—as if his own world was the dream, and *this* was real. He wouldn't be able to shift from place to place anymore: he was stuck. Stuck in himself, bounded by reality. He should have been terrified, but he was too busy wondering where he was.

He seemed to be in a complex of interconnecting chambers, all circular. He was sitting on a curving sofa in the largest one, with a round rug on the floor, and curious pieces of furniture scattered about, all round, or curved, or blob-shaped. There were no external windows: the light, as always on Eos, appeared to come out of the walls, and down from the ceiling, though there were individual lamps in oval recesses that shone with hues of pink and apricot and turquoise. Everything else took color from them. One of the adjacent chambers was fitted with what looked like a bed; another, closed off with a screen of clouded glass, emitted watery sounds, bubbling, and gurgling, and faint splashes. *It's like a bedroom suite,* Nathan deduced, *and someone's in the bath.* For a moment he thought of hiding—but he couldn't hide now, not anymore. He was here, and he was real, and he needed help.

He wasn't really surprised when the glass screen slid back and Halmé emerged from the bathroom.

She wore a loose robe that hung open in a curious echo of

Kwanji's prison garb, and her body was all glowing golden smoothness, with swells and hollows, and shapes of bone gentled under the
mantling of flesh and skin. He thought she resembled an art deco
statue he had seen once in Rowena's shop, unnaturally tall and slender, elongated into an impossible perfection. He gaped and stared as
you stare at beauty, not womanhood, remembering too late to be embarrassed.

"Sorry, I—"

"Who—?" Halmé drew her robe around her, but it seemed to be
a purely automatic gesture. She, too, was staring. Her eyes were very
dark and yet seemed to be shot with hidden colors. "Who are you?
How did you get in here?"

"My name's Nathan."

"You're very small. What race are you—what planet? Are you a
refugee?" She looked anxious or concerned and he thought: *Refugees
carry contamination.*

He said: "I'm human. From earth. It's not here: it's in another
universe." She was silent, still staring, and he went on: "I'm small because I'm thirteen. I'm still growing. Actually, I'm not that small in
my world—people are shorter there—but I'll get taller. I'm really tall
for thirteen."

Her face altered—softened. Shock drained away. "You're a
child," she said. "Is that right? You're saying—you're a child?"

He remembered what Eric had said. No children here for hundreds of years. And . . . hadn't he said Halmé had tried to conceive,
before the magic stopped her womb, tried and failed?

He said: "Yes."

Emotion seemed to be breaking over her in waves; he saw the ripples traversing her expression. She came closer, reached out, touched
him, touched his cheek. "You might be my son," she said. "You are
not so very alien. Your face is—wrong. The wrong shape. Too short,

too broad, too low *here*"—she brushed an eyebrow—"but I think you are beautiful." He noticed that she believed him without questioning, without doubt.

He said awkwardly: "I think you are beautiful, too."

"Do you? All my life people have told me I am beautiful. My beauty has a life of its own, a life of fame and legend that has nothing to do with me. But you come from another world, where people look different—a world of children—yet you say I am beautiful. I think—that is the first time it has ever meant anything." She smiled, and he realized he had never seen her smile till now. "My name is Halmé."

"I know," he said. "I've seen you before. To begin with, when I got here I was invisible, then—like a ghost—sort of transparent. This is the most *real* I've ever been in your world."

"I've felt you," she said. "I've felt you watching. When we went to the laboratory, you followed. That was months ago. How long have you been here?"

"I come and go. It's dreams—I dream myself here. That's how I got in. And time must be different. It wasn't months ago in my world, when I followed you to that laboratory."

"How do you speak our language?"

"I don't know. I just do." In the dream, it came easily, fluently, as if it was native to him.

"Why did you come to me?" Halmé asked.

"I found myself here. I don't choose—I can't control it. I go—wherever I end up. I don't think it's random, but I don't know how it happens. I wanted to get here, and I found the place in my mind where I go when I dream—the way through. But I've no idea why I came out in your rooms. Honestly." He added: "I didn't mean to interrupt your bath."

"It doesn't matter," she said. "I'd finished. Anyway, I'm glad. I'm glad you came here. If there is a pattern, then it was *meant*. My brother believes in patterns. He says all worlds are interwoven, part of a Great Pattern, and if you have the power you can change it, bend it around you."

"Your brother . . . the Grandir?"

"Of course—you saw him, too. He will want to meet you—" She stopped. The light dimmed in her eyes.

"I came to you," Nathan said.

"He would be angry, if he knew I had hidden something like this from him. Something like you."

"Does he—does he get violent, when he's angry?"

"No." She looked faintly surprised at the suggestion. "He's never violent. He wouldn't harm me in any way. But his anger is—terrible. I feel it inside me, clouding me, darkening everything . . . He sets me at a distance, isolates me. I can't bear that. I need him to love me." There was something oddly childish in that plea, even to Nathan's ear. He decided it would be a mistake to tell her that the Grandir already knew of him, spied on him, through a star that wasn't a star. He didn't know if the Grandir was a good man, but he was ruthless, and powerful—too powerful for Nathan—and to ask his help would mean to let him take over. Nathan knew this was a task for *him*. Besides, the Grandir had an unknown purpose, a Plan—perhaps he was bending the Great Pattern of all the worlds around himself even now, and Nathan, though he was only the tiniest particle in that Pattern, had no intention of being bent.

"You don't have to tell him about me," he suggested tentatively, "if you don't want to."

"He'd find out," Halmé said. "He reads minds."

"Not yours," Nathan said, suddenly positive, remembering how the Grandir had refrained from touching her at the gnomons' cage, though he told her to draw back. "Not if he wasn't suspicious. He wouldn't intrude. You know he wouldn't."

"Ye-es," she said slowly. "That is true. But . . ."

"I need your help. Please. There's something I have to do here, and you can help me—only you. I know that's why I found myself here. Like you said, it was *meant*."

She sat down on the curve of the sofa and motioned him to sit beside her. She looked almost resolute, almost hesitant, like someone trying against her nature to be brave. "Tell me everything," she said.

He didn't, of course. But he told her about the Sangreal being in his world, and how it was there for safekeeping, because neo-salvationists and suchlike might steal it if it was here, and do the Great Spell, and get it wrong.

"A Great Spell," she said. "Oh yes. A Great Spell to change the Great Pattern. I know."

He explained how a thief in his world had taken it, and sent it back, and his friend was wrongly arrested by the authorities, and he had to restore the Grail to save her, as well as for the sake of the Grail itself. He kept it simple, and hoped it was true. He *felt* it was true, with some deep unexplained vein of instinct. Kwanji Ley was a good person, he was sure, but perhaps she had been misguided, or the organization had used her. Anyway, he didn't believe the spell could be cobbled together, or performed by people who didn't know what it really was. That would be like some madman trying to build an atom bomb in his own garage. He held on to that thought, and watched Halmé's face, which managed somehow to be expressive and at the same time unreadable, maybe because he didn't know what it was supposed to express. Possibly it was an effect of that exquisite disproportion, the alien quality of her features. He was dimly aware that she was struggling to overcome some flaw in her own nature, weakness or inertia, fighting to become someone she had never been.

At last she said: "I *can* help you, I know I can. I *will*. But it is a big task for a small person. Do children in your world usually perform such tasks?"

Nathan thought of all the books he had ever read, of the Pevensies, Colin and Susan, Harry Potter, Lyra Belacqua, and a hundred others. "All the time," he said.

ANNIE SPENT an uneasy, restless evening. Thoughts of Michael and the kiss frequently intruded, usually at the most inappropriate moments, leaving her confused and vaguely guilty because she had more important things to worry about. She telephoned Bartlemy, who was kind and unruffled and calmed her fears a little. "The evidence against the children is purely circumstantial, and without a confession or further proof it would be difficult for the police to proceed. Besides, the eyewitness statements refer categorically to a dwarf, and both children are too tall. If the cup can be returned, I think they'd drop the case. Trust Nathan. He has courage and determination— and he's very intelligent, which always helps. Where is he?"

"In bed," Annie said baldly.

"I see."

She looked in on him around eight, to find him sleeping on his side, fully clothed even to his shoes. She thought of taking them off, then remembered that whatever he was wearing he would wear in his dreams, and presumably he didn't want to be prowling around the other world with bare feet. So she contented herself with putting a blanket over him, closing the curtains, and leaving him to wherever sleep would take him. She didn't call the police, and they didn't call her, but she was sure Pobjoy would be on the line in the morning. Around nine thirty, Lily Bagot phoned to tell her they had finally been allowed to return home. Hazel hadn't been charged, and the lawyer seemed to be saying the same thing as Bartlemy, but rather more aggressively. Still, Lily sounded strained to the exhaustion point, alternately tearful and furious, and Annie offered to go over there. Lily said no thanks, it was lovely of her, but Hazel wanted a word. And then Hazel's voice took over, asking nervously if Nathan was there.

"He's here," Annie said, "but he can't come to the phone right now. He's—he's gone to get the Grail back."

There was a short pause. "Gone where?" Hazel demanded.

"The other world. He's . . . sleeping. Don't be afraid. He won't fail you."

"Good," Hazel said, and hung up.

Annie thought of calling Michael, but she didn't know what to say and what to leave out, and suddenly she was very tired. She went to bed without disturbing Nathan, but for all her weariness sleep was a long time coming, and her thoughts turned to Rianna, for a little variety in her worries. She wondered where the real Rianna was, in Georgia or under some strange enchantment, and she slipped into a dream where Rianna lay on a bed in a ruined castle, locked in a sorcerous sleep for time uncounted, while roses grew over her couch, enclosing her in a cage of thorns.

AND NOW he was flying through the air on the back of his own xaurian, while the warm desert night poured over him. He was wearing protective clothing that Halmé had procured for him; a scanner in her chambers had read his measurements, and the garments had appeared to order in the space of about an hour. They were seamless, made of some fabric that felt like metal but moved like silk, blue with a gray sheen or gray with a blue sheen. There was also a pair of goggles whose tint varied according to the light, like Polaroid lenses. "You will need a guide," Halmé said. "Someone I can trust"—and somehow he wasn't surprised when the man she summoned was Raymor, though he knew of no previous connection between them. "He was my bodyguard," she explained, "when I was very young, and my father thought I had need of guarding. My father was rigid in his ideas, but Ray was kind. Sometimes we laughed together." She concluded: "He would die for me," not in wonder, nor vanity, but as a minor detail, a mere commonplace. Raymor remembered Nathan as the ghost who had sat behind him once before, and seemed in some awe of him. His mission, Halmé declared, was totally secret. "Since it is important, the Grandir has authorized me to take charge," she said. Even though his face was hidden, Nathan could sense Raymor's doubt. So did Halmé. "He trusts me as he trusts no other," she said, and Raymor appeared to relax a little.

Then they were soaring over the city, cutting up the slower skimmers, skirting the curving flanks of giant buildings, diving under arches, and lifting over crested roofs. The teeming lights—from screened window and high door, from eyelamp and hanging globe—looped and dipped and streamed behind them, until at last the city fell away, and the remaining traffic swerved north or west, and they headed southeast into a night with no lights at all. Despite his worries Nathan couldn't help enjoying himself. He had felt insecure at first, straddling the reptile's narrow back, knowing that his solidity was no longer borderline and if he came off there was nothing to hit but the ground. Also, he had little confidence in his ability to steer the xaurian—he had once ridden a horse, which ignored everything he did with the reins. But the beast appeared content to follow its stablemate, the pommel of the saddle was high enough to hold on to, and he soon grew accustomed to the dipping and wheeling of the flight. Below, he thought he could see the regular outlines of fields, and long tubular buildings like greenhouses, gleaming in the double moonrise; the third moon of Eos always lagged behind. He asked Raymor about them, using the communicator inside his hood. "We grow most vegetables under the filterscreens," Raymor answered. "Very few crops are hardy enough now to survive the sun. The fields are mostly left to the weeds and spittlegrass. What planet are you from, where they still grow crops outdoors?"

"You wouldn't know it," Nathan said.

The signs of cultivation ceased, and there was only the desert, with the dunes rolling like great waves, pathless and shapeless, changeful as the sea. They flew for what seemed like hours, barely speaking. The night drew on, and the moons followed their diverse paths across the sky. The third moon rose over the horizon, late and last, its face bisected with an arc of darkness. It was redder than the other two, blood-bright, and its light showed the landscape hardening into rock, weather-rounded ridges thrusting upward through the ocean of sand. Ancient watercourses made deep creases in the slopes, snaring the shadows. Stars clustered thickly at the zenith of the sky, but their pale glimmer did not touch the earth: this belonged to the third moon alone. "It is called Astrond," said Raymor, "the Red Moon of Madness. Long ago, when pollution first began to change its color, people said it was unlucky to be out under such a moon."

"Do you believe that?" Nathan asked.

"Superstition is not encouraged here."

"But you use magic," Nathan objected, thinking the two things went hand in hand.

"We use power. Magic of the kind you mean, wild magic, out of control—that was over in the remote past. We harnessed it and tamed it."

"Then what is the contamination?"

Raymor didn't answer for some time. The xaurian's wings tilted, making a slight change of direction, and a single beat swept them southward. "Men made that," he said eventually. "They misused the power, warping it to evil. I suppose you could say that what followed was the magic fighting back. That would be one way of looking at it. We thought we could rule the universe, mold it in our own image.

We might have succeeded if it hadn't been for war, and the desire to kill."

"Must there always be war?" Nathan said. "Surely, if you're civilized enough, you can live without it."

"I don't know," said Raymor. "That was a level of civilization we never attained."

They flew on. A faint grayness above the eastern horizon showed a ragged line of mountains. Raymor had estimated they would reach the cave around dawn, and Nathan tried to convince himself the mountain range looked familiar. The recollection of the monster had taken over his thoughts, but he hoped it might be easier to pass it in the dark. "Are we nearly there?"

"Maybe half an hour."

"How will we dodge the lizard thing? Will it be asleep?"

"The Grokkul hears and feels even in its sleep." Raymor's tone was even.

"Will it see us, if we try to slip past?" Nathan asked.

"It sees heat. To the Grokkul, your body glows in the dark. Or in the light. I will distract it. You must go in the cave alone."

"That sounds awfully dangerous for you," Nathan said unhappily. He knew, even if Raymor didn't, that the entrance would be too narrow for an adult male.

"It's more dangerous for you," Raymor responded. "The Grokkul's main object is to guard the cave."

There was silence for a while. Nathan struggled to feel brave, conscious that he was failing. Hazel in a police cell seemed impossibly far away, and the monster was very near. At last he said: "Thank you. I mean, thank you for helping me, for risking your life. Whatever happens. And good luck."

"May the luck be yours," said Raymor, and somehow Nathan knew it was a traditional rejoinder, but it made him even more uncomfortable.

The light was growing now, reaching out across the sky, paling the desert to gray. Astrond, caught above the western horizon, still showed dimly red. And now far ahead Nathan thought he could discern the cliff face that hid the cave, and the irregular slope with its double row of triangular boulders. His internal organs gave an unwelcome jolt; he wished they weren't approaching so fast, but the light was faster. The sun inched above the mountains, washing the sandscape with color and shadow. The slope was nearly under them now. Nathan tried to distinguish the outline of the monster, the broad flat head and splayed feet, but though there were humps that he guessed might be the eyes, its camouflage was so perfect he could almost fool himself it wasn't there. He could see no sign of the wild xaurians. Raymor called "Hold back!" and swooped low toward the rocks.

Nathan tugged on the reins, probably too hard, and his xaurian swerved awkwardly, circling away to the left. As he swung around he saw Raymor make a low pass, close to the ground, double back, and return lower still. "Next time," he said over the communicator, "you come from the other side. Fly swift and low, jump off, and run for the cave. Don't worry about your mount: it can take care of itself. Ready?"

No, Nathan thought. Raymor quickened his xaurian and plummeted. Nathan hesitated—nudged his steed just too late—saw the ground moving, rising, sand streaming from the forty-foot muzzle— saw the monster give itself a shake like an earth tremor, so the dust whirled into clouds. Raymor's mount would surely be blinded, though the extra lid might protect its eyes from hurt. Nathan looped back, uncertain what to do, and a swish of the giant tail took him unawares, catching his xaurian a glancing blow. They were knocked sideways—Nathan almost fell, clutching at the saddle, hanging on somehow. The xaurian, more intelligent than its rider, drove its wings down, gaining height, clearing the flying sand and sweeping tail. Nathan pulled himself upright and looked apprehensively for Raymor.

His guide had managed to sheer off and was hovering just out of range. The blue tongue shot out, but it wasn't long enough. The great head swayed to and fro, eyeing first Raymor, then Nathan, waiting for its prey to come within reach. Somehow, it knew better than to move away from the cave mouth. "Sorry," Nathan said. "I was too slow. Scared . . ." Oddly, his close shave had wiped out some of his fear; he felt sharper now, ready to act.

"It's natural," said Raymor. "I, too . . ."

"What do we do now?"

"Try again. This time, I'll give you the word. Don't move till I say—then move *fast*."

Nathan said *"Na' ka,"* the Eosian equivalent of "okay." He watched Raymor retreating, putting more height and distance between him and the Grokkul. The monster followed him with its right eye, keeping the left—the one injured in the earlier encounter—on Nathan; then, satisfied Ray was leaving, it swung around to seek the other meal, jaws parting to reveal the three-tiered teeth and coiled-spring tongue. It took all Nathan's courage not to kick the xaurian into flight, but he waited, hoping he was far enough away, determined not to mess up again. Far beyond the Grokkul, Raymor turned his mount, poised—and plunged.

The dive was so swift there was a tearing noise as the wings sliced through the air. With a speed unnatural to its size, the monster's head jerked back. *"Now!"* cried Raymor, but Nathan had already moved. He aimed straight for the slot of the cave mouth—the ground zoomed toward him—he was aware of horrible things happening above, of pinions thrashing helplessly, of the crunch of jaw meeting jaw. But he daren't look—he was rolling out of the saddle, tumbling over and over on the sand—scrambling to his feet and running, running for the cave. Behind him there was a *thud* that loosened stone chips from the cliff, and a scream. Not human. He flung himself into the dark, wriggled between the rock walls, staggered a couple of yards—then checked, and turned back.

He knew what he would see. Peering out of the cave, the broad head was too close for comfort, part of a wing and a tail, still twitching, protruding from the jaws. Raymor had vanished. The monster was masticating an obstinate morsel: suddenly, it made a deep coughing noise, spitting out a hunk of metallized cloth and a spray of blood. A few droplets penetrated the cave entrance, spattering Nathan's coverall. He didn't move. He felt sick with disgust and horror, but the guilt was worse. Raymor had died for *him*. The thought flickered through his mind that Halmé had expected it, had given the order, but it didn't make any difference. His own xaurian was crushed under a huge foot, stabbed through the body with a claw a yard long. One limb jerked abruptly—a muscular spasm, it must have been already dead—and then was still. The Grokkul chewed, swallowed, and then lowered its head, swinging it this way and that, attempting to see into the cave. Nathan wished he had a weapon, preferably something nuclear, but he was unarmed. "I'll get you one day," he muttered, knowing it was futile. He retreated back into the dark, raised his goggles, pulled the flashlight Halmé had provided from an inner pocket, and switched it on.

It wasn't like an ordinary flashlight since instead of producing a single beam it had a tiny sphere at one end that gave an all-around light, like a candle only far brighter. He held it up in front of him, seeing the shadows move across the ribbed walls and veins of color patterning the rock like watermarks. After a few turns the passage opened out into the main chamber: the glow of the light showed him three recesses in the far wall, crude but plainly man-made, each shielded by a metal grille. They were all empty. But there was something on the ground beside them, leaning against the rock face.

Some*one*. He recognized her only because there was no one else she could be. What skin remained to her was red and split: blood leaked from the cracks. The burning had gone beyond mere blisters; much of her body seemed to be covered with pus, some of it drying into scabs. He drew closer to her and saw that her eyes were open and aware. He couldn't see her properly, and realized he was crying. He groped inside the front of his suit for the water bottle that was stored there, hearing himself murmuring he knew not what. "Oh God, dear God . . . so sorry . . . I tried to come back, I tried to come straight away, but I couldn't. I didn't want to leave you. I told you, I can't control it, I just seem to go where I'm sent—Here, drink this." He dribbled some of the water between what was left of her lips. It was difficult while holding the flashlight, and he wondered if she could hold it for him, but her hands were clasped around something else, so he put it on the ground. He managed to give her some more water, and presently he saw her throat flex and swallow. "You need medical help," he said, stating the obvious, feeling foolish and ineffectual. "I have to get you out of here." But his xaurian was dead, and the Grokkul was waiting, and the killer sun blazed down on the shelterless desert. He could adjust his communicator to reach Halmé, but she had warned him that any long-distance call would inevitably be overheard—and Kwanji Ley was an escaped prisoner. Still, surely prison was better than death . . .

"Too late." Kwanji's voice had shrunk to a croaking whisper. "No treatment . . . for this." She swallowed again, a brief pain convulsing her face. "I knew the risk. To die here, like this, is better . . . than to live in the Pit."

"You must be in agony," he said helplessly.

"Not now. Nerves mostly . . . dead. The rest of me will catch up soon." He gave her more water, hoping it would ease the remainder of her suffering. He could think of nothing else to do. She went on talking, as far as she was able, pouring visible effort into every word. "It is good . . . that you came. You must take it . . . take it back." She attempted a gesture, but evidently it was too much for her. Looking down, he saw what she held—the object she was trying to pass to him. He would have known what it must be, if he had taken the time to think, but his thoughts had been full of her. Her hands were locked around it; she had no more strength to release them. He had to uncurl her fingers one by one. "Take it," she went on. "To . . . Osskva. He will know . . . the spell."

"Who is he? How will I find him?"

"My father." She hadn't mentioned her father before; only her grandfather. He thought the twitching of her face might have been an attempt to smile. "He didn't approve . . . but no matter. Your dream will find him."

He said wretchedly: "I can't be sure of that." He had to take the Grail back to his own world, but he couldn't tell her that, not when she was dying.

"You found me," she said. "Fate guides you. I must believe . . ."

"The other things—the crown, the sword—where are they? Shouldn't they be here?"

She made a tiny movement with her head, negation or bewilderment. "Only found . . . the cup. Grille locked—but I knew the word of release. Grandfather . . . told me. I think . . . you will find . . . the rest. Hope . . ." Her voice was growing fainter, more labored. He took her hand and then let it go, afraid of hurting her, but she nudged it back into his clasp. "Chosen," she whispered. "You . . . chosen, to save us . . ."

He sensed she was clutching at that idea because it was all she had left; it gave meaning to the last moments of her life, to her death. He didn't think it was true, but he couldn't say so. She didn't try to talk anymore. They sat in silence for some time, he didn't know how long, perhaps hours. He thought: *I'm waiting for her to die,* and that seemed dreadful to him, but to leave her, dying alone, would have been worse. Anyway, he had no notion how he was going to get back to Arkatron, let alone to his own world. There should be an opening from here to the sunken chapel in the Darkwood, but he didn't know how to use it. He couldn't solve the problem, so for now, at least, he tried not to think about it. Instead, he found himself remembering how Annie had told him once about sitting at Daniel's bedside— Daniel whom he assumed was his father—while the life ebbed out of him, sitting and waiting for the end. He had said: *That must have been awful,* and she had said: *You will do it for someone one day, maybe for me, and if you are lucky, someone will do it for you. Death gives life meaning, and when we share it with another we accept that, we face it without fear, and maybe we can go beyond it, into a wider world.*

He waited with Kwanji Ley, to share her death.

ANNIE WOKE early the next day, knowing there was a burden on her mind. Nathan—the police . . . and in the background, still the pulse-churning recollection of Michael's kiss. She went through the routine of washing, dressing, making herself tea and toast for breakfast, putting off waking Nathan because that would hasten the moment when she had to call the inspector. Perhaps he had found the Grail, in his dreams—although then Pobjoy would be certain he'd taken it, even if they didn't proceed with charges. It was a ludicrous paradox. Returning the cup might be the end of the matter, but in the eyes of the law it would be a confirmation of guilt. She worried about this for some time, knowing it was futile. You could only try to do right, and never mind what people thought. Teenagers hardly ever seemed to be prosecuted even for wanton vandalism or habitual theft, so surely they wouldn't prosecute for a crime when they believed the motive was pure . . .

She emerged from reflection to notice that it was nearly nine and there was still no sound of Nathan stirring. She went up to his room, tapped on the door, called out, and went in.

The bed was empty.

She was sure he hadn't gone out earlier: in her present restless state, his movements would almost certainly have woken her. Besides, he was good about things like straightening his bed, and the blanket was still rumpled over the duvet, and the pillow, unplumped, was dented from the pressure of a head. He'd have folded the blanket, she thought. He'd have changed his clothes. He'd have left a note. For the first time, she noticed where the Mark of Agares had been torn off the wall.

She ran downstairs to the telephone.

Bartlemy was out. His machine answered, requesting her to leave a message, and she tried to talk coherently, not to babble. "Nathan's gone. He went to bed early, like I told you, to try to find the Grail. He hasn't left the house: I'd have heard. If he gets up before I do I nearly always hear him. The bedding's all rucked up, as if he's still there, but he isn't. He must've—dematerialized, gotten stuck in the other world. The Mark you drew him, it was on the wall over the bed, but it's torn down, I don't know why. Supposing he can't get back . . . Please call me. *Please* call me."

She hung up, and waited, watching the clock, but no call came.

By ten she could stand it no longer. She had to talk to someone, go somewhere, do *something*. She locked up the shop and headed for Riverside House.

KWANJI'S EYES had closed, and he thought she must have slipped away without his realizing it, but then they opened again. They were bloodshot, but they appeared to clear and brighten, or maybe that was his imagination. She gave him a look that seemed to reach deep inside him, into his mind, into his soul; then a tiny sigh escaped her, barely audible even in the silence of the cave, and the look faded. Long afterward, he said: "There were people there. I couldn't see them, but they were there. I don't know that I was aware of them at the time, but I *remember* them. They came for her." Then he was alone.

He closed her eyes again, the way he had seen it done on television. He wondered if he should arrange the body more formally, laying her down, crossing her arms on her breast, but it didn't seem to be necessary. She was still propped against the cave wall, and she looked quite comfortable, which mattered to him, even though there was no one there to feel comfort anymore. Then he picked up the Grail, holding the flashlight to illuminate it, looking at it properly now. He half expected it to glow at his touch, like the vision in the chapel, maybe to fill with blood, but the stone, though pared to fineness and polished to a dull luster, had no sheen but that of the light reflected in the curve of the bowl, and there was nothing inside. A gem or two glinted in the coils of the design, like the eyeblink of a furtive animal: that was all. The gnomons must have followed it, or so he reasoned, and he listened for soft snake voices creeping from the shadows of the cave, but heard none. He didn't know that although Ozmosees could migrate from world to world on a thought wave, the Gate—the legitimate passage between states of being—was forbidden to them, and so they avoided the dying and the dead, and though they brought fear and madness they never killed. Death was inimical to them. But Nathan knew only that they had gone. He gazed at the Grail for a long while, awed by its ancientry, the might of legend that it carried, the power it was rumored to encapsulate; but if any spirit lived within the stone, it was hidden. At last he tucked it inside his suit, where it made an irregular bulge that dug into his side. Then he drank a mouthful of water—there was hardly any left now—and made his way cautiously to the cave entrance.

Even with his goggles, the sun was dazzling. It must have been around midday: the glare was right overhead, bleaching the blue from the sky, and shade was reduced to mere wisps and dimples etched on a colorless landscape as if with a fine-tipped pen. The vastness of the Grokkul had disappeared into sand and rock, melding with its surroundings. He knew it was there—he could see the double row of its spines—but somehow the threat seemed barely real. Some torn fragments of cloth lay outside the cave; the blood spots had long since evaporated. He thought: *I'm trapped. Even if I could get past the Grokkul, I have no transport, and the city is hundreds of miles away, and the suit might protect my skin but the heat would kill me in less than a mile* . . . His only chance was to sleep, and return home the way he had come.

Back in the cave he explored the recesses, sliding his fingers between the bars of each grille, but the rock did not waver. He kissed Kwanji's swollen hand, thinking he should have done it before, and returned to the entrance, leaning against the wall in an attitude similar to hers, eyes closed, searching his mind for the portal that would take him back. But although he found it, the wrong-colored blotch was dark and opaque, with no fizzing effect like snow. It was like approaching what had been an open exit and encountering a sealed door without handle or key: his thought beat on the panels, but it would not yield. In the end, unexpectedly, he slept.

When he woke he was still in the cave. Beyond the entrance the sun was sinking toward evening. His neck was stiff from the awkwardness of his position, and he was very thirsty. He drank the rest of the water and stood up, squirming through the narrowness of the cave mouth, halting just outside. He couldn't just wait here to die, he had to try something, even if it was pointless. Anyway—better quick than slow. Maybe the power of the cup would help . . .

He stood in the lee of the cliff, screwing up what was left of his courage, watching the sun crawl down the sky, behind the barrier of the mountains.

ERIC HAD taken to sleeping in the back room of the antiques shop, guarding Rowena's treasures, or so he said. She lived in the apartment above. He had come upstairs for a meal a few times, when specially invited, but appeared hesitant about intruding on her private territory. However, they usually breakfasted together in the back room, sharing her daily paper, the *Telegraph* of course, while he asked questions about Tony Blair, and the aftermath of the war, and what the world was all about. That morning Rowena was on the phone from an early hour, still chasing up contacts in the faint hope that she might pick up the trail of the stolen cup. She had just drawn a blank with a dealer in Oxford and was exchanging general courtesies and comments on the summer weather. "Well, we had that big storm on the day of the robbery but it's been very hot ever since . . . Yes, it was unlucky—if the lights hadn't blown the thief might have had no opportunity . . . A dwarf, really. Police want me to say it was a child but I know what I saw—would've had to be a bloody young child . . . Ran off into the woods. The kids went after him but he got away in the rain. Coming down like a monsoon . . . You didn't? Lucky you . . ." She hung up, remarking to Eric: "They didn't have a storm in Oxford. Nice for them. We only had it here—almost like someone laid it on."

"Is possible," Eric said. "Force can do many things. Control weather—control minds."

"Really believe that, don't you?" said Rowena. "Sometimes you almost convince me. Uncanny, the whole business." She poured more tea for herself, and coffee for Eric, who had acquired a liking for it bordering on addiction. "Stealing a cup you can't sell, Von Humboldt's dying like that—now they say it's natural causes—too many things that don't fit, little things, niggling at me . . ." Her voice petered out; she replaced the coffeepot, frowning. "That conversation just now—there was something, something that didn't quite . . ."

"You think they lie?" Eric asked.

"No—nothing like that. A false note. Bugger—can't find it. It's there, but I can't find it."

"What is this bugger that you always mention?" Eric said. "Is word I hear often, but I not understand."

"It's a swear word," Rowena explained. "You use it when you're angry."

"What does it mean?"

Rowena told him. Eric looked rather surprised. "In my world," he said, "we have swear words, but not like that. We use words for story, corruption, untruth. What people do in sex is not bad. Is just a matter for them. I must use this word?"

"Not if you don't want to," Rowena responded. "Use any word you like." She left Eric to choose and reverted to her former problem, glaring furiously at the middle distance. Then her face changed. "But . . . how odd. Why should he—?" She picked up the phone again, redialed Oxford. "Sorry to bother you again. Need to check about the weather. Are you sure it didn't rain?—Not anywhere around there?" She hung up, and looked at Eric. "It didn't rain anywhere near Oxford that day," she said.

Eric was murmuring to himself, presumably trying out potential swear words for size. "Fantasy!" he essayed. And then: "I tell you, storm not natural. Someone make bad weather."

"It's not that." Rowena thought for a long minute, then dialed a new number. Evidently no one was there.

"You are upset," Eric said, watching her expression, concern imprinting his own features. "Who do you call?"

"Annie." She shrugged off the worry with a visible effort. "Never mind. Nothing important. Time to open up." Her assistant wasn't due in that day, and she wasn't going to take time off sorting out minor inconsistencies. Eric started work polishing a walnut side table, and Rowena decided to think of something else.

She tried Annie's number again half an hour later, without success. She tried Bartlemy, and got the machine. Then she closed the shop.

"Come on," she told Eric. "We're going to Eade. Probably a wild-goose chase—but I think something's wrong."

"What is wild goose?" Eric demanded in the van that was Rowena's standard means of transport. "Is dangerous?"

"Don't know. But we've got one dead body—two if you count Effie Carlow—and the Grail's gone, and . . . why tell such a damn silly lie?"

"What lie?" Eric said. "Who lie?"

Rowena explained.

Bluebeard's Chamber

The spellfire had told Bartlemy little that he didn't know, and beneath his customary placidity he was growing anxious. A further period of reflection had given him a new idea, the same idea that had occurred to Nathan. He was mildly irritated with himself for not thinking of it before. "The woodwose," he told Hoover, as he pulled on suitable boots. "Nathan's retiring friend. If anyone saw anything, it would be him. No, you can't come. You'll make him nervous. I'll go alone." He wandered through the trees for some time, well away from the path, moving very quietly for all his bulk. Few twigs snapped under his feet; the leaf fall of a dozen winters scarcely crackled. Birds watched him, but piped no warning. On the border of the Darkwood he came to a hollow oak, struck by blight or lightning years before: nothing now remained but the outer husk of the trunk, colonized by insects and parasitic plants, deep in a thicket of nettles. Nathan had passed it twice in his searches, but he hadn't stopped to look inside. Bartlemy glanced through a fissure in the bark, drew back a short way, and sat for a while on a bank nearby, patient and immobile, while the wood grew indifferent to his presence. When he got up, his movements were slow and altogether noiseless. He parted the nettles with hands that felt no sting, clearing a way into the secret heart of the tree. Through the fissure he saw something like a bunch of bent twigs, half buried in leaf shreds and wood dust. It sat motionless, petrified, the elongated head turned sideways, returning his gaze with one whiteless eye. Remembering Nathan's name for it, he said very softly: "Woody?"

If something already still could become even stiller, it did. Bartlemy thought the very beat of its heart froze. He said: "I'm Nathan's friend, you know that. I'm your friend. We've lived side by side a long time without disturbing each other. I've always known you were here. I've always left you alone. I mean you well, little one. You have no need to fear me."

The woodwose still didn't answer, but he thought its heart began to beat again, a tiny fluttering drum somewhere beyond the edge of hearing.

"I know you're in trouble," Bartlemy said, keeping his voice very low, very gentle. "I can help you."

The woodwose jumped like a grasshopper, hitting his skull against the inside of the tree, then shrank even farther into the hollow, willing himself into invisibility against wood grain and dust shadow. But Bartlemy's eyes were long trained to see things that didn't want to be seen.

"It's all right," he went on. "I can protect you. Come to the house; stay in my garden for a while. Nobody enters there without my permission." *Except a dwarfish thief*—but he had taken precautions since then.

"It will find me," Woody said at last, his voice less than the whisper of a whisper.

"Not if you stay with me," Bartlemy said with quiet authority. "I have power: you can sense that. In my garden you will be safe."

"Nathan can't help," Woody said. "He looked for me, but I was afraid . . . He can't help. It would come after *him*."

"I'll take care of Nathan," Bartlemy promised. "You were following the man in the wood, weren't you? The man in gray. I expect Nathan asked you to watch, so you watched him. You saw what killed him. That's why you're afraid."

"Water," Woody said more softly than ever, as if he feared the breeze would overhear. "It looked human, but it was made of water. It drowned the man, with its fingers. It chased him off the road, and hit him on a tree, and drowned him."

"Did it see you?"

"Saw me. I ran, but it came after. I hid, but it was searching. Then the other man called it. *Nenufar*."

"There was another man?"

Bartlemy walked briskly back to Thornyhill, letting Woody follow at his own pace. "Stay near the walls," he had told him, "in the herb garden. Nothing evil goes near my herb garden. I'll see the dog doesn't bother you." Woody had seemed comforted, as if telling what he had seen had freed him from a burden. Bartlemy entered the house without looking back; he knew better than to check on him. *Another refugee,* he thought with the flicker of a smile. *One moves out, a new one moves in. Who next, I wonder?*

But he had other things on his mind. *Nenufar.* It was a French word for "water lily," but in the language of magic it meant a seaflower, venomous and many-tentacled, beautiful and lethal. No doubt one of many names for the elusive water spirit, the name used by the man who had summoned it, who controlled it, who told it to kill. A deadly partnership in quest of the Grimthorn Grail . . . Woody hadn't recognized the man, of course. But Bartlemy thought he could recognize him, and he wasn't happy about it.

In the kitchen Hoover greeted his master with an imperative bark.

"What is it?" Bartlemy asked.

The dog trotted into the drawing room, and barked again at the flashing light on the answering machine. Bartlemy played back Annie's message and tried to call her, but there was no reply. "She may be on her way here," he reflected. "No matter. The important thing is to do what we can for Nathan. Now. Annie can take care of herself."

THE SUN had moved around, and the shadow of the cliff lengthened across the sand. Nathan stood close to the rock face, nerving himself for a final, desperate dash, trying to decide which way to run. Kwanji had gotten past the Grokkul, so it must be possible; he should have asked her how she did it, which path she chose, but it was too late now. He thought of taking out the Grail, holding it in front of him, in the hope that the magic might afford some kind of protection; in stories, objects of power would do something—well—powerful under such circumstances. That was what they were for. But when he looked at the cup in daylight it appeared somehow reduced by the glare, drained of its greenish hue, the coiling pattern almost worn away, the few gems that adorned it dull as pebbles. He wanted to picture it glowing with a holy radiance that would burn anyone who touched it, or lightning flashing from the bowl that would scorch the Grokkul to a cinder. But it looked too ordinary, too cup-like, and he suspected that even if it was capable of such things, he would need to know the spellwords first. He essayed the one he had heard the Grandir use, in the chamber of crystals: *"Fia!"*—but nothing happened. He tucked the cup back inside his suit and returned to checking out the terrain.

There came a moment when, gazing upward, he thought he saw

spots dancing before his eyes, perhaps because of the sundazzle. But the spots didn't vanish, they grew and darkened, descending lazily on the thermals, becoming winged shapes with arrow-tipped tail, serpentine gorge, and pointed muzzle. Wild xaurians. Their leader was white; the others were black, or piebald. One of them dived suddenly, snatching some small creature that was scurrying across the sand. *They helped Kwanji once before,* Nathan said to himself. *Maybe they helped her again. Maybe they'll help me.* He felt a sudden, impossible surge of hope, and, forgetful of the slumbering monster he waved and called to them, though he knew they understood no tongue. But they continued to wheel and turn, scanning the ground for prey, ignoring him. Presently two of them swooped down simultaneously, landing on the twin boulders that marked the arch of the Grokkul's spine. They began snapping at each other, tails lashing, obviously fighting over whatever they had managed to catch. The sand below them twitched and slid—Nathan cried out in warning—the monster's head detached itself from the desert floor and swung around. The remaining xaurians dived all at once, darting in and out, slashing at the impenetrable hide with toothed beak and taloned wing. For a few seconds Nathan watched, riveted; then he recollected himself, and began to run. The ground shook with the pounding of the Grokkul's tail, the shifting of its huge feet, but all its attention was on the xaurians. He sprinted down the slope and plunged into an old watercourse, using the meager cover to pause and look back.

His escape was still unobserved. The Grokkul's blue tongue flicked out, uncoiling like a whip, but the mob knew their enemy well; they were too quick for it. Nathan wanted to stay, cheering them on, though he knew they could do the monster no real harm; but he had to move on. He doubted that he would get very far; the distance to Arkatron was too great, and he was without food or water. Still, no desert was utterly deserted, according to all the nature programs he had ever seen: cacti retained moisture, and there might be insects he could eat, if he grew hungry enough to try. And surely Halmé would send someone to look for him, if he didn't return. He followed the dry watercourse, gauging his direction by the sun, thinking that once darkness fell the multiple moonrise should keep him more or less on track.

The path descended into a hollow, where the long-lost river must have attempted to carve itself a shallow valley; his view was cut off by banks of rock. Cooling shade covered him. Then, rounding a bend, he found his way blocked. The white xaurian stood there, wings folded, head atilt, watching him with one red eye. A probing ray of sunlight touched its body, glittering off scales too fine to see. Nathan stopped. "Thank you for your help," he said. Annie had always emphasized the importance of courtesy, and he hoped the meaning, if not the words, might be understood.

The xaurian didn't move.

He considered simply walking past it, or retracing his steps a little way and climbing out of the hollow, but somehow that seemed offensive. Besides, it was clearly intelligent; he wouldn't be able to evade it, if it was determined to find him. He took a pace nearer. It was smaller than a domesticated xaurian, but still many times bigger than a boy, and it looked in some way sharper, faster, warier than its cousins. More *dragonish*. Its head swiveled so it could study him with the other eye, suddenly reminding him of Woody. He walked right up to it and laid a hand on its neck. The shoulders lowered; the wings dipped. "Okay," he said, more to himself than the reptile. "Here we go." He swung his leg across its back, just in front of the wing joints where the saddle would have been on an ordinary mount, and heaved himself astride. There was nothing to hold on to, no pommel, no reins, and he supposed rather wildly that he would have to trust to balance or grip the neck. And then he felt the ground shudder, and the coughing roar of the Grokkul was growing louder, nearer—

He clung on with all his limbs as the xaurian reared, beating its wings into a gale, rising almost vertically out of the hollow. The Grokkul's wide skull loomed directly ahead, rushing toward them like an airship, splitting into a gargantuan maw overcrowded with several kinds of teeth. The tongue was unleashed, a band of muscle a foot thick, its pitted surface gleaming with mucus that clung like glue. The breath from a jaw clogged with the fragments of old meals made Nathan retch. But the xaurian swerved—he clamped his arms around neck or body, slipping sideways—the tongue whooshed past, barely missing him—a dollop of spittle landed on his suit. And then they were away, soaring skyward, and far behind the other xaurians screamed in triumph, and the Grokkul roared, and the thumping of its tail churned the desert into a sandstorm.

It was a while before Nathan dared to slacken his hold and try to sit up. Not only was the creature bare-backed, leaner and more lithe than his former mount, but it was unaccustomed to being ridden, and angled its flight to right or left with no regard for his safety. Eventually he was able to get his legs firmly tucked around its belly under the wing joints and felt confident enough to straighten up, though ready to drop forward onto its neck at the first serious jolt. He had been too busy staying on to note their direction, but when he saw the position of the two moons—Astrond had not yet risen—he judged they were going more or less the right way. Presumably the xaurian knew the route. Every so often he thought he might start to enjoy himself, as he had on the flight out, but then the reptile would tilt to one side or the other and he would be hanging on for dear life again. It was like trying to ride a roller coaster with no security bar and a seat like a greased log. And all the while at the back of his mind there was the thought that Raymor was dead, and Kwanji was dead—they had died because of *him*—and he didn't really know why he had been chosen to live, or what crooked fate would have made such a choice.

Astrond had just put in an appearance when he saw the dunes giving way to abandoned fields, and the city lights showed as a glow beyond the horizon, staining the sky. Soon the suburbs were spreading below them, a sprawling maze picked out in arches and trails of glitterpoints, like a luminous game of connect-the-dots. Then the buildings grew taller, and rank upon rank of windows wound past them, and skimmers dodged and dived, eyelights yawing across their path; but the xaurian never blinked. Ahead the towers climbed higher and higher, until they reached the central point where a single spire outtopped them all, crowned with its own stars. Nathan knew that was where he had to go, and the xaurian responded to his nudging feet and urging voice. They circled the tower while he looked for the right landing platform, opting for a small one on the roof of a secondary turret that he decided was familiar. "There," he said, leaning forward to indicate the place. The xaurian plunged—he almost slipped over its head—and pulled up abruptly on the narrow eyrie. Nathan rolled off.

There was no sign of the gauntleted assistant who had brought food, so he said: "Wait. I'll get you something," trusting it would understand. Then he activated the internal communicator in his hood with a code word and called Halmé.

He was still afraid of interception but she came, and alone. On her orders a man with a food bucket appeared, but he wouldn't go near the xaurian, who hissed at him, mouth open, flexing its wings. Nathan took the bucket himself, offering it to his companion, feeling secretly rather proud that the reptile gave him special treatment, though he was aware he had done nothing to earn it. When it had eaten, it flew off, arrowing between buildings, the lights strobing its flanks so that it flashed white and black, white and black, until it was lost to view.

"What happened?" asked Halmé. "How did you tame it?"

"I didn't," Nathan said. "It just decided to help." *Like dolphins in stories. Like god-beasts in legends. If the stories and legends are true.*

She didn't ask any more questions till they got back to her chambers. He took off the protective suit, keeping hold of the cup, waiting for her to ask about Raymor, but all she said was: "You must be hungry."

She went out and returned with a tray of food, food that looked pretty and tasted bland, artificial, as if the flavor had been injected afterward. There was fruit without zest, and fish that had clearly never seen the sea, and green speckled sauce with an echo of parsley, and deep yellow sauce that had nothing to do with butter, and a fluffy, airy dessert that seemed to be made of air and fluff. Nathan ate politely, since it was expected of him, and Halmé watched every mouthful, her expression brimming with what must be concern, touching him from time to time as if to be sure he was real. He had put the Grail on the table, but although she glanced at it all her attention was for him.

"You know Raymor died," he said at last, unable to go on eating. "The Grokkul took him."

"It doesn't matter."

"Doesn't *matter*? He gave his life—he died for *me*. You said you knew him since childhood—"

"Please . . . don't be angry with me, don't be disappointed in me. I can't bear that. Ray feared death, but he also wanted it. We all do. It has been like this for so long, not living, not dying, just waiting, waiting for an end that doesn't come. Like the last second of life, stretched out to endure for an eternity. When you feel that way, death is welcome—if you have the courage. I know Ray must've died bravely."

"Yes," said Nathan. "He was very brave."

"Then his death meant something. He was fortunate. It is a long time since life meant anything to me."

He told her everything then, even about Kwanji Ley, though it felt a little like betrayal. But surely he couldn't betray someone who had died.

"She was mad," Halmé said, and he thought she looked regretful. "The neo-salvationists could not perform a Great Spell. They haven't the knowledge, or the power. They would break the pattern, and the world would end, swallowed in fire, and it would all be over."

"I thought you wanted it over," Nathan said.

"Oh yes," she said, "but I fear the death I want. I am not as brave as Ray. Or you. You are young in years, younger than the youngest thing that lives on our planet, yet you have ventured into an unknown world to save your friend, and you found the Grail, and defied the Grokkul, and won a wild xaurian to be your steed. If legends were true, you would be a hero." She had echoed his thought, and something about that disturbed him. "In legends, there were angels who appeared as children, beings of light and love. Angels and heroes. But I was taught, all legends are lies. I think we should be wary of them. I want to believe, but I dare not." She smiled her magical smile, filling her face with sudden light. "Still, for tonight, you are a hero to me. My special hero."

She is just a woman, he thought, *but she's beautiful. In her face, the legends* do *come true.*

He said: "I want to go home now. The Grail will be safe in my world. That's where it's meant to be—till the time comes. But I can't get back." He pushed up his sleeve, where the Mark of Agares had been scrubbed off his arm. "I can't find the way."

"You said . . . you were dreaming."

"Not anymore. I'm here, really here. I slept in the cave, and woke. The place in my mind is shut." Now that the immediate danger was over, panic was sneaking back, paralyzing thought. "I don't know what to do."

"We will find the way," Halmé said.

IN THE empty bookshop, Annie's phone was ringing for the third time that morning. No one answered. Annie didn't have a machine; she rarely needed one. At the other end Pobjoy hung up, gazing moodily at his desk. The shop should be open by now. Was she busy?—was she out?—had Nathan done a bunk? It seemed wildly unlikely. Nonetheless, he was uneasy. After a few moments' thought, he summoned Sergeant Hale.

"We're going back to Eade," he told her. "I want this business cleared up. As far as it's possible to clear it up, anyway. I'm damned if I'm going to let the theft turn into another unsolved crime statistic."

They went out to the parking lot—"We'll take mine"—and Pobjoy drove off purposefully toward the village.

ANNIE WAS admitted to Riverside House by the maid, who told her in faltering English that Madam was in London and Mr. Addison had gone to shopping in Crowford. Sainsbury's, Annie deduced. She asked if he would be long, but this seemed to defeat the girl's linguistic abilities so Annie did her best to explain, using simple words and gestures, that she would wait. The maid returned to her chores for about twenty minutes, cleared away the dusters and the Dyson vacuum, stared at Annie in evident bewilderment, shrugged, and left. Alone in the house again, Annie wondered how long Michael would be. She prowled around downstairs, keeping her ears open for any sound, wondering if Rianna really *was* in town and trying not to second-guess the clock. As always when you are waiting for something, time stretched out. She had escaped the waiting at the bookshop, only to find herself caught in the same trap here. Frustrated, she tried the door to Rianna's tower, but it was locked as usual. It must be the spirit who locked it, however, she reasoned, not the real Rianna. Michael would notice if his wife never went into her own private rooms. And the spirit, surely, couldn't carry the key, not if it was turning back into water at regular intervals. So . . . the key must be around somewhere. She opened drawers in the kitchen and living room, ran up to the master bedroom to check the dressing table, and fumbled in coat pockets and a couple of unused handbags. Now that she had something to do, something other than waiting, she did it, feverishly. Drawing a blank, she stopped to think, considering the nature of the spirit and the unknown individual, witch or wizard (Bartlemy said it would have to be someone Gifted), who had called it up. Someone who remained in the background, unseen, perhaps using Effie Carlow as a spy and the water demon as a killer. Someone who wanted the Grail to open the Gate between worlds. But the spirit would've retained the key; there would be no need to pass it on. Where would a water spirit hide something?

Even before she had finished the thought, she was in the bathroom. There was nothing in cupboard or cabinet, but when she lifted the lid on the toilet there it was, glinting through the water. A key. It had to be the one. A human would have placed it under a stone or a flowerpot, but for a sea spirit the logical place was in water. Annie rolled up her sleeve to retrieve it. Of course, there could be nothing of importance concealed in the tower, but . . .

She didn't want Michael to come back now. Not yet. Not till she *knew*.

If the tower hid no sinister secrets, she could put the key back, and she needn't even mention taking a look.

She made her way to the locked door, inserting the key with a hand that trembled slightly. It fit. She turned it and pushed the door open.

She was in a kind of study–*cum*–sitting room, much like Michael's in his tower but more cluttered. Publicity stills of Rianna in various roles crowded the walls, often alongside far more celebrated stars. There was a sofa with embroidered cushions, a desk littered with newspapers and magazines, an expensive flat-screen TV, video, DVD, sound system. A silver laptop stood open on the low table, with an empty mug beside it. A bookcase curved with the wall, filled with elaborate editions of the classics—unread, Annie thought—and the fat glossy spines of coffee-table books on subjects like costume and origami and the jewelry of the Russian royal family. Oddly, it was the one room in the house that bore the stamp of a personality—a rather actressy personality, with artistic inclinations, all very predictable. Except for the smell. A faint, sweetish, sickly smell that caught her straight in the gut. She peered into the mug and saw it was full of fur, though somewhere underneath there was what might have been a piece of lemon. Lemon tea, Annie concluded. Watching her weight. She glanced at one of the newspapers on the desk, and saw it was months out of date. She was conscious of her pulse beat intensifying, shaking at her chest. But she couldn't go back now. A twisting stair led to the upper chamber, all white-painted iron fretwork. The treads creaked beneath her feet.

The smell worsened.

She recognized it now. As a child of ten or so she had stood at her grandmother's bedside while the life gradually oozed out of her, the body failing while the spirit hung on. But all people know that smell, whether they have smelled it or not: it is in our race memory, as old as breathing. The fear of it is part of the formula for living. Annie's steps slowed, then quickened again. She cupped a hand over her nose and mouth.

At the top of the stair she emerged into a bedroom decorated entirely in shades of white. Snow-pale carpet, furniture that might have been designed for Barbie, a canopied bed screened with muslin curtains. Through the muslin, she could make out a shape lying in the bed, dark hair spread across the pillow, the coverlet tucked under its arms. Keeping her hand over her nose, she pulled back the curtain.

I won't be sick, she told herself. *I* won't *be sick.* She didn't scream. What was left of Rianna Sardou had evidently been there some time. The hair had outlasted the face, framing a skull sparsely padded with decay. The eyes and cheeks had fallen in. Fingers shriveled to the bone rested on the duvet. *Why does death always come in white?* Annie wondered, with some dim recollection of Daniel in the pristine hospital room. Not the color of weddings and innocence but the color of ending, of grief and horror. She wanted to turn away but she couldn't stop looking, gazing and gazing at that dreadful festering thing. Downstairs were the pictures, the pale angular beauty, more striking on stage and screen than in life, the aura of fame and vaunted artistic commitment. And here, *this*. It was terrible and pitiful.

At last she moved away. Her pulse was still pounding, but then came a sound that stopped it in midbeat.

The stair clanged.

There was a second when a chaos of thoughts tumbled through her mind, jostling for position. Was it Michael—*oh Michael, poor Michael*—or the false Rianna? Where could she hide? But there was no time. She looked around for a weapon, but the only thing she saw was a spiky hairbrush on the dressing table . . .

A head appeared at the top of the stair. Michael.

Annie rushed into his arms, half sobbing, babbling incoherent phrases: "Don't look . . . Don't look . . . Oh Michael, I'm sorry—so sorry . . . I should've told you what she was. I should've warned you . . ." His hands moved to her shoulders, prizing her off his chest. She glanced up, and saw that his face was very still. Not shocked, not stunned, just still. He looked at the bed with its grisly occupant, then down at her.

"Dear me," he said.

Annie backed away a step.

The crooked smile flickered across his mouth, only now it was no longer a smile, merely crooked. The scruffy, careless good looks seemed to change, in some subtle way, like a mask that shrinks to fit the changing face beneath. With an odd glimmer of detachment she noticed the lines of mockery and cynicism that she had once found so attractive pouching his eyes, dragging at his cheek. Since the kiss the previous night the touch of him had stayed with her, his lips, his arms, warming her thoughts even at the back of nausea and terror; but now it evaporated as if it had never been. She felt clear, and empty, and horribly afraid.

"Dear, dear me. So you've found our little secret. You should know better than to unlock Bluebeard's Chamber; as far as I can remember, it didn't do his wife any good, either, though I may have that wrong. You shouldn't have been so damn nosy. You've been very useful to me up till now; I'll really regret losing you."

"You killed her," Annie said faintly. Things were falling into place in her mind. Of course he would have known about the imposture; Michael, of all people, could never have been fooled. She must have been blind—blind or besotted—not to see it.

"Oh no," Michael said. "Not me. I'm actually not much good at killing."

She felt a gleam of hope, which she knew was a cheat, and he knew, and she knew he knew. He was taunting her with that hope, his eyes derisive, hard and shallow as glass.

She said: "It was . . . that thing?"

"I'm afraid so. My lovely Nenufar. She gets carried away. The Carlow woman called her, and then couldn't control her, and after a while I understand she outlived her usefulness. Or not, as the case may be. As for Von Humboldt—well, Old Spirits have a very simplistic view of the world. She thought getting rid of him would give us the Grail. I arrived too late to stop her. Still, it muddied the waters—bugger, I do seem to be racking up the bad puns. She got carried away with you, too, but on that occasion I was in time. Murder is pretty much her solution to everything. She's a primitive."

"Why didn't you use her to deal with Dave Bagot," Annie said, "instead of getting yourself a nosebleed?" She was inching backward as she spoke, more from reflex than plan. He didn't move. He was between her and the stair, and there was no other way out.

"It was a great chance to look heroic." Michael grinned at her. "You did bloody well yourself. You know, I really am sorry about this. Why you had to come poking your nose in . . . What *are* you doing here?"

"It's not important." She was fighting to get control over her shaking limbs, her pumping heart. "Are you saying you *liked* me, and it's such a shame you have to—"

"Good Lord, no. But I was fairly confident I could get the Grail from you, without piling up any more dead bodies. That inspector's beginning to get suspicious; he could be a nuisance. Besides, I needed you to help me get close to Nat. Nenufar thinks he's important—I'm not sure why. Of course, once you're gone, I'll be around to—er—share his grief. We could become pretty close."

"No," she said, the flash of anger driving back fear for a few moments. "I'll open the Gate and return to warn him. I swear it."

His expression stalled. "How do you know about the Gate? You're not Gifted."

"But you are?"

"I suppose it was that bloated hippo Goodman. I thought there might be a little power hiding under the flab. The Carlow hag said so. But the Gate opens only once, my dear—without the Grail, at any rate. You go through it and never return. That's the Ultimate Law. And you're far too sensible to be a ghost."

"Even the Ultimate Laws can be broken," Annie said. "I passed through once before." She sensed the chink in his certainty and knew she had to take him off balance, distract him, divert him. "Your ally was right about Nathan. He isn't—ordinary. His father's from another world. I followed someone through into death, and came back pregnant. I did it once, I can do it again. From death back to life. That is *my* gift."

She believed only part of what she was saying, but she saw it was unsettling him. He moved toward her, away from the stair. At her back, the dressing table dug into her thighs. Her hand groped for the hairbrush, because that was all there was.

"You couldn't do that," he said, and the smile crooked into a sneer, but it didn't work: there was doubt behind it. "It would take enormous power—the power of death, the power of the Grail. What power do you have?"

"The power of love," Annie said. "But you wouldn't know about that." She brought her arm around, hairbrush in hand, and smashed the spiky side into his face, aiming for the eyes. His glasses were knocked off; he gave a yelp of pain. She kicked him on the shins in passing and bolted to the stair.

She half fell, half slid down the spiral, clutching the rail. Then she was through Rianna's study and in the main house. Behind her she heard a *thump* as Michael vaulted the stair. She reached the front door, yanked it open, started down the path—

"You may as well stop running," Michael's voice said from the doorway. "You're not going anywhere." He sounded relaxed now, mildly amused.

It was there on the path in front of her. It had Rianna's hair, Rianna's face, but she could see the water moving under the skin. And in its eyes was the ancient darkness of the abyss.

"That hurt," Michael said, touching his eye. "Wasted effort, I'm afraid. I told you, I don't do the killing around here."

NATHAN LAY in Halmé's bed with the Grail in his hands and the colored lamps turned down low. He had told her about the Mark of Agares and tried to draw it, but the rune was complex and he couldn't reproduce it accurately. "It looks familiar," she had said, and on her screen she had flicked through a file of magical symbols in her world, until she found one that was the same, even to the name. "Perhaps magic has one language and one set of rules in all worlds," she suggested carelessly. She copied the Mark on his arms and forehead in a dark purple ink that had a strange odor, at once herbal and chemical. "Now sleep," she said. "Go into your mind. Find your way home." She offered to play what she called sleep music, but he declined. He thought of how he had torn the Mark off his bedroom wall, and pushed the doubts away. He would have to trust to hope. Halmé left him, with a murmur of *sim vo-khalir*, which he knew meant *"au revoir,"* and he lay awake, feeling as if he would never sleep again. He had expected her to kiss him, a loving, probably maternal kiss—had half feared, half desired it—but she hadn't. And then he thought of the masks, and the contamination, and the Grandir's restraint with her, and he guessed that maybe they didn't kiss here, or not often. He had yet to do any serious kissing in his life, but a world without it seemed curiously bleak. He drifted away into a fog of adolescent speculation, trying to imagine Halmé at his own age, smaller, slighter, an exquisite fairy creature with her perfect alien face somehow soft and unformed, and he took her hand and gazed long into the rainbow blackness of her eyes. Then in his thought he kissed her cheek, and she shrank from the strangeness of it, but not far, and he kissed her lips, and thought became dream and spiraled out of control, and he slipped over the borderline into oblivion.

He woke very suddenly in an unfamiliar place. Not Halmé's room, nor his own. He started to sit up, felt a hand on his shoulder. "It's all right," Bartlemy said. "You're with me."

He was in a bedroom at Thornyhill, and his uncle drew back the curtains on midday sunlight, and when he looked around he saw the Mark of Agares on a sheet of paper taped above his bed. An oil burner exuded the unmistakable aroma of Bartlemy's herbal brew. Between his hands was the Grimthorn Grail.

"I see you brought it back," Bartlemy said. "Well done. Are you all right?"

"Yeah." He thought he was all right, at any rate.

"I want to hear all about it," Bartlemy continued. "But first, I think we should get you home. Your mother's been worrying."

Nathan got up to find he was weak and unsteady on his legs. Obviously his longer sojourn in the other world had drained his strength. Bartlemy produced a quick snack of crackers and cheese, fruit and coffee, and went to call Annie.

"She's still out," he said. "That's odd. I thought she might be coming here, but she'd have arrived by now. Unless she's with the police. I think—we should leave immediately. Hoover!"

Nathan snatched an apple, gripped Bartlemy's arm for support, and they went out to the car.

SHE DIDN'T run. There was nowhere to run to. The thing came toward her with a peculiar swaying gait, something on its face that was almost a smile. *It shouldn't be stronger than me,* she thought, *but it is.* Stronger than the real Rianna, strong as the undertow of the tide, as the onrush of the wave. She couldn't fight it. She was human, weak, powerless. She had no Gift, no resources but herself. Behind her, Michael said: "They'll find you in the river, tomorrow or the next day. Another tragic accident. Oh, the inspector'll be skeptical, he'll sniff around for a while, but there'll be no evidence to find, and he'll cool off in the end. My DNA won't feature, and as for Nenufar, no forensic lab could identify her substance. As far as science is concerned, she doesn't exist. You see, that's the beauty of magic, that's its real power. Nobody in the world believes in it."

But they believe in science, Annie thought, *in genetic fingerprints, and* you're *human* . . . She whipped around and ran to Michael, clutching at him yet again, reaching up to drag her short nails down his cheek. A thin redness spread along the cuts. Then the water spirit caught her and pulled her back, locking her in its clammy grasp, the cold hand sliding across her face to enclose nose and mouth and send its liquid matter gushing into her lungs. "Your DNA is on me now!" she cried. "The river won't wash it off. They can pick up the minutest traces. My mark is on you and yours on me! She may be a spirit but you're not. They'll know—Nathan will know—" The hand shut off her nostrils, sealed her lips. She tried to breathe, and breathed water. The dark was coming, and this time there would be no respite. She saw Michael's expression change, twitching with fury and fear. *Nathan will know* . . . At least she had achieved that.

"Let go! Let go now! *Oss-toklar!*"

"How dare you! Release her at once!"

Two voices, one very deep, oddly accented, one a little higher in tone. Both familiar. The spirit checked; for an instant, startled, it lost its grip on solidity. Annie broke free from an arm that was suddenly more fluid than flesh, and reeled, coughing and gasping, against a strong, supportive body. Eric. Rowena was striding toward Michael like an avenging angel.

"Knew you were up to something! You said your barbecue in Oxford was rained out, but it only rained here. You're after the Grail, too, aren't you? You and this psycho bitch were in the woods that afternoon, murdering Von Humboldt. Don't know *how* you did it, but you did it all right." She rounded on Rianna. "Trying to strangle Annie, were you? Never did trust you actress types. You're going down for the rest of your life . . ."

Confused, uncertain, Nenufar wavered. Its form shimmered as if river gleams showed through the veil of flesh and skin. Then it turned and fled, more gliding than running, its feet barely meeting the ground. As it drew near to the shrubs along the riverbank its shape thinned into a damp coil of mist, which wound its way between the leaves and vanished toward the water. Rowena stood staring after it, suddenly silent, panting from the impact of anger cut short. When she found her voice again, it was to swear.

Michael, seizing the moment, ran the other way—around the house to the car. It was parked at the side of his tower, in the shade of a tree. Annie heard the *click* as the system unlocked and saw the lights blink even as he reached the door. Eric released her to go in pursuit but she grabbed his jacket, holding him back. "No. No. *Look*."

Something was crawling out from under the tree, swiftly engulfing the car, distorting the smooth flanks of the Merc into ripples and bulges. The windows were closed but it flowed through them and up the air vents, making the space within quiver as if in a heat wave. Michael had thrust the key in the ignition; the engine stuttered and stalled. Then he seemed to be beating at nothingness, as though attacked by invisible insects. His mouth twisted and gaped; he clutched at his head. The screaming went on for some time. When it was over he slumped sideways, his face slack, drained of all personality. A phantom glimmer of movement crossed his features as Rowena approached and her reflection curved over the windshield.

"Don't go there," Annie said. "Here. I've got iron." The number in her pocket, little use against human or water spirit, but effective for gnomons.

"I, too," said Eric. "There is no iron in car?"

"Chrome. Wood. Plastic. Is he—is he dead?"

"Not dead, mad. They eat his mind. Nothing left."

Suddenly, Annie found she was sobbing, from relief or some other reaction, while Eric patted her clumsily; he was still not comfortable with physical contact. She strove to pull herself together, curbing the tears, though she was still trembling inwardly. The gnomons seemed to have gone. She glanced around at the man in the car, and then hastily looked away.

By the time the inspector arrived, with Bartlemy, Nathan, and Hazel in his wake, Michael was beginning to drool.

TEATIME FOUND all of them except the police in the drawing room at Thornyhill, eating their way through the reserves of Bartlemy's larder and drinking tea, with stronger stimulants for those who weren't driving. "You never said how you all managed to get there at more or less the same time," Annie was saying. After a rather careful interview with Pobjoy, tiptoeing around the more questionable aspects of her story, she was at last beginning to relax.

"Obviously we all started worrying about you at once," said Bartlemy. "Anyhow, Nathan was back safe, and I wanted to bring him home. When you weren't there, we asked along the High Street, like Rowena and Eric. You've lived in a village long enough, Annie: you know what it's like. In a city, no one would have noticed a thing, but here, half the population saw where you were going. Anyway, Hazel joined us and insisted on coming, too, then Pobjoy turned up. I was very concerned when I realized you'd gone to Riverside House. After I talked to Woody I was pretty sure Michael was behind the appearance of Nenufar in these parts. I'm not certain how Rowena reached the same conclusion—"

"He lied about the weather in Oxford," Rowena said. "Stupid sort of lie. Why bother? Unless he was giving himself an alibi. Couldn't have done the robbery—too tall—must've been the murder. What was that *thing* acting as his wife?"

There were several muddled attempts to explain. "We may never know who she really was," Bartlemy said. "*Nenufar* was no more her real name than *Rianna Sardou*. But with nobody to conjure her, she cannot return. The police will look for her, of course, but they won't find anything. They have a very old corpse and a murderer too far gone to plead Not Guilty who'll have to spend the rest of his life in an asylum. Pobjoy won't be completely satisfied—he's too intelligent for that—but he'll make do. The Grail's been returned and he won't press the matter of the theft, though I daresay he'll always suspect you two were involved." He nodded at Nathan and Hazel.

"But you told him *you* found it, not Nathan," Hazel said. "I heard you."

"I thought that was best," said Bartlemy. "He didn't believe me, though."

"Who did take it?" asked Rowena. "Who was this dwarf?"

"That I also wish to know," said Eric. "If he return it to my world he must have much force."

"Not necessarily," Bartlemy replied. "I'm afraid I don't know all the answers, and we can only speculate. However, some old records suggest that Josevius Grimthorn had an assistant, a hunchback—or a dwarf—"

"Ought to be a hunchback," Rowena said unexpectedly. "Traditional."

"At a guess, his master imprisoned him for some unknown offense. He's werefolk, a true dwarf and not just a short human—he must be to have survived so long. Anyway, he'd know there was a transition point in the sunken chapel where the Grail could pass from world to world—"

"Could a human get through?" Nathan interrupted. "Sorry. I just wondered."

"I wouldn't recommend trying it. Remember, the Grail was going home—and it's an inanimate object, though it clearly has certain powers. A living thing would probably be annihilated by the forces involved in the transition, even if it was able to pass through."

"Why would dwarf wish to return cup to my people?" Eric demanded. "Did he do right thing? Is it wrong, we keep it here?"

"Again, we don't know," Bartlemy continued. "Maybe the dwarf *thought* he did right. Maybe *we've* done wrong. The spell that can save your people—if such a spell exists—is not yet prepared. Until then, the Grail seems safer here, out of reach of local terrorists."

"*If* I can get it back," Rowena pointed out. "Julian's taking it to Sotheby's again—for the Von Humboldts."

"We must do what we can."

She took a restorative gulp of tea. "So," she said, "I'm really supposed to believe all this stuff—about other worlds and sea spirits and so on."

"Believe what you want," Bartlemy said. "You know what you saw."

"Oh yes, I know. Won't forget in a hurry." She gave a shudder, and reached for another cookie. "What *were* those things that went for Michael? Not exactly invisible, but . . ."

"Gnomon," said Eric. "From my world. Bring madness. Iron keep them away."

"They could be protecting the Grail," said Bartlemy. "Though on this occasion they seemed to be protecting Annie. We don't know why."

"All over, isn't it?" said Rowena. "Time we knew everything."

"Life doesn't work that way," smiled Bartlemy, both amused and a little sad.

"Not over," said Eric. "My people still die."

It can't be over, thought Hazel. *Everyone else had big adventures except me; I only had small ones. Unless you count getting arrested, and that wasn't much fun. I wasn't even arrested properly, in the end, just interviewed . . .*

It isn't over, Nathan reflected, *until I can stop myself dreaming.* And Halmé had said *"Sim vo-khalir"*—till we meet again.

I wish it was over, Annie thought, *but it isn't. I haven't told him about his father—that's part of this, it must be—but I can't. Just let me have a little more time—time for innocence, and childhood, and trust, before I have to destroy them forever.*

It isn't over . . .

Later, Bartlemy said to her: "You must be very upset about Michael. I'm so sorry. I know how much you liked him."

"It's odd," Annie said, "but I'm not. Not yet, anyway. It's as if, when I saw through him, all the liking—all the attraction—drained away. Perhaps it's because it was false, all along—*he* was false—false charm, false courage—his whole persona was just a mask, and when you tore it off there was nothing underneath left to like. I don't feel betrayed, just a bit silly. Falling for him like a teenager—sorry Nathan, Hazel."

"He was very clever," Bartlemy affirmed. "He probably used more than charm on you. He was Gifted, but he hid it well. I never picked up on it, and I should have done. He must have suppressed it very carefully in public."

"What d'you mean by *Gifted*?" Rowena wanted to know.

"How did Nathan get cup back?" Eric said. "That is story I like to hear."

"What is the real meaning of the universe?" Annie added mischievously. She was feeling sufficiently recovered to be a little mischievous now.

They sat there well into the evening, talking and talking, while Bartlemy went into the kitchen, setting the questions aside, knowing that some of them would never have answers, and began to prepare a dinner that would celebrate the occasion, and salve the spirit, and fill the spaces where the answers would not come.

Epilogue: Afterthoughts

About four months later Inspector Pobjoy found himself in the vicinity of Thornyhill. He hadn't really found himself, of course; this was a visit he had been meaning to make for some time, delaying it, desiring it, touched with curiosity and something more, maybe an element of apprehension. Bartlemy didn't look surprised to see him. Pobjoy wondered if he was ever surprised to see anyone. If the queen had knocked at the door he would have greeted her with the same tranquil smile, there would have been tea and cookies . . .

There was tea, and cookies. Different cookies from last time, winter cookies with a hint of cinnamon, a whiff of spice. Hoover sat at his feet studying him with an expression that would have been disconcerting on the face of a witness, and was completely unnerving on a dog. Fortunately for him, Pobjoy didn't notice.

"I gather you decided to set aside the matter of the theft," Bartlemy said. "I'm so glad. I can't help realizing I was the prime suspect. It took place in my house, I'm known to be a collector, in a small way—no doubt you could prove I have an obsession with the history of the Thorns—and it would have been very easy for me to engineer the power cut. I was out of the room at the relevant moment, after all. No one else could have done that; I'm sure the point must have occurred to you."

Shaken out of his normal inscrutability, Pobjoy could only stare. Bartlemy was quite right—but it never *had* occurred to him.

"Then when things got a little too hot for me—when I felt the investigation was coming too close—I simply restored the Grail to the appropriate people, and happily, that was the end of the matter. Most kind of you."

"The—the dwarf?" Pobjoy stuttered.

"My dog," said Bartlemy blandly. "He's very highly trained."

Hoover cocked an ear, thumped his tail, and did his best to exude both high training and low cunning.

"That wasn't a confession, you understand," Bartlemy concluded. "Merely a hypothesis. Have some Christmas cake. I know it's a little premature, but one can't eat all the good food over the holiday: it's too much. Far better to spread it out a bit."

Pobjoy, who generally tried to work over the Christmas break because he had nowhere else to be, accepted mutely.

"How is poor Michael?" Bartlemy asked.

Poor Michael, the inspector noted. *Aha. A soft-centered liberal. I might have guessed . . .*

"Insane," he said. "Or so they say. The psychiatrists claim some sort of shock has virtually blanked out his mind. Most of the time he says nothing. Occasionally he babbles—or gibbers. None of it makes much sense. They say he'll need permanent care; he's effectively an imbecile. He could be faking it in the hope of the chance to do a runner. His accomplice is still out there somewhere—the woman who was posing as his wife. We never found her."

"Are you completely satisfied of his guilt?" Bartlemy said.

"I'm never completely satisfied. He did it, no doubt about that, but some of the things he says . . . He seems to have been obsessed with the Grail; quite possibly that's why he came to live in the area. And he was a psychopath—he didn't need to kill his wife, there was no financial motive, and divorce is a lot less risky. We don't know how he did it; the corpse was too old to tell. We don't know how he managed to drown Von Humboldt in the middle of a wood. Carried a bottle of water with him, perhaps. Knocked his victim out, poured water into a bowl, and drowned him—but for God's sake, why? There are easier ways to kill. Even our local psychological profiler is stumped. He says there must be a fixation of some kind, but Addison's too far gone to find out what, or why. At least the death of Mrs. Carlow is fairly straightforward. At a guess she saw something, and he did for her. Maybe she was trying blackmail. He lured her down to the river and pushed her in." But he wasn't happy. There was Hazel's insistence that her great-grandmother had been killed in the attic . . .

"There are a lot of loose ends," said Bartlemy, "but that's the nature of life."

"There are always loose ends. But this . . . When he *does* talk, he seems to be going on about the river. Something about a spirit from the water. I suppose he's one of these New Age cranks."

"Multiple murderers are often quite cranky," Bartlemy said gently. "Or so I believe."

But Pobjoy was immersed in his own doubts, and irony washed right over him. "Nenufar, he keeps saying. Apparently it's French for 'water lily.' Nenufar."

"Maybe it was the name of his accomplice," Bartlemy suggested.

Pobjoy gave him a long look, and some of the hardness was gone from his face. "You know, don't you?" he said. "You know the truth about all this."

"The famous hunch that policemen always have in fiction?"

"I'm not asking as a policeman."

"You've got the villain of the piece," Bartlemy said at last. "That's the important thing. He won't do any more harm. That should content you for now. And the Grail's back where it should be."

"I heard it was returned to Mrs. Thorn?"

"That's right. Possibly the remaining Von Humboldts decided it *was* cursed. Or maybe they thought they could afford the gesture, since they clearly weren't going to make much money out of it. Nobody was ever able to verify its date of origin or even what it was made of. I understand Epstein suggested to the owner that it wasn't worth the trouble of a court case. They have enough problems dealing with Birnbaum. It seems there are several paintings in dispute, also a Cellini saltcellar. At least, I believe it's a saltcellar. That should keep them busy for a couple of years."

Pobjoy shrugged. That wasn't his problem. "I'd better be off," he said.

"Come back sometime," said Bartlemy. "You're always welcome."

As he went down the path Pobjoy looked back, and was visited with the curious notion the phrase hadn't been mere politeness. He wanted to go back—one day. He wanted to ask after Annie. But he had suspected her son: she would never forgive him for that. Probably better not . . .

A FEW days after Christmas, a little group was gathered outside the Registry Office in Crowford. It was a cold, gray day, damp though not actually raining, but although coat collars were turned up and shoulders hunched against the weather the faces were rosy-tipped, bright with anticipation. Bartlemy appeared even more benevolent than usual; Annie, flushed from the windchill, had a sparkle in her eyes that had been missing for some months, though she always insisted the revelations about Michael hadn't affected her. The three teenagers stood close together: Nathan, who had grown an inch or so, looking dark and striking, older than his years, Hazel wrapping her hair around her cheeks for warmth (her mother had recently tried to persuade her to cut it, but without result), and George fidgeting, mumbling in an undervoice that he thought it was a bit disgusting really, at Mrs. Thorn's age, though of course she was probably doing it for the company. A couple of old friends of Rowena's were there; also, rather surprisingly, Alex Birnbaum. Presently Rowena arrived, wearing an unexpectedly smart suit and an old hat that Annie had refurbished for her with pheasant feathers. Eric escorted her, looking magnificent in a camel coat that was actually long enough. Rowena had bought it for him, but as he had no concept of the price of clothes he was fortunately unaware how much it had cost. They waited for a minute, people kissed other people, then they went inside.

They emerged shortly after. There were more kisses, and hugs. Rowena tried to be her usual brisk, practical self, and didn't succeed. George, who had a new digital camera that his parents had given him for Christmas, took photographs. Annie, with an old Olympus that had done yeoman's service on holidays and suchlike for years, did the same. Then they all piled into taxis and were driven to the Happy Huntsman for a lingering lunch. There was champagne, and this time the teenagers got their own glasses.

"I don't see why people shouldn't get married at any age if they want to," Hazel said to George, picking her words. She didn't want to be caught defending romance.

"Well, all right," he conceded, his attitude softened by the champagne. "As long as they don't *do* anything."

"Good luck," Bartlemy said to Rowena. "Where are you going for the—er—honeymoon?"

"Honeymoon!" Rowena snorted. "Ridiculous! Just a little vacation. Thought Africa would be a good idea."

"I see. Especially as Eric is supposed to come from that region." She threw him a shrewd glance. "Whereabouts?"

"Morocco. Got a friend in Marrakech we're going to visit. Deals in this and that . . ."

"Good luck," he said to Eric. "May the force be with you."

Eric, who had discovered the handshake, pumped his vigorously. His big face was creased into many smiles.

"Now that he's married to Rowena, the government won't be able to send him off anywhere, will they?" Annie remarked to Bartlemy. "Because he's here illegally, I mean."

"I trust not," he said. "But with today's rules and regulations you never know. Still, we'll cross that bridge if and when we come to it."

"D'you think he minds," she said, "that in our world he won't go on living indefinitely?"

"He won't go on *existing* indefinitely," Bartlemy said. "He will *live*."

And at the end of the afternoon, as the party wound down and Nathan supported George, who was being sick in the men's room, just one more detail. Rowena handed Bartlemy a small package wrapped untidily in brown paper. "Look after this for me," she said. "You know what it is."

He nodded. "Are you sure?"

"Not safe at my place. It'll be safe with you. I'm the guardian, but it should be at Thornyhill. You know where to keep it."

That evening, back at home, Bartlemy opened the secret panel beside the chimney and tucked the package inside. He didn't even unwrap it. He could feel the contents—the paper fell open for a moment—but he sensed it was better not to touch it any more than was necessary. Only Hoover saw where it went.

The New Year arrived. The sun, traveling down the hill, probed the Darkwood with its long rays, but nobody was there.

For now.

Continue reading for an
exclusive preview of Book 2
of The Sangreal Trilogy,

The
Sword of
Straw

It began with a city, a city in another universe.

Nathan Ward dreamed of the city, as he had dreamed of other cities long before. Most people dream of other worlds, dreamworlds parallel to our own yet subtly different, where strange things are familiar and familiar things strange—the spin-off regions of the subconscious mind. But the worlds in Nathan's dreams were real, or seemed real, depending on the nature of reality. He went to the kind of school where teachers talked about philosophy and quantum physics, so he knew the chair he was sitting on was probably nonexistent, and the entire cosmos was made up of particles too small to believe in, popping in and out of reality whenever scientists studied them too closely. (Sneaky things, particles.) Nonetheless, Nathan was a down-to-earth boy who had yet to find a magical country at the back of a wardrobe, so it was unnerving to find one in his own head. The previous summer he had almost gotten lost in such a dream, and had been unable to make his way back without help.

Sometimes on these journeys he was merely a disembodied thought; at others, as the dream grew more solid so did he, while his sleeping form would fade, even vanish altogether. He was a weekly boarder at Ffylde Abbey, sharing a dormitory with other boys, and a tendency to dematerialize in the night didn't always pass unremarked. Particles can get away with such behavior more easily than teenage boys. At home his mother, his best friend, and the man he called Uncle all knew of the problem, so there was no need to try to explain the inexplicable, but there were moments when he still felt unsafe. As if there were a hole inside his head through which his life and his very self might slip away. Dreams can too easily become nightmares, and when your dreams are real, the nightmares have teeth . . .

The strange thing was, when he dreamed of the city, he knew it wasn't the first time, though the earlier times were all but forgotten, immured in a locked cupboard at the back of his memory. The dream gave him a *feel* he couldn't mistake, like when you return to a place visited in early childhood. There's nothing you recognize, yet you know you've been there before.

There had been a city in his dreams many times in the past, the city of Arkatron on Eos—a city at the end of time, last stronghold of a high-tech, high-magic civilization in a universe that was dying. It had been a futuristic metropolis of soaring sky-towers and airborne vehicles that wheeled and dipped around them like giant birds, and a population mantled and masked and gloved against the poisonous sunlight—a science-fiction city with a ruler called the Grandir— a ruler thousands of years old, whose face was never seen and whose true name was never spoken—a ruler who had once had a whole cosmos for his empire.

But this city was different. (In his mind he called it a city, giving it the benefit of the doubt, though quite possibly it was only a town.) It sprawled over two hills, the higher rising into a bastion of rock with a gray-walled house perched on the top, built of the same stone and blending with it, so you couldn't tell where the crag ended and the house began. The lower hill was a humpbacked ridge crested with pointy gables and spiked with chimney stacks, but only one or two emitted a thin spindrift of smoke, and as his vision drew nearer Nathan saw windows without panes, doors ajar on empty halls, new grass growing over untrodden roads. It was a ghost town—or ghost city—except there seemed to be no ghosts left, only endless vacancy. There weren't even any birds.

In Arkatron, focus of a universe that was ending, the city thrived after a fashion, crawling with people and lights and life, yet here, though the universe showed no signs of imminent demise, the city was dead. A *Marie-Celeste* of a city, whose footsteps had barely faded and whose voices might have been stilled only a little while ago. It reminded Nathan of towns pictured in history books, the outer houses made of mud bricks and rickety timbers, with shaggy thatching on the roofs, the inner of stone and tile. The hilltop house was the largest, poised in the eye of the wind, weather-beaten and grim, sprouting irrelevant battlements and tiny turrets as if it were trying to become a castle, though no one would be fooled. It had neither moat nor portcullis, and on one side a steep little garden sloped down to the wall and road. As Nathan's thought winged earthward he saw four children were playing there.

They might have been the only children—perhaps the only people—in the whole city. Three boys and a girl. The boys were fighting with wooden swords, banging their weapons on toy shields, shouting incomprehensible war cries. The girl was making mud pies. She looked about seven or eight years old and wore an expression of extreme concentration half hidden under the tangle of her hair. She reminded him a little of Hazel, his best friend, who often hid behind her hair, but whereas Hazel's was brown and straight this child's was blond, dark blond like wheat, and the tangle was rippled and crinkled into untidy waves. One of the boys came over, evidently to check on her, and she looked up with a sudden sweet smile, which made Nathan think that when she was older, though she might not be pretty or beautiful, her smile would always win her friends. As in other dreams he could understand what the children said, though he realized afterward that the language they spoke wasn't English.

"Let me play with you," the girl said. "I can fight, too."

"Swords aren't for girls," the boy retorted. "You might get hurt."

"Have one of my pies, then." The smile disappeared; her face closed.

"I don't eat mud and sand," the boy said, half teasing, half scornful.

"'Tisn't mud and sand," said the girl. "It's chocolate."

"'Tisn't chocolate, stupid."

"'Tis so."

The boy opened his mouth to go on arguing, and then was suddenly quiet. Nathan found his gaze fixed on the mud pie, which was round and carefully molded, and he thought it did indeed look a lot like chocolate. There were even little flakes around the rim, like decoration . . .

"Chocolate," said the girl with satisfaction.

A shadow swept over the scene, the advancing edge of a storm cloud. The boys ceased their game, staring upward. A door opened at the top of the garden and a woman in a linen headdress leaned out, calling to the children to come in. There was a note of urgency or fear in her voice. The boy who had been quarreling with the girl seized her wrist and pulled her toward the shelter of the doorway, though she seemed reluctant to go with him. A winged darkness swooped low over the city, swift as a sudden squall; on the slope a stunted tree twisted with the wind. There was a noise that might have been thunder or the booming of immense pinions. Whether the shadow was cloud or creature Nathan couldn't tell, but he felt the icy chill of its advent, and the wind that tried to tear the tree from its roots whirled his thought away, out of the city, out of the dream, into the gentle oblivion of sleep.

When he awoke he was in his own world, and the dream seemed very far away. Nonetheless he thought about it, from time to time, all that day, and the next. It was the Easter holidays, and he was going to be fourteen, and he had to decide what he wanted by way of a birthday treat. *I want things to happen,* he said to himself, both hopeful and afraid, for things had happened to him the previous year, to him and to others—things both exciting and terrifying—and he knew that wishing for trouble is one way of inviting it in.

He said the same thing that evening, when his uncle (who wasn't really his uncle) came to supper.

"You sound like a child in a story," said his mother, "wishing for adventures. After last summer, you should know better. There may have been a kind of happy ending for you, but not for others. People died."

"Of course I don't want anyone to die," Nathan said. "It's only a little wish. For my birthday."

"When you're older," Uncle Barty said, "you'll learn that things happen without your wishing for them, all the time. You may even wish for peace and quiet one day. But you probably won't get it."

Nathan said no more, quelled by the phrase *When you're older,* because he knew his uncle was older than anyone, and had seen more things happen than Nathan would ever dare to wish for. Bartlemy Goodman had the Gift, a strange legacy that gave him not only long life but other powers beyond the norm as well, powers that might have made him a sorcerer or a magus, though he appeared to use his abilities mostly for ordinary things, like cooking, and brewing homemade liquor and herbal medicines. He didn't look at all sorcerous: true wizards should be lean and cadaverous, hook-nosed and long-bearded, but Bartlemy was fat and placid and clean-shaven, with a broad pink face, fair hair turned white with age, and mild blue eyes gazing tolerantly at the world. Still, Nathan had seen beneath the surface, though only a little way, and he never doubted his uncle's reliability, or his wisdom.

It was about a week later when he dreamed of the city again. It was just a brief glimpse of people piling bags and bundles into a cart, and the reins shaken, and the plodding hooves of a horse moving ponderously away. The girl was standing there—she was older now, almost his own age, but he knew her by her hair and the smile that gradually faded as she ceased waving and her hand fell to her side. The cart lumbered down the road and out of the city, heading along a sort of causeway across a low-lying country broken into many pools and water channels that mirrored the gray pallor of the sky. Without her smile the girl's face looked grave and somehow resigned, as if she had seen many such departures. She turned and began to walk back up the road, until it narrowed into a steep path coiling about the hill, and then eventually became steps that climbed the last ascent to the house on the crag.

This is her *home,* Nathan thought, suddenly sure. *Those boys were just visiting. She's the daughter of the lord or king or whoever it is rules this place.*

Her dress was patched with darns and her long hair looked as if it hadn't been brushed for a day or more but there was something about her, a gravity touching her face that might have been merry, a hint of resolution or confidence, the assurance of a princess. A princess without crown or ermine, with no visible attendants and few remaining subjects, but a princess nonetheless.

When she reached the huge main door she opened it herself, without the aid of butler or footman. It must have been heavy since it took a strong thrust to move it. It creaked suitably, as such doors should, closing behind her with a reverberating thud as she went inside.

Nathan's dream followed her—into a hall that seemed to be hung with shadows, up stairs that branched and zigzagged, along passageways and galleries with cold echoing floors and walls where thread-bare tapestries flapped like cobwebs. At last she entered a room that was thick with books—books close-packed on regular shelves or piled in winding stacks or slithering earthward like rows of collapsed dominoes. Nathan was reminded a little of the secondhand-book shop that his mother managed and where they lived, though this room was larger than his whole house, with a vaulted ceiling from the center of which depended an iron chandelier festooned with dribbles of old wax, above a desk where an elderly man was bent over an opened volume, trying to read it with a magnifying glass. A window squeezed between two banks of shelving admitted a shaft of daylight that stretched toward the desk, picking out more books, and dust, and the man's hair, which stood up around his head like a dandelion clock. Long strands of tallow trailed from the chandelier like stalagmites in a cave.

"Frim," said the girl—the man looked up—"the Hollyhawks have gone today, and old Mother Sparrowgrass and her boys. They wouldn't have told me, but I went to take them a cake, and there they were, all packed up and the cart rolling."

"Deserters!" said the old man. "What did you do?"

"What could I do? I wished them luck."

"They deserve no luck," said the old man. "Running away. Bum-skittles! They are your people."

"They are their own people," said the girl. "What have I ever done for them?"

"Your best." He reached out, squeezing her hand in his own thin, bony one, then patting it. He had a strange knobbly face with startled eyebrows, round inquiring eyes, and a long nose that turned up at the tip. For all his age he had a quality of youthfulness that, Nathan reflected, few young people ever exhibited—he seemed vividly alive, curious, alert, exuding enough energy for a small mobile generator. "Never mind," he went on. "The loyal and the truehearted remain."

"Only because they have no choice. Bandy Crow is a cripple; Granny Cleep passed a hundred and twenty last year. The Twymoors and the Yngleveres—"

"They'll not leave," the old man said. "They've always been faithful to your family. They won't abandon your father."

"My father's sick," said the girl, "and growing sicker. I sometimes think the kingdom's been under a curse since my great-great-I-don't-know-how-many-greats-grandfather first lifted the Traitor's Sword. And since I brought the *Urdemons* . . ."

"Don't be silly," her mentor admonished. "*You* didn't bring them. They are drawn to acts of magic—"

"My magic."

"You were a child, playing games of illusion. There's always been a little magic in your family; as magic goes, it's fairly harmless. You had no idea—"

"It's still my fault," the princess insisted, brooding into her hair. Like Hazel.

"Babbletosh!" the old man said briskly. "You take too much on yourself. Just because you're the princess, you think you can claim responsibility for everything? I never heard of such presumption. You're like a little girl who treads in a puddle, and then blames herself for a flood. Utter foolishness! Isn't it?"

"Yes," she said with a furtive smile. "Sorry. It's only . . . Prenders told me . . ."

"That Woman," her mentor said with unmistakable capital letters, "talks a load of—"

"Frim!"

"Squiffle-piffle! That's all I was going to say. Doesn't know her coccyx from her humerus. Why, when everyone else leaves, she has to stay around . . ."

"She loves me," the princess said gently. "And Papa."

"Overrated, love. People use it as an excuse for anything." Absently, he stroked her hand again. "Don't worry. We'll find a cure for the king—and then, so they say, the kingdom will be healed. Somewhere there'll be a formula—the recipe for a potion . . ."

"Then light the lamp," said the girl, indicating an oil lamp on the desk, "or you'll miss it." She removed the glass chimney, struck a match, and held the flame to the wick. The sudden glow flushed her cheek and spun a shimmer of gold from her hair. As the dream faded Nathan tried to fix the image in his mind, wanting to remember exactly how she looked, but of course, when he awoke, he couldn't.

It was deep night. He got out of bed and climbed up to the Den, his childhood retreat under the pitch of the roof. Through the skylight he saw a single star look down, watching him. But he knew it wasn't a star: it was a spy-crystal through which, in an alternative universe, the faceless ruler of Eos could survey anything in its range. Sometimes, when the world was ordinary, that knowledge seemed like a brief glimpse into madness, but not now, not tonight.

Things are happening, he thought, with a complicated shiver, reaching back into the dream. Something had been said, something significant—something that struck a faint chord of familiarity—but he was too busy trying to re-create the face of the princess, and he couldn't remember what it was.

ABOUT THE AUTHOR

AMANDA HEMINGWAY has already lived through one lifetime—during which she traveled the world and supported herself through a variety of professions, including that of actress, barmaid, garage hand, laboratory assistant, journalist, and model. Her new life is devoted to her writing. Look for the second book in The Sangreal Trilogy, *The Sword of Straw*.